The cotton ca_____ ke a
binder to redu_____ She
slipped on a c_____ plaid
kilt. She could_____ as he watched her,
totally absorbed in her ritual before the full-length
mirror. Was he caught yet? Ensnared by his own
racing heart? She looked away as she bent to draw
knee-high cotton stockings over her bare feet. She
preferred silk, but everything had to be totally
authentic.

She turned, hoping to see him lying on the bed,
fully aroused and trembling with shame. That was
how she controlled him. But hope faded as she saw
him standing by the window, looking down at the
courtyard below her apartment where her finishing
school students took breaks between classes. He
was transfixed by an exquisite creature with
cascading red curls.

"Is it her, then?" she asked. "One of my girls? You
want a *child?*"

Her bitterness could have drawn blood, but he
seemed oblivious. "She isn't a child. She's in the first
flush of womanhood. Fresh and lovely, untouched."

Rage foamed in her throat. Not yet thirty and she
was being tossed aside for a simpering virgin? After
everything she'd done for him? Instantly her anger
turned cold. He was a powerful man. He could easily
ruin her. But he had crossed the line, and they both
knew it.

He would get what he wanted. But he would pay
the price.

SUZANNE FORSTER

The Lonely Girls Club

MIRA®

ISBN 0-7783-2201-7

THE LONELY GIRLS CLUB

Copyright © 2005 by Suzanne Forster.

www.MIRABooks.com

Printed in U.S.A.

My everlasting gratitude to those of you
who love me anyway.
You know who you are.
Thank you.

1

Rowe Academy for Girls
Tiburon, California
Winter 1980

The cotton camisole was too small. It acted like a binder to reduce her breasts to a tidy A cup. She slipped on a crisp white blouse and buttoned it up, leaving just a bit of milky throat exposed. Her ticking pulse could still be seen.

She could see his reflection, too, watching her, totally absorbed in her ritual before the full-length mirror. Dressing for sex had always struck her as odd, but this was the way he liked it. Was he caught yet? Ensnared by his own racing heart?

The pleats of her plaid stitch-down skirt just reached her knees. The skirt opened like a kilt, and the flap flew as she twirled on one foot. She was joyous now, childlike. Her dark French-braided hair danced with pleasure. Surely he could see that she was transformed. She didn't look in the mirror as she bent to draw knee-high cotton stockings on over her bare feet. She preferred silk, but everything had to be totally authentic. No makeup was allowed, only freshly pinched cheeks and lip gloss. No jewelry. That would be trashy.

He was no longer in the mirror. She turned, hoping to see him lying on the bed, awaiting her, fully aroused and trembling with shame. That was how she controlled him, and it had to go right today or their relationship wouldn't survive. She had something important to tell him. But hope faded as she saw him standing by the window, looking down at the courtyard three stories below her bell tower apartment, where her finishing school students took breaks between classes.

The academy, a U-shaped structure, designed in the manner of the ivy-covered Victorian castles of old England, was more than a school, it was her family home, donated through a foundation to the cause of education when her grandmother died, fifteen years ago. Right now it felt like her prison.

She joined him, but he didn't acknowledge her presence. He was transfixed by an exquisite creature with cascading red curls and the pensive smile of a Sistine Madonna. The young woman stood near the fountain in the courtyard's center, seemingly unaware of the mist from the water that hovered around her like a communion veil. Brisk weather had kept most of the students indoors today, but this one must have wanted to be alone with her thoughts.

"Is it her then?" the headmistress asked him. "One of my girls? You want a child?"

Her bitterness could have drawn blood, but he seemed oblivious. "She isn't a child," he pointed out. "She's fully grown, but still in the first flush of womanhood. She's fresh and lovely, untouched."

Rage foamed into the headmistress's throat. Not yet thirty, and she was being tossed aside for a simpering virgin? After everything she'd done for him? She had planned her whole life around him, but there was no way she could tell him her news now. He would think her ridiculous.

Instantly her anger turned cold. She was subzero, molten ice. He would get what he wanted, and he would pay the price for it. He was a powerful man. He could easily ruin her.

But he had crossed the line, and they both knew it. Yes, he would get what he wanted. Yes, he would pay.

San Quentin Prison
Summer 2005

Haze shrouded the sun, turning it into a silvery moon as the main gate clanged open. A tall, thin ghost of a human being hovered in the entrance. He took a few steps, although it looked more like floating than walking. The dark suit he wore swung loosely on his fence-slat frame, and his heavy blue-black hair fell forward, shuttering the light from his eyes. What could be seen of his face was all jawbones and cartilage. He was a death row inmate, but he was walking free, the only prisoner scheduled for release that day.

He didn't seem aware of the road ahead, only of the medieval fortress behind him. After a few steps, he stopped and turned, swaying like a spindly, overgrown tree. He raised one hand and curled back all of his fingers except the middle one. It might have been less an act of defiance than a test of his constitutional rights. Was he really a free man? A car door banged in the distance, and he ducked, clearly expecting to be shot.

Another man stood across the road by a gleaming black SUV with darkened windows. Jameson Cross was as tall as the ex-con, and his jet hair had the same shimmering blue lights, but that was where the resemblance ended. In every other way than the physical, the two men were profoundly different. They could have been alter egos.

"William Broud? Can I give you a ride?" Cross stepped forward cautiously, offering his hand—and his car. "It's a long walk to civilization."

Broud did not look up or acknowledge Cross in any way. Cross could have been invisible, except that he knew the other man had heard him. This was deeply deliberate. William Broud had been ignoring Jameson Cross since before Broud went to prison. They weren't enemies. It was worse than that.

Cross began to walk with him. "I'd like to talk to you about the finishing school murders. You're going to need a job now that you're out, and I can pay you for your time."

Cross was a bestselling true crime writer, and his stake in this case went beyond the book he might write. Broud had been a gardener and handyman at an exclusive finishing school in Tiburon. He'd spent twenty-three years in prison, most of it on death row for the murder of Millicent Rowe, the school's headmistress. But Broud had been recently exonerated by DNA evidence, and Cross didn't understand the man's reluctance to talk about an injustice of that magnitude. When they'd arrested him, he'd professed his innocence, babbling about conspiracies and cover-ups, a sex ring involving the students. But he'd had drugs in his possession, a record of priors and B-negative blood had been found at the scene, which was his type.

"Who are the 'lonely girls'?" Cross asked. "You claimed they killed the headmistress. Were they students at the finishing school?"

Broud continued walking, head bowed, face buried in hair.

Frustration burned through Cross. This had to stop. "You rotted in jail for twenty-three years and no one cared," he said. "They would have let you die. Whoever did it should pay for putting you through that hell."

Black hair flew, exposing Broud's tortured visage. He glared at Cross. "You're right. No one cared. Why should I? Leave me alone."

"It doesn't have to be like that. Billy—"

"Don't call me that," Broud ground out savagely. "Billy's gone. He doesn't exist anymore."

Cross came to a halt, watching Broud lumber away. If he'd continued, they might well have come to blows. Billy Broud might be gone, he thought, but if zombies existed, this man could have been one. His face was a howling Halloween skull. He'd been spared execution, but any part of him that had been human was dead now. Only the pupils of his eyes burned with terrifying life. And Jameson Cross would not soon forget them.

Cross was certain that Broud knew who had done this to him, but for some reason, he wasn't talking. Perhaps he wanted to exact his own revenge. Nevertheless, it was a story that Cross intended to tell. He'd just made that decision. His suspicions alone would create headlines.

It would be interesting to see who ran for cover when he fired the first shot. If he was right, he was hunting big game. The people he suspected operated at the highest levels of government, jurisprudence and business. And even more interesting, they were all women.

2

"Tell me there's a white lace thong lurking somewhere under those black robes, and I *swear* I'll give up my *Girls Gone Wild* video."

Bent deeply over a banker's box of legal folders, Mattie Smith ignored her law clerk's whispered plea to the great god of young male hormones. She shifted position as the twenty-four-year-old ex–gang member entered her chambers, denying him the bottom-on view as she rifled through files. She was searching for a case she remembered from her prosecutor days that dealt with tainted confessions, but God forbid she should encourage him.

How many law clerks spoke of thongs in the presence of a federal appeals court judge? Even in whispers? Only Jaydee Sanchez. Had any other clerk tried, it was quite possible Mattie would have fired him, after she'd plucked out his beady little eyes. But James Dean Sanchez wasn't just any law clerk. And she wasn't just any judge.

He dropped the morning paper on her desk. The slap of newsprint against gleaming mahogany got him a mumbled thanks from Mattie. "You'd show promise as a porn czar, Jaydee, if you weren't a lawyer."

"Yet to pass the bar," he reminded her, "and I haven't ruled out porn czardom as a career path. It's more dignified than law, and it *has* to pay better. But alas, there goes my seat on the Supreme Court."

Mattie glanced around at his deadpan expression. "You looked into it? Porn?"

"I even looked into male modeling," he said, as if that should explain everything.

A tight sensation in her lower back brought Mattie upright. Either she'd been bent from the waist too long, or her thirty-eight years were catching up with her. She winced, rubbing the tender spot.

Her quick frown told Jaydee not to say a word, even though she had no idea what he might say in this case. If he was preoccupied with anything, it was her sexual orientation, not her age or her infirmities. Mostly he complained about her wardrobe choices. Too much khaki.

"As I recall, you wanted to borrow my bulletproof vest for your audition," she said, remembering his detour into the Bay area's fashion scene. It had surprised her because Jaydee was famously preppy, always with the polo shirts under his blazer jackets, like today.

"I just wanted to see *you* take it off."

A grin made fender dents out of his cinnamon-brown dimples. He popped the top on his bucket-size cup of convenience store coffee and took a test sip from the frothy, steaming well. His dark lashes fluttered with enjoyment.

"Like you really need to be more hyper." Mattie had always envied him his ability to take pleasure where he found it. Jaydee's gift, she called it. But today it just made her cranky. She'd had another restless night, grappling with the problems of the child kidnapping case before her. She normally didn't try criminal cases at the district court level. Three years ago, she'd been appointed to the Ninth Circuit Court of Appeals, where cases were presided over by a three-judge panel, but she'd recently been loaned out to the district court due to the severe shortage of judges.

This particular case had been difficult from start to finish. She'd had to shuttle between her chambers in the Ninth Circuit and her temporary chambers at the district courthouse, which gave her limited access to her library and research material, and she could bring only two clerks with her, which meant operating at half-staff. Plus, the abuse issues were disturbing for personal reasons, and initially, Mattie had wondered if she could be fair and impartial. Now she was worried that she'd gone too far trying to be fair.

The twenty-one-year-old defendant had kidnapped his six-year-old brother from the home of their abusive father, and taken the child to a safe house across the Canadian border, promising to come back as soon as he could. But the house was raided by the FBI the following day, and the boy returned to his parents.

The case history was extensive and troubling. The parents were wealthy and well-connected politically, and the defendant had failed in all his efforts to have his little brother removed from the home. Finally, in frustration, he'd attacked his father and been charged with assault. He'd done his ninety days, but Child Protective Services had no longer considered him a fit advocate for his brother, and the six-year-old had remained in the family home until the defendant kidnapped him.

Now the child was in protective custody and doing well, but it remained the court's job to decide the fate of Ronald Langston, the older brother. He'd said some things when the police questioned him that could have been construed as a confession. Mattie had the power to suppress the statements, but she'd wanted to be rigorously fair in allowing all the admissible evidence, so she'd let the statements stand. In truth, she'd never imagined that Langston would be convicted. Now, given the way the trial was going, she wasn't so sure.

"There's your precious paper."

Mattie looked up to see Jaydee pointing to the copy of the *San Francisco Chronicle* lying on her desk.

"You read that thing for the personal ads, right?" He gave her a knowing nod. "I'll bet you flip straight to the SSPs."

"SSPs?"

"Same Sex Personals. Don't pretend you don't know what I'm talking about, missy."

Mattie didn't bother to give him the dirty look he so richly deserved. It was hopeless anyway. Their relationship went back years, and in some ways, they were closer than kin. She'd been mentoring him in all aspects of the law, but because of their unique relationship, she'd been particularly careful to teach him about the care and feeding of judges. Outside her chambers, he treated her with the utmost deference and respect, but inside was another story. He was usually incorrigible, like today.

He'd decided she was gay back in her prosecutor days when he was her star witness against a drug kingpin who supplied most of Orange County's Hispanic youth. She'd started wearing the Kevlar vest on the strong advice of local police, but it wasn't her clothing that had put Jaydee off. It was her toughness.

He was the product of the macho gang culture and not used to a woman calling the shots. Still, Mattie hadn't forced him to testify. He'd volunteered for personal reasons. He'd been thirteen when he risked his life to help bring the kingpin down, and his testimony had put the man in prison for the rest of his natural life. It had also put Mattie on the map. She had benefited tremendously from their association, but Jaydee had lost. Everything. The kingpin's thugs had found and killed his only family, the aging grandparents who'd raised him.

Mattie's shock and grief had been nearly as great as Jaydee's. He was too proud to let her comfort him openly, but she'd found other ways. She had become his family, bringing him back with her to the Bay area, where she'd grown up. She started a law practice and gave him a job, but because of her long hours, she found him a supportive foster family to live with.

She was delighted when he chose law as a career.

As far as she was concerned, Jaydee Sanchez could ding her about her Kevlar vest or her waterproof diver's watch any time he wanted. Besides, he wasn't the only one wondering about Mattie Smith's sexual orientation. She was widely known as the one hundred and five pound pitt bull with the china-blue eyes and balls to match. She saw it as a plus. If the mystery of her sexuality distracted her opponents long enough to give her the advantage, then God bless 'em, let them wonder.

"Could we talk about the Langston case?" she said. "It's giving me fits."

"No shit." Jaydee pulled a yellow legal pad cluttered with notes from his overstuffed briefcase. "The public defender is inept, and the prosecution is brilliant. They're making the kid look like the monster from *Alien*."

Mattie couldn't agree more. At one point the prosecutor had strolled over to the jury box and casually turned back to look at Langston, a hulking kid with a shaved head and a jagged scar on his face from the fight with his father. Can you imagine, the prosecutor had said to the jury, how terrified the child must have been to be snatched from his bed in the dark of night? How would *you* like to be kidnapped by that man?

Mattie'd had to quell despair that was completely inappropriate for a judge. If a tender heart lurked under Langston's fear and defensiveness, it wasn't easy to see.

"The prosecutor's trying to make it look like a grudge match between Langston and his father," Jaydee said, "and he's doing a good job. He wants the jury to believe they tossed the kid around like a football."

Of course, during testimony, the father had denied the abuse and said his oldest son hated him for changing his will and would stop at nothing to get back at him. He even claimed his son's original intent was to conceal his identity and kidnap the child for ransom money. The prosecutor had run with it, an excellent strategy.

"The way I see it, Langston doesn't have a shot at due process." Jaydee rattled his legal pad. "But, here I am to save the day. Want to hear my ideas on how to fix this?"

"I don't think so, Jaydee. I really don't."

"Mattie, he's going down, and with all due respect, that confession you allowed is wrapped around his neck like an anchor. His only chance is an appeal, and he can't get one unless there's a legal error in this trial. Someone has to make a mistake, a big one."

"Legal errors can't be arranged in advance, Jaydee, certainly not by me."

Mattie's knee made a suspicious click as she knelt and resumed digging through the files. She really was falling apart. The knee injury was a childhood incident that elicited more mental pain than it did physical. Ironic that she thought she'd packed her past away more tightly than she'd packed this box, but the case had forced her to open both up.

"So Langston goes to jail, possibly for life, for trying to be a good brother?"

Mattie sighed. Jaydee couldn't possibly know how torn she was over this case, or he wouldn't be tempting her to use her powers in questionable ways. She looked at him askance. "Do you think maybe we could let the trial proceed until we have the jury's verdict? That's what our court system is for."

"*Unless* the deck is stacked against the defendant through no fault of his own."

"Here it is!" She yanked the file from the box. "People versus Randolph."

"All we need is one reversible error," Jaydee persisted, "improper pretrial discovery or conflict of interest, maybe. The defendant's father probably plays golf with the prosecuting attorney. Hell, ineffective assistance of counsel might be enough."

"Can't, Jaydee. Professional ethics."

His pad hit the desk. "The only ethical thing to do is get this kid due process. Where's your sense of fair play, woman?"

She shot him a warning glare, and got to her feet, forgetting all about her back. "A moment ago, my womanhood was in doubt, was it not?"

"It wouldn't be if you'd stop wearing that vest."

His eyes harbored a dark twinkle. But then, they always did.

"Make yourself scarce," she told him. "I need some alone time with Lady Justice here." She touched the marble statue that sat on her desk. It had become one of her rituals before a difficult trial to sit quietly with the symbol that balanced the scales of justice. Not to pray or meditate or ask for guidance. Just to be still and take in the gravity of the task ahead of her.

Today, she might even pray.

She knew Jaydee wasn't questioning her conviction. He just didn't understand that this case was personal for her, and that she had bent over backward trying to be careful. Usually, it was her total inability to be politically correct that he objected to. She didn't flinch at moral ambiguity. She took it on and made it more ambiguous. She muddied and murked things up in her search for the truth—even when the truth wasn't what people wanted to hear. They wanted justification for their beliefs, no matter how slanted they might be.

They wanted her to make it easy for them to cling to the lies, and she made it hard.

Jaydee warned her constantly of the dangers of making enemies. In many ways, he was more conservative than she was. And at times, wiser. But he wasn't a judge. He didn't have to worry about where the limits of the law collided with the limits of his power.

"So, *are* we wearing anything interesting under the robes today?" Jaydee asked as he fitted the plastic top on his coffee cup.

She unzipped the black linen placket and took a little bow, showing him that she wasn't wearing the infamous vest. "Do I get points?" she asked. The khaki skirt and mantailored white blouse she'd fished from her closet were high fashion compared to what she usually wore under her robes—khaki pants and a polo T-shirt.

All he did was laugh. "When's the gender reassignment surgery scheduled?"

"You'll be the first to know. Meanwhile, don't let the door hit you on the way out."

She waved him off, but Jaydee didn't seem ready to leave. "Seriously, Mattie," he said, "why so butch? What's the point?"

"It works."

"To keep men away?"

"No, to accomplish my goals. I'm a badass. People don't mess with me. Well, other than you."

She sat down at her desk and returned to her mission, ready for the conversation to be over. She had a file to review. But her thoughts drifted back to the first time Jaydee had felt it necessary to question her preferences. She'd just started her law practice, and she'd hired him as an afterschool gofer. He'd been all of fifteen at the time.

"You're gay, right?" he'd asked one evening as he stopped by her office to say good-night. "A sapphist? You have to be."

"Why?"

"Because I've never seen your legs, and you haven't made a pass at me."

"Here's a tip," she'd said. "Don't hold your breath for either."

Now, she sensed his presence and looked up, startled to see him standing right next to her, gazing down at her. His nearness forced a little gasp out of her.

He bent and touched the indentation below her lip. "This is a pretty mouth," he said in an odd, soft voice. "Why don't you use it for something other than eating people's lunch?"

A pretty mouth. Mattie shuddered at the words, as much as at the way he said them. She struggled to get to her feet, staring at him as if he'd lost his mind.

"Get out of here, Jaydee," she said. "Get out of here now—and don't ever touch me like that again."

"Hey, Your Honor, I didn't mean anything."

She turned her back on him, too enraged to risk another word. Her temples were throbbing, but she heard him go. The door to her chambers shut, and only then did she let her shoulders drop. Silently she inventoried her reflection in the window. She didn't bear the slightest resemblance to a man, despite what Jaydee said. Her squared shoulders projected strength, but her petite frame was blade slender. She burned energy standing still. And for all her toughness, she was as transparent as glass. When the fires were spent and the shadows emerged, her face took on a fragile, despairing cast, and she looked haunted, like now.

She chose severe clothing intentionally. No accessories. No makeup. Her skirt and blouse could have been fashionable and sexy, coupled with stiletto heels and Britney Spears's tousled mop of hair. But Mattie had secured her shoulder-length locks with a plain black headband. Not the height of fashion and not flattering to her sharply blue eyes and pronounced cheekbones. Boomerangs, a teacher had once called them. Mattie Smith had edges that could cut, and she used them.

But God, it was lonely. When she allowed herself to feel the emptiness, it was almost more than she could bear. She had lied to Jaydee. To everyone. She didn't dress like this just to accomplish her goals. She did it to ward people off, men who touched her mouth....

3

Rowe Academy for Girls
Fall 1981

"Such a pretty mouth," the man observed in his chalk-dust voice. "She's scruffy, yes, but that might be fun. Tomboys, you know."

The woman who'd arranged the "interview" nudged the girl into the spotlight to give him a better look at her. The girl's uniform, a plaid pleated skirt and white blouse, accented by a monogrammed navy blue scarf, hugged her lanky frame. Her navy knee socks were uneven, one of them clinging to her calf and the other sliding toward her ankle, as if they'd been hastily pulled up. An errant strand of fine dark hair stuck to the girl's damp cheek, but it was her wary soul-blue eyes that dominated her face.

It would have been too easy to call her unkempt. Untamed was a far better word, and that feral quality might even have been the source of her odd, edgy appeal. Her attitude bordered on sullen, but it was clearly fueled by fear, churning beneath the surface.

The tip of her tongue slicked along her teeth and darted out to wet her lips. She wasn't trying to be seductive. Her mouth was dry and tacky. She couldn't even manage a smile.

"She looks young," the man said.

"She's very clever," the woman countered. "She's our best archer, but she also reads palms, I'm afraid to say."

"Reads palms? One of *your* girls?" His hushed voice carried in the empty classroom. Hardwood floors and shuttered windows bounced every sound like the walls of a canyon.

The woman smoothed her own hair, tucking dark wisps into the braided coil that nestled like a shiny snake at the base of her skull. "This one's different. I've spent a great deal of time with her, but she seems immune to my civilizing touch."

"Shades of *My Fair Lady?*"

She sighed. "I suppose."

The fourteen-year-old girl being discussed fought a scowl of defiance. She had been told to smile and flirt with the man, but the lights were so bright she couldn't see him, even when she squinted, and she was going to catch hell for doing that. Ms. Rowe hated her charges to act common, even if that's what they were. But she wasn't like the other students, who came from wealthy families. She came from the projects, from nothing. She was one of the Grace scholarship girls.

"What's her name?" the man asked.

"Matilda. Sweet name, don't you think? She's very spirited, quite lovely in her own way."

The girl did scowl then. Lovely? She was a gangly mess, and no one knew it better than her. It was a mistake that she was here. She hadn't thought any of the men would want her. Matilda, the geek? The brainy nerd? Why had she been selected for this supreme indignity? The school only had four scholarship girls, and the other three would never believe he'd picked Mattie Smith. They were all beautiful and had breasts. She'd even rumpled her clothing, hoping he would think she was gross.

The man drew something from his overcoat pocket, a long sash that he snapped through his hands to straighten.

"No blindfolds," Ms. Rowe cautioned. "She's quite terrified of confinement. She won't see anything, not in the dark."

Mattie's heart lurched, hammering painfully as the sash disappeared in his pocket. What would she do if he covered her eyes with that thing, blinded her?

Kill him, she thought. Gut him with the boning knife she'd swiped from the kitchen and hid in her sock. If she'd had her bow, she would have put an arrow in his heart.

"How do we know she won't talk?" he asked the headmistress, who pretended to pout.

"You underestimate me, sir. It won't be a problem, I assure you. These girls know what's at stake. They're very lucky to have been admitted to a school like Rowe, isn't that right, Matilda?"

Mattie managed a nod.

"She does look young," he said again, as if that were weighing heavily on his mind. He moved within reach of Mattie, but all she could see was the dark sleeve of his coat and his pale hand as it reached toward her face.

Mattie's instinct was to recoil, but she couldn't look away. He had thick palms and short, webby fingers. A spatulate hand meant a physical nature, aggressive, a leader. She noticed hands. It was automatic, a reflex. But something glittered, distracting her. His cuff links. The one she saw had a gold star mounted on a circle of onyx.

"This," he whispered, "is one of the loveliest little mouths I've ever seen."

He touched her lips and sent a painful jolt through her. Revulsion made her stomach float. Shock rang in her ears. It was hard to hear him after that, but he murmured something about kissing her, and she felt a hand dig into her lower back.

The headmistress was pushing her toward him. Matilda pushed back, and sharp fingernails bit into her skin.

"Matilda?" he said, "is something wrong?"

Now he was too close. She could smell the stale coffee on his breath, and another odor that made her gorge rise. He smelled like the men who'd come to see her mother. Lela Smith was a palm reader, who saw her customers in the bedroom of the small apartment she'd shared with her daughter. Mattie had been too young to know exactly what was going on, but she'd caught the laughter, the whispers and the primitive smells of animal excitement.

Terrified she would be sick, Mattie turned her head away. Nausea foamed into her throat, and the spotlight swirled. She had no knack for feminine wiles, or she would have seized the opportunity and fallen to the floor in a faint. Any of the other girls would have done that, but they weren't ungainly, awkward clods.

A desperate plan came to mind as she struggled to keep her balance.

"Nothing's wrong," she said, letting him touch her face and gently draw it up. He was going to kiss her now, and she knew Ms. Rowe would allow it, even watch with some satisfaction.

The light burning Mattie's eyes kept her from getting a look at him. Better that she couldn't, she realized, or she would never have been able to go through with it. He drew her toward him with the finger that tipped up her chin.

Ms. Rowe jabbed her, urging her to go.

"Matilda with the pretty mouth," he said softly.

Her spine rippled with the horror of what was about to happen. As he bent to kiss her, she spat at him. And not in a timid way. She hocked up all the moisture her parched throat would allow and spat ferociously.

He howled with outrage, and Ms. Rowe sprang into action. She pinched Mattie's flesh hard enough to break the skin, and Mattie fought back a shriek of pain.

The man dropped back into the shadows, and the head-mistress shoved Mattie out the way so that she could speak with him.

"I'm terribly sorry." She raised her hands beseechingly. "I can't imagine what's wrong with her. Please excuse me while I have a word with her."

Mattie didn't hear the man's reply. It wouldn't have mattered anyway. He couldn't have saved her if he'd wanted to. No one could. Once he'd gone from this gothic monstrosity of a school, she would be tortured in ways that would ensure she never defy the headmistress again, that she never even dare to think about it.

Mattie's mouth was stuffed with something that burned like hellfire. As she tried to spit it out, she realized it was her own tongue. It had swollen to more than twice its size, and every inch of the surface was raw and pulpy. She could taste blood, but she didn't dare try to swallow. She would surely choke.

That was her first terrifying awareness as she fought her way back to consciousness. The second was worse. She was enveloped in darkness and trapped in a space so tight she could feel her own breath rush over her face. The barrier above her couldn't have been more than three inches from her mouth. It acted like a backboard for the steam flooding out of her lungs.

Was this a coffin? Was she in a grave, buried alive?

Terror gripped her, ripping at her control. She had to get out of here or she would die! Her hands were caught at her sides and her knees thumped painfully against the walls. It was as tight as a mummy case. She couldn't move enough to beat on the walls or kick her way out.

A bright flash of light startled her. It illuminated her prison, and from what she could see the filthy area looked more like a crawl space than a coffin. But where was the light coming from?

Calm down, she told herself. *Lie still and watch, listen.* But every breath brought a tightening, panicky sensation in her chest. Somehow, she had to find a safe place within herself. Sink into it and be still. There was no other way to survive. This was the nightmare that had—and would—haunt her for all time. Everyone had a death dream. She'd studied them in her social anthropology class. They sprang from the primordial forests, the swamps, the aboriginal fears. This was Mattie's. But how did Ms. Rowe know that?

Not such a pretty mouth now, Matilda?

The light flashed again, and a tapping sound caught her attention. It reminded her of water leaking from a faucet, but each drop seemed to ignite a sizzling shower of sparks. Within seconds the crawl space was filled with the deadly crackle of electricity, and a smell she recognized as danger, the stench of scorched hair.

Suddenly Matilda understood. She was in a crawl space, perhaps in the attic of Ms. Rowe's tower apartment, and it was raining outside. Somewhere near her head was a live wire, probably lying in a pool of water. The sparks had already singed her hair. If she came into direct contact with the wire—if she became a conductor—she would be electrocuted.

Was that what Ms. Rowe wanted?

A shallow breath slipped through her lips. Her whole body trembled. This place was a medieval torture chamber. She didn't dare move. How would she ever get out of here?

She tried to recall what had happened before she lost consciousness. Ms. Rowe had taken her into the parlor of her apartment and brewed her a cup of tea. To calm her down, she'd said. She insisted that Mattie drink it before they spoke. Mattie couldn't remember anything after that, except that the tea had tasted too sweet, as if she'd added extra honey to disguise another taste.

What had she put in the tea? Lye? Acid? Either one would probably have killed Mattie if she'd drunk it. But perhaps death came slowly. Mattie didn't know much about that sort of thing. She could be dying right now. Ms. Rowe dabbled in herbal concoctions, some of them poisonous, but most were homeopathic remedies. She could have dosed the tea with a sleeping agent, and when Mattie was unconscious, swabbed her tongue with something caustic. It felt as if she'd been scalded with boiling water, and Mattie wouldn't have put such a heinous thing past her. Ms. Rowe was evil.

Mattie had heard rumors of scholarship girls disappearing in the past. She'd never really believed them until now. There might even be other girls up here in the crawl spaces. Dead girls. The academy was an old Victorian-style castle with several wings. It had tunnels and towers, and only about a third of the buildings were currently being used. There were plenty of places to hide bodies, especially if they'd been dismembered.

She was not going to die this way. She was going to fight.

She tried to move her legs, but it felt as if she had been poisoned, by fear, if nothing else. A strange lethargy dragged her down. Her eyelids drooped, and her body longed to give into it, but she had to stay awake. If she didn't, she might accidentally move and hit the wire. What little air there was had grown hot and thick. Suffocating.

Her anguished sigh nearly drowned out another sound, a *click-tap-click* in the distance. It sounded like footsteps. Was someone coming her way?

Ms. Rowe, she realized. Who else could it be? The headmistress was coming to see if she was dead yet.

4

Federal District Courthouse
San Francisco
Summer 2005

The gavel jumped as Mattie rapped it against the sounding block, calling the court to order. It felt odd presiding over a jury trial again, even though it had only been a few years since she'd done it on a regular basis. She'd spent two years here at the district court level before being appointed to the appeals court, and she'd sat in this room at this very bench.

It might not be as grand or palatial as the courtrooms at the historic courthouse where the Ninth Circuit convened, but the gleam of mahogany and brass was everywhere, as was the mystique of venerable power. This morning, as they awaited the verdict on Ronald Langston, that air of power and finality was disconcerting, even to Mattie.

She addressed the jury foreman, a graying, slightly built male with wire-rim glasses balanced on the tip of his nose. "Have you reached a unanimous verdict?"

"We have, Your Honor."

"Please give the verdict to the marshal."

Mattie glanced over at the defendant's wary expression. She could feel his raw nerves even from a distance, but she could only imagine the anxiety of being at the mercy of the men and women in the jury box. With any luck, she would never know.

His fate would be decided this morning, and the course of his life determined with a few words. She hoped they were the right words, but as a judge, she was charged with restraining her passions and her prejudices, which meant keeping her emotions in check, no matter how strongly she might feel. She'd done her best not to influence the jurors in any way, other than to ensure that they understood what they'd heard and had been guided by the facts and the law in making their decision. She'd also made sure they were fully aware of the consequences of that decision.

The marshal handed Mattie the verdict. Her hands were steady, but her heart surged painfully as she read it. She handed it back to the marshal. As he walked it over to the jury box, she got out the words, "Mr. Foreman, please read the verdict."

The foreman cleared his throat. "On the count of kidnapping, we, the jury, being duly impaneled, find the defendant guilty. On the count of child endangerment, we find the defendant guilty."

Mattie reached for the gavel, but her fingers wouldn't grip it. It felt as if she'd taken a blow that was reverberating in her spine and might never stop. She had feared this outcome, but clearly she hadn't let herself believe it would happen. Somehow she had to gather herself together. Her duties weren't over. She had to set a date for the sentencing and bring the session to a close. But what she dreaded most was the necessity of having to look at Ronald Langston again. She did not want to do that. She did not want to see the trapped animal fear in his eyes.

Mattie didn't even bother to go around the desk to her chair. She dropped her leather folder and court files next to the unopened newspaper, absently aware that there'd been no time for her morning ritual. Tomorrow was another day, however. She would be reading the *San Francisco Chronicle* over a cup of hot, honeyed tea. And Ronald Langston would be eating something akin to gruel in his cell.

Take off your robe, she told herself, but she didn't get any further than the zipper pull. The door opened behind her, and she clipped the desk as she turned around. Something fell to the floor, but she didn't take the time to pick it up.

Jaydee was shaking his head, apparently dazed.

"Don't look at me like that," she said. "As much as I didn't want to see Langston go to prison, I couldn't knowingly lead that idiot public defender into an error. I just kept hoping he'd make one himself."

"Right," he said, emitting a heavy sigh. "I should never have brought it up. What do we do now?"

Mattie had already given that some thought. "I'm going to assign the two best appellate attorneys I know to appeal the case. They'll hate me for it, but I'm going to do it anyway. I'll write a letter to be placed in the file listing all the reasons I believe the defendant didn't receive a fair trial, including my own clouded judgment in allowing a tainted confession to be used as evidence, and of course, I'll give him the minimum sentence for his offense."

Jaydee tapped his yellow legal pad. "Your own clouded judgment? Sure you want to do that? It won't look good on the résumé."

"What are they going to do, impeach me? Federal judges are appointed for life." Mattie knew it wouldn't look good, but what else could she do? A twenty-one-year-old man didn't get a fair trial because of evidence she'd failed to suppress.

"They're going to want to know what clouded your judgment," he pointed out.

Mattie had shared a lot with Jaydee, but she'd never told him about the ordeals of her past. She didn't doubt he'd be sympathetic, but she'd always been the caretaker in their relationship, and she was deeply reluctant to upset that delicate balance. Too much was upset already.

"I'll handle that," she told him.

"Listen, I'm always available, if you want to talk."

"We'll be okay," she said, gently cutting him off. "I have the advantage of being a circuit court judge, so I have a pretty good idea what it takes to get a case on the appeals docket, and so do you."

A smile broke. "Want me to search the transcripts for errors?"

"Please."

"Want me to draft the letter, too? You can add the clouds yourself."

"Please."

He hesitated, and then probably because he was on a roll said, "Are you okay with what happened between us this morning?"

He meant the way he'd touched her, but Mattie couldn't go there. The case had triggered flashbacks, and his familiarity had sent her to a place she'd never wanted to go again. He couldn't have known that, of course, but he'd crossed the line, regardless.

"Let's leave that alone, okay?"

"Mattie, come on. This is me. We can talk about anything."

His wheedling tone set her fraying nerves on edge. "Okay then," she said, drawing a deep breath, "let's talk about how you don't know when to back off, like now. You make jokes about my underwear and my sexuality, and you burst into my chambers without any warning. It's unprofessional, Jaydee. It's unprofessional, and it's rude."

She sounded like Ms. Rowe, lecturing about manners when corruption was eating away at the very soul of the posh finishing school, like worms in rotting wood. *When I'm through with them, my girls will know how to smile and speak and put others at their ease. My girls will be grace itself.*

Jaydee drew back, his brow furrowing. He didn't seem to know what to say next. She'd succeeded in getting him to back off, but it gave her little comfort. She had intended to talk to him about what happened, but not like this.

"Hey, I'm sorry," he said. "You want me to knock, I'll knock."

Mattie tried to dismiss the entire episode with a shrug, but he wasn't having it. "I guess you are upset about what happened," he said. "I've already apologized twice. I could cut off my hand, if it would help."

"Keep your hand, lose the attitude," she said, trying to sound stern. "Nothing is wrong, and if there were, it wouldn't have anything to do with this morning, okay?"

Mattie shivered. She'd just broken out in a film of perspiration. Even her scalp was damp. "I just need some time to clear my head."

"Sure," he said, peering at her. "Are you all right?"

"I am, really." She engineered a smile. "I checked with Michelle and other than the sentencing hearing, my calendar is clear for a few days, so I'm going to start packing things up."

The Langston case had ended early, and Mattie wasn't due back at the Ninth Circuit until the following week. Whatever had to be done on Langston's behalf could be done from there.

"You talked to Michelle about this?"

"Yes, in fact, I gave her the afternoon off. You might as well take some time, too."

Michelle, Mattie's judicial assistant, kept track of her calendar and Jaydee's schedule, among other things. Jaydee was Mattie's senior clerk, and he'd been doing double duty for several months because her rotating clerk was out on maternity leave. Mattie had hired him as he was finishing his junior year at Berkeley, and she had to admit he was good. He'd be taking the bar exam in a few months, and he wasn't kidding when he talked about clerking for one of the Supremes. It didn't seem to faze him that only the top one percent in the nation were even considered.

Mattie's offer seemed to mollify him a bit. "Okay…but you'd tell me if there was anything really wrong, wouldn't you?"

"No, Jaydee, I wouldn't, but thanks for asking." She turned away again so he wouldn't see her fumble as she unzipped her robe.

She waited for the door to close, but didn't hear the click. She could feel him standing there, watching her, probably debating what to do.

"Mattie, you know I've got your back, don't you?" he said. "No matter what happens, I'll always have your back."

She felt heat in her throat, a sharp sadness. "I know that, Jaydee, thanks."

She wished she could accept his gesture of support. She knew it to be sincere, but he didn't realize what he was offering. The only time in her life anyone had ever had her back was during a brutal year in boarding school when she and two of her classmates had pledged to protect each other to the death, a pledge that turned out to be prophetic.

Jaydee *was* sincere, but there was so much about Mattie Smith he didn't know, so much she could never tell him.

Mattie didn't know quite what to do first. She was anxious to get settled in her own chambers, but she didn't have the energy it would take to start packing, not even her own personal things. A nice long lunch held some appeal, especially since she'd had no breakfast, but that would mean going home to change, and she couldn't even seem to get out of her robe.

Her shoe came up against something, and she looked down to see the newspaper on the floor. It must have fallen earlier when she bumped the desk. She knelt and opened it where it lay on the floor, giving the front-page headline a glance before leafing through the sections.

Her knee ached from the strain of kneeling, but she kept turning pages, not so much out of habit as some growing curiosity. She had no idea what she was looking for, but this was odd. Something compelled her. It was as if her eyes had seen an image that her brain hadn't registered.

An article in the metro section caught her attention. Earlier that month a local labor dispute had come before a panel of the Ninth Circuit judges, of which she'd been one, and she'd written the dissenting opinion, arguing that certain safety regulations were unnecessary, redundant and onerous for already overburdened contractors. It had not made her popular with union officials, but then she wasn't the darling of the business community, either. Last year she'd written the opinion on behalf of striking grocery workers.

Her lack of ideological bias tended to confound even her colleagues. Sometimes she wondered if that was the toughest part. She was a lone wolf in her own profession, and as yet, she'd made no strong ties with the other judges. That hampered her in some ways, but it had also given her tremendous freedom to think and act on her own.

She flipped through health, home and sports on her way to the features section. Whatever intuition had compelled her still seemed to be at work. Perhaps, without realizing it, she'd seen a teaser or a quote in one of the paper's sidebars.

The lead story about Jameson Cross, a local crime writer,

baffled her the first time she read the headline. The second time it stunned her.

"This can't be," she said under her breath.

The paper rattled loudly as she rose to her feet. She gripped it tighter, reading so fast she skipped chunks of information. All that mattered was finding the disclaimer, and it had to be here somewhere, the paragraph that said this was all a joke, all a mistake. It couldn't be happening.

Jameson Cross was calling for the finishing school murder case to be reopened. He cited William Broud's exoneration and argued that Broud's claims of a sex ring and a conspiracy to cover up the crime should be taken seriously. Cross was quoted as saying that he had launched his own investigation with the goal of reopening the case, and he claimed to have several prominent suspects in mind.

Mattie read the last paragraph aloud. "'Cross, who's known as a literary bounty hunter for his books delving into miscarriages of justice, is planning a book on this case. Through his past efforts on other cases, several prisoners, wrongfully convicted of homicide and other charges, have been found innocent and freed, and he's also aided police in bringing the real killers to justice.'"

Mattie left the paper on her desk. She hurried over to lock the door, her robes billowing around her. She didn't want anyone to interrupt her now. There was a phone card in her desk drawer that she could use to make the calls. It wouldn't be smart to have either number on her office phone bill, but there were two people who had to be informed about this turn of events. One was arguably the most visible woman in the world, and the other lived a life cloaked in sex and secrecy.

Moments later, Mattie sat at her desk, studying the sequence of numbers the phone card required. Her first call would be to a luxury spa in Mexico. Her second would be to the White House.

5

Jane Mantle was not pleased to see her personal assistant, Mia, waving from the other side of the circular Diplomatic Reception Room. Mia had slipped through the double doors and was hovering near one of the room's yellow damask settees. The younger woman's hand signals said it was important, and her judgment had to be trusted in this case. Jane was meeting with wife of the Peruvian ambassador, and Mia wouldn't have interrupted without good reason.

She gave Mia an imperceptible nod.

"Forgive me, Madame Velasquez." Jane made it a point to touch the petite woman's forearm as she promised to be back in a moment. Protocol varied as to personal contact with a foreign dignitary, but Jane had been advised that our neighbors to the south preferred less conversational distance and more contact than Americans, although hand shaking was usually reserved for males. She'd found that odd, but she was a stickler for getting it right.

At thirty-eight, she was among the younger First Ladies in history, but that didn't make her a maverick or a rule-breaker. She took comfort in knowing what to expect, so much so that when in doubt she'd been known to make up the rules herself. The press liked to call her the most organized First Lady in modern times, although it wasn't necessarily a compliment. She'd been busted in print for scheduling exactly three four-minute bathroom breaks into her twelve-hour day. Nor were their cracks about her pastel suits meant to be flattering.

She was a spring, for heaven's sake. What did they want her to wear? Black?

As Jane left the woman's side, an aide magically appeared to offer Madame Velasquez refreshments.

"You have a phone call, ma'am," Mia said. "It's urgent."

"Is it the president?" Jane's first thought was of Larry's health. He'd been complaining of a constriction in his chest, and she was a strong believer in herbs and natural medicines. She'd been nursing him herself rather than alarm the entire nation with a presidential doctor appointment. He was going to be fine, of course. He had to be. The country needed him, and so did she. But if it got any worse, she would have him at Bethesda's cardiac unit in no time flat.

They'd been married fifteen years, but she hadn't sacrificed herself and her gifts for Larry Mantle's political career as so many people thought. She'd given herself. They didn't have children or dogs and cats like most of the other first couples, but she and her husband were a team in ways that few people could understand. She wasn't always sure she understood it herself. But what would she do without Larry's ship to steer? He was the pilot, but she was the navigator.

"No ma'am, it's a Matilda Smith. I'm sorry, but—"

"Matilda Smith?" It had been years, but Jane wasn't likely to forget Mattie Smith. She just couldn't imagine her calling here, this way, without any warning.

"She said she was an old friend," Mia explained. "She went to school with you. She insisted it was urgent, and that you'd want me to interrupt. I hope I haven't made a mistake."

Jane's fingers went to her throat, straight to the string of cultured pearls she wore. "No, it's all right. Get a number and tell her I'll call back as soon as I've made my excuses to Madame Velasquez."

All kinds of questions raced through Jane's mind as she went to join her guest, who was now sitting on the blue-and-gold needlepoint divan, but had apparently declined a cup of anise tea and caramel custard with meringue, both Peruvian treats. Not a good sign when dignitaries didn't want to eat in the White House. Usually they took whatever was offered out of respect for the occasion. Jane had used refreshments to her advantage often, either as a stalling tactic or a distraction.

What could Mattie Smith possibly want? Jane could think of nothing else as she crossed the room. It had been several years since she'd spoken with Mattie personally, and urgent could mean anything. Had something happened to Mattie? Or to Breeze Wheeler, their other friend from finishing school? Jane didn't like where her thoughts were going, but the only other possibility was even worse.

Rowe Academy.

The rich blues and yellows of the reception room went pale before her eyes, and she slowed down to get her bearings. She had left all that behind, so far behind it couldn't touch her now, not here. She actually felt light-headed at the strange pounding in her ears. What was that sound? Her heart?

It took her a moment to realize what was happening. She hadn't felt emotion like this in so long she barely recognized it. Her schedule was fast and furious, but in a good way, she'd always thought. She liked the discipline of being busy. There was no time to get bogged down in feelings. Emotional highs and lows were dangerous when your life was a racetrack. You either accelerated and made the corners or you crashed.

This was not about Rowe. She wouldn't let it be.

She pulled a hanky from the sleeve of her suit jacket and

held it to her nose. Before she tucked the white lace back into its place, she gave it a glance, checking for blood. She was prone to nosebleeds when under stress, and she hadn't yet found a way to stop them, so she made it a point to check every so often. Thank God, no one had yet noticed or they would accuse her of scheduling that.

She looked at her watch, curious how long it would be before she could take another sliver. Years ago, she'd begun cutting a mild tranquilizer into sections so tiny they looked like slivers. Spaced out during the day, they were just enough to take the edge off without impairing her. She prided herself on her nerves-of-steel image, even if it did take a little help from her friends. She also liked not waking in the dead of night soaked in sweat and fighting to keep her mind from dragging her into dark places where demons lay in wait.

Another hour to go? It was bad this time.

Jane rushed over to Madame Velasquez with an apologetic smile. "I so want to resume our talk about the rain forest," she said. "Did I mention that the steps you and your husband are taking to preserve the country's natural resources are admirable?"

But Jane's hands were icy cold, and the other woman jumped as Jane grasped her arm. The shock on the Peruvian First Lady's face triggered something in Jane that felt like a premonition. She had a sense of things in motion that could not be controlled. Mattie's call was one of them. Whatever was happening, it wasn't good. After years of emptiness, she was suddenly in the grip of the one emotion she didn't ever want to feel again: Dread.

Breeze Wheeler was going through her lingerie armoire, searching for a few perfect pieces, when she heard the bedroom intercom chime. Intent on her search, she pulled a black satin peignoir set off the rack to have a better look. The lacework was exquisite, but it wasn't right at all. Classic, when she was going for sensual and playful. The image in her mind was lush décolletage, floaty boa feathers and Marilyn Monroe's limpid, blue-eyed breathlessness.

She spotted a red chiffon baby doll and arranged it on the bed with her other selections, still ignoring the persistent chimes.

"Two, three, four, five, six," she murmured, counting the pieces she'd laid out. These should work nicely. Her last touch was a Polaroid camera, which she gave pride of place on one of the bed's velvet throw pillows.

The intercom again. Her guest must be here, and he wasn't used to being kept waiting. In his country, people dropped to their knees to kiss his ring when he entered the room. His subjects trembled in his presence, but here in Breeze Wheeler's Spa Marbella, the usual rules did not apply. He was just one more man in need of the spa's many, varied and highly eclectic services.

That might be the best part of her strange and wonderful life, seeing the powerful at their most vulnerable. Behind the confident facades, doubts and fears ran rampant, and it was her job to make her clients feel safe, protected and, most of all, deserving of their exalted status. Some weren't, she had discovered. Some were despicable. Those she dealt with in her own special way.

Her silk kimono billowed against her bare legs as she picked up a remote and pressed a button. The intercom chimed to life, and the spa's receptionist answered.

"Ms. Wheeler? There's a phone call for you from the States."

"I can't take it now, Therese."

"She says it's urgent."

"She?"

"Matilda Smith. She said you would know who she was."

"Oh, my God."

"Ms. Wheeler?"

Breeze stepped back from the intercom. She dropped the remote on the bed and heard it miss, clunking on the floor. Her naturally fair skin must have been as stark white as the marble slab on her dresser. As far as she knew, Mattie wasn't aware that the goddesses had smiled down on Breeze Wheeler. She'd grown her modest day spa into a luxurious resort with a large, superbly trained staff, and one of the most exclusive clienteles in the world. Breeze's spa wasn't public, and its location was known only to a select few, but somehow Mattie had tracked her down, even though they hadn't had more than sporadic e-mail contact in years.

Once they'd been as close as family, but their bond had gone deeper than that, deeper than blood. Back in their boarding school days they'd been part of a small, inseparable group of three, but after they'd graduated, their lives had diverged. None of them had families worth a damn, so it had seemed terribly important to stay in touch, but they'd only managed it for a few years. Mattie had eventually gone into law and Jane, their fearless leader, had married a politician, which had put her under some scrutiny. After that, it had seemed wiser to go their separate ways, although the decision was largely unspoken, and Breeze had never stopped missing her two kindred souls.

"Ms. Wheeler, your guest is also here. In fact, he's been waiting for some time, and—"

"Therese, apologize to him for me, please. Profusely. Distract him with something yummy, Cristal and beluga, if necessary, but give me a few minutes before you send him up."

An impossible choice, Breeze thought. The old war buddy who had saved her life—or one of the most important foreign dignitaries on her client list?

"What about the urgent phone call?" Therese asked.

Breeze hesitated, still torn. If it was Mattie Smith then this wasn't a wedding or a baby announcement. It was something big, and Breeze, who was usually as free-floating as her name, needed time to prepare. Even she didn't wade in crocodile-infested waters without the proper boots.

If it wasn't Mattie—and that was a possibility—then she wanted to know as much as she could in advance, which would require some detective work. Breeze had more than herself to protect. She had the anonymity of her clientele.

"Take a number," she told Therese.

Breeze's bedroom suite had a sitting room and a wet bar. She headed for the liquor, which she rarely touched, but kept in plentiful supply for guests, and poured herself a gold-rimmed glass of something, possibly Cointreau. The searing heat brought tears to her eyes. She didn't even get down half the small glass, but it wouldn't have mattered anyway. What was missing couldn't be replaced by belting down a drink. It was her own resolve.

She would be fine. Whatever had happened, the strength to deal with it would be there when she needed it. It always had been.

Now it was time to prepare for her guest.

It took her mere seconds to slip out of the kimono and into the red baby doll, which was so sheer she felt naked. Less was more, she'd learned in her precocious youth, especially where skin was concerned. Lots of it wasn't nearly as tempting as a glimpse.

She slipped on the remainder of the outfit, a matching chiffon vest with poufed boa trim, which she left open and fluttery, and a pair of red satin slippers with boa trim.

"Set the scene," she murmured, giving her head a shake to scatter her hair. A drop of perfume on the décolletage was always nice. And then another in the belly button. And now for the kicker, she thought as she draped herself languorously on the chaise lounge to await him. Too bold for His Royal Highness? Too obvious? Perhaps.

A tap at the door set her heart racing. This was her moment of vulnerability. If she'd calculated wrong, she would know it immediately.

She couldn't decide whether she liked him better in his robe and *keffiyeh* or the immaculately tailored dark suit he was wearing.

"Will you join me?" she asked, bestowing him a smile.

His position demanded that she rise to her feet and show deference in some way. She did none of that, of course. She let a strap fall off her shoulder as she dragged herself to a sitting position.

"Have you ever read the American magazine, *Playboy?* Yes?" She returned his eager smile. "Actually, I knew that, Your Highness. Someone told me the magazine is a favorite of yours, and I have a little secret. I've always wanted to be a centerfold."

A Polaroid camera sat on the bed amongst her lingerie. She picked it up and handed it to him, letting her robe fall open. "Would you do the honors?"

He took the camera, and she could see by the gleam in his eye that she'd done the right thing. For the next few hours nothing would matter except making a man who had everything very happy, and all it took was a fifty-dollar Polaroid and a little imagination.

6

Rowe Academy
Fall 1981

Mattie didn't know whether to scream or play dead. The footsteps had stopped just outside the crawl space. Someone was out there, which meant Mattie might not be that far from a hall or a corridor. She didn't see how anyone but Ms. Rowe could have known where she was, but then Mattie had no idea how long she'd been unconscious—or trapped in this place.

If she stayed still, the headmistress might think she was already dead and leave her here to rot. Not a comforting thought, but better than suffering more torture at the hands of someone who was sadistic and deranged. Mattie didn't want to be dismembered and hidden in the walls of Rowe Academy. She wanted a chance to escape, and this might be it, if she didn't give herself away.

She closed her eyes and heard the rush and tumble of her breathing. She sounded like a freight train, which brought its own kind of panic. There had to be a way to summon some calming force, but she couldn't hear anything over the noise. She let her respiration slow and then subside altogether for a moment. It was a wonderful, sinking sensation that made her feel like a deep-sea diver, and in that odd state of being, the solution came to her.

The image of a bull's-eye filled the screen of her mind. Her archery lessons had always taken total focus. They relaxed and centered her in a way that nothing else could. At times it felt as if she'd merged with the yellow orb at the center, and if she could sink into that trancelike state now, she might be able to block out everything else. The still point of the turning world, she thought, recalling the T. S. Eliot reference from a literature class. Concentrate on that.

Her arms relaxed and her fists uncurled. The quiet was soothing, and as she meditated on it, she realized that the wire had stopped sparking. Maybe it had gone dead, and she was safe from that at least.

She'd begun to think her plan was working when she heard a scraping noise. It was down by her feet, and it sounded like someone was trying to remove a rusty grate, maybe a floor or wall vent. She wondered if the crawl space was some kind of air vent, but that seemed unlikely in such an old building.

"Is there something inside this wall?"

Mattie's eyes popped open. Whoever was out there was whispering to her.

"Mattie, is that you? Are you in there?"

The voice was familiar, but— Was that Jane?

Mattie's heart ripped out of control. She didn't know for sure, and she couldn't get a word past her grossly swollen tongue. Letting out an anguished croak, she began to thrash her legs, desperate to be saved. But she was also terrified of being electrocuted.

"Shhh, be quiet! I can hear you, but I can't get you out by myself. I have to get help."

No, no! Don't leave me, Jane!

Mattie could hear her running away, the sound suddenly

cut off by the bang of a shutting door. Mattie's zenlike calm had vanished, and she couldn't get it back. The silence had grown as thick as the heat. Sweat dripped from her brow. It stung her eyes like salt in a wound, but she didn't dare wipe it away. Nor did she dare move a muscle moments later when she heard the thunder of footsteps coming her way. All she could imagine was a hatchet blade splitting her mummy case and cleaving her chest in two.

What had Jane done? Set off the fire alarm? Mattie prayed she hadn't alerted Ms. Rowe, or she and Jane would both be entombed in the walls for eternity.

A heavy thud jarred Mattie, forcing a mute scream from her throat. Another shook the crawl space, and the wire crackled to life behind her. A blinding flash lit the area, but it wasn't electricity, she realized. The metal grate had been pried off, letting light flood in.

Someone grabbed Mattie by the ankles and dragged her out of the smothering sweatbox. She landed on the ground on her butt, choking on the clouds of dust that enveloped her. Her arm was bleeding. It looked like a gash, but there wasn't time to check for injuries. The dust had cleared, and she was staring straight up at the terrifying face of her rescuer.

Shadows wreathed the small room, but Mattie recognized the scowling creature immediately. How could she forget his bloodshot eyes and cold, angry mouth? She didn't know his name, but he was the school's handyman and gardener, and she'd been avoiding him since the day she saw him throw his pickax at a diseased pine and split the tree in two. Everyone was terrified of him except Ms. Rowe.

Mattie tried to thank him, but could only mouth the words. She wondered where Jane was and why she hadn't come with him. Maybe Jane hadn't found him, and he'd come up on his own. Mattie began to shiver.

Finally she got out, "Where's my friend?"

"Fell and hurt herself," he mumbled.

"How?" Mattie wasn't so certain that he hadn't hurt her himself. He'd disposed of Jane and now he was going to dispose of her.

"What the hell are you doing in the attic?" His mouth curled into a sneer of disdain. "I knew she was hiding something up here. Didn't think it was one of her students. What did you do? Use the wrong fork?"

It seemed safer not to answer. She had no idea what he was talking about.

"Spoiled-rotten little bitches need a good lesson," he muttered.

Mattie winced. She'd thought that's why students came to this school, for lessons. She struggled to get up, and he made absolutely no effort to help her. He looked disgusted enough to stuff her back in the wall.

Bastard, she thought. Anger burned through her fear, and she fixed him with a glare. "Bitch, maybe," she croaked, "but I'm not spoiled."

If she was surprised to get the words out, she was more surprised to see his scowl soften. Just for a second before he turned his back on her and left, he registered the barest hint of interest. Odd how he strode toward the door as if he couldn't wait to get out of there, as if he might get in trouble if he were found with her. Maybe that meant he wouldn't tell anyone.

The door slammed, and she shuddered with relief, violently. She'd expected him to split her in half like a tree.

The room he'd called an attic was thick with dust and roped with spiderwebs. It was also empty, except for some stacked metal chairs. She groaned and pushed to her feet, staring at the door he'd taken, the only door. She had to get out of this place, but the thought that he might be waiting for her somewhere down the stairs was enough to make her want to crawl out one of the dormer windows.

* * *

The school's infirmary was on the ground floor of Graedon Hall, another three-story tower at the east end of the U
that surrounded the courtyard. Mattie seemed to be the only
student in the unit's tiny bay of hospital-type beds, which
was fine with her now that her friend, Jane, had shown up,
proudly sporting bruises on her arms from her tumble down
the tower stairs. It seemed the handyman had been telling the
truth about why Jane hadn't come back with him.

Mattie sucked on an ice cube, relishing the relief it gave
her poor, thrashed tongue. She'd come to maybe an hour ago,
smelling of iodine and wearing a hospital gown, but had no
idea why she was there or where her clothes were. A bad fall
from the attic window had knocked her out cold, according
to Jane. Somehow Jane had gotten past the nurse's aide, stationed in the infirmary's front office.

"How long have I been here?" Mattie croaked.

Jane shushed her while she yanked the curtain shut around
the bed, enclosing them. "Ms. Rowe told us at dinner last
night that you'd had an allergic reaction," she whispered,
scooting as close as she could to Mattie on the bed. "She said
you were in the infirmary, but we should all stay away from
you because your tongue was swollen up like a tennis ball,
and you were embarrassed at how ugly it was."

Mattie gestured for Jane to get her some writing materi-
als. Jane quickly produced a notebook and pencil from her
backpack.

Rowe did this to me, Mattie wrote. *I spit on one of her disgusting men.*

Jane clapped a hand over her mouth, stifling a snort of
laughter. "That's my girl," she gurgled.

Mattie scribbled down another question. *How long have
I been here?*

"Since last night," Jane explained. "After that gardener

guy came down from the attic without you, I went up to see what had happened, but you were gone and the window was hanging open. You scared me to death, Mattie. I thought you'd jumped, and before I could get back down, that snotty senior, Lane Davison, had found you in a heap on the ground. It's amazing you didn't break any bones."

Mattie wasn't so certain about that. Her arm was tightly bandaged, and the way her knee throbbed, it felt as if she'd broken something. *I didn't jump,* she wrote. *I climbed down two whole stories to the ledge before I fell.*

"Well, Lane went to get Ms. Rowe," Jane said, eager to continue with her story, "who pretended to do CPR on you— no, not mouth-to-mouth!" Both girls grimaced at the thought. "She checked your pulse and stuff, and then she found the gardener and asked him to carry you to the infirmary. I followed them close enough to hear her tell him you must have had a severe allergic reaction, otherwise why would your tongue be swelled up that way. He never said a word, but he had to know it wasn't true."

Ugh, Mattie wrote. *He carried me here? Darth Vader?*

Jane nodded, hugging herself as if she were shuddering.

Where are Ivy and Breeze? Mattie wrote, curious about the other two members of their small band of outcasts. All four girls were at Rowe on scholarships, which made them untouchables as far as the nouveau riche kids and the blue bloods were concerned. But honestly, Mattie didn't mind so much anymore. She had real friends for the first time in her life, people she could count on.

"They're in Breeze's dorm room, lighting candles and sending up prayers for your swift recovery to the goddess."

That brought a smile to Mattie's lips, which wasn't easy when your tongue was a tennis ball. The band had discovered Artemis in a freshman lit class on mythology, and they'd adopted the fierce Greek deity as their patron. More than a goddess of the hunt and fertility, she was the protector of young women, who had decreed that she and her hand-maidens could never be seen by a man. Enter poor Actaeon, a hunter, who made the mistake of gazing upon Artemis and the girls as they bathed naked. Miffed, Artemis turned him into a stag and watched as his own hounds tore him to pieces.

When Artemis said no, she meant it.

"Oh, I almost forgot—" Jane dragged something else out of her backpack. "Ivy wanted you to have this. She said it would keep you company until you got back to the dorm with us."

The cuddly teddy bear must have come from Ivy's collection of stuffed animals, but Mattie didn't want it. She wasn't the teddy bear type, for God's sake. She rappelled down tall buildings! But she didn't want to hurt anyone's feelings, either.

With great reluctance, she reached for the bear, which sent Jane into gales of muffled laughter. "It won't bite," Jane said, stuffing the animal into her arms.

Mattie sighed and hugged the bear to her chest, feeling like the dork Jane always accused her of being. She managed a pained grin. Her knee made a strange clicking noise every time she moved it, and her bandaged arm stung, but she had one more question. She wrote on the pad and held it up for Jane to see.

How did you get in here without getting caught?

Jane actually blushed. "You know that cute guy from town who makes deliveries, Jimmy Broud? He has the key to the back door of this place, where the supplies are kept. I caught him on his way out."

Jane's smile was far too mysterious. Mattie was insanely curious, but she was determined not to reveal the slightest hint of interest in Jimmy Broud. *So he let you in here?* she asked Jane.

"Yes, and he wanted to know if I'd come to see Sleeping

Beauty. I think he meant you, but I lied and told him no, I just needed to get some aspirin for a headache. He's a pretty sweet guy, don't you think?"

"No!" Mattie barked the word and got a mouthful of fiery pain for her trouble. If Jimmy Broud had been looking at her while she slept, he would have seen the scratches and bruises on her face, the grotesquely swollen mouth. He couldn't have been talking about her unless he was being sarcastic.

"Is something wrong, Matt?"

Mattie fell back on the pillow. "T-tired," she got out.

"Yeah, sorry, I better get out of here. I'm supposed to be in first-period science, anyway. Are you going to be all right?"

Mattie's sigh was her answer.

Jane was suddenly serious. She dropped a hand over Mattie's, which she'd never done before. "Ms. Rowe wasn't always this cruel," she said. "Remember our first year, all the times she invited us up to her apartment, just the four of us? She gave us makeovers and swore to us that women had secrets, powers they didn't use. She promised to teach us things that would make up for all our disadvantages in life, and she told us we could be anything we wanted to be. I believed her."

Mattie had believed her, too.

"What happened to her?" Jane asked. "Why did she change?"

Mattie didn't know, but when she glanced over at her friend, she saw tears swimming in Jane's eyes. Pain welled up suddenly, cinching Mattie's heart and squeezing it hard. She had no idea how to make it go away, or to help Jane. Of all of them, Jane had wanted most to have the kind of life their headmistress had described, the beautiful things, the grace and refinement that seemed to belong to the privileged set alone.

"What are you going to do?" Jane asked her. "I mean, with Rowe on the rampage the way she is?"

Mattie's solution was easy, but she didn't write it down for Jane to read. It might take her a while to store up enough provisions, but she was going to run away. She hated the thought of leaving her friends, especially Ivy, who was fragile and needed more protection than any of them, but some guiding force, possibly Artemis, had already whispered the truth in Mattie's ear. If she stayed at this place much longer, something terrible was going to happen. Someone was going to be hurt, but it would not be her. It would be *because* of her.

7

Mattie let out a mute cry of pain. Something cold and sharp had jabbed her in the back. She rolled over and opened her eyes to the horror of someone standing beside her bed. A silvery object glinted in the darkness, and the figure hovering above her screamed of evil.

A bad dream? A nightmare? She blinked her eyes to make it go away. But she wasn't dreaming. It was Ms. Rowe and she had a knife in her hand.

Mattie slammed herself against the wall that buttressed the bed. She curled into the corner, making herself as small a target as possible. She couldn't scream loud enough for anyone to hear. It had only been a few days since she was trapped in the crawl space, and her tongue was still swollen.

Her thoughts darted about wildly. She'd found a lug wrench in a shed in the nearby woods, and hid it under her bed. But it was too far away, and the headmistress was too close.

Mattie gaped at the frightening figure, still unable to believe it was Ms. Rowe. She was wearing a gleaming dark robe and wisps of her hair had pulled from the braid she usually wore coiled at her neck. Moonlight made the wisps look white and wiry. Ms. Rowe had always been perfect in every way, from her grooming to her manners. She taught perfection. Expected it of her students. What was happening to her?

The headmistress broke the silence with a snick of laughter.

"Are you cowering, Matilda? Quite ridiculous. What did you think I was going to do? Stab you?"

She held up the silver object, letting Mattie see that it was a letter opener. "I was only trying to wake you. I thought we'd have a friendly little talk."

Mattie knotted herself tighter, aware that the T-shirt she slept in exposed her legs. She didn't know any other way to protect herself. This could be some kind of trick. She could get stabbed to death the second she showed her belly.

Menace crept into Ms. Rowe's smile. "Very well," she said in a low, trembling voice. "If you insist on looking ridiculous, have it your way, but you really are a very stupid girl."

Mattie wanted to croak that she was smart enough not to trust crazy people with sharp objects, but she knew better than to antagonize her at a time like this.

"It's time we came to an understanding," the headmistress said, "and since you don't *respond* well to the school's rules, I'm forced to be creative."

She produced Mattie's backpack, which meant she'd been snooping in Mattie's closet. Mattie had stashed the backpack there, and each day she'd been filling it with food she'd taken from the cafeteria.

"If you're thinking of running away, Matilda, think again. If you do, your friends will suffer in unspeakable ways. And I'll find you and drag you back by your hair to watch the fun. You must know that. I'll find you wherever you go."

She dropped the backpack, letting it crash to the ground. The sound of shattering glass made Mattie wince. She had dishes in there, too.

"Sh-sh-shi—" The word got mangled in Mattie's throat. *Shit.*

She flinched as the letter opener slashed close to her face. She heard the blade slice through the air.

Ms. Rowe loomed over her, hissing like a snake. "I'm deadly serious, you stupid, slovenly pig. And if you tell anyone about this talk we just had—if you ever discuss *anything* that happens here at school—your three friends will have accidents. Fatal accidents. They will die, one by one, starting with Ivy."

Mattie shook her head, disbelieving. She *had* gone crazy. Ms. Rowe hadn't been right in the head since she got back from her sabbatical this summer. Now she was threatening to kill people? Maybe she'd been killing them all along and stuffing them in walls.

"Ah, so I finally have your attention?" Triumph lit the headmistress's glittering eyes. She drew in a deep breath, as if savoring her power. "Let's hope you have the sense to cooperate. It will be so much easier for everyone, especially poor, sweet, *helpless* Ivy."

She thrust out her arm and rolled up the sleeve of her bathrobe. As Mattie watched in mute horror, Ms. Rowe dragged the sharp end of the letter opener across her pale skin, leaving a bloodred mark. "I'm not afraid of pain, Matilda. Nor am I afraid to inflict it, as you know."

Her smile was suddenly benign, as if she had actually enjoyed the ceremony. Mattie felt sick at the sight. She veered back as Ms. Rowe bent close and spoke in a soft, caressing voice.

"You won't tell a soul, of course, not about this, not about the man you were so rude to, not about anything." She patted Mattie's face almost tenderly. "I'm quite confident of that, Matilda. You may tell your friends, however. In fact, I'm counting on you to do that. They, too, need to understand the rules."

Her face was flushed, and she was breathing in short, sharp gasps as she turned to leave. Almost as suddenly as she had appeared, Ms. Rowe was closing the door behind her.

Mattie rushed to the bathroom, ignoring the pain in her knee. She was going to be sick, and she could only imagine what raw stomach acid would do to her wounded mouth.

Ivy White chose clothing that made her feel invisible. Today it was a gray cable-knit turtleneck and faded denim jeans, a couple sizes too large. But no matter how hard she tried to blend in with her surroundings, everyone saw her anyway. Maybe it was the awkward wall-clinging, but she drew attention like a magnet. At times she was certain her classmates were lying in wait to embarrass her and say nasty things.

"What do you use on your hair, White? A Weedwacker?"

"You got Twinkies stuffed in those jeans, Blubber Butt?"

They tried to make her feel overweight and ugly, but Ivy knew she wasn't either. She wasn't lithe and angular like Mattie or obviously pretty like Breeze, but she was a constant witness to her own ethereal beauty. People remarked on it to her face. Strangers stopped her on the street. There was no escaping it, and maybe that was why she was driven to wear drab, baggy clothes, or to binge on sweets one day and starve the next. To mar the perfection? Or to reveal the ugliness it hid?

This morning, she only had to make it as far as Mattie's dorm room, a few doors down from her own. That was where they were meeting to go to breakfast in the cafeteria. It was the best part of the day for Ivy, breakfast with her friends. She wasn't even sure what a sense of belonging was supposed to feel like, but she imagined it was something similar to the warmth that came from being with Mattie, Jane and Breeze.

She wasn't particularly good at her classes, except art. She did love sketching with charcoal, and it had shocked her when her father approved. She hadn't expected him to see anything of value in her scribblings. He was a classic work-aholic, and he'd always wanted her to be as driven to succeed as he was.

Ivy spotted a small pack of students coming her way, so she dashed over to Mattie's door and slipped inside. A small alcove hallway led to the dorm room itself. She hesitated there, her heart hammering as she heard the students pass by. When they'd gone, the whispering voices from inside Mattie's room drew her attention. It sounded like her three friends, but Ivy heard her own name mentioned and wondered why they were talking about her. She moved close enough to the doorway to hear.

"We can't tell Ivy. It will scare the shit out of her."

"Rowe threatens to kill her, and we aren't supposed to tell her?"

"Ivy's the weakest of us all. That's why Rowe picked her to die first. She knew we'd do anything to protect her. Now, we don't have any choice but to obey Rowe's disgusting rules. She knows that."

Ivy went utterly still. The one who didn't want to tell her was Mattie. Ivy recognized the croaking voice. The second voice was Breeze's and the third, Jane's.

It took a moment for the horror of what she'd heard to sink in. She was a pariah wherever she went, even among her own friends. She was the weak one, the target, and they had to sacrifice themselves to protect her. Now it was so bad Ms. Rowe was threatening to kill her, and maybe them, too, because of her.

She let herself out of Mattie's room and dashed back to her own, veering around a small knot of gossiping girls. They all turned to watch her, but no one called out. Maybe even Ivy White looked too crazy this time.

Once she was back in her room, she went straight to the long dresser and pulled it away from the wall. It was an antique, built with an indentation in the back just big enough for her to curl up inside. As soon as she'd arranged herself, she gripped the dresser by the legs and pulled it back. None of the floor mistresses had ever thought to look for her here when they were searching for her. Even her friends didn't know about this place.

Why did she only feel safe when she was hidden from sight?

She ought to pack her things and go home, but she couldn't. Her father would never allow it, and he would never believe anything against Ms. Rowe, certainly not that the headmistress was plotting murder. The idea would probably amuse him. He'd not only picked this school himself, he'd generously endowed it. But, in his typically bizarre fashion, he'd insisted that Ivy enroll under another name so that she wouldn't be shown any favoritism. And he'd made her apply for a scholarship, as if she were from a destitute family. Ms. Rowe didn't even know who Ivy White really was.

No, she couldn't go home in disgrace. Her father would probably kill her himself. He wanted offspring as hard and fearless as he was. He would expect her to handle this herself and not come whining to him. Her sensitivity had always seemed to enrage him, even when she was small, but she had the feeling it frightened him, too.

Curled up in her cubbyhole, Ivy contemplated her immediate future. She could not go home. This place was her last chance.

8

Mattie let loose a string of expletives as she tried to wedge her tea mug into her trial case. The case bulged like an over-inflated tire, and she could relate. Her orderly life was suddenly very disorderly, and the worst of it seemed to have come out of nowhere. The kidnapping trial had gone terribly wrong, and now some vigilante crime writer was threatening to play Pandora and open a box that was booby-trapped, probably with explosives. She wasn't entirely sure herself what was in that box, but she knew at least three people who would get hurt if Jameson Cross continued mucking around. She was one of them.

Mattie turned slitty eyes on the mug. "I'll leave you here. You want to stay here, where the dispenser water doesn't get hot enough to make a decent cup of tea?"

Threatening a mug. Pathetic. Even worse, her cell phone hadn't rung. It had been nearly two hours since she'd placed calls to Breeze Wheeler and Jane Mantle, but she'd heard nothing back, and considering the time zone differences, it was probably too late to call again. She would have to wait for them, and in this case, patience wasn't a virtue. It was a pain in the ass.

She gave her fingernails a furtive glance, noticed a tiny hangnail on her index finger and absently nipped it off with her teeth. Not up to Ms. Rowe's standards, certainly, but better than biting nails on the Relative Scale of Unattractive Habits. At least she didn't do that anymore.

My girls eschew the rude behavior that so many young women today find fashionable. And no, eschew does not mean sneeze, but if it did, my girls would most certainly have a hanky tucked up their sleeve.

Mattie gave the mug another look. She had not given up.

She spotted her shoulder bag, hanging from the coat tree. Perfect. The mug could go in there. That decided, she scrutinized the banker's boxes of files and the stacks of research material, and finally, she picked one last item from her desk. That morning's crumpled *San Francisco Chronicle.*

She crushed it into the case and locked it. Done. The rest of it would be packed up and moved by Jaydee, and whomever he could muscle into helping him. As Mattie took her shoulder bag from the tree and dropped her mug into it, she felt the tension ease. Maybe things would settle down when she got back to the Ninth Circuit.

It was possible she'd overreacted to the Broud article. People called for murder cases to be reopened all the time, but very few were. Law enforcement had enough on their hands without resurrecting cases over twenty years old, and the Tiburon city fathers wouldn't want this one reopened anyway. The finishing school murder was a cesspool of potential scandal for everyone involved. It had soiled whatever it touched, from the students to the faculty to the town itself.

Maybe she *was* overreacting. Maybe it would all go away. And meanwhile, she had Ronald Langston's appeal to deal with.

A knock on the door brought her around. Interesting. Was that Jaydee, mending fences? "Now, that didn't hurt, did it?" she called out, smiling. "Come on in."

The door rolled open, but the man who entered was not Jaydee.

Mattie's smile vanished. Her staff had gone, but she couldn't imagine how he'd slipped past security. Federal judges were well protected. She couldn't place the man, but there was something familiar about his lean face and dark hair. His eyes were odd, a shade of gray so pale it pierced, and his raincoat billowed like judicial robes, evoking images of a grand inquisitioner. Clearly, she'd spent too much time in the halls of justice.

"Didn't hurt a bit," he said, holding her gaze.

She held on to her bag, thinking the mug would make it a good weapon if she had to swing. There was also a panic button on the underside of her desktop, providing she got there before he did.

"How did you get in here?" she asked him.

He flashed a card, which she couldn't read from where she stood.

"My credentials usually get me through the front door without a problem," he explained.

"I *meant* my chambers."

"Ah, well, apparently everyone in the building thinks you're already gone. Your staff has vanished, and even the marshal's been reassigned. By the way, are you Judge Matilda Smith?"

He was still holding the card, but she wasn't going over there. She hadn't decided whether she was safe or not, but she'd had plenty of experience with rapists and murderers and he wasn't giving off any of those vibes. Nor did he look like an escaped convict bent on revenge. He was attractive, actually, but in the same eerie way that he was disturbing. Did she know him from somewhere?

"Judge Smith?" he repeated.

His voice was not what she expected at all, deep and oddly musical. It tugged at her to answer, but she wasn't easily led these days. He looked younger than her first impression, perhaps forty, and she sensed that she was dealing with an acute intelligence. Everything about him burned with the fires of awareness.

He spotted her name engraved on the trial case's brass locking plate.

"Your Honor," he said with perhaps a touch too much reverence. "I read your opinion on the Sunshine Toys appeal. It was brilliant. I write for the *Chronicle Magazine,* and I'd like to ask you a few questions."

He put the card away. Apparently he'd given up on her taking it. The magazine he mentioned was a supplement that came with the newspaper on Sundays. It dealt almost exclusively with Bay-area people and places of interest. A coincidence that he was here after this morning's article? Mattie wanted to think so. She really did.

"About Sunshine?" she said. "That was resolved months ago."

"About you, Matilda Smith, the woman."

Mattie must have breathed too deeply. She almost coughed. "Sorry, but your timing is way off. As you can see, I haven't moved out, but I'm trying to."

"I would have called for an appointment, but I had a hunch you'd say no."

"You should listen to your hunches."

"I do. I woke up feeling lucky this morning, and here I am."

"Look, I really do need to finish up here."

He checked out the boxes. "Where do you want them? I have a van. I can move you anywhere you want to go."

"Thanks, but I haven't finished packing."

"You drive a hard bargain. Okay, I'll help you pack."

He cocked his head expectantly, which she ignored. A wiseass reporter. Just what she needed to complete her day. He probably thought his quick wit would give him an advantage. She was about to point out that the desk had a panic button when she noticed something. It wasn't his eyes that were piercing. It was his stare. His irises were a strange lavender-gray, and one of the loveliest, eeriest colors she'd ever seen. He *was* almost perversely attractive.

"What could you possibly want to know about me?" She meant that with all her heart. "I lead a very mundane life. Judges aren't exactly celebrities."

"Most aren't."

She set her bag down on the desk. "Meaning I am? I've written some controversial opinions, but so have many of the Ninth Circuit judges. I can't hold a candle to Judges Reinhardt and Kozinski."

"Apparently you haven't seen the blog."

"Blog?"

"A Web log on the Internet called 'Underneath Their Robes.' You're the star attraction."

Don't ask, Mattie thought.

He told her anyway, of course. "As of this morning, you're the odds-on favorite to win the Superhotties of the Federal Judiciary contest. However, you do have some stiff competition. You're up against twenty-one other federal judges— women and men—who are said to be the equivalent of *People* magazine's Most Beautiful list."

Mattie laced her fingers together, but held her fire, as any prudent person might, under the circumstances. She could have had him thrown out, but he was a member of the press, not that she particularly cared at this point. It was something else that told her to be quiet, to listen—a prickling sensation at the nape of her neck that she'd learned to heed.

"I'm just reporting what I read," he said, apparently forgetting about the hazards of being the messenger. "The blog also has a great gossip column. The items are blind, but it's pretty clear who they mean when they're whispering about the Ninth Circuit hottie who gives her fellow male jurists heart palpitations, as well as philosophical fits."

"Male jurists?" Mattie graced him with a cool smile. Ms. Rowe would have beamed. "No talk of gender preference on this blog?"

"*Your* gender preference? Is there something to talk about?"

"Apparently not or they wouldn't have missed it." She dismissed the subject with a curt tone to let him know she meant business, which would, of course, intrigue him all the more. Her lesbian alter ego was a fabulously effective distraction.

"Someone has too much time on his or her hands," she said. "If I'm the attraction this week, next week it will be Justice O'Conner."

His expression told her he was struggling to get back on track. It also said he'd probably like to check out her khaki skirt and blouse without being too obvious about it. She could almost hear the questions running through his head. Was she really gay? Were there obvious signs?

Mattie was delighted she'd worn her Ferragamo Mary Janes. The only thing better would have been ballerina slippers. She wanted to smile. So badly.

"I'm the flavor of the week," she said, as if that were the end of it.

He studied her intently. Walked over to the room's only guest chair, sat down and studied her some more.

Go ahead, let him bring it up, she thought. She most certainly would not talk about it, and he wouldn't be able to think of anything else.

Just where she wanted him.

She would have felt deliciously in control, except for one thing. Those eyes of his were enough to make her hair stand on end. It felt as if he'd brought an electrical charge in the door with him. She would have expected to get a shock off her own carpet with him around.

"I might agree with you on flavor of the week," he said at last, "except that your name hits the legitimate media on a regular basis, too. Sunshine Toys, for example."

He was talking about a copyright infringement suit heard by the Ninth Circuit. An artist had used the toy giant's best-selling dolls in an exhibit to call attention to a dangerous trend of desensitization concerning violence against women. The eye-popping tableaux of female dolls suggested bondage and nonconsensual sexual activity, and the indignant toy company charged that the work was lewd and soiled the dolls' wholesome image.

The three-judge panel on which Mattie sat found no basis for the infringement charge, and her written opinion argued that the depictions were constitutionally protected forms of social commentary. In closing, she'd given the toy company a slap on the wrist by suggesting that the anatomically correct dolls distorted the natural contours of women's bodies in ways that were neither wholesome nor realistic, and may have done more damage to young, impressionable minds than the artist's work ever could.

"I did enjoy writing that decision," Mattie admitted.

"Of course," he said, "given your *gender* preference."

Mattie couldn't suppress a smile, and neither could he. "Why would that have anything to do with it?" she asked.

"I can't imagine."

She didn't point out to him that it wasn't her most controversial opinion. But it had made for a good sound bite and gotten lots of media play. It had also helped confirm speculation that Matilda Smith wasn't nearly as interested in legal technicalities—or even legal justice—as she was in getting at the truth, no matter how elusive and contradictory.

Mattie actually took pride in that rumor. She believed that too often justice went to the highest bidder, and the best attorneys were master illusionists, but she also believed that truth played no favorites. All it required was a dedicated seeker, and that she'd tried to be.

"What are you doing?" she asked.

He was on his feet again, and he'd noticed the pile of paperwork on her desk, which included a tattered palmistry chart. It illustrated the human palm, its various lines and their meanings, and it had belonged to her mother. Mattie had been surprised to find it folded up and tucked in a sleeve of her briefcase. She wasn't sure how it got there, or why she'd been carrying it around with her. Not for sentimental reasons, certainly.

"Palmistry?"

Don't all hot lesbian judges read palms? "One of my many useless skills," she said.

"Most judges carry court files in their briefcases."

"I guess we've established that I'm not most judges."

"Exactly." His voice suddenly burned with meaning, and he moved as if to come straight for her. "Can we talk, Your Honor? Is that a possibility because I believe you have some things to say that people might want to hear."

"Yes." Mattie said it more to ward him off than anything else. Clearly he'd worn her down, or maybe she was just curious, especially after what his newspaper had written. "What do you want to know?"

"Anything you'd care to tell me. Let's start with your past—recent or distant—I could go either way."

"Recent," she said. "My signal fades after ten years or so."

"Whatever you'd like." He glanced at the chair he'd just vacated, as if awaiting an invitation this time. His good manners baffled her, but she nodded for him to sit, very aware that he'd glanced at her body again.

"Any truth to the rumors that you wear a bulletproof vest?" he asked.

She presented herself to him with a sweep of her hand. "Does this look like a bulletproof vest to you?"

"It looks good to me."

She came very close to coloring. Jaydee would have found that interesting, she knew. At the very least, it might have eased his mind about a few things, so of course, he would never know.

She changed the subject. "I wish I could offer you something to drink, but as you already know, these are temporary quarters."

"I'm fine." He settled back in the chair, which just barely accommodated his unusual height. "Tell me how you became one of the youngest federal circuit court judges in the country. That's quite an honor."

"Well, I got appointed, and then I got confirmed. I'm sure they're all sorry now."

"You're too humble," he said in a wry tone. "Your record is commendable. You distinguished yourself as both a defense attorney and as a prosecutor. Who doesn't remember the wide-eyed nursing mother you defended against the transit company's indecent exposure suit? Or that barrio drug lord you sent up the river? The people versus Victor Trabuco, wasn't it? That was a powerful closing argument."

She thanked him, aware that it was Jaydee who deserved the credit. She wouldn't have had a case or a closing argument without him.

A cold sensation unfurled in her stomach. It was as much a warning as the prickling sensation at her nape, and she glanced at her watch. "Are we done? I'm expecting a phone call."

He showed no signs of leaving, but he was alert now, watching her.

"One last question?" he said. "How strong is your signal for the finishing school murder? You were at Rowe Academy about the time it happened, weren't you? My research shows that you graduated twenty-two years ago, one year after the murder was committed."

Mattie's laughter was quick and sharp. "Twenty-two years ago? You really know how to hurt a girl."

That information wasn't in any of her official biographical material, but it didn't surprise her that he'd found it with all the research he'd done. If she didn't go along with him, it might look suspicious. On the other hand, she wasn't giving anything away. At least now she wasn't off balance. She knew exactly what to do, get him out of here as quickly as possible.

She walked over to the nearest window. The blinds were open at the angle she liked them, letting in misty ribbons of light. She wondered if she had the strength to shut them. Would he see the panic rising like steam, her terror of being closed in? She'd always liked the idea of seeing without being seen, but she couldn't be in a room where everything was closed up tight, the doors, the blinds, everything. That made her feel trapped.

And so did he, she realized.

She turned to face him. "I'm afraid that signal's pretty faint, sorry. It was a long time ago."

"I thought it might be." He rose from his chair. "What is it that's not supposed to hurt?" he asked out of the blue.

"Excuse me?"

"When I knocked on the door, you said 'that didn't hurt, did it?'"

"Oh, my law clerk has an aversion to knocking. I thought it was him."

"Maybe he likes to catch you off guard. It's not an unpleasant thought."

"Mr.—I don't know your name," Mattie realized aloud. "Are you flirting?"

"It's Cross," he said, "Jameson Cross."

Shit. The expletive caught in Mattie's throat, fortunately. She was entertaining the crime writer who wanted the finishing school case reopened. He'd obviously been lying in wait the entire time he was in her office, hoping to catch her unaware. Without giving it another thought, Mattie walked over to the desk, reached under the top and hit the panic button.

"Goodbye, Mr. Cross," she murmured.

9

A tiny red light flashed in the shadows like a radio beacon on a tower. Jameson Cross saw it the moment he entered the old marine warehouse he'd converted into his living quarters. Whether he wanted to or not, he saw it. Every time. How could you miss Red Death, his nickname for the omnipresent telephone answering system?

He dropped his computer case on the trunk table and hesitated there, in the entry of the airplane-hangarlike space that he had called home for the past several years. He usually went over his notes at the end of the day, cleaned them up and organized them, but he wasn't in the right frame of mind. There was too much unformed information in his brain. He needed to give his thoughts time to take shape.

Red Death continued to flash, but he'd become an expert at ignoring it. That might be his only accomplishment today. His investigation had hit a couple of speed bumps, one of them being a federal judge named Matilda Smith. He wouldn't quickly forget the look on her face when she'd pushed the panic button. Fortunately, she'd told the guards it was all a mistake, but no one had believed her, least of all him.

He closed his eyes for a moment, holding on to the snapshot in his mind of her sudden defiance. What was she covering, fear? He didn't yet have concrete proof that she was one of the lonely girls, but the way she'd avoided his questions and then bounced him had sent up flags.

He'd only been actively working on the case a few weeks. The news of Broud's exoneration had piqued his interest, but he hadn't been able to get at the court transcripts or the original police records. They'd been sealed since the first trial back in the eighties. Only the attorneys who'd worked on Broud's case over the years had gained access to them, and Jameson had already been in touch with the young woman who'd engineered his release, but Tansy Black had refused to see him in deference to her client's wishes.

She'd been pleasant enough when they'd spoken on the phone. "It's nothing personal," she'd said, "but William has asked me not to discuss the case with the media."

Jameson could have told her he was family. She might have hung up in his ear. He'd shamelessly dangled a prominent mention in his book on the finishing school murder, but she hadn't taken the bait.

Hot late-day sun poured down on him from a skylight that ran the length of the warehouse's vaulted ceiling. He'd worn a raincoat because of the clouds this morning, but the weather had fooled him again—and so had this case. It seemed to be locked up tighter than a vault, even after twenty-three years. He'd found it impossible to get information that should have been readily available, like trial transcripts, and not simply because the case was cold. Broud had been dismissed as crazy all those years ago when he claimed there was a conspiracy and a cover-up. He wasn't looking so crazy now.

Still deep in thought, Jameson kicked off his woven leather sandals, leaving them on the slate entry tiles, and released the stainless steel band on his watch. So far he'd had to rely on old newspaper clippings, magazine articles and the yearbooks in the school library. He was lucky there'd been plenty of media interest in Millicent Rowe and her prominent family, her father being a state senator. Jameson had also questioned the faculty, staff and alumni at Rowe. Anyone he'd found who'd been on the scene that day had been interviewed.

No one had known the identities of the lonely girls. Most claimed never to have heard of them outside of having read the same clippings Jameson had found, but there was some speculation that they might have been the Grace scholarship girls, a small group of students who hung out together and were generally thought to be a little odd and antisocial.

Some harmless chicanery had gotten Jameson copies of three of the girls' transcripts, and their grades had been exceptional. One in particular had excelled at her studies, particularly the classics and the sciences, Matilda Smith.

Mattie. That's what the other students had called her.

Odd that he couldn't remember her. Jameson rubbed the back of his neck and realized he was perspiring. He moved out of the sun, doing what amounted to a slow strip as he walked toward his bedroom at the other end of the twenty-five hundred square foot building.

He set his watch on a marble-topped console and then reached behind his head for a handful of his tan crewneck sweater to pull it off. The stretch felt good. He wasn't exercising enough, even though he'd put in a workout room when he bought the warehouse. He'd chosen the place because it was enormous, but there were no windows, so he'd had the vaulted ceiling split from front to back and a skylight panel installed. The effect was so interesting he'd decided not to cut any windows into the walls.

In the mornings, sun crept in from the east and moved through the rooms to the west, making a sundial out of his home. But the bright line of light also cast the periphery of the house into perpetual shadow, which gave the impression of day and night at the same time. Jameson liked the contrast.

His sweater landed on the granite countertop that separated the dining room from the kitchen area. He unsnapped his jeans and let them drop enough to ride on his hips. The stress of the day seemed to ease with every possession he shed. Possibly he should have been a nudist.

"I'd do naked cartwheels if it would help me sort out this case," he said, thinking aloud. The yearbook pictures had triggered some memory traces, especially of the painfully beautiful Ivy, who was found dead in her dorm room a month before the headmistress was murdered. Jameson had been eighteen at the time, and working his way through college, delivering institutional supplies.

Rowe was on his route, and he always stopped there, whether he needed to or not. He'd had a secret crush on Ivy, and her death had been incomprehensible to him. It was called accidental, but the timing was highly coincidental, as was the poison, heartwine, which came from tropical berries that oozed a bloodred liquid when crushed, that had been found in her system. Over time the fermenting juice lost its color and odor, but turned highly toxic. A cortical depressant, it worked on the higher centers of the brain and eventually paralyzed the vital organs, starting with the heart and lungs.

Jameson had heard from several sources that Millicent Rowe had used heartwine for mysterious cosmetic purposes, and it had also been found in her system during the autopsy, although not a lethal dose. She'd died by asphyxiation, smothered to death with her own pillow.

The air had cooled his bare skin by the time Jameson got to his favorite room, the library. It was an extension of the living room and two of the walls had teak bookshelves that ran from floor to ceiling. The third wall was actually a hanging screen where his unique collection of magazine covers was displayed.

The cleaning service must have been in that day, he realized. A stack of books had been reshelved, and the rest of the house was neat, as well, except for the mess he was making. Red Death or not, it was good to be home, even if home was a "trashy, film-noir-inspired bunker," as *Golden Gate* magazine had once described it in an article.

Cold-blooded sharks, those newspaper reporters. He'd been a journalist all his adult life. You couldn't tell him about cutthroat. The article had described him as dark and elegant, terms that often came up in his publicity, and had originated with his publisher. Jameson went along with it because it sold books, but no one would ever have described him as elegant if they'd seen what he could do to a hotel room in ten seconds flat.

He hit a switch and the wall opposite him lit up, illuminated by a track of spotlights. Maybe it was pride that made him smile as he contemplated his prized collection. This could be what the reporter had objected to. Jameson had taken covers from pulp classics like *The Detective, True Crime* and *True Police Yearbook* and had them blown up to poster size and framed. The artwork was mostly damsels in distress. Lots of distress.

Jameson wasn't quite sure whether he wanted to be the guy who tied the damsels up or the guy who untied them, but both thoughts intrigued him. He'd been immersed in crime magazines since he was a kid, and they were probably responsible for the direction his career had taken. Detective work was in his blood, and he satisfied the urge with the investigative reporting for his books and articles. Other than that he had no excuses for his taste in art. He loved the stuff…with one exception.

The cover of *Detective Casebook Chronicles* featured a scantily clad woman in bondage, not unlike many of the other covers, except that this woman's bondage was potentially

lethal. Her wrists and ankles were tied with rope, and a longer length of rope had been secured to her bound ankles,
drawn up and looped around her throat in a way that would
eventually cut off her breathing if she struggled.

That was grotesquely obvious to Jameson now, but it hadn't
been when he bought it. He'd been twelve, too young to understand. The dealer had told him it was the magazine's first
and only issue, one of a kind. But the cover had disturbed him
on sight, and later, when he'd realized what the tie could do,
he'd told himself to remove it from his collection. He wasn't
sure why he hadn't done that. But now, decades later, the woman's plight served as a constant reminder that no matter how
innocent the impulse, tragedy was always there, lying in wait.

His stomach rumbled, reminding him that breakfast had
been his only meal that day. There were pork tamales and a
quart of orange juice in the fridge, but Red Death still beckoned. He might as well get it over with.

On his way back to the blinking orb, he absently detoured
to close a cabinet door on the entertainment center. The
cleaning service must have missed it. They'd missed a drawer
in the kitchen last week. He noticed things like that. Opened
drawers. Lost tapes. One missing girl from a set of four.

One. Missing. Girl.

Jameson's thought processes brought him to a halt. He'd
found yearbook pictures of three of them—Ivy White, Jane
Dunbar and Brenda Wheeler, but nothing of Mattie Smith.
He could still see her expression when he'd asked about the
finishing school murder that morning. She'd look terrified for
a split second before defiance had burned it away.

Where had he seen that look? Could she have been the
wary little urchin who hid behind trees and watched him un-
load the truck? He'd tried to approach her once, and she'd
spit at him and run away. Had the Honorable Judge of the
Ninth Circuit Court of Appeals been *that* wild thing?

He walked over to Red Death, hit the button that played back the messages and folded his arms, listening to the first call. It was Carson Silvers, his literary agent of many years.

"Jim," he barked, "where's that blockbuster proposal you promised me? I hope to hell you're not working on that finishing school crap. You're much too close to that project, Jim. Leave it to someone with objectivity."

Jameson smiled. Carson was right as always. A man could hardly be more involved than Jameson was, but that didn't mean the true story wouldn't make a tremendous book, if someone could get to it. Jameson had gone all the way to his friend, Frank O'Neill, the current district attorney of Marin County, trying to get access to the records and evidence, including a set of videotapes the headmistress was supposed to have made as teaching aids. He also wanted lab and autopsy reports.

Frank had actually laughed at him. They met once a week at the Athletic Club for racquetball, and afterward, in the steam room, Jameson had brought up the sealed records.

"You know I can't do that, buddy," Frank had said as they sat across from each other in their white terry towels. "Only the judge who ordered them sealed has that authority. In lieu of that, you'd have to hire yourself an attorney and file a motion with a state court judge."

Jameson had questioned why the records were still sealed, but Frank wouldn't go into that, either. And Jameson had already started looking for another angle, which included going to the source. He wasn't done with Mattie Smith and her friends.

He deleted Carson's message and went on to the next one.

"It's William," the caller said in a strained whisper, "William Broud. You offered to help, and I hope you meant it. I'm at the Excelsior Hotel in San Rafael, and I want to talk. But don't come now. I need some rest. Wait until tomorrow, around noon."

Jameson played the message again, alert for clues as to what had made Broud change his mind. The whisper suggested he thought someone was listening. That was all Jameson got, but it was interesting that Broud was staying in San Rafael. The small coastal town was about a half hour's drive up Highway 101, and for Jameson, it would be going home.

William Broud feared the mattress was going to swallow him whole. With every turn, he sank into its softness. There were no hard spaces, nowhere to get purchase, even at the edges. The spongy foam pillows lay on the floor where he'd flung them. He couldn't breathe with the damn things pushing into his face like grasping, smothering hands.

He rolled his head and looked at the clock. He wasn't used to one of those, either, and wasn't sure he ever wanted to be. He hated being reminded minute by minute that his life up to now had been a stinking waste. On death row, day faded into night, night into day. After a while, everything faded, even the cell bars. You just didn't see them anymore. Some inmates had money for luxuries like a TV or a clock. Others had relatives who cared enough to—

A barking sound ripped out of him. Laughter? Anger? He didn't know anymore. What did it matter?

His throat burned, and he struggled to a sitting position. There'd been some plastic bottles filled with water in the room when he got there. Strange thing, putting water in a little bottle. He'd drunk it though, figuring the stuff from the tap must be backed up with sewage.

The bottle on the nightstand had a swallow or two left. He swigged it down, grimacing at the aftertaste. Tap water couldn't have been much worse, even backed up. Funny the way his fingers tingled. His lips, too. He rubbed his icy hands, trying to get some feeling back. Maybe he was sick.

The thought made his heart race. Where did a man go when he was sick? He didn't even know where he was going when he left this hotel. He had sixty-six bucks and no prospects. The job leads the community resources officer had given him were a joke. No one was going to hire this death row freak show.

In prison he'd dreamed about nothing else but being free and how it would solve all his problems. Now he was free, and he didn't even know how to sleep on a bed. The dark hotel room felt like a cavernous void. How did people think with so much empty space?

The heat was stifling. He'd turned the thermostat off and stripped down to his shorts, but he couldn't get the room cold enough. Maybe he was trying to recreate the dripping wet chill of a San Quentin cell block. But there was no cold like that. It froze your mind, your soul.

He rose from the bed, joints cracking. Fatigue dragged at his footsteps. It made him stagger. There was nowhere to go. He'd dreamed of taking walks, but the darkness outside looked like the mouth of the universe. If you fell, you'd fall forever. A man would need a space suit to survive.

Damn window curtains didn't work, or he would have shut them.

Had he locked the door? He checked it, latching and unlatching it several times to be sure. He knew what could kill him in jail. Out here, anything could kill you. Hotel rooms could do it.

He ended up in the bathroom, pissing into a moldy toilet bowl. The room stunk, but at least the smell was familiar. As he stared at his stubbly jaw and red-rimmed eyes in the mirror, he realized that he'd found his space suit. This was where he belonged. This filthy latrine of a room, this hard, cold floor.

Shivering, he lay down on peeling tile and rested his head near the base of the toilet. Ammonia burned its way into his sinus cavities. This was what he knew. Every night he slept with the stink and the cold and the terror. Every night his last conscious thought was of being attacked in his sleep, of never waking up.

The barking sound erupted from his chest. He couldn't get it to stop, but it wasn't laughter. It was a dry, hacking cough.

He opened his eyes and stared at the ceiling, startled by his thoughts.

It hadn't happened. He hadn't died in his cell.

He'd made it out alive. For some reason, he'd survived, and yet he didn't believe in predestination. If everything happened for a reason, who could explain what had happened to him for the past two decades? An innocent man locked in a putrid stink hole, waiting to be executed? Explain that.

He'd lived with the brutal truth of his own innocence the entire time, and no one had cared. Now they would. Lots of people would. Fear had kept him silent all these years. There'd been death threats, anonymous warnings to keep his mouth shut, but it wasn't his life at stake. They must have known that wouldn't work. They'd threatened to kill the only family he had left.

He hadn't said a word to anyone, not even to the attorneys who'd filed his stays of execution. There was nothing he could tell them, nothing he could say until now. He'd already had requests for interviews and turned them all down. He didn't know who to talk to, but he'd given his papers to someone who could do that for him. It was all in his papers, the ones he'd written in his cell and hidden in the deep cracks in the cement.

He closed his eyes, wondering if he'd ever done anything in his life that counted as good. He didn't want to think about that. He didn't want to care about his life. It made him sad.

He couldn't remember when his heart had ached this way. He'd helped a young girl once, although someone else probably would have if he hadn't. And he had stayed quiet all these years, but not just for himself. Maybe that's what this sickness was about, this terrible fire in his chest and throat. Maybe that was the reason he'd lived. To stay quiet.

But he couldn't do it any longer. He had to tell someone what he'd been carrying with him. If he died for it, no big loss. Even if he lived to be an old man, he would never know how to sleep anywhere but on a dirty floor with his head next to a toilet.

10

Mattie hoisted two overstuffed bags of groceries into her arms and attempted to close the trunk of her car with a jab of her elbow. She really would have to break down and invest in something more reliable. Her old compact car had seen its day. A more determined jab and a bump of her hip finally did the trick. Nice to know her less-than-toned bum was good for something.

Last night Jaydee had e-mailed her a draft of the letter that would go in the Langston file, objecting to the verdict, and Mattie had made revisions from home on her laptop computer and e-mailed them back. If he'd been surprised at the very general reference to the abuse in her past, he hadn't mentioned it. This morning, she'd made several phone calls regarding Langston, including courtesy calls to the two appellate attorneys she planned to assign. She doubted they'd be sending her flowers, but both had been guardedly optimistic about Langston's chances for an appeal, which had heartened her.

Meanwhile, she'd heard nothing from Jane or Breeze, even after leaving follow-up messages for both of them. She'd also checked her e-mail repeatedly for replies. They were either very busy or much less concerned about the reopening of the finishing school case than she was, if they knew about it at all. By late morning she'd decided to do something more constructive than worry, like run errands and grocery shop.

Struggling with the bags, she made her way up the steps to the Sausalito beach house she'd bought when she returned to northern California and had been appointed to her first judgeship. The house was small, rustic and tranquil, which suited her perfectly, especially given how overwhelmed she was by the appointment, which had seemed to come from nowhere.

Eventually she'd learned that Jane's husband, who'd been the junior senator from California at the time, had championed her candidacy. The state's senior senator had also thrown in his support, and the confirmation process had been unusually smooth, but Mattie had felt as if a magic carpet had swooped down and scooped her up. She'd never been politically inclined, and she'd been so preoccupied with winning her cases, she hadn't paid much attention to the reputation she was building, nor had she realized she was being seriously considered as judicial material.

She didn't feel very much the august judge right now as she juggled bags and fished in her pants pocket for her keys. Probably didn't look like much of one either in her regulation khakis and striped polo top. Not that anyone cared, least of all her at the moment.

She had decadent plans for the evening. *A sinful gourmet quest.* She had all the ingredients for *paella,* and her mouth was already watering. She lived on deli food and takeout, and taking the time to prepare and cook a favorite meal seemed almost self-indulgent, especially since she hadn't had a day off since she'd been appointed to the appellate court. She'd worked through weekends, holidays, even her own birthdays, but that was by choice. She really wouldn't have known what else to do.

"If you had a brain, Smith," she observed, "you'd try to

enjoy this break instead of obsessing about things that will almost certainly go away."

Meaning the Broud case and Jameson Cross.

She'd given the latter much too much credit. Cross would need rock-solid evidence to reopen the case, and what he had so far sounded like conjecture. He didn't even seem to know who the lonely girls were. *Why was she angsting over this?*

An ironic smile surfaced.

She wouldn't have known what else to do.

"Hey, stop that!" One of her grocery bags was trying to get away from her. She gave it a bump with her knee and hiked it back into her arms, gripping it firmly as she climbed the rest of the stone steps that led through her prized rock garden.

As she looked up at the white clapboard house with the dark green shutters, her smile faded. Was that an optical illusion or were her blinds shut? She never closed them all the way. Just the thought made her uneasy. Must be the sun, a reflection.

She had to set down one of the bags and wedge herself inside the screen door to get her front door unlocked. But her hand-eye coordination was good, possibly from all the archery practice as a kid, and she had the job done quickly.

As she backed into the house, she hesitated again. The living room was dark. The blinds *were* closed.

The hair on her neck pricked like needles.

She whirled, gasped as the screen door banged shut behind her. "What are you doing in my *house?*"

The bags dropped from her arms, and a bottle of red wine hit the rug, cartwheeling like a bowling pin. Onions and peppers spun in several directions, tripping her as she tried to back out the door.

One of the men caught up with her before she could get away. She tumbled against the door, unaware that her shoulder bag had caught on a metal latch. It was yanked right off her arm as he pulled her to her feet.

A second man picked up the bag, unzipped it and rifled through it. He was looking for ID, she realized, not money. These weren't vandals or thieves. Thieves didn't wear nondescript gray suits and earpieces. These were—

"Matilda Smith," the crouching man said as he scanned her driver's license. "It's her. We have the right place."

Mattie didn't attempt to fight. She was outnumbered, and these guys were pros. Her mind sprinted, analyzing the danger. *Do nothing until you know what you're dealing with,* she told herself. She might have a short fuse, but she wasn't crazy.

Two more men entered the room. They'd come from the kitchen. She could see the open drawers and cupboards through the dining room cutout. They'd gone through her whole house. The sofa cushions had been upended in her living room, and the carpeting had been ripped up along the border.

"Matilda Smith? *Judge* Smith?"

The authoritarian voice came from the hallway that led to her bedroom. Another gray suit appeared in the archway, but Mattie knew from this one's tone and military stance that he was running the operation. She'd also determined that the men were either government agents or posing as such, possibly FBI.

"Where's your search warrant?" She flashed the leader a look cold enough to entomb him in ice. "And what the hell are you doing in my house?"

He smiled as if her questions amused him. "I'm John Bratton, United States Secret Service, and this is a matter of national security. I'm sure you know what that means."

"I'm sure I *do.*" Mattie's disdain for abuses of authority came as naturally as breathing. She'd endured plenty of it as a kid, and it had shaped the judge she'd become. At the district court, she'd routinely signed court orders authorizing legal searches, but things had changed since documents like the Patriot Act were signed into law. It put the Secret Service in the unique position of being able to search private premises with impunity, providing they could justify acting in the country's interests. They weren't accountable to the public or the media, either, since most national security matters were top secret.

It wasn't a case of absolute power, but it was close. However, if these men really were Secret Service then this search could be related to her call to Jane.

Mattie forced herself to scrutinize the ID he flashed.

"I've done something to imperil our nation's security?" The laughter in her throat had an acrid taste. "You think I'm a spy? A terrorist?"

Bratton's tone was measured, sardonic. "No, Your Honor, I don't think you're a terrorist. I apologize if I gave that impression."

Mattie released her clasped hands, surprised at the pain. She hadn't realized how tightly she'd gripped them. Her impulse was to rub away the ache, but something told her not to show any weakness with this man.

"Do I need to call my attorney? Or perhaps I should call the U.S. attorney and see what he thinks of your visit?" *Bastard, I'm not without recourse here.* This was probably not the time to stare him in the eyes and defy everything she saw there. She did it anyway. The roll-over-and-play-dead routine had never come easily to her—and she had the scars to prove it.

"That won't be necessary, Your Honor. This shouldn't take long." He gestured for her to come with him, and then spoke to his men. "Carry on, gentlemen, but be sure you put everything back where you found it."

Mattie quickly scanned the room for damage. Nothing broken that she could see. Her favorite rattan rocker was all right, as was the stand of good-luck bamboo that Jaydee had given her for Christmas. She was superstitious about that bamboo.

"After you," Bratton said, standing back to let Mattie pass.

Aren't we polite, she thought, unless he planned to shoot her in the back. Or get her alone and rough her up. What better location than her own bedroom? She suspected that's where they were headed, so she turned left instead, toward the den.

A hand shot out to block her. "The other way, please," he said. "I have something to show you."

He'd found her mother's palmistry paraphernalia. The charts and instruction books were spread out on Mattie's bed. Other than that the room looked undisturbed, but she was certain he'd been through every closet and drawer.

"Who ordered this search?" she demanded to know. "Who gave you the authority?"

"I assure you," he said, "I *have* the authority. And apparently you have an interest in palmistry?" He presented her with the evidence the way Vanna White would present a vowel.

"An interest, yes." She stared pointedly at his outstretched hand. "Don't be too concerned about that broken life line, Mr. Bratton. I'm sure you'll recover from the tragic accident. I can't say as much about your loved ones, if you have any."

He didn't smile. It felt like a small, petty victory. It felt good.

Next, he went to her armoire and opened it. Mattie's spine stiffened. She had a small, combination-lock safe in there, and he was going to ask her to open it and reveal the contents. She hadn't used it in so long she wasn't sure she remembered the combination, but if she didn't comply he would probably shoot the damn door open.

Her bad knee gave out a noisy click as she knelt in front of the safe. It took her several minutes of fiddling, but she finally got the numbers right, and the door clicked open. There were two objects inside, a large envelope in which she kept important papers and a nine-millimeter handgun.

Bratton asked her to move away from the safe. "You have a license to carry this?" He crouched to inspect the automatic weapon.

"In the envelope." Mattie had bought the gun when she was a prosecutor, working on Jaydee's case. "It was for protection."

"It's not protecting you in a safe." He didn't bother to look at her license. He'd suddenly become interested in a blindfold that hung from a hook inside the armoire door.

Mattie stared at him in disbelief as he held it up. What was this? Show-and-tell?

"Is this something we need to discuss?" His scalp seemed to tighten as he peered at her, creating little furrows in his close-cropped hair.

"It is not." She longed to tell him to shove the blindfold up his ass, and then she'd be happy to discuss it with him. She had a tendency to go on the attack when she was terrified—or mortified. And she was both. But she couldn't risk antagonizing him with five other *gentlemen* in the next room. There was no way to be certain they were Secret Service. ID could be faked.

"Something like a sleep mask?" He returned the blindfold to its hook and gave her a sidelong glance.

"Something like that." He would never have guessed what she used the blindfold for, nor would he have understood, if she'd told him. She couldn't imagine that anyone would. There was no way to explain that if not for a black canvas blindfold, you would be an emotional cripple.

He shut her armoire door. "I know this is inconvenient for you, but it isn't personal. We have a job to do."

"Inconvenient? When's the last time someone ransacked your home for no apparent reason?" She was seething, and just barely able to control her voice.

"My men and I aren't here for our own entertainment. Think of us as civil servants, doing a job."

He didn't want to know what she thought. It astounded her that he would pretend to be contrite about what had happened here. This was her home. It had taken her years to fill it with treasures and make it her own, and at least that long to build a sense of security and serenity. She had done everything in her power to keep it sacred, her cloister. He and his civil servants might as well have broken down the doors and shattered all the windows.

"Exactly what job are you doing?" she asked.

"We're searching the premises. Clearing it, you could say."

"But why *my* premises?"

"I'm not at liberty."

"Well, you had damn well better be at liberty!" This had gone on long enough. She strode to the bedroom phone, but before she could pick up the receiver, she heard an urgent buzzing sound.

Bratton reached in his pocket, possibly for a beeper, and the buzzing stopped. "We're leaving, Your Honor. No need to make that call. Again, I apologize."

She whirled on him. "Answer me one question before you go. I want to know if you found it."

"Found what?"

"What you were looking for. You must have been searching for something."

"We're always searching for something."

"Did you find it?"

"Sorry, not at liberty."

"Get out of here," she said softly. "Get the hell out of here before I lose my temper and do something really stupid."

She'd known they wouldn't find drugs or weapons, but that didn't mean they couldn't plant something incriminating, if that was their goal. Maybe she'd been in law enforcement too long. She didn't trust anyone, especially if the government was involved.

Another buzzing sound. Bratton fished in his pocket, pulling out what looked like a miniature walkie-talkie.

"Go ahead," he said, holding it close to his mouth.

"We're done here," the caller said.

"Good, vacate and move to Phase Two. I'll join you—" he glanced at his watch "—at twelve hundred hours."

Mattie checked the clock radio on her night table. That was noon, three minutes from now. They were leaving, but what was Phase Two?

He performed another check of the bedroom, and Mattie realized he was looking for electronic bugs and surveillance devices, not drugs. Apparently his walkie-talkie was also a detector. He swept it over lamps, telephones, floorboards, knickknacks and artwork. He also touched, tapped and slid things around like a street-corner con artist playing a shell game.

She didn't move the entire time, but something in his behavior had made her think he was telling the truth. He *was* Secret Service. But what did that mean? When he was done, he folded the palmistry charts and stacked the books, handing them to her.

"Sometimes I don't like what I have to do," he said. "You can understand that. You take away people's freedom, their lives. You're not always comfortable with that, right? But you do it."

It was safe to say she wasn't always comfortable. Her concern over the kidnapping case made it hard to breathe at times.

"It's a job." He shrugged with the air of a man who'd

grown bored with his lot in life. Mattie knew from experience that those were the dangerous ones. They often ended up in her courtroom, and she was rarely *un*comfortable about curbing their freedom.

He backed away from her a few steps, then turned and left the room.

Moments later she heard the front door close, and she sank onto the bed. The palmistry charts escaped from her hand, sprung by her fierce grip. She had no idea what had just happened. The courtroom required her to deal with situations like this, but always from the safety of the bench. She'd never been the subject of a search, and she still didn't know what had made her a target. Her call to Jane at the White House couldn't have triggered anything so extreme. Or the article in the *Chronicle,* for that matter. But things may have gone much further than she realized. It alarmed her to think that she could already be under investigation for the crime that William Broud had just been absolved of.

Laughter bubbled into her throat again. Terrible laughter, hot and sharp as nettles. This was absurd. It was unthinkable. She really should call an attorney, just to be safe. But there again, who could she trust with this information?

Calm down, she told herself. Before you do anything else, do that.

She sat on the bed for what seemed like a considerable time, but her fighting spirit seemed to have deserted her. Righteous anger didn't transform her, cleansing her in a fiery wave as it always had before. She would have to go in search of her legendary nerve, summon it with an effort of will. That's how off balance she was.

Alis volat propriis.

The Latin phrase she'd picked up years ago in boarding school came into her mind, a reminder of real adversity. What she'd seen, heard and endured in those days made this incident seem like an inconvenience. If a young girl could endure that, then how could a woman be cowed by this.

She flies with her own wings.

"*Alis volat propriis*," Mattie echoed as she rose from the bed and steadied herself on her feet. She would check out her house. Restoring order to the rooms, one by one, would help restore her.

But as she walked into the living room, she saw a woman there.

Dressed in an elegant black pantsuit, the tall, slender blonde stood with her back to Mattie, studying the small fountain of metal, rocks and bubbling water that graced the corner of the living room.

She had changed significantly, but Mattie knew her instantly. Even without the constant television coverage, she would have known her.

"Jane?" she said softly.

11

"How old is she?" the man asked.

"Fourt—"

"Fifteen." Jane cut in before Ms. Rowe could finish. Her insides were shaking. She had just boldly added four months to her age, and she didn't know how Ms. Rowe would react, but Jane was desperate. She'd told the truth at her other interviews and been rejected each time. Maybe it had nothing to do with her age, but she wasn't taking any chances. She wanted to be chosen this time. The dismissals were getting embarrassing. There'd been three already, and she was the only one who hadn't been picked. Even Mattie's guy had wanted her before she spit on him.

What was wrong with Jane Dunbar? As far back as she could remember there'd never been a male who'd shown any interest in her, including her father.

Jane forced herself to speak to the man again, and this time her voice sounded breathy and weak. "Do you like to kiss?"

It was probably a stupid question to ask a man who'd come here for much nastier things than kissing, but Jane didn't know where else to start. He didn't answer, but she told herself that he may have wanted to. She heard a noise that sounded like shuffling feet. Maybe he was nervous, too.

They were in the same darkened classroom Ms. Rowe used for all the interviews, and as always, Jane stood in a bright ring of light. She could see nothing but the man's mud-specked oxfords, gray slacks and trench coat, which made it damn difficult to convince herself that he was a boy her age, someone she might actually *want* to kiss.

You'll close your eyes, Jane. You can do it. You'll hold your breath, and you won't even think.

Her mind raced as she waited for him to answer. Maybe he was waiting to see what she would do next? Even Ms. Rowe was quiet. Jane took that as tacit permission to continue.

She cocked a hip and tilted her head, refusing to give in to the terrible awkwardness she felt. "I like to kiss." She could not be shy. She had to play it for all it was worth. "Want to see?"

"*Jane,* a lady waits for the gentleman to ask."

The headmistress's tone was stern, but Jane wanted this man to choose her even more than she feared Ms. Rowe. She hadn't allowed herself to think too much about what would happen when he did. She just didn't want to be pushed aside again and made to feel as if no one cared if she lived or died.

You weren't blessed with natural good looks, Jane. You'll probably never be pretty enough to interest a man. Jane's stepmother had been preparing her for rejection since Jane was little. Maybe she considered it a parental obligation. She'd told Jane to be ready to make her own way in life, and Jane had believed her implicitly. After all, her stepmother knew these things. She was dazzlingly pretty, and Jane's father was obsessed with her to the exclusion of all else, including Jane. He worked two jobs to bring home enough money to keep his "bride" happy, but she complained bitterly of the opportunities she'd squandered to marry him, and in the end, he'd died trying to live up to her expectations. His blood pressure had been dangerously high, and a stress-induced stroke had killed him the year he turned forty-three.

Jane had been left with no living relatives. Her natural mother had divorced her father and given up custody when Jane was small. Jane had never seen pictures or been told stories about her because her father wouldn't allow it. He'd told her only that her mother was a drunk, and she'd come to a bad end, dying before she was thirty.

Jane's stepmother had wasted no time looking for ways to be rid of her teenage charge. Fortunately, Jane had heard about the scholarships that Rowe Academy offered needy girls, or she might have ended up on the streets. When Jane was accepted, her stepmother dumped her off at Rowe, and disappeared, but that hadn't surprised Jane nearly as much as the temporary guardianship Ms. Rowe offered so Jane wouldn't be sent to a foster home. Ms. Rowe had hinted at the time that there would be ways Jane could make it up to her.

"Maybe I'm no lady." Jane peered into the darkness, hoping the man concealed there would mistake her bright smile for eagerness rather than nerves. So far he'd said nothing, not a word, but that didn't necessarily mean he wasn't interested. Maybe he was very interested.

He spoke up at last, a smirk in his voice. "If you're fifteen, you must have been around some. Kissed a few boys?"

Well, the neighbor boy when she was ten, and then a summer crush at camp a couple years later, but only because *he* didn't have a choice. A bunch of them were playing Spin the Bottle. Boys did not line up for Jane Dunbar, but that wasn't something she should admit. Still, if this man had a thing for finishing school students, he might prefer them pure. There was no way to know.

She glanced down, raising her lashes slowly. "I said I liked it, didn't I?"

"What else do you like?"

He was serious, Jane realized with a stirring of alarm. He would want her to do all kinds of weird, kinky things, and she couldn't dare refuse him. What would he think when he found out she had no experience? None.

"Jane, dear," Ms. Rowe said, "you were asked a question."

Dear? Clearly Ms. Rowe approved of the way things were going.

"I like lots of things," Jane said, scrambling for some gruesome details. "A wet tongue in my ear and hot kisses on my—"

"Do you like having your breasts touched?"

His voice cracked like an adolescent boy's. He cleared his throat, and Jane struggled not to shiver with disgust. "I—uh, yes, very much," she got out.

But the distaste she felt must have been obvious. She groped for what to say next. No one spoke for several seconds, and she could feel the brass ring slipping away from her. "Of course, I like having my breasts touched," she said in a tight, strained voice.

"I don't think this is going to work," the man said. "Maybe another—"

"Yes, it will!" Jane hurried to unbutton her blouse. She was fairly well developed for her age, and maybe that would change his mind. Her last audition, the man had crudely said he'd like to check out the goods before he bought them. Ms. Rowe had given him permission to feel her up, but Jane had flinched even before he'd touched her. She wouldn't make that mistake again.

She ripped through the last few buttons, opened her blouse and yanked down the cup of her bra. Her breast looked swollen and strange, the nipple frozen hard. She couldn't imagine why anyone would want to touch it. Something inside her had gone numb, she realized. She was staring at her breast as if it belonged to someone else.

Her fingers felt icy cold against her skin. She stroked herself and smiled. "See," she said, "I told you I like it."

"Jane, move closer," Ms. Rowe prompted. "Don't make the gentleman come to you."

Somehow Jane managed to take a few steps toward the oxfords. She stood there, easily within his reach, staring at the floor and suddenly feeling horribly exposed.

"I like it," she whispered.

"Go ahead," Ms. Rowe prompted him. "She's young and firm, and she'll do anything you want."

He stayed quiet for so long that Jane began to shake again.

"I don't think so," he said. "Maybe another time."

Another girl was what he meant.

"Touch me," Jane implored, "please."

"No, really, I—can't."

"Why?" Jane clutched her blouse together. She must have looked strange to him, too, frozen and ugly. "Is there something wrong with me?" She didn't really want to know the answer, but she asked anyway, recklessly.

"No, of course not. I like blondes. Petite blondes. It doesn't work for me, otherwise."

Liar, I'm not pretty enough. I'll never be pretty enough. I'm frozen through and through, and you will never be able to make me feel...anything.

No one moved or spoke for what seemed like an eternity. At last Ms. Rowe said, "Jane, do up your clothes and wait outside. I'd like to talk to the gentleman alone."

Jane didn't have the strength to protest—or to do up her clothing. She walked to the door and let herself out, not sure where she was supposed to wait. Probably any other girl would have felt ashamed or dirty at having flashed her breast, but if Jane felt those things they were buried under the awareness that she had failed miserably. Ms. Rowe would never give her another chance. She'd humiliated herself and worse, embarrassed the "gentleman."

She leaned against the wall next to the door, gradually sinking to the floor in a demoralized heap. She was unable to think of anything but her own stupidity and inadequacy. She wallowed in the pit of self-doubt for several long moments, flagellating herself until she simply couldn't do it anymore. She might be a worthless wretch, but she had never tolerated despair well. It had always seemed like a waste of time once the dark mood had passed.

The hallway was quiet as a crypt. The campus's vacant buildings had always given her the creeps, and this one was the worst. The exterior doors were boarded up and the windows broken out. Normally, Ms. Rowe wouldn't have allowed such neglect, but she probably wanted this place to look abandoned to ward off the other students.

Jane wondered how angry the headmistress would be if she sneaked away. Her friends had probably come back from dinner in the cafeteria by now and were hanging out in Mattie's room. Jane wished she hadn't told them she had an interview tonight. She wasn't up to dealing with their questions, and the last thing she wanted was their pity. At least she'd gotten an A on her social ecology paper that morning. Too bad she hadn't brought it with her. She could read Ms. Carlton's glowing comments again.

Jane rested her head against the wall and sighed. Gradually she began to work the audition situation around in her mind, replaying it and editing it in ways that soothed her battered ego. She imagined herself driving the man slightly mad with her sensual voice and her taunting smile. She said all the right things, and when she displayed her perfect breast, he was so overcome that he dragged her into his arms and kissed her passionately, heedless of Ms. Rowe—and the fact that he'd revealed his identity. From that point on, he was hers. He belonged to Jane Dunbar.

"You didn't like her?"

Jane opened her eyes. That was Ms. Rowe's voice. Jane must have left the door ajar. The man answered Ms. Rowe in a low, sensual tone that made Jane wonder what was going on between them. She imagined that he was touching her and staring deeply into her eyes, seducing her with his raw male urges. Jane shuddered.

"I liked her fine," he said. "But she's not precocious like the other one. She doesn't *get* what a man needs from a woman."

"Really? And what is that?"

"Oh, you know. Some women are born knowing."

Ms. Rowe's throaty laughter made Jane lean closer to the door. She wanted to look, but she was terrified they would see her.

"You may be right," the headmistress said, still laughing. "I think I know exactly what you need."

Her voice dropped to a whisper, and Jane couldn't hear what she was saying. But the other sounds she picked up made it very clear what they were doing. Snatches of laughter and little crooning noises turned to heavy sighs and other steamy mumblings. Jane could only imagine what nasty stuff was going on. Suddenly, she was listening to outright moans and groans of pleasure. *Were they going to do it right there with the door open and her sitting in the hallway?* The wet squishy sound of lips and tongues made her wince. *Were they Frenching? Or was she giving him—*

Jane clapped her hands over her ears. She didn't want to hear it. The sounds of their drooling, disgusting lust made her queasy, and yet she was torn. She also felt a mad desire to keep eavesdropping. How else could she learn? As much as it repulsed her, she wanted to know everything there was to know about what Ms. Rowe and her gentleman were doing in that room. It was as if they belonged to a secret society that wouldn't admit a graceless oaf like Jane Dunbar. This was a party to which she wasn't invited, but plenty of other girls her age were. Even Breeze seemed to know her share of secrets. Already, Breeze had been chosen several times, but she wouldn't open up about what she and the men had done, and Jane didn't think that was fair.

Jane wanted to know the combination to the locked room where men and women met in the dark and offered themselves, body and soul—for surely the soul was involved in a transaction like that. She wanted to understand what it all meant, and most of all, she wanted to know what was wrong with her so that she could fix it.

As she sat there, slumped against the wall, defiance rose inside her. She didn't tolerate failure any better than she tolerated despair. She might not have been born knowing the secrets women were supposed to know about men and sex, but she could learn. And she was a damn quick study.

"Why is it called a cock? Does it look like a rooster?"

Breeze winced at her friend's question. "It's called an erection, Jane. That's something you'll need to remember if you ever get chosen."

Hot red slashes burned Jane's face. She flipped Breeze the finger, struggling to look indignant, but Breeze could see the hurt in her eyes—and instantly regretted what she'd said. She probably shouldn't be instructing the other girls on the finer points of male anatomy. Ms. Rowe had told her to keep quiet about her "dates," especially the scary ones. But the way her friends were hanging on her every word was intoxicating. For the first time in her life, she felt important.

She wasn't tough like Mattie, and she didn't get the grades

like Jane. Her claim to fame was that she'd been chosen repeatedly, more than all the rest of them put together, and
she'd just returned from her fourth "blind" date. Somehow,
that made her the expert on men, and whether it was true or
not, it felt good.

"Is it weird, wearing a blindfold?" Jane asked.

"Only at first." Breeze shrugged, as if it was all in a day's
work. "It's not about kinky sex, if that's what you're thinking. It's to protect the man's identity."

"Yeah, right," Mattie scoffed. "The whole frigging thing
is about kinky sex, Breeze. Get real."

"Not true. The man I met today was really sweet." He *was*
sweet, compared to her first two dates. A hollow sensation
invaded Breeze's stomach as she thought about her very first
"date," as Ms. Rowe had called it. The headmistress had forbidden her to tell the other girls that the man had taken her
off campus to a motel, which was against Ms. Rowe's rules.

Other than Ivy, whose gentleman had come to pick her up
in a limo, the girls were supposed to meet Ms. Rowe in the
same building where the interviews took place. There, she
would blindfold them and take them to a room where the
gentleman was waiting. Breeze had never seen the room, of
course, but she'd felt the velvet and leather furnishings, and
imagined that it looked like a Victorian parlor.

But this man had intercepted Breeze on her way over to
the building. He'd come up behind her in one of the campus tunnels and blindfolded her himself. He'd told her they
were going somewhere else, and that Ms. Rowe had agreed.
Breeze didn't find out until too late that Ms. Rowe knew
nothing about it, and that he had punishment games in mind.
He'd paddled her so hard it had brought tears to her eyes.

"Young lady, that skirt is indecently short," he'd said once
they were in the room. "You need a good old-fashioned
spanking." He'd instructed her to bend over his knees like a

five-year-old, and he'd actually dropped her panties and used a table tennis paddle on her bare skin. If she hadn't been so shocked and mortified, she would have sunk her teeth in his thigh. As it was, she'd slipped out when he went to the bathroom, probably to masturbate, and run all the way back to the campus, where Ms. Rowe had given her fifty dollars in hush money and promised her nothing like that would ever happen again.

That was when Breeze had begun to realize she had some power. Money? Promises? Breeze would have been less surprised if Ms. Rowe had held a gun to her head and threatened her with death. The only other time the headmistress had bothered to use kid gloves was during the girls' first term, when she was selling them on the idea of being sexy and desirable, and how it would give them advantages in life the other students took for granted.

"I'll teach you all my secrets," she'd told them. "You'll have knowledge and skills that will leave those other girls in the dust."

Breeze had allowed herself to be talked into a second date with a different man, mostly because she feared Ms. Rowe's wrath, which crackled like lightning in her green eyes, even when she was being nice. The second man hadn't touched Breeze, but it had been awful anyway. He wanted her to say dirty words while he did things to himself. Thank God, she'd had a blindfold. The sounds he made were gross enough.

She'd wanted to quit at that point, but her third date had been better, and her fourth, a revelation. Once again, she'd discovered that she had power. Real power. She'd just had to find the courage to use it.

"Look what I got," she said, holding up her hand to show her friends the shiny gold bangle on her wrist.

"What did you have to do for that?" Mattie asked, "something totally putrid?"

They'd just come back from dinner in the cafeteria, where even the meat was cooked to baby food consistency, and had crashed in Breeze's room. Mattie was lying on the bed, and she'd been making gagging noises while Breeze talked, but that was just for show, Breeze had decided. Mattie was glued to every word. She was as fascinated as Jane, who'd scored the only decent furniture in the room, a padded high-back chair Breeze had swiped from one of the storage areas.

Only Ivy seemed uncomfortable. She sat on the floor, against the far wall, a sketch pad in her lap, listlessly drawing faces as lost and morose as her own.

Honestly, at times Breeze just lost patience with her. She didn't seem to care that she was spoiling Breeze's moment in the sun with her lack of interest, and how bad could her life be anyway? At least she had a father, although she wouldn't talk about him, except to say that he lived a couple hours north of the campus, and he worked a lot. But none of the rest of them had any family around at all. Breeze's parents were doing time for growing marijuana. They were always crusading for something. In this case, it was medical legalization, and they'd turned themselves in, naively believing some civil rights organization would come to their rescue and give meaning to their sacrifice. That was nearly three years ago.

"What did you have to do for the bracelet?" Mattie pressed. "Tell us everything, even the icky stuff."

"Especially the icky stuff," Jane chimed in.

Breeze rose from the beanbag chair and sashayed from one friend to the next, giving them a closer look at her prize. She rarely got the chance to be the golden girl, and it was fun.

"I didn't have to do anything," she said. "It was my idea to get naked. He couldn't stop shaking, and I was trying to reassure him. I even took his hand and put it on my breast to show him that it was okay."

"Oh, my God," Jane whispered. "What did he do?"

"He cried."

"Cried? Tears?" Mattie sat up in disbelief. "Was he weird?"

"Yeah." Breeze nodded. "Nice weird, though."

"Did you do it with him?" Jane asked. "Did he put it in?"

"That's called penetration," Breeze explained.

"I don't care what it's called. Did you do it?"

Even Ivy was paying attention now, her long lashes fluttering as she looked up from her pad.

"No," Breeze said, feeling very superior, "but I convinced him to let me touch his penis."

"Ewwwwww...did it erupt? Like a plugged faucet or something?"

"That's an orgasm, Jane, and no, it didn't. He was too scared, I think."

Mattie and Jane doubled up with moans and groans of revulsion, which didn't surprise Breeze. She'd been brought up differently than other girls her age. Her parents were throwbacks to the hippy generation, free thinkers in the extreme, who'd taught her that sex and nudity were natural things, not shameful or sinful. The commune she'd grown up in wasn't a nudist camp, but members were inclined to skinny-dip when the weather got hot, and clothes weren't a big deal.

Breeze had a comfort level with her body that most girls her age didn't, and at fourteen, she'd already had some experience with sex, although it was with a boy her age, and nothing like being with Ms. Rowe's men. Still, she'd survived the first two dates, and she'd learned a little something about men, and a lot about herself. She seemed to have a natural aptitude for reading the subtle signals men and women sent each other, though she couldn't have explained what they meant, even to herself. But she knew it was her skill. Her gift, and she honestly didn't see anything wrong with it.

"What if he wants to see you again?" Mattie asked.

Breeze gave the bracelet a spin. "I hope he does, and not because of the jewelry."

"Why then?" Jane asked. "Did you like it when he touched you?"

"I didn't hate it." Breeze hesitated, knowing her friends would make fun of her if she told the truth. "He was sad, and I made him happy. I think next time he'll be less afraid of me or any other woman. I don't know why, but it made me feel good."

Mattie leaped from the bed to confront Breeze. Her eyes were painfully blue, and her hair Medusa-black. "These men aren't sad," she said. "They're sick, and if you start to like it, you're going to get sick, too."

"Calm down, Mattress Pad. It wasn't the sex. I helped him. He felt better about himself, and that made me feel better, too."

"So now you're the Mother Teresa of sex? You're going to travel around the world, helping men feel better about themselves?"

Breeze managed not to flinch, which wasn't easy with Mattie Smith in your face. "I might," she said softly.

Jane broke in, asking where Ivy was, and Breeze realized that Ivy had left the room. "Stay here," Breeze told the other two as she headed for the door. "I'll find her. It's probably my fault she took off."

Breeze dashed into the hallway, leaving her friends to huff and puff and make their silly noises. She saw Ivy standing in the window alcove at the far end of the hallway, staring out into the darkness. She called out her name, but Ivy didn't turn. She didn't even seem to hear, and Breeze had a horrible moment of knowing what she didn't want to know. Her friend would have jumped, if there'd been any way to get the windows open.

12

Breeze approached the window with some hesitance. "Ivy, what's wrong? Was it the stuff I said?"

Ivy turned around, shading her eyes with her hand, as if the hallway lights were too bright. "What? No. I just needed to get some air."

Her skin looked pale and clammy. Breeze wondered if she'd stopped eating again. The floor mistress had caught her hoarding junk food, and now the other students were hassling her. They made rude animal noises and teased her about porking out. She barely touched her food at meals lately, which Breeze found ridiculous. Ivy wasn't overweight.

Breeze reached for her hand, but Ivy crossed her arms and tucked her fists inside. She didn't seem to want to look at Breeze, either.

"Are you eating?" Breeze asked.

"Yes, I'm fine. This isn't about food."

"What is it then? You ran out of the room so it couldn't be fine. If it's not food, then hair? Boys?"

Ivy looked away, and Breeze knew instantly. Ivy didn't have a boyfriend. None of them did. The boarders weren't allowed to date the boys from town, and the nearest prep school was across the bay in San Francisco, but this had something to do with the opposite sex.

Breeze glanced around to make sure they were alone.

"One of Ms. Rowe's men came for you in a limo last weekend. I saw you being picked up down the road, and I figured it was so no one would notice. But you never said anything about the date afterward, so I'm just wondering. Did it go okay?"

A sigh moved Ivy's whole body. "Oh, God," she whispered.

"What happened?" Breeze asked. "Did he hurt you?"

Ivy turned her big sad eyes on Breeze. "Yes, but not in the way you're thinking."

Breeze felt like she'd been jabbed in the ribs with an elbow. How could anyone hurt Ivy? She was about as threatening as a gnat. "It doesn't matter what way I'm thinking. If he hurt you, we have to tell somebody."

She grabbed Ivy by the sweater sleeve and tugged her toward the elevator. "Come on. There must be somebody at this damn school who can help us."

"No!" Ivy jerked away. "Ms. Rowe will kill me—and she'll kill Mattie, too."

"No way. That was just a threat to keep us in line. I'll prove it to you. We'll go talk to her ourselves."

Ivy was near tears. Her voice cracked. "No, please. She'll send me home, and I couldn't bear that."

"No, she won't. She really wants this campus brothel thing of hers to work. I swear she does. One of my dates was a spanking freak, and I went straight over there and told her. She was okay about it. Said it wouldn't happen again."

"She likes you—and those men of hers, they like you, too." Ivy hugged herself, clearly stricken. "She'll send me home, Breeze, and I would rather she killed me."

"Ivy, don't say things like that. What's going on with you? *Tell me.* You have to tell me, or I can't help you."

The elevator opened, and a small hive of students emerged, buzzing about whatever they'd been doing. They headed down the hall in the other direction.

Ivy hissed under her breath at Breeze. "Stay out of this. You'll only make it worse, and if you tell Ms. Rowe, I swear I'll run away."

Her beautiful face was ablaze with anguish. She spun and ran for her room. Breeze watched her key the door open and shut it behind her. Moments later, Breeze found herself standing outside Ivy's door, wondering if she should knock. She listened for sobs or any sign that Ivy might have broken down. If she'd heard that, she would have forced her way in. Instead, she heard the scrape of a heavy dresser being pushed across the floor. It made her think that Ivy might be barricading the door.

An icy stone sank to the pit of Breeze's stomach. Something was terribly wrong, but there was nothing she could do about it without betraying her friend. *Nothing.* It took a while for that realization to take hold, but when it finally did, she drew a breath, fixed a determined smile on her face and headed back to her room.

If the girls were still there, she would pick up where she left off, sharing her secrets about men and sex, whetting their interest, and maybe they could take up where they'd left off. She hoped their avid questions would help her forget this awful, helpless feeling she had. She really had done everything she could.

Ivy stood alongside the dirt access road, staring down at her scuffed tennis shoes. Her jeans bagged at the knees and her extra-large T-shirt hung lower than the navy peacoat she wore to ward off the blustery autumn winds. She didn't bother to look up as a black town car pulled off the road that led to the school and rolled toward her.

That morning's rain kept the road dust from flying in her face, but her shoes sank in the mud as she walked to the car. *This won't go over well,* she thought. *He loathes untidiness.*

A driver came around, gave her a curt nod and opened the door. She slid inside the murky depths of the limo and mumbled a greeting to the man seated inside. The interior smelled of citrus cologne and pungent breath mints. Burning scents. Astringently clean.

He looked her over, disapproval chiseled into the contours of his face. "I'm surprised Ms. Rowe allows you to dress like that."

As Ivy picked at her jeans it dawned on her that she didn't want to be there, and this outfit allowed her to feel as if she weren't entirely a willing participant. She had shown up, but she hadn't dressed for the occasion.

In a small, distant voice, she said, "I made sure Ms. Rowe didn't see me. She would have made me change."

"Then why didn't you change? You have a lovely figure. Why dress like you're ashamed of it?"

"I like comfortable clothes."

He touched her face, and she reared back. Her heart was pounding. It was a reflex, but she half expected him to slap her. "Sorry," she said, not knowing exactly why she was apologizing. Another reflex.

"You're getting a blemish," he said. "I hope you're not eating junk. That will ruin your complexion."

"I eat the cafeteria food. Is that junk?"

"Don't be sullen."

"I'm not."

"You are. You're sullen. I'm trying to help. Everything I suggest is for your benefit, not mine, and this is how you behave."

She tugged at the loose button on her coat sleeve. "I'm getting all As in art." Her voice was barely audible. She knew it was hopeless. Nothing she could do would ever placate him, and she hated herself for trying.

"Art's a hobby, not a career."

"I wasn't planning on making it my career."

"Then what were you planning? To get by on your looks?" His voice dropped to a fierce hush. "Have you thought about who's going to want you? You're sloppy and sullen. Your complexion is bad. Look at me, Ivy. Someone has to say these things to you. When will you realize that I'm trying to help?"

"I don't want *help*." The raw pain in her voice surprised her. She couldn't believe he could still get to her this way, that he could demolish her with a few words. She'd poured cement slabs around herself, built a safe room to keep him out. Her friends thought she was with one of Ms. Rowe's men. She only wished she was. She would rather have been having sex with a stranger than trapped in this car with her own father.

Suddenly she was railing at him in a soft, strained voice. "Why can't I be sullen? I'm a fucking princess, right? I'm not like anyone else. You tell me that all the time. I'm special. I have promise, but I'm not living up to it. Well, I don't *have* any promise."

He hit a button that brought a soundproof window whistling down. It closed them off from the driver, and that would have been enough to stop her if she'd been anywhere near rational. But not today.

"When are you going to get that I'm not like you?" she said. "I'm not brilliant. I'm not good at school. I'm just a fourteen-year-old retard, so let me be, please."

He didn't respond, and she was afraid to look at him.

She crossed her arms and tucked her fists inside them to stop the trembling. Eventually she realized that she couldn't even hear him breathing. When he got upset, he went into a strange state of automation. His voice went cold and stiff, like a robot's, and you never knew what he might do. When she was a kid, he would lock her in her room and watch her on a security monitor. She was afraid to breathe with him spying on her like that.

One night, thinking the darkness would shield her, she slipped out of bed and crawled across the floor on her belly. She hid in her closet all night, but the next day he had a camera installed in there. He was concerned that she would hurt herself, he said, without bothering to explain what that meant.

But Ivy knew. Her mother had been in and out of clinics throughout Ivy's childhood. She'd always been emotionally unstable, and Ivy suspected she'd had several breakdowns, but she hadn't known that her mother was suicidal. Even now, she had trouble grasping that there had been a terrible tragedy just a few months ago, and her mother was dead. But maybe that was because Ivy knew so little about what had actually happened.

Her father wouldn't discuss the details other than to say that she'd suffered a fatal fall at a clinic where she was being treated for some mysterious disorder. But Ivy didn't believe for one second that it was an accident.

She'd lost her mother just after she'd returned to school this term, and she should have been devastated. Any other girl her age would have been, but Ivy didn't know how to feel—or to grieve. She was numb and confused. How did you lose someone you'd never had? She hadn't known her mother at all, and now she never would.

A flash of blue sea caught her eye. She glanced out the window and saw that they were rolling down the two-lane highway that bordered the Tiburon peninsula. She hadn't even realized they were moving. Her father would probably take her for an early dinner somewhere in Sausalito—or San Francisco, if he was in the mood for something more exotic. She didn't know where they were going, of course. He always chose the place, even on special occasions like her birthday. She'd never been able to please him in any other way. How could she possibly pick a decent restaurant?

She broke the silence with a question. "Why wasn't I allowed to come home for her memorial service?"

His little finger glided along the pleat of his wool trousers, smoothing the ripples and leaving it perfectly straight. "It wasn't that kind of a service," he said. "It was just your mother and I, very quiet, the way she would have wanted it."

"It must have been quiet since she was *dead*."

He glanced at her as if he didn't know what to make of her tone. "I didn't want to put you under that kind of stress. You weren't doing well at school, and—"

"She was my mother!"

"Ivy, lower your voice. I'm trying to do what I think is best for you. I love you."

"Right, the way you loved her? You drove her to it, didn't you? You killed her."

He sucked in a breath. "You little bitch. How dare you."

Ivy felt as if *she* must be suicidal. She had never confronted her father before, and now, she couldn't stop. "I should have been allowed to mourn my own mother. What happened to her? Did she kill herself because of you? Did you drive her mad?"

He sat forward and rested his elbows on his knees, his head bowed as if he were thinking. He studied his hands, inspecting his fingernails. "Maybe it's time to put you back on medication again," he said quietly.

Ivy wanted to open the car door and jump out. "No, please."

His voice took on a low, mean edge. "I don't know how you can talk about your mother that way. It dishonors her memory. She was very ill, but she would never have taken her own life, and you know it."

Ivy didn't know it at all. Not at all. There were times

when she herself felt that might be the only way out. Surely her mother must have felt that way, too. "How did she die then?"

Air jetted through his nostrils. "I was going to tell you everything tonight at dinner. I even had a surprise, but that's ruined now." He sat back heavily and stared straight ahead, talking to the glass partition in front of him. "You want to know how your mother died? First of all, I have to tell you something that may come as a bit of a surprise. She was pregnant."

"Pregnant?" Ivy couldn't imagine it. She hadn't seen the two of them touch in years, much less anything like that, especially as her mother had become more disturbed and withdrawn. She wanted to ask if it was his baby, but she didn't dare.

"Yes, pregnant," he said, "but she was having complications, so her doctor hospitalized her. She was afraid she might lose the baby, and she didn't want anyone to know, not even you. She died in childbirth."

Ivy rarely ever looked at him directly. Now, she gaped. "I don't believe you," she said.

"What are you talking about? Why would I lie about something like that? I would have told you sooner, but we didn't know if the baby was going to live. You have a sister. Three months old."

Ivy couldn't listen any longer. She couldn't look at him. Trees whirred by outside, but she didn't see them, either. *He hadn't allowed her at her mother's funeral or told her about the pregnancy? What else was he keeping from her?*

"Ivy, did you hear me? Your mother had a baby. You have a little sister."

Ivy's numbness had turned into something more profound. His voice came to her from somewhere else. She wasn't even in the car with him anymore. It didn't matter where she was. A string of words scrolled through her head, but there was no feeling attached to them. She was empty of everything. Dead.

A baby. She had a little sister. And he had someone else to destroy.

13

Mattie hesitated as Jane Mantle turned and saw her standing in the archway. Mattie expected a reaction, but not the one she got. Shock transformed Jane's perfectly made-up features into a fright mask.

"What happened?" she whispered, gaping at Mattie's condition. "Are you all right?"

Mattie glanced down, startled to see that her clothing was askew. Her khakis were oddly twisted around, and her polo top was torn, probably during her fall against the door.

"What are you doing here?" she asked Jane. The Secret Service made more sense to Mattie now, but she couldn't imagine why Jane would show up in person unless it *was* a matter of national security. Mattie had no illusions that this was a social call.

Jane took a half step forward, as if unsure what to do. "You left an urgent message. I thought this would be safer than a telephone conversation."

"Is that why the Secret Service searched my house?"

Jane breathed out her frustration. "I'm sorry about that. They won't let me go anywhere without doing an advance security check."

Mattie's hand shook as she touched her midsection. "They're very thorough."

"Mattie, what's wrong? Did you hurt yourself?"

Mattie made a halfhearted try at straightening her clothing. Her hair was probably a mess, too. No wonder Jane was frightened. Mattie took a step and winced at the pressure in her knee. Great, she'd strained it somehow.

"You're limping? Are you limping?"

"A stumble." Mattie shrugged, making light of it. "You know me. No awards for coordination here."

Jane's lips pursed, a sure sign that she wasn't satisfied with Mattie's answer. Twenty years vanished with that one look, and Mattie instantly regressed to adolescence when Jane said in her stern mother voice, "Walk over here, Mattie. I want to see for myself."

"I'm *fine*." But reluctantly, Mattie hobbled toward Jane. In school the four scholarship girls had called her Lady Jane, and not just because she took on airs. She'd always been the mother hen of the group, and it was no use trying to fend her off now. Mattie hadn't been surprised when Jane had married a career politician and turned him into a presidential front-runner. She had ambition, drive and a staggering work ethic. What surprised her was that Jane hadn't run for president herself.

Try as she might, Mattie could not eliminate the limp altogether.

Jane clucked her tongue. "Was it the Secret Service? Was that asshole Bratton out of line?"

"Your boys scared the hell out of me, and I tripped, but that's all it was."

"Well, I apologize for that. Mr. Bratton can be a little extreme. Apparently I'm thought to be difficult to protect, can you imagine?" Her tone was dry. "So they've given me Godzilla as my keeper. He and I have been known to make life somewhat difficult for each other, all very politely, of course."

Mattie was delighted to hear that, just delighted. Poor Bratton, his bad behavior was already catching up with him in the form of some Jane Mantle Karma.

"I should report him," Jane said. "This situation was clearly excessive."

"Whoever you reported him to would want to know all about your private meeting with me, and we don't need that, do we?" Mattie sat down in the rattan rocker to rest her knee. "Excessive is probably a good thing with an election coming, and all the concern about a terrorist attack. They're trying to protect you, Jane. Your safety *is* in the national interest, and for all we know, they may have some concerns about me. My judicial record is pretty wonky."

Not to mention the rumors about my personal life.

Jane seemed mollified. "Mattie, I couldn't warn you," she said, her voice softening. "The operator red-flagged your phone call, which means certain security procedures go into effect. I couldn't be sure they weren't recording calls to and from your number. Plus, I had to let them check you out. Otherwise, they would have been suspicious."

"It's fine, Jane. *I'm* fine. But what about us, here?"

"Are you asking if it's safe to talk?" Jane mouthed the words. "Yes, I insisted the gestapo wait outside. We have privacy."

Mattie's chair was next to the writing desk by the window. She got herself over there, took a piece of notepaper and wrote out the words: "They went over the place with a sweeper. No bugs found, but could they have placed some?"

Jane waved a finger as if to say just a minute. She checked the window blinds and gave the cord a yank, pulling them even tighter. Mattie felt a flash of panic. She could feel the breath thickening in her lungs, but she said nothing, willing the sensation to go away. Jane had known about her fear of confinement back in their school days. There was very little they'd kept from each other, but that was a long time ago, and people often outgrew their childhood phobias. Mattie hadn't, which probably meant she wasn't dealing with a simple phobia. She'd seen enough posttraumatic delayed stress in her career to know the symptoms, but she'd rejected the possibility for herself, maybe because she didn't want to believe she was that badly damaged.

Jane searched through her tote bag and pulled out a device that looked like Bratton's cell phone. Within moments, she'd gone over the key pieces of furniture, the telephone and the room's baseboards. She gave Mattie a thumbs-up as she finished.

"I swiped this from Bratton's predecessor," she said, tucking the device back in her tote, "which is one of the reasons they replaced him with Godzilla, I suppose. Hey, politics is a dirty game, and the enemy is everywhere. I don't like taking chances. Of course, I'm much more cynical than Larry."

She meant Lawrence Mantle, her husband, who was the innocent of the two—if that word even applied in today's politics—and who often played the good cop to Jane's bad cop when it came to tough choices. He rarely made an important decision without her input, which they denied to the world, but was a deep, dark secret that every married woman in America knew. And, of course, they'd been compared to other first couples like the Clintons and the Reagans, where charismatic males and strong females made a nearly unbeatable team.

Jane sat on Mattie's couch of pale silk grass cloth and patted the cushion next to her. "Are you ever going to tell me what's going on?"

"Of course," Mattie said, but she couldn't seem to do much more than stare at her friend. She'd seen Jane on television, but they hadn't been together like this since Jane's wedding to Larry, fifteen years ago. Mattie and Breeze had been bridesmaids at the joyous occasion, but the following year, when it became clear that Larry was headed for Washington, D.C., and Jane would be living in a fishbowl, the three women had decided it best to limit their contact.

Their careers were taking off, and none of them could risk any connection to the Broud case or to the mysterious lonely girls he'd accused, especially Jane. They'd kept in touch with e-mails, and every year they'd remembered the anniversary of their graduation from Rowe with donations to a favorite charity in Ivy's name, but after Jane had become First Lady, even the e-mails had stopped.

Jane was terrified of harming Larry's career, but she had rocked Mattie's world with a phone call three years ago. She'd tipped Mattie that President Larry Mantle was going to nominate her to the Ninth Circuit. And Mattie, who never cried, couldn't stop. It wasn't a dream. It was a miracle, a gift from Artemis, protector of young women, as Jane had called it. They'd talked like fools, forgetting their fears and sharing every sacred tidbit they could. Afterward, Mattie had realized how desperately she missed her friend.

Finally, Mattie spoke. "Jane, is it really you? You could be a beauty contestant."

Jane made a face, but Mattie meant it as a compliment. Jane had suffered from deep insecurities at Rowe. She'd thought herself plain and dull, and much worse, uptight. Too prissy to ever interest a boy, she'd once told Mattie. But Mattie had wondered if it wasn't grown men Jane was worried about. Ms. Rowe's men.

Now, Jane's dark blond hair curved to her shoulders in a trendy, bowl-shaped pageboy. The sleek black pantsuit was probably Armani. Mattie had read somewhere he and Cha-

nel were her favorite designers. At any rate, she looked totally put together down to her Via Spiga pumps, and no one
had ever described Mattie as put together. Thrown together,
maybe. Tossed, like a salad. If she'd been the First Lady, the
fancy designers would have been forced to contend with
headbands and flak jackets as fashion.

Antifashion, Mattie would have called it.

As she sat down next to her fellow outcast, she thought
about what a long way they'd come.

"You look beautiful," she said with such conviction that
the unflappable Lady Jane from Rowe Academy actually
squirmed. That hadn't changed, Mattie realized. Jane still
wasn't good with compliments. None of the scholarship girls
were, except Breeze.

"Now, tell me the bad news," Jane prompted.

"Maybe I should make us some tea first?" Mattie held out
her hand to check it for steadiness. The pain was gone, but
the shakes weren't. "Let me see if I have any chamomile. It's
calming."

"Any tea will do," Jane said, "just put liquor in it."

Moments later, Mattie returned from the kitchen with a
steaming pot of tea and a fifth of apricot brandy. She'd just
poured Jane a cup and laced it with a slosh of brandy when
they were interrupted by a knock on the front door.

John Bratton entered and beckoned to Jane.

After a quick, hushed conversation, he slipped back outside, and Jane returned to the couch. "It seems we have a visitor," she said.

The front door swung wide this time, and Bratton escorted a sunny blonde with an infectious smile into the room.
Breeze Wheeler's flowing, honey-dipped waves bounced as
she walked, and her brown eyes twinkled with as much mis-
chief as they always had. As a teenager, she'd redefined the
word precocious. She'd been alarmingly advanced for her

years, a baby bombshell at fourteen, but with an inner sweetness that no man could resist.

Nothing had changed. Mattie was glad, actually. The world needed its Breezes. They were a reminder that life could be about fun, too. It didn't *all* have to be deadly serious. But Breeze had her complexities, too, even though she covered them well. Mattie had always thought that Breeze was the only one of them to come out of Rowe Academy unscathed. She wasn't so sure about that anymore.

Breeze had never considered herself as victimized. She'd seen the headmistress's "clients" as sad and needy men, and it had pleased her that she could make them happy. Perhaps it had given her a sense of accomplishment, or even power, but somehow she'd turned oppression into opportunity. It may have been the way she'd grown up, in a sixties-style commune, before she was taken from her freewheeling, pot-farming parents and put in a foster home. That could have accounted for her resilience, but Mattie had always wondered what part denial played in Breeze's coping skills.

Mattie'd had to become an acute observer of people over the years. As a child it had been a question of survival. As a lawyer, she'd been trained in jury selection, and as a judge she'd had to reach deeply into the psychology of human nature to carry out her duties. Breeze had always struck her as *too* breezy, too quick to shrug off problems. It was almost as if she'd closed off some part of herself and learned to negate her needs in favor of others, perhaps because it was safer.

"Thanks for the pat down," Breeze told Bratton with an encouraging flutter of her eyelashes. "Very thorough job. Maybe I'll get another one on my way out? Just to make sure I haven't taken anything of value? You never know. I could be smuggling something in my bra."

Breeze's outfit was black, too, though not Armani. She wore trim capris, a matching sweater and teeter-tottery stiletto pumps. Her V-neck cardigan unzipped at both ends, revealing a bit of midriff as well as bosoms, and she lifted her shoulders to give him the full benefit of her creamy décolletage, just in case he'd missed the point.

Bratton had no eyelashes, or they surely would have fluttered, too. He tried to make a joke, but his voice nearly gave out on him. "I'll do what I can," he said and left. Ran, actually.

"Such a nice man," Breeze said with a charming little shrug.

"Breeze? How did you get here?" Mattie wasn't sure she could handle any more surprises today.

Breeze gave Jane a smart salute. "That one, of course, which is why she was our fearless leader back in the dark ages of Rowe Academy. And by the way, thank you, Jane. I always enjoy a nice ride in a private Citation jet."

Mattie turned to Jane in confusion. It sounded as if she'd engineered this meeting to the point of getting Breeze up here from the Gulf of Mexico.

Jane set down her teacup. "You could say I anticipated you, Mattie. I take the *Chronicle*—have for years—and I knew all about William Broud. I assumed your urgent message had something to do with his being released, and that you'd also contacted Breeze, so I didn't waste any time setting up this meeting. Sorry I had to keep both of you in the dark, but please believe me, it was the *only* way, given my crazy fishbowl of a life."

"You told me it was a school reunion," Breeze said.

"Well, I had to tell you something, or you wouldn't have come. And besides, this *is* a reunion, isn't it, girls?"

She held up her teacup, as if to make a toast. Breeze took her cue and hoisted the bottle of brandy.

Mattie had fleeting regrets that she hadn't put more brandy in her tea. Lots more. She raised her cup, aware that this wasn't her meeting anymore. Jane had taken over, but why should that surprise her? It had always been that way. Jane was the oldest of the group, only by a few months, but she'd assumed the leadership role from the beginning.

She was the expert on life in general, but specialized in being organized and sucking up to authority figures. Breeze had been good for makeup, sneaking out and French kissing, which the girls had been forced to practice on each other since there weren't any boys around. Mattie hadn't minded that exactly. Maybe she *was* a lesbian?

Mattie's sole contribution had been her ability to pee standing up, which drew crowds, but not much status. And, in Jane's defense, she probably wasn't aware there was any competition. Jane was goal-directed to the point of blinders, a trait as oddly endearing as it was annoying.

"Amicus usque ad aras," Jane said. "Friends to the end."

"Tria juncta in uno," Breeze added. "Three as one."

Mattie repeated the solemn toasts and they drank.

Breeze took another swig from the bottle and set it down. "Now who the hell is Jameson Cross? Would one of you two ignorant sluts please tell me?"

Jane laughed. "He's a bestselling true crime writer who wants the finishing school murder case reopened. His publicity says he's relentless and reclusive."

"Not *that* reclusive." Mattie butted in with no apologies. Jane could organize with the best of them, but this was Mattie's story to tell. "He paid me a visit in my chambers at the district court yesterday."

"Jameson Cross?" Jane sloshed her tea, and Breeze let out a little squeak of delight.

"So what's he like?" Breeze burbled. "Is he cute? Is he hot? Is he *murderously* sexy?"

Mattie shot her a look. "Take a shower, Breeze. We met. We didn't have sex."

"Poor baby. Next time, dress like a girl. You might get lucky."

"Hey!" Jane rose from the couch to restore order. "Breeze, this is serious. The man could ruin our lives."

Mattie rose, too, with careful thought to the gimpy knee. She tried not to look at the barricaded windows. It would have given her great relief to open the blinds, even fractionally, but she wasn't sure what signal that would send to the gestapo, as Jane had called them.

"He *is* a threat," she said. "He pretended to be interested in my court cases, but it was a ruse. He was there to dig up dirt about the lonely girls and Millicent Rowe's murder."

Jane's perfect makeup turned as gray as ashes. "Are you sure? How much does he already know?"

"Rumors, conjecture, circumstantial stuff at best. As far as official records go, everything's sealed up like a drum. What could he know?" Mattie combed her fingers through her hair, aware that she was the unkempt one, the uncut stone in this three-gem setting. "He was fishing."

"I'll bite." Breeze grinned. "Okay, okay, this is serious."

"It's only a matter of time," Mattie cautioned. "If he hasn't already figured out that we three are the lonely girls, he will soon. Basically, we're dealing with a ticking bomb."

Mattie went through the rest of the details of her meeting with Cross, and by the time she was done, Jane had gone silent. She sat on the edge of the couch, her legs as tightly wound as a French braid. Her lips were pursed, her eyes rigidly focused on the floor.

Breeze sat forward. "Jane?"

"If he goes to the press, this story will explode," Jane said. "My life will explode."

"He isn't going to the press," Mattie pointed out. "He doesn't want to lose control. He wants to find the real killer— and make a killing himself by turning it into a book."

Jane looked up. "And when he finds out who I am? That one of the lonely girls is the First Lady?"

Mattie instantly assumed the authority, aware that someone had to take charge. For the moment, Jane had abdicated. "When he finds out who you are, he'll back off. He can't make unfounded charges against the First Lady. There would be consequences—enormous consequences—and he's smart enough to know that. It would ruin his credibility."

Jane shook her head. "I don't trust him. We have to make him back off. Frighten him, dammit, if it comes to that."

"And make him even more suspicious?" A lightbulb popped in Mattie's head. Jane was terrified. It had taken Mattie this long to figure it out because Jane was never terrified, and Mattie hadn't recognized even the most obvious signs. Her friend had so much to lose it was incomprehensible. This wasn't about three isolated women. The entire country would be affected. It could bring down her husband's administration.

Mattie went to the couch and knelt next to Jane, aware of the pressure in her knee. "The only thing we have to do is say nothing. Silence is golden, twenty-four carat, in this case. We're not hostile, but we don't admit to anything, just the appearance of cooperation is enough. Is that clear?"

"You're describing my life," Jane said.

"Good, *excellent*. Now I'm going to suggest one more thing. I want to hire a detective to check out Cross. I know several because of my profession, and there's one who's impeccable. I'd trust him with my life, *and* he owes me a favor."

Jane was already shaking her head. "We can't bring anyone else in on this. It's too dangerous."

Mattie exchanged a glance with Breeze, whose raised eyebrow seemed to say that she had misgivings, too. Mattie was about to argue the point when Jane gripped her hand. "Larry can't find out. It would kill him. His health isn't good anyway. He *can't*, Mattie."

Jane's strength nearly took Mattie's breath away. She was afraid her hand would be crushed. "Of course not," she said. "And he won't find out. No one will. We'll handle this together, just the three of us."

"Thank you."

Jane sagged with relief, and Mattie's instincts were immediate and fiercely protective. She had never seen her friend this vulnerable.

"I'll take care of it," Mattie said. "Don't worry about anything. I'll head Cross off."

Breeze flashed her a thumbs-up, but Mattie wasn't at all certain she could do what she'd just promised and keep her word to Jane. She already had a plan in mind, but it wasn't something she could share with the other two, and that gave her grave misgivings. She wasn't generally superstitious, and perhaps most adults would think childhood vows silly, but Mattie didn't like the idea of breaking them, especially now.

14

The once-stylish Excelsior looked more like a chunk of rotting meat on an anthill than a hotel. Besieged by pawn and porn shops on every side, the decomposing structure was another casualty of urban decay and the economy's failure to trickle all the way down.

Jameson Cross had grown up fifteen minutes south of here in a three-bedroom rambler in a neighborhood that was solidly middle class. He could remember when the Excelsior was one of the area's top draws for businessmen and campaigning politicians. But that was twenty years ago, before the exodus to the coast and the high-rent real estate of Sausalito and Tiburon.

Now, no one would stay at the Excelsior by choice—and Jameson didn't want to be here, either. He had an appointment that had to be kept.

The glass entry doors were reinforced with rusting metal gates that served little purpose, since they'd been left open. Jameson let himself in and took the stairs to the fifth floor. From somewhere in the building, a baby was crying and hip hop music blasted from a boom box. Suddenly a door slammed, muting the sounds. Jameson read off the room numbers as he walked down the hall, approaching the one he wanted with expectations that confused him. Hope, dread, even fear.

No one answered his knock, so he tried the door. It was locked with a deadbolt, but they weren't as difficult to jimmy as most people imagined.

He knocked again. On the third try, he made a decision.

Crime writing had taught him many useful tricks over the years, and one of them was lock-picking. He carried a tiny screwdriver and a heavy-duty paperclip in his wallet, and he used a technique called scrubbing that required applying pressure to all the pins in the lock at once. It was a quick way to pick a basic five-pin tumbler, and fortunately that's what he was dealing with.

Once he'd determined the right amount of force to use, he was ready. It took him all of two minutes to lift the pins and release the locking mechanism. Much too long for a burglar. Just fine for his purposes.

The bed had been slept in and the floor was littered with pillows and bedcovers. An empty water bottle lay on the floor next to the wastebasket, and the nightstand had an array of crumpled candy bar wrappers. Other than that, there was no sign of the occupant.

Jameson glanced at his watch, saw that he was a little early, and decided to go back outside to wait in the hall. The appointment was for noon, and the last thing he wanted was to be an unwelcome surprise. This was too important. So much of Jameson's life was here in this room.

As he left, he noticed that the bathroom door was partially open. He came to a halt, unable to believe what he saw. A man's bare foot. It stuck out beyond the bathroom door, the only part of him that was visible. Someone was on the floor in there, and Jameson reacted like a witness to a terrible accident. Even as he broke for the door, he didn't want to look.

Dread, fear. Hope ripped him apart.

Sweat drenched him.

The door pressed against the weight of a human body, and Jameson let out a snarl of raw despair. He squeezed through the space and found a tall, gangly man lying on the floor. He was curled up like a kid at the base of the toilet. It looked like he was sleeping peacefully, but when Jameson dropped to the floor and knelt next to him, he could see the grimace. It wasn't peace, it was pain. His face was contorted in pain.

"Oh, God, Billy," he whispered. "What have you done?"

Jameson touched his brother's blue-black hair, the only thing he and his older sibling had in common besides their height. He touched his cold, still face and felt his nostrils for breath.

There was none. Billy Broud was gone. He'd been released from death row only to die in a seedy hotel room within driving distance of the town where he'd grown up—the same place that had vilified him and wrongly convicted him of murder.

Jameson's heart was breaking. Twenty years of unshed tears burned his eyes and throat. Their family had disowned Billy years before the murder conviction. He'd never gotten along with their father, a no-nonsense life insurance salesman who preached on Sunday mornings at the neighborhood church. When Billy hit his teens, he was regularly skipping school, experimenting with drugs and getting into trouble with the law. By sixteen, he'd been banished from the house for his unrepentant sins, which included getting a neighbor's wife pregnant.

Jameson's greatest regret was that he'd abandoned Billy, too. He'd sided with his strict father, turning his back on his brother when Billy needed him most. None of the family had gone to the murder trial. But after their father died, Jameson realized he'd made a terrible mistake. He wrote to Billy and went to see him in San Quentin, but Billy refused to acknowledge Jameson's existence. He'd begun calling himself William and saying that he didn't have a brother. He didn't have a family.

Jameson had vowed to make it up to Billy, to win his forgiveness, if possible. Now it was too late.

He sat back on his haunches and dug his cell phone from the pocket of his jacket. Moisture blurred his vision, making it impossible to see the numbers. He swallowed back the pain that welled into his throat. All he wanted to do was tap out 9ll, but his hands wouldn't work.

"Why here, Billy?" he said. "Why this stinking hole?"

Jameson could see no signs of foul play. He feared his brother had taken his own life, and he didn't want to think about what had driven him to suicide at a time like this. He was a free man. This was the beginning, not the end. He had everything in front of him.

What had they done to his brother in there?

The phone dropped to the floor, and Jameson doubled over, as tortured and contorted as the body on the floor.

SKREEET CLANG CLUNK.

The deafening noise jolted Jameson out of his troubled slumber. He jackknifed from the leather recliner where he'd dozed off and scanned his living room, expecting to see an armed intruder. It sounded like someone was forcing his way into the house.

Mail? He squinted at the legal-size manila envelope on the floor in front of the door. What time was it? The mail was normally delivered around noon, and it looked to be sunset by the soft, peachy glow of the skylight. His watch said 7:00 p.m. Could it be that late? He'd sprawled in the chair when he got home from the hospital, physically and emotionally exhausted. He must have fallen asleep.

He squinted down at the envelope, which was prominently stamped Special Delivery. Probably something from his publisher.

"The U.S. Postal Service strikes again," he muttered, shaking his head to clear the cobwebs. He left the mail there and headed for the kitchen. Coffee. He doubted it would help his throbbing temples, but he needed something to wake himself up. Sleep had dulled the edges of his pain a little, but he couldn't sleep forever.

The noise he'd heard was the metal flap to the mail slot. It always crashed like a thunderclap after the mail was pushed through. If Jameson had owned a gun, he would have pulled it in self-defense. Maybe the mailman was lucky he didn't.

He checked his jacket pocket for his cell, and realized that he was fully dressed. He'd fallen into the chair without even taking off his coat. The day was a blinding red blur. Billy had been taken to the hospital, where they'd pronounced him dead, but they hadn't been able to determine the cause. By that time Jameson had walled himself off emotionally. He was just going through the motions.

The police were called in, and Jameson told them everything he knew, except the real meaning of his brother's phone message. Jameson felt certain Billy had been hiding something over the years, which was why he'd urged his brother to tell him what he knew about the finishing school murder. Based on the phone message, Billy may have been about to break his silence, which could have put him in danger. But when the police asked if Jameson knew of anyone who would want to harm his brother, he had said no, and left it at that.

His mostly stainless steel kitchen was spotless from the cleaning crew—and lack of use. Normally, it probably fulfilled some need he had for order. Tonight it felt cold. Everything did.

He opened two or three brushed-chrome canisters before he got the one with the coffee. *Maybe you should try labeling the canisters, genius,* he thought as he breathed in the powerful essence of plain old Columbian from the grocery store. He'd tried the fancy stuff, but he didn't want dessert, he wanted a drug. Coffee should taste as bitter as dirt and pack a punch.

His thoughts drifted back to his brother as he filled the coffeemaker's reservoir with tap water and piled the filter high with grounds.

In truth, Billy was a complete mystery to him, as apparently he was to everyone else. Jameson had never believed the stories that Billy was crazy, and yet, he knew so little about his brother's inner life that it was difficult to hazard a guess as to why he would silently waste away in prison for twenty-three years if he hadn't done the crime. Why didn't he shout his innocence to the heavens, like every other death row inmate, even the guilty ones? Nor was it clear why he would have taken his life after he'd been released. But if he'd become a threat to the real killer, that might have been his undoing. That did make some sense.

Jameson poured himself a mug of mud-black coffee and went back to the living room. Fortunately, the police officers he'd dealt with hadn't recognized him, so he'd given them his legal name, James Broud, rather than the pseudonym he was known by. Billy's death was sure to hit the news, and Jameson didn't want to get caught in the media spotlight at a time like this. He'd also lied to the police about his relationship with his brother, saying that he and Billy were close.

After he'd finished filling out the paperwork, he'd made arrangements for his brother's remains, and then he'd gone to a noisy, crowded sports bar, where a major tennis match had filled every screen, and he'd drunk beer until the thought of going home didn't fill him with despair.

Silence. He couldn't face it. The silence would remind him of his lost brother, and of twenty years that felt like an eternity...*was* an eternity now that Billy wasn't coming back.

He stood in the middle of his living room with its sleek, armless leather divans and benches, gripping the burning coffee mug for several mindless seconds. Lately, when it got too much, his nervous system checked out and he went on automatic pilot. It was survival, he supposed. The grief came all at once, like a tsunami. If you let it, it could engulf you and take you under.

At some point later, the envelope caught his eye again. He flipped it over with the toe of his shoe and craned to look at the return address. The Excelsior Hotel? Abandoning the coffee mug, he picked up the envelope and ripped it open. Several pieces of paper and fabric fell out.

The envelope was full of scraps, probably a hundred of them, that had been written on in what looked like red ink. Blood? Pieces of a ripped paper bag had been imprinted by a sharp object, but the impression was readable. On some of them, Jameson could make out his brother's signature at the bottom.

Billy sent this?

Jameson checked the envelope's postmark. It was mailed the same day Billy left the phone message—yesterday. He sat on the floor in the falling light and began sorting through the scraps, reading what looked like snatches of Billy's ordeal in prison. They weren't in any order that made sense, but he couldn't stop to sort them out. He nearly scorched the paper with his need to know what his brother had to say, but his stomach knotted as he read, churning with a mix of curiosity and dread.

On each scrap of paper Billy had scribbled a few cryptic words, perhaps to keep the meaning deliberately unclear in case the notes should be found. But Jameson did notice the word

"Framed" written somewhere on almost every scrap, which he took to be the point of Billy's efforts. He was declaring his innocence and trying to expose whoever had set him up.

About a third of the notes had numbers, a quarter had dates and the rest weren't ordered in any way. It seemed as if Billy might have started with one method and switched to another as an easier way to organize his entries.

As Jameson began to sort by date, he thought he saw a certain chronology. Each note had the word "Framed" in it, but the other references were what intrigued him.

Didn't kill her.
They hated her. They did it.
Sick to the soul. Secrets.
Eyes like ether. Hair like fire. Cold as stone.
Wicked little blonde.
Find the girls. They did it.
Couldn't protect them.
VIPs. Big dogs, all of them.
Videotapes. One missing.
Drugged.
Death threats. Every day!
Framed!
Kill my brother. Can't let them do it.
Stay quiet.
Protect him.

Jameson read on, but his mind had stopped at the reference to death threats. Billy had been threatened? That would explain his long silence, but it sounded as if the threats were against Jameson, not Billy. Good God, his brother was protecting him. Jameson could hardly fathom that, especially since he'd done nothing to protect Billy. He almost didn't want to believe it was true.

He sat back, trying to get control. It didn't help with the guilt he already carried, nor could it right the wrongs done to his brother, but he consoled himself with the thought that there was nothing he could do to change the past, and if he let himself get sucked into that hole, he would never get out. His salvation was to move on, find the murdering scum who did this and give Billy the only justice he would ever get. That was all that was left to Jameson now, the only course he could take.

He forced himself to look over the scrambled chronology again, focusing in on the references to the person Billy described: Eyes like ether, hair like fire, cold as stone, wicked little blonde.

That couldn't be one woman, he reasoned. Billy was talking about two different hair colors. Two women then? Or more? Possibly he was trying to give the salient feature of each of the four lonely girls. Eyes like ether meant blue, he assumed, and that would be Mattie Smith. Hair like fire could have been the redheaded Ivy White, although she was already dead by the time the headmistress was killed. Cold as stone. Jameson wasn't sure about that one, but from everything he'd read and heard, Breeze Wheeler was the wicked blonde, which left Jane Dunbar. Cold as stone.

He sat back on his haunches to think. He looked at the scraps again and began reorganizing by date this time.

Find the girls. They did it. Videotapes. One missing.

This was the message.

Jameson rose and drew in some air, as much as he could get. The house was nearly dark now. He ought to turn on some lights, but the shadows that crept out of every corner seemed much better suited to his mood. A blanket of gloom had enveloped him, and he did nothing to ward it off. Better to be alone in the dark with your thoughts when they were this bleak.

There were conflicting forces stirring inside him. Maybe he didn't want it to be the four girls. They were kids, students.

Maybe he didn't want it to be her, the crazy judge. But it seemed Billy was convinced that they were the ones who'd killed Millicent Rowe and the videotapes would prove it.

That meant getting his hands on evidence that couldn't be begged, borrowed or stolen. He wondered if Mattie Smith had had anything to do with keeping the records sealed all this time.

If Billy was right then Jameson already had his killers. It was just a matter of proof. But another question burned in his brain, bright and excoriating. If the lonely girls killed their headmistress and framed Billy, had they also killed Billy to keep him quiet?

Jameson stared at the paper littering his floor.

Jesus, did they kill anyone who got in their way? Who was next?

15

Breeze Wheeler had never seen a woman more in need of help than Mattie Smith. It was too late for crisis intervention. This called for life support. Breeze wasn't certain how a woman could function in such a derelict condition. She paced the bedroom in bare feet, unpolished toenails and sweatpants that bagged at the butt. But worst of all was the way she eyed her fingernails. Like a garter snake eyeing a big fat bug.

Breeze was glad Jane had gone back to D.C. that afternoon and wasn't here to see it. Mattie had chewed her nails to the quick in their Rowe Academy days. The gnarled stumps had given Breeze nightmares, and she'd been relieved to see that her friend had finally conquered the problem. Even without polish, Mattie's nails were in decent shape, but tonight she looked like a wino about to relapse. She would be gnawing on them any minute if Breeze didn't do something.

With a delicate little shiver, Breeze climbed off the bed and threw open her boxy Louis Vuitton suitcase. *Sin,* her favorite fragrance, exploded from the case, and she breathed in deeply, relaxing at once. That's what Mattie needed, a beauty break and a soothing scent to calm her. Poor thing, she worried too much. Mattie let herself dwell in the dark corners. Breeze had learned how to barricade herself with enough luxury and beauty to hold back the night. Some people might call it living in a fantasy world, but so what? It beat reality.

"Let's see what we have in here," Breeze said, feeling very much like a doctor on call. "There isn't time for more than a quick fix, but I've been known to save lives with a half hour's notice. Shouldn't be a problem."

Mattie didn't seem to have heard a word she said. Every atom of her attention was focused on *the problem*—coming up with a strategy to deal with Jameson Cross. She'd nearly worn a path in the carpet, and now she was sitting in one of her creaky rattan chairs, bent forward, her chin cupped in her hand.

She'd had a call from her assistant earlier that day. It seemed they needed her to sub for a fellow judge at a hearing tomorrow, and she'd also spoken with her law clerk about a case she'd assigned. But neither of those things had her gnashing her teeth. It was a man, of course.

Breeze sighed. Mattie really did need her help. She was much too intense—and she didn't have a clue when it came to the opposite sex.

"Maybe you're overthinking this?" Breeze suggested. "He's a man. Appeal to his chivalrous instincts. That always works."

Mattie glanced up from her funk. "You think he *has* chivalrous instincts?"

"Of course, men love to play the white knight. Employ some charm and wit, as Ms. Rowe used to say. 'Beauty isn't a blessing or a curse, ladies. It's currency. Invest it wisely.' Remember that one?"

Obviously, Mattie did. She looked like she was going to be ill.

"What charm and wit?" she mumbled into her fingers. "You forget who you're dealing with here."

Breeze swept the tails of her black silk kimono out of her way. "Oh, Christ, you're brilliant. But stop worrying about the battle or you're going to lose the war. Show a little leg, blow in his ear and let him think he could save the day if he would just amuse himself with a different murder case, maybe one that wasn't two decades old."

"So…I'm supposed to play on his sympathies and tell him the lonely girls were innocent bystanders? Maybe I could remind him that we were mere children when it happened and couldn't possibly have done anything so diabolical, and oh, by the way, we all came from broken homes and lives of terrible hardship."

"Now you're talking! Fight like a woman. You can do it."

"Ugh," Mattie said, making a face. "You want me to give our entire gender a black eye? Take us back to the days of Sandra Dee and her feather-duster eyelashes? You do know she became an alcoholic."

Breeze let her impatience be known with a sigh. "If you want to play fair, then you might as well tell him what we did. We'll all go down together, just like we planned. Only Jane will be hit the hardest—and she has by far the most to lose."

Mattie was nodding, tapping her fingers against her cheek. "Frankly, Jane has me worried. I've never seen her so fragile. That's why I'm overthinking. I can't blow this. For her sake, I can't."

Mattie sank back into her funk, leaving her houseguest to her own devices. Breeze abandoned the suitcase in favor of inspecting the spare bedroom they were in, which was where she would be staying for the next few days, until the Jameson Cross thing blew over. And Breeze was certain it would blow over. These things always did. Mattie and Jane were both overreacting.

Meanwhile…

Breeze cast a skeptical glance around the guest room, if it could be called that. Mattie could use some decorating help, too. Make that life*style* support, Breeze thought. She wasn't a fan of anything that had been minimalized or feng shui'd or covered with grass cloth, which meant most of Mattie's house would have to go.

"No way," Mattie mumbled, apparently speaking to herself. "I can't believe I'm considering anything so ridiculous."

Breeze turned, startled. "Considering what?"

"Persuading Jameson Cross to help us. Playing him like a cheap accordion. *Seducing* him. That's just sick."

"I know. Isn't it great! And hell, *yes,* you can do it. You've got smarts to spare. And nerve. God knows you're a nervy bitch." Breeze folded her arms, assessing the damage. "But the rest of it will take some work."

"How much work?"

"Mattie, you're a wreck."

Mattie blinked at her.

"You need help, Mattress. Let's just say it's good that I'm here."

Now, she glowered as only Mattie could, with every nerve and muscle in her face. "Don't call me that."

Mattress was Mattie's nickname from school, and it fit her to a tee, in Breeze's opinion. Back in those days, she'd never cared a thing about how she looked. In fact, she'd resembled an unmade bed. But she'd earned the name because of the weird things she kept hidden under her mattress. Breeze recalled tattered palmistry charts, a mud-spattered blindfold and the teddy bear that Ivy had given her.

Breeze had to smile. Mattie had always been the odd one, a misfit among misfits. Ivy was wistful and sensitive, a lost soul in many ways. Jane was take-charge and everyone's mother-confessor. There was no one better than Jane when you needed advice. But Mattie was fierce, loyal and shy, their Robin Hood. She would have fought to the death for her friends, and Breeze had never had anyone else like that in her life.

Breeze knelt in front of the suitcase, inspired, pulling things out.

"I must be nuts," Mattie said. "This will never work. He'll laugh his ass off."

Breeze got stern. "Mattie, you can be the authority on everything else, but I'm the authority on men, all right? It's a scientific fact that males are more inclined to help attractive women. Everyone is, for that matter. They've done studies that prove attractive people get offers of help at twice the rate that unattractive people do. Okay, it's not fair, but looks *are* a huge advantage, and you're not using yours. Hell, you're abusing them."

Mattie gave the bureau mirror a quick glance. She yanked at her hairband, as if that could fix the problem. "Breeze, that's crazy," she said. "Who would do a study like that? It can't be true."

"Care to wager?" Breeze continued to search the case for her magic potions.

"Of course not. It's utter nonsense. If anything, beauty is a drawback. People don't take you seriously. Men want to sleep with you, not work with you. You should know that."

Breeze whipped out a vinyl bag of beauty products and unzipped it. She pulled out the sponge she wanted, grabbed a tube of cream and darted into the guest bathroom.

"I just have to dampen this sponge," she called out to Mattie.

"Take your time," Mattie called back.

Mattie's bathroom got a failing grade, too. The light was bad. It cast shadows. The mirror wasn't large enough and there was no tap for filtered water. And, of course, what beauty products Breeze found were all made with lanolin. Yucky stuff. Very clogging.

"Beauty, luxury and pleasure are my business," Breeze announced as she returned to the bedroom. "I never underestimate their power—and neither should you."

Mattie sat on the bed, waiting for her. "Speaking of your business. How's it going?"

Had anyone else asked the question, Breeze might have been wary. She didn't talk about what she did, for obvious reasons, but Mattie and Jane both knew that her spa offered extras. Breeze had confided her secret at Jane's wedding, and they'd both reacted with mild shock, but no judgment. Their concerns were with her welfare and her happiness, and she'd assured them on both counts. But that was all she could tell them. Neither of them knew that her spa served more than one purpose, even back in those days—and especially now that the world was in such disarray.

"Couldn't be better," Breeze said. "I choose my own hours, I make lots of money and I deal in dreams. That's the best part."

Mattie's eyes sparkled for the first time that night. "Must be nice."

"Oh, it's nice."

"I can't imagine what it would be like, having sex with lots of men. I can't even imagine having sex with *one* man."

Breeze laughed. "Sorry to disappoint, but there's only one man who visits my private suite on a regular basis these days. He is a prince, though."

She wound the tie of her kimono around her finger. "I think of it as a calling. I make people happy."

"But what about you? Are you happy?"

"Of course," she said with a bit too much force. The tinge of sadness she felt confounded her. She'd never thought of herself as unhappy. Of course, she wasn't unhappy. That was impossible with a life like hers. She lived every woman's secret dreams.

Mattie's gaze seemed to hold a mix of envy and curiosity. "Was it weird to be with a man like that? I mean back when we were at Rowe?"

Breeze wasn't fazed by Mattie's question, but it did take her back. It wasn't supposed to have turned out the way it did, she was sure. Ms. Rowe must have intended her "friends" to have their choice of four young lovelies, but the men had shown a great deal more interest in Breeze, the flirty blonde, and Ivy, the wistful redhead, than they did the other two girls.

As far as Breeze knew, Ivy only had one man, apparently wealthy, who picked her up in a limo. Breeze would have preferred an exclusive situation like Ivy's, but she consoled herself with being wildly popular. More men had requested her than she'd had time to see. But no one had picked the other two. Mattie was too much the tomboy, and Jane was too stiff and proper.

"To be honest," Breeze said, "I was flattered. I suppose I felt special being chosen."

"But you were only fourteen. The thought of a man made me sick at that age."

"I was never fourteen, Mattie." Breeze didn't know whether to laugh or cry at the notion. She'd never really been a teenager, or a child, for that matter. And yet, she'd had a childhood most kids could only dream of. No rules or punishments. If she broke a favorite toy and threw a crying fit, her parents sobbed with her. She was homeschooled with the other kids in the commune and always encouraged to express herself.

She had all the space and freedom a child could possibly want, but sometimes she wondered if it was too much. It had left her with a vague sense of weightlessness, as if nothing was permanent, and no one would ever be around for long. Even now her parents were caught up in their latest cause and had been out of touch for months. She didn't begrudge them wanting to change the world. Somebody should. She even helped them with money and legal assistance. She didn't feel abandoned, either. It wasn't that, exactly. It was more that they'd never been there at all.

She planted a hand on her hip. "Are you trying to distract me?"

She grabbed Mattie by the sleeve and set her down on the vanity seat, facing the mirror. "Lose the sweatshirt," she said. "I'm going to need some working room."

Mattie stripped to her bra while Breeze put together a tray of magic potions. When she was done, she gave Mattie's skin a merciless inspection.

"Here's the diagnosis. Your face needs a regular regime of cleansing and exfoliating, your hair needs shaping and highlights and your teeth could probably use a little brightening up. But your breasts are lovely. That will help."

"Great, I'll wear a bag over my head and go topless."

"Every man's dream," Breeze murmured, sitting opposite Mattie, love-seat fashion. "Now shut up."

First, she prepared Mattie's skin with a gentle foaming cleanser, and then she coated the sponge with an oatmeal-apricot scrub. Mattie winced as Breeze applied the grainy mixture to her T-zone.

"Ouch, what are you doing?"

"Exfoliation. Your skin is like a baby's butt."

"Isn't that good?"

"This baby's got diaper rash."

Breeze scrubbed gently, applying enough pressure to bring a rosy glow to Mattie's pale skin. When she had the effect she wanted, she took her reluctant friend into the bathroom and rinsed her until she squeaked.

"You look better already," Breeze said. "And that's without makeup. Now for the pore-minimizing mask."

"If you value your brown roots, you will get nowhere near me with a mask."

"Okay, then, clarifying lotion." Breeze had forgotten all about Mattie's claustrophobia.

The clarifying lotion stung, and Mattie told her so. The mask wouldn't have, Breeze pointed out with some pleasure. She finished up with a moisturizing lotion that promised to make a visible difference with fine lines. Mattie had a few, probably from all that glowering.

When Breeze was done, she presented Mattie with a hand mirror and encouraged her to glory in her sparkling new self.

Mattie glowered instead. "All I have to do is bat my lashes at Cross, and he'll eat from my hand?"

"He'll eat from anything you put in front of him, so keep your legs crossed."

"Just what I was hoping to hear."

"Hold your enemies close," Breeze said, espousing a concept she firmly believed in. "Know them better than you know your friends. The only safe way to deal with snakes is to know where they are at all times. Think about it."

Mattie set the mirror down. "Do I have to?"

"Ingrate." Breeze began gathering up her paraphernalia and returning it to the suitcase. "We'll work on the whole package tomorrow—makeup, hair, the outfit. And what would you think if I called an interior decorator in for a consult?"

"You're planning to reupholster me?"

"No, this place. It needs some sprucing, too."

Mattie was already shaking her head. "Breeze, there's a Four Seasons right across the bay. One more word about redecorating this place, and I'll relocate *you*."

Breeze sighed. "Whatever."

Mattie had her face in the mirror again, which pleased Breeze. For an ingrate, she seemed pretty intrigued with the luminous glow she saw.

"I wonder what Ms. Rowe would think of me now," she said.

Hearing that slightly wistful question come out of Mattie Smith's mouth was all the thanks Breeze needed. "She would think that someone had done what she could not," Breeze said. "No need to thank me, Mattie, but I've just turned you into the alluring woman you were born to be."

Mattie set the mirror face-down on the vanity table, as if determined to change the subject. "Have you thought about who really killed her? I mean, now that we know Broud didn't do it?"

"Ms. Rowe?" Breeze felt an odd sparkle of fear in the pit of her stomach. She dismissed it immediately. Jane and Mattie held the franchise on that emotion. But Mattie's question had disturbed her, and partly because she knew everyone else would be asking it, too. This was a mystery that had already aroused too much attention, and if people knew who—and what—was really involved, there would be no end to it. It would never go way, and none of them would be safe.

The sparkle was still there, she realized. It grew brighter, sharper, like the quills of a feather, a terrible feeling.

She whisked up the mirror, gave herself a quick, expert inspection, and frowned. Was that a pimple? She was going to need a facial soon.

"I'm sure there were lots of people who wanted her dead," Mattie pointed out.

Breeze peered over the mirror. "Even *we* wanted her dead."

"I just wish we'd left it at that," Mattie said softly, "at wanting."

She rose from the vanity, sobered and showing signs of fatigue. "Bedtime for me," she said. "I have to be there early tomorrow."

She hesitated, as if there was something else she wanted to say, and then, didn't. "What about you? Beauty sleep?"

"Me? Sure." Breeze nodded, but her mind was somewhere else, recalling the night the lonely girls club was born. It was their first year at Rowe Academy, and the headmistress had made a concerted effort to take the four scholarship girls under her wing. She'd invited them to her apartment for a very special orientation session to help them adjust to their new home, and to coach them in grooming and social skills. Or so they thought. Still, the four of them had been thrilled to be singled out for such special attention, even Mattie. They were all smiles and anticipation. The future was bright. Everything was perfect.

16

Rowe Academy
Fall 1980, Opening Term

"Look in your mirrors, ladies. Look deeply and tell me what you see. I do hope it isn't rude, crude or attitude. That may be faddish and popular, but it's not what we strive for here at Rowe Academy. We are gracious and refined. We are swans. We are proud."

Mattie stared into the handheld mirror the headmistress had given her and searched for any sign of a swan. She didn't want to be the only ugly duckling in the group, but it didn't look good. Staring back at her were pinched eyes, a knitted brow, lips pursed in consternation.

"See anything?" she whispered to Jane Dunbar, who was sitting next to her on Ms. Rowe's living room sofa. For some mysterious reason the headmistress had invited Mattie and Jane and the other two scholarship girls to her apartment that evening for a cozy cup of tea and a chat. Mattie had assumed that it was some kind of orientation session for first-term students, but she couldn't imagine why the four of them had been singled out. And since she knew virtually nothing about the headmistress, other than the rumors floating around campus, she didn't know what to expect.

"Anyone care to tell me what they see?" Ms. Rowe asked.

Breeze Wheeler raised her hand, which wasn't fair, as far as Mattie was concerned. Breeze had a golden halo of hair that made her look just like an angel. She was naturally beautiful and embarrassingly boy-crazy, which made Mattie wonder about the angel part. Mattie's own mother had been flirty like Breeze, and most of the neighbors had thought of Lela Smith as trailer trash.

Breeze had a breathless catch to her voice. "I see a girl who wants more than anything to be a swan," she said.

That brought a smile to Ms. Rowe's lips, which were shiny and plum-red, the exact color of her elegant long skirt and turtleneck sweater. Mattie'd heard the rumors that Ms. Rowe wasn't even thirty years old, and certain people on the school's board of regents thought the headmistress should be older. Maybe that was why she was so snobby at times.

Of course, Ms. Rowe *was* the academy. The buildings and grounds had been in her family for generations. The small school was a hotbed of gossip and everyone said that Ms. Rowe herself was born and raised here, and had not wanted the estate to be donated for educational purposes, but her grandmother had done it anyway, which left her granddaughter with two choices—she either ran the school or looked for another place to live.

Ms. Rowe tapped her palm, apparently applauding. "Very nice, Ms. Wheeler. Who would like to go next?"

No one spoke. Breeze beamed with pleasure while Mattie and the other two waited in painful suspense. Rather than stare at her silent guests, Ms. Rowe took a turn around her circular living room, smoothing the lace runner on the baby grand piano, rearranging a snapdragon in a bouquet of fresh-cut flowers and brushing her hand lovingly over certain pieces of furniture. She paused at an ornate birdcage and poked a finger inside to stroke a bright green parakeet.

Mattie had also heard that the headmistress was so in love with everything English that she held old-fashioned sherry hours for the faculty right here in this apartment. The tower room was done up like a Victorian parlor with a carved mahogany fireplace and heavy damask curtains on the windows. Mattie didn't know much about antiques, but she'd heard everything was real, from the bone china to the Chippendale tables and the needlepoint chairs, which were Hepple-something.

Ms. Rowe finally stopped in front of Jane. "And how about you, Ms. Dunbar? What do you see in your mirror?"

Poor Jane went violent red. Stop signs weren't that bright. Mattie felt bad, but was deeply grateful it wasn't her.

Jane shook her head. "Someone who wishes she wasn't—"

Here, Mattie thought.

Whatever Jane had intended to say, she couldn't get it out, and Ms. Rowe came to her rescue. "It's all right, dear" she said. "I didn't mean to embarrass you. And it doesn't matter anyway because I think I know what you saw in the mirror."

"You do?" Jane gazed up at her, hopeful.

Ms. Rowe smiled and touched Jane's chin, lifting it. "You didn't see a swan, but you did see yourself, and that's even better. You saw Plain Jane, who wants to be Lady Jane, isn't that right?"

Mattie was as hushed as everyone else. Jane didn't move a muscle, but Mattie suspected what Ms. Rowe had said was true. Jane often watched Ms. Rowe with a reverence that was close to hero worship. She wanted to be elegant and polished, just like the headmistress.

"And you will be Lady Jane," Ms. Rowe said. "You have my promise. You will be everything you want to be, all of you. I'll teach you how."

She turned to the others. "I would like you to look carefully at my hands. What do you see? Would anyone care to guess? Ivy, how about you?"

Ivy White looked up from her own hands, her dark green eyes wide with alarm, her smile frozen. She stared at Ms. Rowe's long elegant fingers and plum-red nails, as if they were daggers.

"They're very beautiful and white," she said.

Mattie wished Ms. Rowe would turn her hands over so that she could get a look at the lines. Long fingers meant intellect and the conical tips were artistic, but they also meant her heart ruled her head, and her emotions could run amuck.

"Thank you, Ivy. That was a sweet thing to say."

Ivy seemed pleased. She relaxed in the chair, shoulders dropping, and Mattie was surprised at the relief she felt. She didn't know Ivy well, but the titian Madonna, as the older girls had started calling her, was a recluse, and Mattie felt protective toward her. Ivy seemed very much alone in the world, and Mattie was helplessly drawn to other outcasts.

"Before you arrived, ladies," Ms. Rowe said, "I applied a botanical to my hands called heartwine. It's made from the berries of a tropical plant, and it constricts the blood vessels, which is why my skin looks translucent and pale. Do you see that?"

The girls peered at her hands as if they were witnessing a biblical miracle.

"Heartwine also causes edema," she explained, "which fills out wrinkles, not that any of you need worry about that yet. But you can't start taking care of your skin too soon. Agelessness begins now."

Mattie was surprised to see Ivy rolling up the sleeve of her sweater.

"Can I use it on this?" she asked, revealing what looked like a birthmark on the inside of her forearm. The angry purple scar bubbled like a bad burn, and Ivy grimaced in disgust as she showed it to Ms. Rowe.

The headmistress's voice grew faint. "Ivy, dear, *no*. Heartwine absorbs through the skin, and it's toxic in large doses. You can only use tiny amounts—and one other caution, ladies, all of you, it may be called heart*wine,* but don't ever attempt to drink it. That could be fatal."

Someone rapped at the apartment door, and Ms. Rowe actually swore under her breath.

She slashed a finger at the door. "Classic bad manners. We've lost respect in this country for the private time of others, so I shall be rude and raise my voice at whomever is on the other side of that door."

She bellowed, "Come in!"

The door creaked open, and Lane Davison, a popular junior girl, peeked in. "Sorry to interrupt, Ms. Rowe, but I have the best news!"

"What is it, Lane?" Ms. Rowe seemed to warm slightly, probably because it was Lane, the boot-licker.

Mattie wanted to puke. Lane was a day student. She and her gang of friends were from local, well-to-do families, and they were also the meanest girls on campus, but Ms. Rowe had no idea. Lane did everything but drop to her knees and kiss the headmistress's ring whenever she got the chance, and Ms. Rowe ate it up.

"I've heard from my mother," Lane trilled. "She'll be back from Europe in time for my birthday tea. She wants to bring us both a very special gift from Rome. I hope that won't be awkward for anyone."

"Lane, that's so kind of your mother, but why don't you come to my office tomorrow, and we'll discuss it. These are my *private* quarters."

Her voice had a shrillness that made Mattie question the

warmth she'd been showering on all of them. She hoped it was just the intrusion.

Lane's unhappiness darkened the entire room. "Then why are *they* here?" She threw the scholarship girls a baneful look.

"Well, they're special cases, dear. They haven't had your advantages, and they need a little extra help fitting in. I know you and your friends are doing everything you can to make them feel welcome."

Lane had nothing to say about that, but Mattie knew a little something about Lane's friends. Lane had gained such favor that she and her friends had been made hall mistresses, which allowed them to roam the halls during classes and terrorize other students. Breeze called them the Death Squad.

Once Lane was gone, Ms. Rowe was friendly and inviting again. She lowered her voice and spoke in a near whisper. "Another good lesson here, ladies. What we do in these sessions must stay between us, just the four of us, and you must not tell anyone, especially a girl like Lane, who has many friends and may not be as discreet as we would like."

Lane had been blown off. Mattie couldn't have been happier, but she was only half listening. She'd noticed an oddlooking tree, planted in a pot near the baby grand. There were no leaves on the tree, but its naked branches were studded with pink blossoms. Mattie vaguely remembered Ms. Rowe telling a story at assembly about a Judas tree. Mattie didn't recall much of the story, but she wondered if this could have been the tree. Something about it disturbed her.

"What will we be doing?" Breeze asked Ms. Rowe.

"Having a lot of fun, I hope. I'll coach you on things like grooming and deportment, social skills and how to behave with the opposite sex. Call it lifestyle boot camp."

Breeze whooped as if she'd won the lottery. Jane was smiling, and even Ivy seemed pleased. Mattie stayed quiet, but she was intrigued. She'd never had a mentor of any kind.

Her single mother had handed her off to an aunt when Mattie became inconvenient, and then her aunt had taken a job that required extensive travel, and Mattie had been handed off to this very boarding school.

"Come, ladies," Ms. Rowe said, busying herself at the coffee table, where earlier she'd set a silver tray laden with goodies for tea. "Let's get our tea and biscuits and gather around the fireplace. I have much to tell you. Oh, and bring your mirror with you."

When each girl had a steaming cup of tea she brought them over to the fire, where she'd thrown down floor pillows for everyone to sit on.

"You will learn wonderful things here at Rowe," she told them once they were settled. "Our classics program will introduce you to ancient Greek and Latin literature. You'll explore philosophy, all the sciences, math and whatever athletics interest you."

Mattie spoke up for the first time. "I saw archery targets on the north field. Could I take a class in that?"

"Of course, Matilda. I want you each to pick what interests you, and my goal is that you will learn everything you need to know to transform your lives. But you'll have an advantage because I will share my secrets with you, and you'll know things that none of the other girls do, even Lane and her friends."

"Why us?" Mattie asked the question, wondering if she should have.

"Because I know all about your backgrounds, and none of you have family to support you. I want to try to provide that support to give you the best possible chance. I know most of you are alone in this world, but I don't want you to feel alone here. You have each other, and you have me."

She reached out to each one of them and touched her

hand. "To be honest, I think of you four as my lonely girls, and I want to help you. I hope you believe that."

Even Breeze was quiet, but Mattie noticed that Jane had tears in her eyes, and Ivy had bitten her lip. Mattie was having a little trouble with her throat. There wasn't enough room for the lump.

Ms. Rowe filled the awkward silence by sipping her tea and eating one of the cookies she'd stacked in her saucer, probably against all the rules of etiquette.

"Of course, we believe you," Jane said.

Everyone's relief was so great they all began talking at once, chattering about how happy they were to be there, and finally, Ms. Rowe stopped them.

"Okay, ladies, tell me a secret. No, I shall tell you one first. I have a lovely man in my life right now, and I think he might be the one. He's very handsome, of course. And what else? Well, he makes me want to sing and shout."

She giggled like a girl and refused to say anything more. "Now, let's hear about your boyfriends. I want to know *everything.*"

"Boyfriends?" Breeze grumbled. "There aren't any men around. Let's find a boys' school and pick out a couple of exchange students."

Ms. Rowe gave Breeze a thumbs-up, and Mattie didn't know what to think. She had totally underestimated their headmistress.

No one else had any boyfriend stories to share, so Ms. Rowe suggested they pick up their mirrors and take another look. "Tell me what you see now," she said.

Mattie picked up her mirror and saw a face less guarded and more open to new experiences. That pleased her, but something else struck her, as well. She felt a quickening deep inside, an odd little shiver of anticipation at the possibility that Mattie Smith might grow up to be something more than a palm reader who lived, plied her trade and raised her children in a single-wide trailer.

Her need to do something else, to *be* something else, was huge, but she couldn't allow herself any more hope than that.

17

Had someone stuck a rude Post-it note on her back?

Mattie was perplexed. She'd been getting odd glances since she entered the courtroom moments ago to hear pretrial evidence for an injunction sought by the National Labor Relations Board. The first glance had came from the U.S. marshal, a furtive once-over that had her wondering if she'd put her robe on backward. There'd been second glances from the labor relations board counsel, two male attorneys who'd been in her courtroom before, and even from the court reporter, who'd done a double take, blushed and looked away.

Mattie reached to flick the hair from her face, and suddenly every eye was on her. Their expressions were intensely curious, but she picked up a hint of something else, especially from the men.

All at once, Mattie understood. It was Breeze's handiwork.

Breeze had gotten the jump on her this morning. She'd been up before Mattie had opened her eyes, preparing for a makeover that would end world hunger, apparently. As a result, Mattie was wearing pink shimmer on her cheeks, smoky shadow on her lids, even eyeliner. Her trusty headband had been burned in effigy, after which her hair had been styled to fall around her face in dark waves.

Breeze also had a lucky diamond tennis bracelet, which

was supposed to be "fairy dust" where men were concerned. She'd insisted Mattie wear it, and Mattie had finally agreed. She'd had so many other things on her mind that it had seemed the easiest route, but now she felt foolish. If there'd been time, she would have ducked back into her chambers and washed her face in the bathroom. Fortunately, this was a quiet little hearing in one of the smaller courtrooms without an elevated bench that would have made her feel even more on display.

Get on with things, she told herself. *And don't let Breeze near you again with a mascara wand.*

Mattie was about to open the proceedings when Jaydee slipped through the judge's door and gave the U.S. marshal a note. The marshal brought the slip of paper to Mattie and waited for her answer. It seemed a member of the board had been held up in traffic. The note asked if Mattie wanted to proceed without the member or reschedule for later that morning.

Mattie saw no reason to delay, even to wash her face. She scribbled her answer on the paper and gave it to the marshal, but apparently Jaydee hadn't thought it necessary to wait for her response. He was nowhere to be seen in the courtroom. The marshal ducked out to go find him, and Mattie picked up her gavel.

She was about to announce the session when the courtroom doors flew open. The sound exploded in the hushed gallery. Light flowed into the room, and at first, all Mattie could see was an outline in black. She knew intuitively that it was a man—the height, the shoulders, the ramrod stance. Everyone else seemed to see him, too, because the room had grown very still.

Mattie didn't have to be told that a confrontation was coming. It took just one good look at the man striding up the aisle, straight for her bench. He came through the swinging doors of the spectator's rail, and Mattie tightened her grip on the gavel. Neither Jaydee nor the marshal had come back yet, and she was on her own.

"This morning's session will be delayed," she told the assembly.

She banged the gavel once. That was all the time she had before Jameson Cross took it out of her hand.

"He's *dead*," Cross said. His words were barely audible, but they held a harsh indictment of some kind.

Mattie's arm was still in the air, but Cross had the gavel.

"What in God's name are you doing?" she whispered. If he'd been anyone else, she would have called security and had him thrown out of the courthouse, even jailed for threatening a federal judge. But this man had a vendetta of some kind, and Mattie had to instantly calculate the threat he presented. If they came to verbal blows, he could do her far more damage than she him.

Mattie saw the marshal burst through the courtroom doors. He drew his gun and came up the aisle behind Cross. She didn't know what terrified her more—Cross, or the fact that he might be shot.

"No!" she shouted at the marshal. "Put the gun away!"

She lunged to shove Cross out of the way just as he turned and saw the marshal. Cross moved as if to shield Mattie, and their collision was inevitable, audible, *painful*. She hit him, and in the confusion, her bracelet caught the side of his face.

Mattie felt it slice his skin. She gasped and sat down hard. The dark red gash on his cheek made her feel sick.

"Set the gavel down," the marshal said, menacing Cross with the gun. "Move away from the bench. Now!"

Cross set the gavel down, but he didn't move.

Mattie could see that she had to take charge. The courtroom was still packed. The crowd was on their feet, frozen in place. They had the startled look of witnesses to a lynching.

The marshal ordered Cross to move away from the bench and turn around. As Cross did so, the marshal reached for his handcuffs.

"That isn't necessary." Mattie's voice wasn't strong enough to command attention. She rose to her feet, shaking as she planted her fists on the gleaming mahogany.

"Holster your weapon," she told the marshal in a stern tone. "I know this man, and he meant me no harm."

Cross's dark head came around. His gaze slammed into Mattie's with resounding force. He certainly looked as if he wanted to harm her. Bodily harm, in fact.

What was worse, Mattie thought she knew why. He must have ferreted out something that connected the lonely girls to Ms. Rowe's death. Not conjecture, evidence, and he was going to the police with it, but not before he'd given the judge a chance to confess and atone right here in her own courtroom. Generous bastard that he was.

"Your Honor?" One of the labor attorneys cautiously approached the bench. "Are you all right?" the man asked Mattie.

"I'm fine," Mattie assured him. "Help me clear the room, would you? This gentleman and I have business to discuss." She beckoned for the marshal, including him in her instructions. "Let's have everyone file out as quickly as possible. The hearing will begin as soon as the missing board member arrives."

"If I were you, I'd postpone until tomorrow." Cross made the suggestion in a low voice. It was for Mattie's ears only, and his discretion was a relief. At least he seemed willing to wait until the room cleared before resuming his verbal assault.

Mattie avoided looking at him as the crowd filed out. Unfortunately, there was no way to avoid him forever. Thank God, he couldn't see what was happening inside her. No one could see that, or she wouldn't be allowed to roam free on the streets.

As the doors closed behind the last of the crowd, she braced herself. She inspected her hands, saw a hangnail and began to perspire.

"Who is dead?" she asked him.

"William Broud."

Mattie could feel the blood draining from her face. William Broud? How could he be dead? He'd just been released from prison. In her mind she could see the frightening man who'd pulled her out of the crawl space—and may have saved her life. Perhaps she ought to have been sad, but all she could feel in that instant was fear.

"How did it happen?" she asked.

"Funny, that's what I was going to ask you, Your *Honor.*"

Mattie picked up the gavel without thinking. Her knuckles were white with tension, and he noticed it, too.

"Obviously, you know who I'm talking about," he said. "The man who took the rap for you twenty years ago? You may even have followed his writs for habeas relief over the years?"

"Be very careful what you accuse me of, Mr. Cross. False accusations are actionable. You could be looking at jail time."

"Who said the accusation was false?"

"*I* did." She stared him down, but the anger in her voice faltered as she thought about the damage he could do with his accusations, false or not. A couple of words to the media, and lives would implode.

Her gaze flicked past him to the courtroom where she had made decisions that had altered the courses of lives. Presumptuous decisions. How could they be anything else when all she had to examine was evidence? Not minds, not hearts, just evidence, most of it circumstantial. She didn't have the ability to see into souls for the truth. Only an oracle could do that. She was forced to decide the fate of her fellow human beings on nothing more than educated guesses that often felt like whims—and now it was her fate in the balance. It didn't matter which side of the bench she was on.

Would Jameson Cross be as presumptuous with her? Would he show her any mercy? Did she deserve any?

Her legs didn't want to hold her, but something else kept her standing, and it was more than the adrenaline steaming through her. Thank God, this bench of hers was such a formidable barrier. If this were one of the larger courtrooms with a raised dais, she would be towering over him.

As she had at so many other times when her world was under attack, she drew in a breath and focused her thoughts. In the back of her mind she could see the yellow orb at the heart of the bull's-eye—*the still point of the turning world*— and she felt resolve seeping into her as if it were a tangible thing. In theory, each breath she took would make her more resolute and when she merged with that yellow eye, she would be unassailable.

This man couldn't break her, she told herself. No one could.

Without a word to Cross, she left the bench. There was only one step down, but the high heels Breeze had insisted on forced her to take it carefully. On solid ground, she squared her shoulders and headed for the judge's door.

"Where are you going?" he asked.

His tone was low, almost savage. She matched him, equally savage. "To my chambers," she said. "This is a personal matter."

"Bullshit. You emptied the place. We can talk here."

She hesitated at the door just long enough to answer him. "I could call the marshal and have you thrown out of here. He saw you trying to assault me."

"I could call the police and have you arrested for murder."

Arrested? What is God's name *did* he know?

Mattie opened the door. "I'm going to my chambers. You can join me there or not."

Her robes billowed as she entered her chambers. The dark room was eerily quiet in contrast to the questions thundering in her head. She couldn't bluff, and she couldn't fake indignation. She had to know what he knew. Knowledge wasn't always power. It could be very dangerous, in her experience. But in this case, it was her only shot.

She switched on the light and went to her desk. *Take your time, Mattie. You're in no hurry.* She knew he was behind her only because she heard the door shut, but she had no intention of turning so soon. Let him witness the sobering majesty of an appellate court judge's chambers. He wasn't accosting a jurist loaned out to the district court and holed up in temporary offices. This was a *sanctum sanctorum,* hers, and she could still remember the fear and awe she felt when she'd walked through those doors for the first time. Did he understand who he was dealing with?

But he was ready for her the moment she turned around.

He drew a Ziploc bag of tattered papers from his black canvas jacket. He also had an envelope that looked like it contained school transcripts.

"Matilda Smith," he said, "Rowe Academy, 1980 to 1983." He dropped the envelope on her desk. "Dean's List, Latin Club, English and math honors, archery, and a member of the lonely girls club. Breeze Wheeler and Jane Dunbar were also members. Ivy White, the fourth member of your club, died in 1982 of a poison overdose, possibly self-induced. Your headmistress, Millicent Rowe, was smothered to death one month later, and her autopsy showed traces of the same poison, heartwine, although not enough to kill her."

Mattie allowed herself only a casual glance at the plastic bag he held. "You brought your lunch?" she said, refusing to take him seriously.

"William Broud's journal," he said, "and you're in it. The lonely girls, all four of you, identified by Broud. The day he was arrested, he claimed the headmistress was exploiting her own students. Millicent Rowe had a lucrative side job, didn't she, Mattie? She was selling the sexual favors of underage girls to a ring of powerful men. She was selling *you*—and that's why you conspired with your friends to kill her."

Mattie didn't blink. She was well past being susceptible to his threats. She was the eye, the center. Nothing could touch her here.

"Why didn't this journal come out at the trial?" She'd done her homework, too. Years ago, she'd attempted to get access to the police reports and trial transcripts. She'd been almost relieved when she couldn't. All records were sealed, which meant no one else could get access to them, either. But during her search, she'd found several early articles on the trial, before the testimony had been closed.

"He wrote the journal in prison," Cross explained, "but he didn't mail it until after he was released. The envelope was postmarked the day before he died. Apparently whoever killed him didn't know about these papers. They thought they'd silenced him."

Mattie's smile was as cold as his pale gray eyes. "Who-*ever* killed him? Now you're not sure?"

"It doesn't matter if I'm sure. It matters that Broud was. Whoever killed the headmistress killed him, too, to keep from being exposed. According to this journal, he received death threats while he was in prison, warning him not to talk."

"From who?"

"They were anonymous, of course."

"Obviously, he had some enemies."

"Obviously, three of them."

He gave the transcripts a pointed glance, which Mattie

ignored. She didn't intend to acknowledge in any way that again he had accused her of murder. To acknowledge that was to dignify and give it credence. Instead, she began to question him, regretting that she couldn't ask the one question that burned to be answered. What had he told the police, and did they know about the journal? That would have come too close to admitting her fears, too close to the trap he was laying for her.

"Why did Broud send the journal to you?" she asked, certain he was telling her only what he wanted her to know. There was a piece missing in all of this, maybe several.

"He had his reasons, I'm sure."

"Care to speculate on what they might have been?" While Mattie waited for his answer, she began to unbutton her robe. She wanted it off. The room had grown warm and the heavy black material felt like an encumbrance. She'd been foolish to think judicial trappings could give her any special authority in a situation like this.

She kept her robes in an oak armoire. As she drew out the hanger and went through the ritual of hanging this one, Cross said nothing. His silence tugged at her, and finally she broke the suspense and glanced at him. It startled her to realize that he was watching her in the same way that she had watched him when he walked into her courtroom. She'd known he was a threat. Some people gave off enough animal energy to signal their intentions. He was one of them.

His gaze remained on her as she turned around, and she felt an icy ripple of response. He wasn't looking at her eyes now. This was no clash of wills, at least not in the way it had been. When she'd entered the courtroom this morning, she'd had several penetrating glances. She didn't want to call it sexual curiosity, but something had caught those men's attention, and she doubted it was the robe.

She tweaked her scoop-neck sweater by the shoulder

seams to straighten the lines, knowing it clung to her breasts. Maybe Breeze had been right in her theory. Mattie's skirt was off just slightly. She fixed that, too, wondering how long a woman could hold a man's attention this way. Indefinitely, she imagined, which would give her some kind of subliminal bargaining power.

"You didn't answer my question."

"There's only one thing you need to know," he said. "I'm going to have the Millicent Rowe case reopened. No matter what it takes, and no matter who goes down."

"That's not a smart idea."

"Why is that?"

"You have no idea what you're dealing with."

"That sounded ominous, Ms. Smith. What *am* I dealing with? I can call you Ms. Smith, can't I? Now that you're wearing civilian clothes?"

"You're bleeding, Mr. Cross." The cut on his cheek looked like a bright red punctuation mark. Mattie pulled a tissue from a box on her desk and handed it to him, stiff-armed.

"I'll get a transfusion later," he said.

Someone rapped sharply on her door.

"Come in." Mattie seized the opportunity. She wanted Cross out of her office. There was nothing more she could accomplish with him now. She had to talk with Breeze and Jane.

Jaydee Sanchez popped his head in the door. "The hearing is ready to be reconvened," he said. "All the board members are here with their lawyers." He spotted her visitor. "Oh, sorry, I didn't know—"

"Jaydee! Come on in. Mr. Cross was just leaving." At least her clerk's timing was better than in the courtroom.

Jaydee entered and offered his hand to Cross, along with a big smile. "James Dean Sanchez," he said, "law clerk extraordinaire."

"Jameson Cross. I'm sure she needs an extraordinary law clerk."

Jaydee's handshake became more vigorous. "*The* Jameson Cross? Author of *The Sparrow's Dead?*" At Cross's nod, Jaydee let out a whoop. "I loved that book! What are you working on now?"

Mattie sighed. Her law clerk was a Jameson Cross fan? "Jaydee, Mr. Cross was on his way out, and I need to get back to the hearing."

Jaydee seemed transfixed by her visitor. He squinted at Cross. "Are you bleeding?" He grabbed the tissue from Mattie's hand and actually began to blot the laceration on the man's cheek. "Geez, you are bleeding. What happened?"

Cross seemed more amused than anything else. "I'm working on a book about a murder that took place twenty years ago," he said with a sidelong glance at Mattie. "It happened across the bay in Tiburon, and there was a major cover-up involved. I think it's going to be a blockbuster when the word gets out."

"Cool," Jaydee said. "What's it called?"

"It's not titled yet. Maybe your boss can tell you more about it. She was there when it happened."

"Yeah?" Jaydee looked over at Mattie.

She managed a thin smile. "Mr. Cross appears to be writing fiction."

She dismissed them with a curt nod and went to the armoire to get her robe. Cross was a bloody bastard. He was playing with her, but he wasn't going to get away with it. His veiled threats smacked of blackmail.

Cross dropped the crumpled tissue on Mattie's desk. "Thanks for your time," he said. "I hope I jogged your memory. I may have more questions."

"I'm sure you will." *And you may get some answers you don't expect.*

As he walked out the door, Mattie realized something. He'd said Jane Dunbar. That was her maiden name. Maybe he hadn't yet figured out that he was dealing with the First Lady of the United States.

18

Jane Mantle stepped into the crowded elevator, preoccupied with the meeting she'd just had with her husband's chief of staff. He'd asked to talk with her privately about Larry's health, and they'd decided to meet in a conference room on one of the lower levels rather than the chief of staff's office or the family quarters, where they could be interrupted.

Jane acknowledged her fellow passengers with nods and smiles as they shifted to make room for her in the elevator. She was gracious, but careful not to make eye contact. She didn't want to encourage any conversations that would rob her of the few precious moments she had to think about what she'd just done.

She'd lied. She'd said Larry's health was perfect, and the chief of staff's relief had been palpable. It had almost justified her evasion. The elections were coming up, and the White House would soon be in campaign mode. A staggering amount of time and manpower went into a presidential campaign. Just getting it organized was a massive effort, and Jane didn't want to stop the momentum before it got started.

What else could she have done? Scared everyone to death?

No one knew about Larry's symptoms except her, although possibly they suspected, which would explain the chief of staff's relief. Larry's symptoms had come and gone quickly. He'd had some tightness in his chest that was probably nothing more than indigestion or stress. A simple cold. And Jane had already made up her mind that her husband would be fine because she would see to it herself.

The elevator stopped at the next level, and Jane eased back to let people out. As more bodies pushed in, she stepped back farther—and accidentally bumped into the person behind her. A man, she realized without knowing exactly how she knew. The rustle of his crisp cotton dress shirt, perhaps. Some subliminal male scent. Or his height. He stood behind her to her left, his shoulder riding just above hers, if that was his shoulder. She didn't look.

That would have ended the suspense, she realized.

It was better not knowing, wondering.

Was that a whiff of gin from a luncheon martini?

She murmured an apology, but heard no response.

Odd that she was perspiring. She checked the hanky in her sleeve, hoping she wouldn't be forced to mop her brow in front of everyone. First Ladies didn't often use the staff elevators, and when they did, they usually had an entourage of some kind. Jane had accepted the Secret Service as part of her life, but she refused to be impeded by gofers and assistants, if she could handle things herself. She preferred a PalmPilot to having Mia follow her around with a steno pad.

Warm air touched the back of her neck.

Something brushed the curve of her buttock.

The man's hand? His thigh?

Was it intentional?

Jane's stomach tilted as if the elevator had lurched. Her breath locked in her chest, but nothing could stop the cascading sensations once they started. She was in free-fall, head over heels, tumbling down a stairway. She still didn't look at him. It would all be over if she looked at him. The anticipation that threatened to shake her inside out would be gone.

She yanked the hanky from her sleeve and blotted the wetness from her upper lip, but it was useless against the heat swamping her face. Within seconds, her mind had caught up with her body, and she was immersed in a frenzy of pornographic imagery, all of it about the anonymous man behind her.

It would happen at the next stop, the ground floor. Everyone would exit but the two of them, and when the doors were closed, he would unzip his perfectly pressed cotton twill slacks and present her with an enormous erection. Jane would melt to the floor, her legs unable to hold her. Tiny bubbles of joy would burst in her throat, and saliva would flood her mouth like a river. She would grip his buttocks and guide him in. Swallow him whole.

Jane knew what would happen because she'd done it. Not with this man on this elevator, but with many men, in elevators and any number of other places where illicit connections with strangers could be made. Her conquests rarely took place in private, but exposure wasn't Jane's thrill. It was closing the deal. And she almost always did. All she cared about was that they were professional men, well-groomed and well-spoken.

Just like Ms. Rowe's men had been.

And that they wanted *her,* Jane Dunbar.

The fear of rejection was terrible. But the thrill when they chose her was orgasmic. She needed no foreplay. She was ready for anything, which no doubt made it all the more gratifying for her conquest. If they weren't interrupted, it could go further than a blowjob. It could go anywhere.

I know exactly what you need, she told them. *Some women were born knowing.*

Many of them begged to see her again, and their pleading gave her the most exquisite pleasure imaginable. She always let them think she might, but never did. She was ruthless with herself about repeats. She used phony names and wore disguises to make sure no one discovered who she was. Of course, that was years ago…before she met Larry…when she was no one anyway.

Why was it happening again? Now?

The door opened and the elevator began to empty. Frozen, Jane watched the people disappear. The anticipation pouring through her was painful. Sweat soaked her throat and underarms. *Ruining her Chanel suit.* The thought made her want to laugh it was so absurd, and yet, not absurd at all. She had earned every button and stitch on this masterpiece of a garment. She prized it the way her father had prized his battered Craftsman tools.

Her conquest didn't move, and Jane could already hear the zing of his zipper, taste the gushing heat of his come as it set fire to her throat. When he'd spent himself in her mouth, he would rip away the crotch of her panty hose, penetrate while he was still hard, ejaculate again.

Men could have multiple orgasms with her. She could rock their world, turn them into gods, and then slaves, if she chose. They could never reject her. Never.

The elevator doors began to close, propelling her into action. She surged through the opening and into the hallway, a cry of relief locked inside her. *Dear God, that was close. Too close!* For a second she didn't know which way to go. She needed a restroom, a place to hide, but the restrooms would be public on this floor.

Did he follow her out? Was he behind her?

She didn't turn or look at him. She didn't even know if it was a man.

Hysteria gurgled up like stomach acid. She fought back the urge to laugh, knowing she couldn't let out so much as a whimper. She was already acting oddly, and people had noticed. She couldn't let anyone get a glimpse of the chaos inside her.

Hold it together, Jane. Hold it together. Jane!

Mia would be waiting for her in her office, but Jane couldn't go there in this condition. She started down the hall in search of a stairway, a businesslike smile fixed on her face. She was praying her husband's cabinet meeting was still in session. She didn't want to run into Larry in their private quarters. There was only one thing that could bring her down off this ledge, and she had to be alone for that.

Jane couldn't control the knife enough to cut the pill, not even in half, much less the perfect eighths she was used to taking. She'd tried herbal remedies, but they hadn't been as effective as these tranquilizers her psychiatrist prescribed. She'd been taking them for years, but not nearly the recommended dosage. She would have been hopelessly addicted by now, and that was unthinkable.

One-eighth of a pill, four to six times a day, depending on her schedule. That was how Jane Mantle dealt with her demons, and she was quite proud of herself for controlling things so well. She cut the pills into slivers and spaced them four hours apart. On days when she woke up jittery, she took one before she did anything else, washing it down with mouth rinse in the privacy of her bathroom.

But just one. She'd never allowed herself more, even on those mornings when her heart was pounding outside her body, or those nights when she fell into bed, vibrating like a guitar string. And she gave herself gold stars when she took less. This morning she had taken nothing.

Now she doubted the entire bottle would be enough.

She abandoned the knife on the counter, afraid she would cut off a finger and have that to explain, too. The round pink tablet looked huge, but she picked it up and swallowed it whole, ready to take another one if she had to. A swig of cold tea, left over from that morning's scheduling session with

Mia, helped wash it down, but the loss of control she felt was profound. First, the man and the elevator, now she was guzzling pills.

Next, she went to the writing desk in her bedroom and turned on the speakerphone. She tapped out the sequence of digits quickly, surprised she still knew her psychiatrist's phone number by heart. She hadn't seen him in years, not since Larry was elected. There'd been no need, thank God.

"Jane Dunbar," she said when the receptionist answered. "I need to see the doctor immediately. It's an emergency."

That would get her through, even if her psychiatrist was in session. Her records were in her maiden name, but he knew who Jane Dunbar was, and he would call himself to schedule her. They could meet at the White House, if she requested it, but that wouldn't be wise, given the problem. Larry knew about her therapy, but she'd left out the sordid details. Actually, the entire country knew about her therapy. It had come out during his campaign, and she'd had to go public immediately and disclose her condition.

Larry's campaign manager had told her it might work in Larry's favor if she was seen as more human and vulnerable, someone the women of the country could relate to. First, at a press conference, and then on a daytime talk show, Jane had revealed that she'd been treated for depression, which was true. She didn't mention the source of the depression, which would have blown the lid off the campaign—and her marriage.

A male voice came on the line. "Jane, are you all right?"

"No," Jane said, "I'm not. Do you have time for me?"

"Where are you now?"

"Pennsylvania Avenue. My bedroom."

"I'll clear my schedule and be free by the time you get here."

"Thank you," she said, hating the way her voice broke.

* * *

"How do you feel?"

"Ridiculous. Ashamed. Like I should be neutered." Jane took the hanky from her sleeve and blew her nose, trying to be delicate about it. By the time she was done, the fine Irish linen was stained with red.

A nosebleed. Sweet Christ. Well, everything else was coming back to haunt her. Why not nosebleeds?

"I was in a White House elevator," she said. "Can you imagine me blowing some strange man in a White House elevator?"

"I'm trying not to," the doctor admitted.

She looked up at him, stricken. "Why did it happen after all this time? And why is it still so exciting?" She could have said painful or degrading or risky. Any one of those words, but she'd said exciting.

He sat in a large leather easy chair, across the room from her, his legs crossed, his steel-gray hair catching light from the window, and somehow he managed to look as if he didn't find the very sight of her loathsome. That was why she'd been able to go back to him after their first session some fifteen years ago. She'd told him everything, and he hadn't registered shock or scorn or any judgment at all. If anything, he'd seemed sad for her. Immeasurably sad.

"It's exciting because your nervous system only remembers the pleasure," he explained, "and it wants more. That's how addictions work. They reduce emotional pain, relieve stress, alleviate boredom. The effect is only temporary, but it's very powerful. It wouldn't be addictive if it wasn't."

Jane tied knots into her hanky—and wondered how she would ever get them out. "Will it happen again? Am I relapsing?"

He considered her question. "No, I don't think so. You're under a lot of pressure. That's when addictive behavior tends to flare up, no matter how long ago it was."

He didn't have a clue about her pressure. She'd told him all about the sex, but she hadn't told him everything about the finishing school—and now there was Jameson Cross. "I love my husband, and this would kill him. You know what I'm capable of—ghastly things—and I don't trust myself."

She'd gone with strangers in their cars, just like a hooker. She'd picked up men in sports bars and pool halls, country clubs, grocery stores, even churches. Whenever those withering feelings of rejection began to eat away at her, whenever they whispered that she wasn't good enough, she found a man who thought she was very good.

At first she'd told herself it was the power, and Lord, that was a heady wicked rush of ecstasy, almost good enough to take any risk for. But eventually, even the power had left her empty and wanting. It was love she was after, acceptance, adoration. All the things she didn't get as a kid, and never believed she was worthy of…until Larry.

"I can't fall off the wagon now," she said. "I can't go through that again. Or put him through it."

She folded her hands in her lap and bowed her head, as if waiting for the judge to sentence her. Instead, his voice was calm and sympathetic.

"Jane," he said, "fifteen years ago, you desperately needed to prove something to yourself. Today, you're happily married to the leader of the most powerful country in the world, and he couldn't run this place without you. You're the First Lady, Jane."

Lady Jane, she thought, shaking her head.

It took her several moments to absorb the Olympic event—the tragedy and the triumph—that was her life. Finally, she glanced at him, managing a hint of irony. "What's left to prove?"

He smiled. "From where I sit, nothing, but only you can answer that question."

* * *

She fell back against the town car's leather seat and sighed, releasing some of the crushing pressure her psychiatrist had talked about. The session had helped. She was steadier now—and less terrified that she might seduce a poor innocent White House intern—but she didn't know how long it would last. She could always get more tranquilizers, but that wasn't the answer. The way things were going, she would be a junkie if she had to rely on medication to get through this.

She told herself to rest. Her cell was turned off, and she was being driven by a Secret Service agent. How many chances did she get to be out of the fishbowl and totally alone, without anyone vying for her attention? But rest was not what her thoughts had in mind. They wanted to agitate and churn, and she didn't have the energy to obsess over her problems. There were too many.

She switched on the radio, hoping to distract herself, but all she got were talk shows. The national news programs were full of grim economic indicators, which didn't bode well for Larry's reelection, so she switched to a San Francisco station, which was being picked up on a special satellite feed.

Jane sat up, listening as the commentator reported the death of an ex-convict. Apparently, she'd come in at the end of the station's local news segment.

"The former death row inmate was found dead in his San Rafael hotel," the man said, "by his brother, James Broud. The cause of death is unknown, but the police have already launched a full investigation."

Jane turned the volume higher. Were they talking about William Broud? He was dead? At the moment, Jane could not even fathom what that meant. She was being zapped by too many other distress signals, but she doubted there was any way it could be good news.

She searched through her purse, found her cell, and hit a button to bring up her telephone book. She was looking for Mattie's number. She would have to be careful what she said over a cell phone, but she needed to talk to her friend. She had to let someone else know what had just happened.

19

Jameson touched his face and then took a look at his fingers. There was heat and tenderness where Mattie Smith had cut him, but no blood. Lucky break. He could skip the transfusion and head straight to a psychiatric ward to get a jump on the posttraumatic stress disorder therapy.

Overhead, black clouds glowed silver at the edges as they engulfed the midafternoon sun. The ominous weather did nothing to improve Jameson's state of mind as he left the Golden Gate Bridge and headed for Highway 131, the cutoff that would take him back to Tiburon, but he wasn't going to his place. He was on his way to Rowe Academy on the other side of the peninsula.

Who the hell *was* Mattie Smith? A homicidal maniac, capable of not one heinous crime, but two? The controversial circuit court judge who'd divided the ninth district with her decisions? Or the woman he'd just encountered in her chambers, the weirdly sexy, smoky-eyed female?

Jameson had a bad feeling she might be all of the above.

And none of those images meshed with the scruffy little monster who hid behind trees and spat at him when he got near her. Funny that it was Ivy who'd preoccupied him over the years with her confusing beauty and her mysterious death. He'd been concentrating on the wrong woman.

When Jameson reached the peninsula, he took the scenic

route that followed the bluffs above the bay. Rowe Academy sat at the north end of the peninsula on several acres overlooking the water. The city of Tiburon, a placid coastal town that seemed designed for the front of a postcard, was just a few more miles down the road that curved around the point.

As Jameson drove through the iron gates that opened onto Rowe's green, hilly campus, he ignored the signs that directed him to administration, the library and the chapel. Fortunately, he knew exactly where he was going because his mind was still locked on that morning's incident.

The last thing he'd expected to see was a babe when he walked into Matilda Smith's courtroom. He'd envisioned a hard-hearted killer, which didn't jibe with Mata Hari eyes and lips that glistened like cabernet grapes. What was that all about?

Protective facades had always fascinated him, particularly because they were nearly universal. Maybe it was part of being human to live in fear of exposure of the hidden self with all its base and shameful emotions and desires. Only the very young, who didn't know they were naked, and the dying, who had nothing more to lose, would dare risk the world's scorn. But Mattie Smith didn't strike him as a woman who hid behind her sex appeal. Quite the opposite. She seemed more determined to scare men off than to suck them in.

He left his Escalade next to the loading zone where he'd parked the delivery truck twenty years ago. Rowe Academy itself had a protective facade, he realized. The gothic halls and wooded grounds had always reminded him of a magnificent old castle. Everywhere you looked there were rolling greenbelts, leafy trees and winding paths. It was the last place you'd expect to find dead bodies, corruption and sex rings.

The path he took led him through a stand of poplars beyond which he could see the school itself. The ivy-covered stone-and-brick buildings formed a U-shape around a large courtyard, where every summer climbing roses ran riotously up the walls and burst into glorious reds, pinks and yellows. In the center of the courtyard, a cloud of fountain spray encircled a serene Greek goddess, holding a cluster of grapes. Large stone benches sat around the outside, each framed by trellis-work, smothered in vines.

It was like a secret garden, though not nearly so innocent. Some of the notes in Billy's journal had touched on various aspects of what he claimed was the sex ring, and he'd described certain illicit arrangements had taken place right here in this courtyard. Apparently a male client could look down at the courtyard from the windows of the headmistress's apartment, select the girl of his choice, and the headmistress would arrange it. Unfortunately, Billy hadn't mentioned the clients' names. Either he didn't know who they were, or he'd decided not to identify them, possibly because of the threats he'd received. His notes had suggested the students involved were limited to the four scholarship girls, which made sense. They were boarders, separated from their families and support systems, and for the most part, vulnerable.

Jameson scanned the buildings around him, aware that it was summer break and the campus was largely deserted. He saw a pair of joggers who looked more like faculty than students. Only the library buzzed with activity. Even in secondary school, research went on year-round.

Jameson hoped to stir some memory traces as he continued walking. He'd been on this campus recently to interview faculty and staff, and he'd asked those he talked with to go back twenty years. Today *he* wanted to go back, and not just because of his brother. That travesty cried out for justice, but it was the conspiracy as much as the crime that intrigued Jameson. Billy had implied it was a sex ring made up of

VIPs, which sounded like a cabal of men who believed their power and money gave them access to anything they desired, including minor females. And if Jameson's suspicions were correct, it was this web of corruption that led to the head-mistress's death. Unfortunately, the only ones who had an obvious motive were the victims themselves. But if they'd knowingly let his brother go to jail, they weren't just victims, they were part of the conspiracy.

When William Broud Sr. died, Jameson went to San Quentin to give his brother the news. He hadn't seen Billy in a dozen years, and he wasn't surprised when his brother refused to talk to him, except to tell him to stay out of it. Jameson had little choice but to agree, and he'd honored Billy's wishes right up until his brother was exonerated. Then guilt and remorse had overwhelmed him.

Billy hadn't done it? Everyone believed he had, includ-ing Jameson. The entire community had been eager to cru-cify him, and they'd all been part of the conspiracy, including Jameson.

Jameson passed the library and the infirmary, stopping to look at the tower that was Ms. Rowe's apartment. It was time to rip away the protective facade and expose the truth. He'd already looked at his own culpability. He wanted the bastards who knew they were sending an innocent man to his death. He wanted *that* conspiracy.

He'd grown up in the area, and his mind kept reworking the same questions: Who the hell had these men in the sex ring been? Anyone he'd known? And why had his brother be-lieved that it was three fourteen-year-old girls who'd killed the headmistress?

That was what haunted him as he watched a cluster of stu-dents exit the library and stop to gossip. Twenty years ago, he'd witnessed the same scene repeatedly. It was normal be-havior for teenage girls—but not for *those* girls. They didn't sit under the trees and picnic like the other students did. He'd never seen them indulge in grooming rituals or gossip and talk about boys. They spoke in their own code, watched each other's backs and engaged in what appeared to be female tests of courage.

He knew because he'd been wildly infatuated with one of them, and he'd paid close attention. He'd also used every excuse he could think of to come to the campus, including "forgetting" to deliver items so he could make multiple trips. Wonder it didn't lose him his job.

They'd hung together like a pack of thieves, and he'd been forced to work up the courage to approach all four at once. He'd tried talking to them at various times, but it hadn't been easy to get more than a blushing hi out of Ivy, which was part of why he'd been smitten. Breeze had been fun and flirty, but a little too bold for a shy eighteen-year-old delivery boy. Jane was standoffish, but he sensed that she was the leader and protective of her little brood. Mattie was the scrapper, ready to take on any threat.

At one point he'd seen the four of them huddled in an alcove behind Graedon Hall. They clearly believed they were hidden from view and were passing around a vial of a clear liquid, possibly something they'd stolen from the infirmary, or so he'd thought then. They'd rubbed a few drops onto the skin of their hands and face, and then they'd each taken a sip from the vial. Breeze Wheeler had clutched her throat, as if she were choking. Only Ivy hadn't realized it was a joke, and the others had laughed at her chalk-white horror. That was when Mattie had spotted him, and they'd all scurried off into the pine forest, which had convinced him they were up to no good.

He'd decided it was drugs or alcohol, probably some hazing ritual, and let it go at that. Now, he wondered. When the goal was to get high, you didn't rub the intoxicant on your hands and face, but if it was an herbal cosmetic, like heart-wine…

Jameson crossed the courtyard and took one of the enclosed stone passageways that formed a mazelike network of tunnels through the complex. He was curious if the old chapel was still in use. He wished now that he'd paid closer attention to the girls. They'd kept to themselves, and he'd never been in a position to overhear any of their conversations, but they'd always looked as if they were up to something.

What he did remember—sharply—was the morning he saw his brother arguing with Ms. Rowe. Jameson had been asked to make an unscheduled stop, and as he'd carried a box of supplies to the dining hall, he'd heard sounds coming from the chapel. A man and woman were arguing, and the angry tones drew Jameson to the open door.

Apparently they'd gone inside for privacy, but hadn't realized how their whispers reverberated in the sanctuary. Jameson had recognized Billy's nasal tones and bad grammar. The woman's voice wasn't familiar to him until he peeked inside the door and saw her.

No one wore her hair tightly coiled at the nape of her neck except the headmistress of Rowe Academy. Millicent Rowe was accusing Billy of blackmail and threatened to retaliate. Jameson heard her say that she didn't care where he got the drugs, to leave her out of it. She reminded him that he was far from clean. He had a record, had served time, and she warned him not to do anything stupid, or he'd regret it.

Jameson wasn't surprised drugs were involved. Billy had been banished from the family home for his drug use, among other things, and he had done time for selling controlled substances. Jameson *was* surprised about Millicent Rowe. She didn't look like a woman who counted gardeners or drug pushers among her friends, and Billy was both. Her father was a state senator, and her family was comfortable, if not wealthy, but Jameson's research indicated that most of the money was tied up in the educational foundation her grandmother had started. Ms. Rowe couldn't touch it, and yet Jameson had seen her in town several times, once buying pricey emerald studs for her ears. He had some idea what a headmistress earned, and her monthly salary wouldn't have covered the gold settings.

Seeing his brother with her was another reason Jameson had been reluctant to testify for the defense at the trial. What he'd heard could have been construed as a motive for murder, and if that had come out, it would have done Billy more harm than good. But Jameson needn't have worried about the trial. He hadn't been called by either side. The prosecution not only had fingerprints and blood evidence, they had a couple of students who'd claimed to see Billy enter the apartment that morning. An open-and-shut case. Everybody thought so, including Jameson, at the time.

He headed back to his car, much on his mind. Moments later, as he let himself into the SUV, he thought about the next logical step his investigation should take. He was waiting on the medical examiner's report for the cause of Billy's death, but meanwhile, he intended to pay Tansy Black an unscheduled visit. She'd refused to see him when he called on the phone, but he wasn't going to give her a second chance. He also hadn't given up on getting the original case files unsealed. No one seemed to want to tell him who'd sealed them and why, and that much at least should have been public information.

Videotapes. One missing.

That was Jameson's next logical step, but even as he worked on formulating a plan, his thoughts kept spinning back to another dichotomy, one of such monumental *in*significance he couldn't believe he was going there again, trapped like a mouse in a maze, repeating the same wrong turns and winding up exactly where he started.

His mind was struggling with two diametrically opposed images of Mattie Smith—one of a child raised by wolves, who snarled and spat at him when he came near her, and the other of a grown woman, the icily beautiful creature whose chambers he'd just left.

He touched the cut on his cheek.

That was easy. He liked the scruffy little monster best.

She hadn't done a very good job of backing off Jameson Cross. Mattie pulled a three-foot strip of toilet paper off the roll, wadded it and went to the sink to dampen it. She refused to ruin a washcloth, and she didn't know how else to remove the goo Breeze had applied.

The hearing wasn't Mattie's best work, either. She hadn't maintained her usual tight control of the proceedings, and everyone had seemed to sense that she was distracted, much like a child's ability to sense when his mother is at a disadvantage. Afterward, Mattie had come straight here, to the bathroom in her chambers. Even if the makeup wasn't to blame, it had to go. She didn't like the way people looked at her. Worse, they couldn't seem to hear what she was saying. "Excuse me, Your Honor?" She'd been forced to repeat herself all afternoon, and it had thrown her off her game.

"I kind of liked the Bette Davis eyes."

Jaydee stood in the bathroom doorway, watching her dab at the charcoal eyeliner. The sleeve of her robe was dripping. Apparently she'd drowned it when she wet the toilet paper.

She wrung out the sleeve in the sink. "I like them, too, on Bette Davis."

He slipped his hands into the pockets of his jeans, but his fingers wouldn't go beyond the second knuckle before the snug denim stopped them. Jaydee liked to think the ladies appreciated his masculine assets.

"Waterproof eyeliner must have the half-life of plutonium," Mattie grumbled. "Look at this stuff. It won't die."

She'd scrubbed her eyes until they were bloodshot, but all she'd succeeded in doing was creating two charming black halos. Her next job would be clown work. Thank you, Breeze.

"Would I be prying if I asked what happened in the courtroom this morning?" Jaydee said. "Rumor has it that you duked it out with Jameson Cross. He was bleeding from the head when I came in here."

"Where did you go, Jaydee? The marshal went after you, and I was all alone in there."

"Sorry, nature called, and I barely made it to the men's room in time to answer. So, what happened?" He tried again. "Did he make a pass at you, not realizing you were a lesbian?"

"From what I saw, the only one making passes was you. You were all over the talented Mr. Cross."

Jaydee cleared his throat. "Mattie, that's cruel."

Mattie went after the eyeliner with a washrag and some liquid soap, and this time she got results. She no longer looked like a raccoon. She looked like she'd been on a five-day toot.

"What's the status on Langston?" she asked, unbuttoning her robe as she brushed past Jaydee and returned to her chambers. The robe landed in the nearest chair, wet sleeve and all. She was in work mode now, anxious to get as much done as efficiently as she could.

"You assigned the case to the right lawyers. They've already met, mapped out a game plan and the motion to appeal will be filed next week."

"Excellent," she said, greatly relieved. "I'm counting on you to be my eyes and ears on this, Jaydee."

She went to her desk with the idea of checking out her calendar for the next couple of weeks. Her assistant left copies of the court docket, along with the cases Mattie had been assigned to hear in Mattie's in-basket every Friday. But, of course, they weren't there now because Mattie had been over at the district court for the past several weeks.

"I need to know what my schedule looks like," she said. "Can you get me a copy of the court calendar?"

"Say no more. I already checked. You've been assigned two sex discrimination cases, thank God. I live for sex discrimination cases, and the first one is a circus sideshow. I should have it written up and ready for you to review by tomorrow. There's also a First Amendment case, which is completely frivolous, but no one ever listens to me."

Mattie went to the window, knowing what she had to do, but still torn. "Jaydee, I have to clear my calendar. Another judge will have to be assigned."

"To which cases?"

"All of them."

"What?"

She nodded. "I need some time off."

"Mattie, you don't take time off. You haven't missed a day in court since I've known you. What's going on?"

The phone rang, and Mattie waved him out the door, promising she would explain later. "Yes, Michelle?"

Her assistant's brisk tone broke through the static on the line. "Your Honor, it's a Jane Dunbar to speak with you. She wouldn't tell me what it was about."

"That's fine, Michelle, put her through." Jane was using her maiden name. It would have been like shining a spotlight on the situation to do otherwise.

Mattie heard several clicks on the line but no one spoke. The empty air was ominous. "Jane?"

"Mattie, he's dead. William Broud has been murdered."

That last word sent a painful chill through Mattie. Nothing Jameson Cross had said could have affected her as much as this just had. Hearing it from Jane made it real, made it true.

"Where are you calling from?" Mattie asked.

"My cell. I'm on my way back to the White House. I had a...doctor's appointment."

"How did you find out about Broud?"

"It was on the news." Jane's voice dropped to a whisper.

"In Washington, D.C.? It made the national news?"

"No, local. There's a television in the town car, and it picks up Bay-area channels. My office has a special satellite feed, as well. No one thinks anything of it. I'm a born and bred Californian."

As Jane explained, Mattie realized something. "Did they say that he was murdered, Jane? Did they specifically say that?"

"Well, yes, of course. Are you saying he wasn't?"

"I'm asking you what *they* said." Jameson hadn't told her how Broud died, and she hadn't asked. Maybe he was bluffing, trying to frighten her into a confession.

Jane was hesitant. "Well, now I'm not sure. They said he'd been found dead in a San Rafael hotel, and I just assumed."

"Let's not assume, okay, especially not the worst. Let me find out what's going on, and I'll get back to you."

"Mattie, what happened with Jameson Cross? Did you get anywhere with him? God, when he hears about this."

He's heard, Jane.

"What about Breeze?" Jane asked. "I tried to call her, but she's not answering. I tried your place, too. She's not there."

Mattie had to think. "She said something about renting a car and driving into San Francisco, probably to shop. I'll track her down. Meanwhile, don't panic. No one can prove we have any connection to this thing." *A lie, Mattie, maybe even a black lie.* "I have to get my calendar cleared, and then I'll go work on this."

"Mattie, wait—"

"Jane, it will be fine. I'll get back to you as soon as I can."

Jane's sharp protest stayed with Mattie even after she'd hung up the phone, but Mattie couldn't deal with questions right now. She didn't have any answers. What she had was a phone call to make, and a prayer to say, a solemn plea to the heavens for deliverance. And if none of that worked, there was always the blindfold.

20

"So, tell me, Swami. Is there a Four Seasons hotel in my future?"

Breeze was referring to the open palm she'd just extended to Mattie, insisting that she read it.

"Could be," Mattie said, not bothering to give Breeze's life line so much as a glance. "Or it could be a San Quentin cell block." Honestly, the woman was starting to get on her nerves. Breeze had come in the door an hour ago, fresh from her spree and so thrilled with the city's shopping opportunities that Mattie had been reluctant to burst her bubble with the news about Broud's death.

Mattie needn't have worried. Breeze hadn't raised an eyebrow, nor had she inquired about the cause of death. Not that Mattie could have told her, but she had noticed the lapse. Breeze had written it off as drugs and immediately suggested they have a slumber party to lift their spirits.

That's when Mattie knew she was on her own. Jane was too nervous to take into her confidence and Breeze couldn't care less. Breeze had always had an uncanny ability to blow things off, but Mattie had begun to wonder if it was more than just denial at work. Fear, perhaps. Then again, it was almost as if she was holding something back. She clearly didn't want to discuss Broud's death.

Mattie pushed a plate of cookies toward Breeze. "Does

the Four Seasons get any better than this? Organic ginger-snaps and infused herbal tea?"

"Lord, no. Poor jerks over there have to make do with chocolate truffles and Cristal champagne." Breeze turned her hand over and glanced at her nails.

It was still early in the evening, but Breeze had suggested they get comfortable, and Mattie had humored her house-guest, even though she strongly believed they should be compiling a list of possible suspects for Ms. Rowe's murder. At least that would be a start, and the lonely girls were in a unique position to speculate about suspects, although none of them had ever actually seen any of Ms. Rowe's men. They'd either been blindfolded or the room had been dark-ened to protect the man's anonymity.

Mattie plucked at her football jersey. "You can't accuse *me* of not getting comfortable."

Breeze's version of comfort was a silk gown the color of eggplants. They'd retired with a tray of goodies to the antique sleigh bed in Mattie's guest room, but Breeze had no inter-est in cookies at the moment. She was peering at what might have been a chip in her glittery fingernail polish.

Mattie would have needed a magnifying glass to see it, but when it came to grooming, Breeze could have spotted an atom spinning a micromillimeter out of its orbit. She wasn't high maintenance. She was off the scale.

While Breeze luxuriated in the plumped pillows, Mattie sprawled on her stomach, preparing to read Breeze's palm and get it over with.

"Don't misunderstand me," Breeze said, helping herself to a gingersnap. "Your cottage is darling. I love the shutters and the grass cloth and the serenity. It's so *not* the blood-and-guts Mattie I knew. But…if we *were* at the Four Seasons, we could have had a masseuse sent up to the room to massage away every little tweak and twinge. Or a masseur, if we preferred. Their foot reflexology treatments are bliss. And their mattresses, Mattie—" She sighed. "My back, it's touchy."

"Mmm." Mattie was absorbed in Breeze's palm. It had a lovely sensual shape with a shallow valley between two plump mounds, and the lines were feathery and exotic. "Your love line has enough branches to be a tree, woman, and that Mound of Venus, wow."

"Well, duh," Breeze said. "What does it say about business and health? How's the fate line?"

"One thing at a time. I'm trying to remember how this works. I think a missing fate line can mean problems."

"My fate line is *missing?*"

A cell phone rang somewhere in the house, and Mattie recognized it as hers. She kept it on the nightstand, but her bedroom was down the hall, and this sounded like it was coming from the living room. Maybe she'd left her shoulder bag in there.

"Be right back," she told Breeze, who was scrutinizing her palm.

"Which one is the fate line, Mattie?" Breeze called after her as she dashed out the door. "Mattie?"

The cell phone was in Mattie's bag, as she'd thought. She'd left it on the floor near the fountain. Her bad knee popped as she knelt and fished out the phone. The stab of pain made her wince. The knee was getting worse, and she needed to avoid stressing it. There was no time to see a doctor.

The number that flashed into the cell phone's display was the detective she'd hired. "Vince?" she said, "It's Mattie."

Jane hadn't wanted a private detective involved, but Mattie had taken the initiative and called one anyway. She'd used Vince Denny many times while she was in private practice, and she trusted him completely.

"I have some information on the subject we discussed," Vince said.

A sharp breath stung Mattie's nostrils. "Go ahead."

"Jameson Cross is a pseudonym. His real name is Jimmy Broud. In fact, you may remember the guy. He drove a supply truck, and Rowe Academy was on his route. It was back when you were going to school there."

Mattie sank to her haunches. *Jimmy Broud.* "Does he have a brother?"

"I guess you do remember him. His brother is William Broud, the death row inmate who was found dead in his hotel room."

"Oh, my God," she whispered. Now she knew why Jameson Cross had looked familiar. He was the boy who'd delivered supplies to the school, the shy charmer from town. Mattie had always had a secret crush on him, but he didn't know she existed. He was smitten with Ivy, the beauty. It seemed that every male who got within range of Ivy was smitten, but she was a melancholy type, who showed no interest in boys at all. Mattie had eventually decided that Ivy's heart was already broken. She didn't need some silly schoolboy to do it.

She also understood Cross's rage. He'd found his brother dead and assumed that she and her friends had murdered him to cover up their supposed crime of twenty-three years ago. Now Cross was out to avenge his brother—and he'd been dangerous enough when all he wanted was to dig up the past so he could write a book. Mattie could only hope that Breeze was right, that Broud had overdosed on drugs.

"Mattie? There's more."

Vince reclaimed her attention. "What is it?" She wasn't sure she could handle anything else tonight.

"Cross has been asking questions. He's talking to people at Rowe and around the little town there, Tiburon. It's about a murder that took place over twenty years ago, and he's after the names of some students who went to school there."

"Thanks, Vince." She wanted to end the call, but Vince wasn't done.

"I'd suggest you contact a young woman named Tansy Black," he said. "She's the attorney who got William Broud out of San Quentin. She's a constitutional scholar from Stanford Law, ferociously smart and a compulsive perfectionist, according to my sources."

"Stanford Law?" It was Mattie's school, but she'd probably graduated well before this woman's time.

"Apparently, she's borderline crazy, pushes the envelope every chance she gets. She once wore a sexy getup to cross-examine the defendant in a sexual harassment case, and she got the poor bastard to say exactly what he was accused of having said to the plaintiff. Supposedly, she's been sanctioned by the Bar Association, and she's only twenty-three."

"I like her already," Mattie said. "How do I get ahold of her?"

"She's out of the country, a research trip, according to her voice mail message. Want her cell number?"

Mattie scrambled to find a pen.

Moments later she was listening to the voice mail message Vince had described. He'd said Black was out of the country, so her cell must have international coverage, as did Mattie's. As she left her name and number, she debated saying the call was urgent. But why tip her hand at this stage? This could be exactly the watershed she needed. A legal whiz named Tansy Black might be sitting on a pot of gold—and all Mattie had to do was get her to share the wealth. But she couldn't let Black know what she was up to.

Jameson came out of his bed like a shot. "Jesus," he breathed. "What was that?" He searched for briefs, jeans, anything he could throw on. His bedroom was at the far end of the house, enclosed only by a hanging parchment screen, and the explosion had come from the other end. Had some-one blown the door off its hinges?

His clock radio said 1:00 a.m. He couldn't have been asleep long, but his adrenaline was gushing. It had hot-wired his nervous system.

"The fucking mail slot again?" He yanked on jeans that were cold from the slate floor. "I have to board that damn thing up."

When he got to the front door, he found a videotape lying on the floor. Someone had forced the thing through the slot and mangled it. The label on the side said: Proper Conduct for Modern Young Women: The Appreciation of Fine Food, Table Manners, Prudent Dietary Choices and Weight Control.

A folded note lay next to it.

Jameson crouched and picked it up. Handwritten in large block letters were the words: Open your door. There are more.

Jameson checked the peephole, but saw no one outside. He opened the door and found three sealed cardboard boxes sitting on his stoop, big enough to contain several dozen cassettes, but he couldn't take the chance of assuming. He had no formal law enforcement training, but he'd done re-search in the field for years. Plus, 9/11 had changed every-one's perception of unmarked cardboard.

He gave the first box a nudge with his foot. It was heavy, but could be lifted. He turned it gingerly, using his hands and listening to the contents shift. He didn't detect any marks, stains or odors that might signal explosives, so he dug a pocket knife from his jeans and split the seam.

Tapes, at least two dozen of them. The second box was full of tapes, too.

He had a hunch, and if he was correct, these were Milli-cent Rowe's instructional tapes, the ones that were part of the sealed evidence. He'd asked Frank about access to the tapes and been laughed at. Apparently the last laugh would be Jameson's. Frank might not want him to watch the tapes, but someone sure did.

"Are you listening carefully, ladies? I have an important question. What would you say is the most obvious indicator of social class? Anyone? Don't be afraid."

Millicent Rowe strolled around the perimeter of the classroom as she spoke, one hand slipped into the pocket of her crested navy blazer. A wooden pointer tucked under her arm gleamed of old-fashioned lemon oil, and her gray flannel trousers and Italian leather loafers spoke of old money and quiet good taste.

Jameson registered mild surprise as the tape rolled. Millicent Rowe was a knockout. Her rich green irises were almost the exact color of the emerald chips she wore in her lobes, and her features were finely cut, although maybe a little too patrician for him. He'd read her age as around thirty when she died, but he hadn't expected her to be a babe.

"Profession, Ms. Rowe?" one of the students asked.

"Family background?" another offered.

The headmistress's voice sharpened. "You aren't listening, ladies. I want the most obvious indicator, the first thing you notice, before introductions are made."

"Um…their outfit?"

She turned on the student who'd just spoken. "That isn't how we refer to our apparel, Deirdre. We wear clothing, not outfits. Rowe Academy ladies are not, and never will be, slaves to fashion. That would be vulgar."

She seemed well aware of the tension she generated by circling around and behind her young charges, and she used the maneuver shamelessly, employing her pointer to give the walls and empty desks an occasional tap. Slumped students got a pop on their rounded spines, which brought them instantly to attention.

Fear was thick in the small classroom, obvious even on the very old videotape. Jameson hit the volume button on the remote. He didn't want to miss a word of this.

"Size," Ms. Rowe said. "The first thing we notice is the person's size, and we slot them instantly, based on that alone. The upper classes tend to be tall and thin, thin, thin. Historically they did no manual labor and didn't need the physical bulk of the lower classes, so in general, the heavier the frame the lower the class."

Some of her students frowned their disapproval. Others, most of whom met the slenderness standard, seemed secretly pleased.

"I didn't say it was fair," Ms. Rowe added, "but whether we like it or not, our perception of things becomes our reality, and that has always been society's perception. Whoever said you can't be too rich or too thin was echoing that theme."

"The House of Windsor is short and stout, mostly."

The girl sitting next to Matilda Smith had spoken up. The video was fuzzy, but Jameson thought he recognized her as one of the lonely girls. She had heavy chestnut hair that fell almost to her shoulders, light eyes and a heart-shaped mouth that was slightly pinched at the moment. More important, she easily met the slenderness standard.

"There will always be exceptions, Jane," Ms. Rowe said, "but exceptions don't shape our mores. Mostly we find them confusing, so we reject them and cling to the familiar. Thus, the dreaded stereotype, which can in fact be highly useful in helping us organize our world. We take it for granted that our law enforcement officers are guardians of the public safety, even though a few clearly are not. Think what it would be like if we couldn't rely on certain accepted beliefs. Chaos."

She walked to the front and took a moment to contemplate

her class. Her gaze settled on the lovely creature who sat by herself in the last row and looked as if she wanted to be anywhere but that room.

"Let's try a little test," she said. "I'll need a volunteer. How about you, Ivy? Why don't you come up front and join me?"

Ivy White, the object of Jameson's youthful lust from the moment she noticed him watching her walk through the courtyard one morning. She'd averted her gaze, her angelic face glowing with embarrassment. He was Jimmy Broud in those days, and she was the unattainable dream, which had only made him want her all the more.

Ivy pried herself free of the desk that seemed to have imprisoned her. She walked to the front, head bowed, and Jameson noticed something he'd completely missed twenty years ago. Ivy still had her baby fat. He wouldn't have called her plump or even voluptuous, but she was soft and well rounded, no angles anywhere. The opposite of the headmistress.

Ivy proceeded so slowly that Ms. Rowe went to get her, took her by the hand and brought her to the front of the class. She ran a thumbnail down Ivy's spine, demanding better posture, and when Ivy straightened, the headmistress lifted the girl's chin and brushed her unruly titian curls off her face. When Ms. Rowe finished with her wretchedly unhappy charge, she turned to the room.

"Based on her weight what class is Ivy? Anyone?"

There was a rash of tittering before one of the girls muttered under her breath, "Lower, obviously. Her ankles are tree trunks."

"She can't really help it," another explained. "She has peasant bones."

"She can too help it," a third girl huffed. "She *inhales* Twinkies."

Ivy flinched as if she'd been struck. Her ashen face made

Jameson wonder if she was going to faint. The viciousness of the other girls' attack astounded him, too. Ivy didn't have peasant bones. She wasn't even a large girl. That was pure cruelty, motivated by what he didn't know, but he was surprised the headmistress allowed it.

As the camera picked up the classroom, Jameson caught Mattie Smith's reaction and was instantly riveted. The miniature pit bull with the china-blue eyes was coiled to spring out of her seat. There was blood in that one's eye, and it was directed at the headmistress, as much as the other students. To say that she looked capable of murdering Millicent Rowe was an understatement. She looked capable of mass murder, maybe the whole damn class.

Jameson had two distinct reactions. He could feel Ivy's shame and rage, and it made him sad, not just for her, for all of them. These were kids. They were impressionable and easily led. He also wondered what had happened to provoke such a violent reaction in Mattie Smith. It couldn't be this one incident. There had to be a history between her and the headmistress, and Jameson suspected it was ugly.

Jameson hadn't believed Billy's accusations about the school at the time of his arrest. No one had. Billy was a troubled soul, who'd tried to lie his way out of situations more than once. But now Jameson might have a way to back up his brother's wild claims, even if he had to fast-forward through forty-nine videotapes.

He'd stacked the cassettes next to the entertainment unit. He hadn't found an index, so there was no way to know if he had the complete set, but something Billy had scribbled on one of the journal scraps played through Jameson's mind. He'd urged whoever read his words to find the tapes, but then he'd written two more words.

One missing.

21

"**O**n your feet, ladies! Give me twenty lunges, alternating legs. Let's show Little Miss Ivy how it's done."

Ms. Rowe's arm swooped like a symphony conductor's as she urged the class to rise. "Ivy, you'll watch this time," she said, barely veiling the sarcasm in her tone. "We wouldn't want you to hurt yourself."

Moans and groans of protest could be heard as the students rose from their desks. "Thanks a lot, bitch," one of them whispered to Ivy.

Mattie Smith shot a white-hot visual bolt at the girl who'd spoken and watched her blanch with alarm. Lane Davison was a senior now, one of the uppity day students, and *thin, thin, thin.* Lane liked to make gagging noises when Mattie was around, the meaning obvious. *Barf, barf, barf.* Mattie was the scruffiest kid in school, and to girls like Lane, an embarrassment. Lane's clique ran the school, pretty much with Ms. Rowe's blessing, as far as Mattie could tell, although Mattie was virtually certain that Lane and her friends knew nothing about the headmistress's dirty side business.

A fierce look was all Mattie needed to back off most of the other students. Very few of them would take her on, certainly not one-on-one, but it gave her no pleasure to know that she was feared. It was a matter of survival. Breeze could cajole her way out of most anything, and Jane used her reasoning skills, but Mattie didn't possess that kind of finesse. It was crush or be crushed, and she did what she had to, although most of the time she was scared to death.

"Matilda? You're not joining us?"

Ms. Rowe had spoken. Mattie didn't respond except to look over at Jane. The entire class had risen, including Breeze. She and Jane were the only ones left in their seats.

"Get up," Jane whispered to Mattie. "She'll kill you, if you don't."

"If we get up," Mattie said, "Ivy is going to get slaughtered."

"If we don't, all three of us will get slaughtered. *Come on.*"

Jane stood and Mattie let out a sniff of derision. She was disappointed in Jane, but she was really angry at herself. Her guts were quivering like water. She couldn't do this on her own. She didn't have the nerve, and now they would all know it, especially that crazy witch of a headmistress.

Secretly Mattie was terrified of what Ms. Rowe might do. She'd changed since coming back from her four-month sabbatical in Europe this summer. She was angry and hateful, especially toward the scholarship girls, and the very sight of Ivy seemed to enrage her.

"Is there a problem, Matilda? I'd be happy to meet with you in my office to discuss it."

Mattie wet her lips and felt the scars etched into her tongue from the lye Ms. Rowe had used on her not that long ago. She could still taste the acrid mix of blood, sweat and terror.

Mattie kicked the chair out from under her as she rose. It screeched loudly, but didn't topple.

Ms. Rowe smiled. "Thank you, Mattie."

Mattie heard titters and snicks of laughter around the room. She flashed her murderous glare, trying to silence the other students. Some of them actually glared back. She had been wounded, and they knew it. This bunch could smell blood.

"Lane," Ms. Rowe said, directing the senior girl to the back of the class, where a video recorder sat on a tripod, "turn it off, would you? I doubt this session is going to be very educational."

Lane leaped up to do the headmistress's bidding. Teacher's pet was also the designated audiovisual aide. She made sure the recorder was loaded and running when Ms. Rowe wanted a class taped, and she was also responsible for maintaining the tape library. But the headmistress didn't know her pet had been bragging around school that she was going to steal some of the more embarrassing tapes and use them to blackmail the students she didn't like.

As soon as Lane had the equipment turned off and had returned to her seat, Ms. Rowe told the class to begin doing lunges.

"Twenty, starting now!" She turned to Ivy. "Pay attention. When they're done, it's your turn."

Mattie did twenty ferocious lunges and finished well ahead of the rest of them. Jane wasn't athletic, but fueled by indignation even she did well. A few of the students failed to the complete the set, but Ms. Rowe didn't seem to notice. She wasn't interested in anyone's performance except Ivy's, as if she sensed Ivy's vulnerability and despised her for it.

A lamb to the slaughter, Mattie thought, aware that she could do nothing to help her friend. Of all the emotions ripping at her now, she loathed helplessness the most.

On the fifth lunge, Ivy wobbled and thrust out a hand, catching herself before she toppled. The other students howled with glee, but she stubbornly pushed to her feet and started over. She managed a few more, but her legs were shaky and her balance was off. Mattie didn't see how it could have been physical stress. She was demoralized, defeated already.

The next lunge she couldn't save. She landed on the side of her foot, and her hand wouldn't hold her. It was horrible to see her hit the floor and sit there, trying to gather herself together. Mattie silently urged her to get up, and at last Ivy did. But, with her head down and her hands clenched, she refused to do another lunge. Her posture said that she would not be humiliated any further, and Mattie was glad.

Mattie looked over at Jane, who swallowed hard. A smear of red on her nostril made Mattie wonder if Jane was having another nosebleed.

Ms. Rowe shrugged, as if to say it was hopeless. "Apparently Ivy can't even manage ten lunges," she said, addressing the class, "so you girls will have to do them for her. Meanwhile, maybe we should find Ivy something she *can* do, like eat."

A top drawer in Ms. Rowe's desk produced a large box of Twinkies. The headmistress held the box up for the class to see, as if she'd planned it just for this purpose.

"Eat, Ivy," she said, handing the box to the bewildered student. "Eat fast because your classmates are going to do lunges until you finish the entire box."

Tears were rolling down Ivy's face as she stared at the box in her hand. She shuddered as if she was going to be sick, but after a long, horrible moment, she looked up, caught Mattie's eye and gave her a nod. She was going to do it, she seemed to be saying. She had to.

Mattie shook her head. *Don't Ivy. You* don't *have to.*

But Ivy ripped the box apart, tore open one of the cakes and choked it down.

"Girls, start your lunges!" Ms. Rowe shouted. "When Ivy's done with the entire box, you can quit, but not until."

Mattie wanted to cram the box and all down the headmistress's throat. She flung herself into the exercise. It was that or assault the woman. If she could control herself, Ivy might get through this. If she couldn't, anything might happen. She glanced around at Breeze in the row behind her, looking for reinforcements.

Breeze had her eyes closed, as if she were about to be sick, too.

"Keep going, girls—and remember why you're doing the extra work—because this *lazy* pig wouldn't. When she finishes the Twinkies, you can quit."

She pointed to Ivy, who was fighting to stuff cake after cake into her mouth. Tears rolled down her cheeks, and she gagged on every bite.

Sweat soaked Mattie's face. Abruptly she stopped exercising, braced her legs and glared at the headmistress, panting to get the words out. "If there's a pig in this room, it's you."

Ms. Rowe looked genuinely surprised. When she spoke, her voice was oddly soft. "Come up to the front, Matilda."

Mattie flipped her the finger.

"If you don't come up here," Ms. Rowe said, measuring her words as if they were doses of poison, "I'll call security, and have you taken away. I understand incorrigible students go straight to reform school. You would be the first ever in the history of Rowe Academy. Quite a distinction."

"Mattie, go," Jane pleaded. "You're making it worse."

Every step Mattie took was a fight. She wanted to run screaming at the headmistress. When she reached the front of the room, she turned and faced the other students. Most of them wouldn't look at her. Of course, Lane and her cohorts were smirking.

"What social class is this one, ladies?" Ms. Rowe asked, indicating Mattie. "The lowest of the low? Perhaps she'd rather be in reform school?"

"I'd rather be rotting in hell," Mattie said through her teeth.

Cold laughter iced the headmistress's voice. "How nice that I can grant you that wish. Go to my office, Matilda. You know what to do when you get there. I won't keep you waiting long."

Mattie stood at the window, looking out at the pine forest that bordered the campus and wishing she could hide in its cool, dark depths. She was supposed to be sitting in the chair nearest Ms. Rowe's desk, her feet flat on the floor, her hands clasped in her lap, reflecting on her transgressions. That was protocol when you were in trouble, and Mattie was in trouble a lot. But she was caught up in another plan that had nothing to do with protocol, and if she couldn't pull it off, none of the rules would matter anyway.

Mattie knew her punishment would be severe. If Ms. Rowe could break her, then the others would be broken, too. Mattie was the rebel, and the headmistress needed to regain control, especially of the scholarship girls. She'd intentionally isolated them from the other girls, probably because she didn't want her dirty secrets known. Most of the day students were from wealthy and distinguished families, who might not appreciate their little darlings being exposed to a hotbed of sex and scandal.

Mattie heard a latch click, and she made a dash for the other side of the room. She didn't make it. She tripped over Ms. Rowe's shoe and fell crashing to the floor. Embarrassed, she scrambled to her feet.

"You brazen little bitch," the headmistress said, speaking in whispers, "you are not going to defy me any longer. I could have turned you into someone special, a woman every man wanted and every other woman envied, but you don't have it in you. I'd intended to choose you, to guide and tutor you into an extraordinary creature. Now you'll be lucky if I let you live."

A knock on the door interrupted her lecture. She opened it to Lane Davison and half a dozen of her friends, all senior girls who'd been assigned to the hall squad. Mattie's heart began to pound. The Death Squad. She waited for Ms. Rowe to send them away.

Instead, she waved them in. "Ah, here you are," she said. "Just in time to help our Mattie understand the seriousness of what she's done."

Once the girls were safely inside, Ms. Rowe wasted no words. She whipped out her pointer and tapped a rattan basket filled with canes, the kind used for corporal punishment.

"Help yourself, ladies. And don't spare the rod. She needs to be taught a lasting lesson. You'll excuse me now. I have a class to teach."

Ms. Rowe swished out, and the seniors encircled Mattie, their eyes glittering. They stared at her as if she were an animal they were about to sacrifice. One of them had pulled the canes from the basket and was passing them out. No one spoke, and Mattie was too wary to say anything.

She exhaled, expelling air from her lungs. She concentrated on the still center in the turning world, because her world was turning. And seconds later, they were closing in, and she was reeling, spinning, trying to watch them all at once. The first whack came from behind. It doubled her over in agony. The second knocked her to the ground, and once she was down the blows came fast and furious, cutting her clothing into shreds and rending her flesh. She could smell the stink of hatred and the sour musk of her own blood. A well-placed kick splintered her ribs.

"Oops, sorry," Lane said, laughing.

Mattie moaned, doubling to protect herself, but there was no way to do it. They were everywhere. Another kick caught the knee she'd injured falling from the tower, and the room became a spinning red ball. She felt as if she was going to pass out, but the pain was so terrible, it wouldn't let her. She would be wide-awake when she died, she realized, because surely that was the plan, to kill her.

22

Out of a dead sleep, Mattie grabbed her ringing cell phone off the night table next to her bed. Her only conscious thought was to stuff the phone under her pillow, but she must have hit a button because someone was talking. The husky, oddly sensual voice on the other end of the line made her hesitate. She couldn't tell if it was a man or a woman.

"Hello? Anyone there?" the caller asked. "I'm trying to reach Judge Matilda Smith. Do I have the right number?"

"Who is this?" Mattie rolled over and checked the bedside clock. "It's 3:00 a.m."

"Oh, sorry, did I wake you?"

"Of course, you woke me." Mattie couldn't believe she was having this conversation. She couldn't have been asleep more than a couple hours. Vince's report on Jameson Cross had kept her up. She couldn't think of him as Jimmy Broud.

"I'm calling from Italy," the caller explained. "It's been one of those insane days, and I just got to my messages."

"Who *is* this?" Mattie asked again. She tried to place the voice. It was rapid-fire, yet oddly sexy, with a squeak reminiscent of an adolescent boy's.

"It's Tansy Black! Profuse apologies! I know exactly who you are. I was so damn excited to get a call from the famous Judge Smith that I wasn't paying attention to the time difference."

"Famous? Infamous, maybe." Mattie didn't want to smile, but she couldn't help herself. Tansy Black even sounded like a dynamo.

"Should I call you back at a better time?" Black asked.

"No, this is fine." Mattie threw off the covers and turned on the light. "I'm coming to."

Static fuzzed the line, but Black's voice could be heard. "What can I help you with?" she asked. "I'm flattered to be of any assistance whatsoever."

Mattie rolled off the bed and stood up. She needed to get some blood circulating and collect her wits. She had several important goals with this phone call. She hoped to get as much information as she could about William Broud and his two legal proceedings—the one that put him in jail and the one that got him out—and she hoped to learn what Black knew about the lonely girls, if anything.

As Broud's attorney, Black had had access to at least some of the sealed police reports, trial transcripts and forensic evidence. Mattie didn't know whether she and her friends were mentioned by name in any of those reports, but she needed the information in order to protect all of them from Cross, and whatever else might be coming their way. And it had to be done without giving Black information she might not actually have.

Perhaps most important of all, Mattie had to determine whether Black might be a friend or an enemy. She eyed her fingernails, resisting the sharp tug she felt. Quickly spotting an enemy could become a crucial survival skill in the coming days. Her training in behavioral psychology and jury science would help with that, but she would also need discipline, focus.

"Congratulations on your victory with the Broud case," she said, wondering if Black had heard the news about her client's death. It was possible she hadn't since she was in Europe. Mattie decided not to mention it.

"I have a similar habeas corpus petition under review," Mattie explained. "But I'm torn as to whether it should be allowed to go forward. Could you tell me why you decided to take on Broud's case?"

"That was the easy part," Black said. "The initial research came out of a law school assignment. It was supposed to be a team effort, but it took years and several court orders just to get the records unsealed. By that time, everyone else had bailed out. I'd put in so much time already, I figured it didn't make sense to quit, but I'm hardheaded that way."

"Some people might call it heroism," Mattie said.

"I was being practical, not noble." Black laughed. "Besides, it was a fascinating trial. The prosecution's case was riddled with discrepancies, and the defense was woefully inadequate, in my opinion, so it looked like an appeal was a good bet."

"Discrepancies?" This was why Mattie had called her.

"Their rush to judgment was dizzying. They never bothered to look for other suspects, and they neglected to declare certain crime scene evidence that may have helped the defense."

"Exculpatory evidence? Like what?"

"The crime scene people found video equipment in the headmistress's bedroom and a set of instructional tapes, one of which was missing. A later search turned up an index, which identified the missing tape as Ms. Rowe's Private Social Registry. It might not have been significant, except that Broud had accused her of running a sex ring."

Mattie knew about the tapes. They were mostly etiquette classes, and she'd been part of the making of some of them. The collection covered everything from social graces to appropriate behavior with the opposite sex, but Mattie had never heard of the one Black just mentioned.

"Did the sex ring allegations come up at trial?" she asked.

"Never. Broud was considered unreliable, partly because of his wild allegations. The defense didn't want them to come out during cross-examination, so they never put him on the stand. Plus, the cause of death was established as suffocation, but a poisonous substance called heartwine was found in Rowe's tissues, in her stomach and in her bloodstream."

Mattie feared the strain in her voice was audible. "Do they have any idea how it got there?"

"It never came up during the trial. I found references to it in the coroner's report. It was totally overlooked."

Mattie shouldn't have been relieved to hear that. The negligence may have cost a man his freedom and his life. At least she could take some comfort in knowing that she'd really believed Broud to be guilty. They had all believed he smothered Ms. Rowe.

"But the blood was the deciding factor in my taking on William's case," Black said.

"The blood?"

"Yes, the spot on Ms. Rowe's pillow that was determined to be his blood type. It was the basis of the prosecution's case against him."

"You knew it wasn't really Broud's blood?"

"No, not at all. But I was prepared to take that risk and so was he, which convinced me even further. My best—maybe my only—chance of getting him out was to have a DNA analysis done on that blood. To follow up on his allegations about sex rings twenty years later would have been a wild-goose chase, to say the least."

Thank God for that.

Mattie's sense of relief was coupled with concern. It didn't seem that Black had come across their names in the records, but there was plenty of evidence indirectly linked to them that could come out if the case was reopened. At least now Mattie had a better idea what they were dealing with. In short, Jameson Cross was bluffing. She doubted he had anything to go on other than his deceased brother's conjecturing. He couldn't even point fingers with evidence that flimsy. The press wouldn't print his claims, and if they did, he would look foolish. He had a reputation to protect, too.

Maybe Mattie should be the one to tell him that.

"Am I rambling too much?" Black asked. "Have I helped you at all?"

"Immensely," Mattie assured her. "You'll never know how much. Did I mention that I grew up in Marin County? I was just a kid when the murder took place, but I've always been curious. One last question, and I'll let you go. Do you know why the records were sealed, and who ordered it?"

"There may have been juveniles involved, students from the school, but I didn't come across anything about it in the material I reviewed, and to be honest, that wasn't my focus."

She hadn't answered the second question, but Mattie decided to let it go. "Thank you, again! Let me buy you a drink when you get back to the States, please? It's the least I can do."

"An honor," Black said, promising to call as they said their goodbyes and hung up.

Mattie glanced at the bedside clock, wishing she could wake Breeze and tell her the good news. She stacked up bed pillows and fell against them, hoping to go back to sleep, but her mind was racing. Black would never know how much she'd helped. Finally, Mattie had some breathing room. Now that she didn't have to worry about Cross stalking her, she could focus on who the real murderer was. That was the surest way to end this nightmare before careers—and lives— were destroyed.

It seemed the most obvious suspect was the man Ms. Rowe had been seeing, her mystery lover, but none of them had ever caught a glimpse of him. There was nothing to go on. She thought back to the times they were in Ms. Rowe's apartment, privy to her personal life. She'd even talked about the man in her life at one point, but Mattie didn't recall that she'd said anything specific enough to help. And Mattie could only conclude that no one else knew about him, either, or his name would have come out at the trial.

Some time later, just as she was about to drift off, her mind began to make the connections it had refused to make when she was straining to remember. It had always been a source of irony and frustration to her that the brain seemed to resist her when she needed it most. But now, thoughts stirred, bits and pieces of memory, swimming into her awareness. Bits and pieces of paper? A letter written by Ms. Rowe?

Maybe there was something, and she might be the only one who knew it still existed. She had to talk to Breeze.

She got out of bed, tiptoed down the hall and opened the door to the guest room. The last thing she expected to find was an empty room.

As she switched on the nightstand lamp, she saw a hand-written note on the pillow: "Gone to the Four Seasons. Love, B."

Jameson awoke to the crackle and spit of eggs frying in a pan, music to a starving man. A nest of tiny spiders danced in front of his eyes, although they didn't really look like spiders. They looked like snow…or bad television reception. He rubbed his eyes, which immediately began to water and burn.

It *was* the television, he realized when his vision cleared. It had only sounded like eggs frying. His stomach rumbled as he reached for the remote to turn off the VCR. It was early by his watch. He'd been viewing tapes all night long, lecture after lecture from Ms. Rowe's bizarre collection, and apparently he'd dozed off with his eyes open, a skill he'd learned in college to get him through his first-period classes. In those days, coffee had kept him going until lunch, when he'd finally woken up and joined the human race. In a world of early risers, Jameson had been nocturnal, a nighthawk.

He clicked off the TV, tugged up his jeans and headed for the kitchen in search of fuel. Eggs came to mind, probably because of the noises that awakened him. He hadn't eaten since he sat down in front of the VCR. He'd gone through nearly one entire box of cassettes, fast-forwarding whenever the material allowed, and he'd seen more than enough of Ms. Rowe's philosophy of life and learning to make him wonder why she hadn't been taken out sooner.

A warped mind sat atop that long, elegant neck of hers. Seriously warped, to his way of thinking. The tapes documented her elitist opinions and gave hints of her sadistic teaching style. He didn't doubt that she suffered delusions of grandeur, or that taping herself had not been a teaching tool. It had been an exercise in ego gratification. He wondered if it was that same ego that had gotten her killed.

Jameson's kitchen was sleek and modern, mostly stainless steel with teak and granite. Not cozy, exactly, but clean and efficient. A decorator had warmed the place up with lots of leafy green plants that, thank God, his cleaning service remembered to water, and she'd also used poppy-red place mats and wrought iron bar chairs with woven red leather seats. He enjoyed the area, and did a lot of his own cooking, rudimentary as it was.

Once he had some eggs frying in the pan, he returned to musing on what he'd seen, and particularly on the fact that one of the tapes seemed to be missing—the last one in the collection. His plan was to talk to anyone who'd been involved and was still in the area, and he was going to start with Lane Davison, who was married to a friend of his, Frank

O'Neill, the D.A. Lane had seemed to be Ms. Rowe's gofer, and he'd noticed her working with the video equipment.

There hadn't been any smoking gun evidence on the tapes he watched, but then he hadn't expected to see any. What he had seen were four teenage girls, all apparent victims of a cruel headmistress, who might well want to strike back at her. Ivy, in particular, but Ivy was already dead, which left Mattie as the one with the strongest motive, given her attempts to defend Ivy.

The Honorable Matilda Smith, notorious crusader for truth and boat-rocker, even by the standards of the Ninth District.

Hmm...

Jameson ate the eggs right out of the skillet, and followed them up with a foaming glass of orange juice from the refrigerator. Tough as Mattie seemed, he didn't see her as a cold-blooded killer, nor could he imagine that an overinflated ego would trigger her murderous instincts, if she had any. There had to have been a serious threat, but he hadn't seen any indication of it. Nothing on the tapes would motivate an elaborate murder plot, in his opinion, and yet, at the time of his arrest, Billy had accused the girls, and even though the police had ignored him, Jameson couldn't.

Billy's babbling about a sex ring meant there may have been others who wanted Ms. Rowe dead. VIPs he called them, important men, perhaps, who were afraid of being found out and ruined. The journal also implied that Billy had been given the drugs by Ms. Rowe rather than selling them to her. Jameson had heard her accuse Billy of blackmail. She may have been paying him off in drugs.

Jameson left the skillet and juice glass soaking in the sink. Billy's claim of a cover-up was taking on more credibility in Jameson's mind, even though there was no tangible support for it. Maybe Jameson wanted it to be true. Cover-ups made for great true crime stories, but they were as complicated as hell. It became nearly impossible to get to the truth because so much got lost in the labyrinth of lies and deception.

Jameson couldn't let that happen this time.

He was on his way to the master bedroom for a shower and maybe a nap, when his doorbell rang. It was early still, just after seven, and he wasn't expecting anyone. He kept walking the other way, anticipating the steamy heat and welcome oblivion of a shower, until the incessant ringing brought him to a halt. The son of a bitch wouldn't go away.

He whipped open the door to a rumpled-looking character with peppery gray hair in need of a trim and a much-too-large mud-brown sports coat. The badge the man flashed identified him as Arvid Edwards, homicide detective with the San Rafael Police Department.

"James Broud?" Edwards asked.

Jameson nodded, aware that he'd better get used to being addressed by his real name since he'd used it when he reported Billy's death.

He didn't recognize the detective. He'd tried to maintain his contacts with the various police forces and the sheriff's department in Marin County, but he hadn't had to make much use of those contacts until recently. Most of the cases he chose to follow up for a book took him out of the area and sometimes across the country. His last was the Chandra Levy case in Washington, D.C. He was still gathering material and formulating theories on that one. It had intrigued him partly because the senator involved was from Northern California.

"Are you new in Homicide?" Jameson asked. Years ago, Jameson had known all the homicide detectives at SRPD.

"I just got promoted." Edwards beamed. "I worked downtown for most of my career—violent crimes—but I always wanted to get into crime investigation, solve mysteries. They just assigned me to the team investigating your brother's death."

"Congratulations," Jameson said softly. *You've got yourself a mystery now.*

He nodded. "We thought you'd want to know that the medical examiner's report is in."

Another surprise. He'd expected to be called down to the station or told over the phone. A personal visit seemed unusual, and Edwards probably expected to be invited in, but Jameson didn't want him to see the tapes. "I appreciate that," was all he said.

It was warm for so early in the day, and Edwards seemed flushed and overheated in his overcoat. He wiped his brow with his sleeve and then shouldered out of the coat and draped it over his arm.

"We're calling it a homicide," he said. "Your brother died of asphyxia. He was suffocated, probably with a pillow."

"Suffocated?" Dread had formed in Jameson's gut. Despite the warmth, his palms were sweating ice. "Did you find drugs in his system?"

"No drugs—nothing illegal anyway, but he had traces of a poison called heartwine, which could indicate premeditation. If the killer intended to poison him and failed, then suffocation may have been a last resort."

Smothered with a pillow? Traces of heartwine in his system? That was exactly how the headmistress died.

"I know you've already been questioned," Edwards said, "but I have a few more."

"I'm running late for an appointment." Jameson needed some time to assimilate Edward's bombshell. "Why don't I drop by the station later today?"

"Make it tomorrow morning. I'm in the field this afternoon."

Jameson agreed, already thinking through his strategy. He

doubted the detective knew much about the earlier case, certainly not arcane details like the traces of heartwine found in Ms. Rowe's system—and Jameson didn't intend to tell him, at least not yet.

Jameson had felt some sympathy creeping in toward the girls, given what he'd seen on the tapes. They were underprivileged kids, and it looked as if they'd been singled out for humiliation and abuse. But someone had not only taken his brother's life, they'd been sick enough to duplicate the murder of the headmistress. If they'd done it—if one or all of the lonely girls was guilty of anything that heinous—they would pay.

23

Nothing broken except maybe some ribs.

Mattie winced as she touched the pulpy mass below her left breast. The pain was excruciating, but she'd broken ribs before, and they'd always healed up in a week or two. Sprawled on the bed in her dorm room, eyes closed, she examined the rest of her body, as much as she could reach without getting up.

She had welts and bruises everywhere. Her mouth was bloody. She could taste the iron. Even the skin on her face was sore to the touch.

"Dirty rotten bastards." She groaned out the words, but they held little conviction. Vengeance took too much strength. It hurt to breathe.

She opened her eyes to darkness, but knew almost immediately that she was in her tiny dorm room. She couldn't see the armoire sorely in need of paint or the dresser with the missing pulls, but she could smell the banana peel on the bedside table next to her head, and if she got up too quickly she would trip on a heap of clothing next to the bed. Her room. It wouldn't win any awards for neatness, especially with all the grungy stuff she had stuffed under her mattress, but it was hers.

As she lay there, afraid to move, she realized that she must have passed out from the beating and someone had brought her here and dumped her. They would take that as a sign of defeat, but they hadn't defeated her. Nothing could. Nothing ever could. Even death would not be defeat, as long as her spirit wasn't broken.

At some point she'd realized that no matter what damage was done to her, a part of her could not be touched. She went to a place where nothing bad could happen. It was how she survived. But nothing good could happen, either, she'd realized. She paid a price for protection that total. And yet, for better or worse, she had learned very early in life not to bargain, at least not with the enemy. She couldn't. There was a part of her that refused to be tempted or tortured or given away, and it had something to do with never wanting to be like her mother, who gave everything away.

You'll be fine, baby, once you learn how to be soft and pretty, just like me. Men love that.

All of Lela Smith's men had abused her in one way or another. The last one had bashed her in the head and left her in a coma, from which she never emerged. But Mattie had known long before her mother's tragic end that she didn't intend to be soft and pretty. She'd made that decision at the age of eleven when one of her mother's nicer boyfriends caressed her face and asked her if she was that soft everywhere. Mattie had gone straight to her mother and kicked up a fuss that got her shipped off to live with her aunt.

Mattie heard a strange click and shot up, moaning in agony.

She clutched her ribs and felt under the pillow, where she kept an old lug wrench she'd found in the storage shed. The blood roared through her head, dizzying her as the door to her room opened. A face appeared in the doorway, but Mattie couldn't see who it was. Moonlight gave the area a ghostly cast.

"Mattie? Are you all right?"

"Shit." Mattie dropped to her elbow, gasping in pain as Jane and Breeze slipped into her room. "You guys could have killed me, scaring me like that. I probably broke another rib."

"Mattie, you look terrible. Oh, my God!"

Breeze got to the bed first. She fished inside the neck of her blouse and pulled some tissue from her bra. Gingerly, she blotted the blood from Mattie's mouth.

Jane switched on the bedside lamp, which flickered with dingy yellow light. "What does the other guy look like?" she asked.

She smiled down at Mattie, who had reverted to gasps again. God, that hurt like hell on earth. Every move hurt. She rolled to her back, wheezing. She couldn't breathe, and her lips were burning. Breeze's touch felt like salt on open wounds.

Jane sat next to Mattie on the bed and began unbuttoning Mattie's school blouse from the bottom up. "Let's see how bad it is," she said.

Mattie swatted her hand away. "Back off," she snarled. "I'm fine."

"Shut up," Jane said. "You're too much of a dork to know whether or not you're hurt."

Jane was one of the few people at Rowe Academy who wasn't afraid of Mattie. She wasn't foolish enough to dismiss her, but she didn't run from a confrontation the way others did.

Mattie breathed out an expletive when Jane laid open her blouse. She knew it was a mess in there. She'd felt the welts and swollen lumps. But she hadn't expected to find a sea of livid purple. Her entire abdomen was mottled with torn tissue and blood pooling under the skin.

Jane went pale and Breeze let out a strange little whimper.

"We need to get you to a hospital," Jane said. "You could be bleeding internally."

"Ivy? Is that you?" Mattie spotted a shock-white face peeking from behind the two girls. Ivy must have just crept into the room, and she looked horrified at the sight of Mattie's injuries. Mattie wished she hadn't had to see this. She didn't want Ivy to feel responsible.

"I'm not going anywhere." Mattie assaulted Jane with the most ferocious glare she could manage, mostly for Ivy's benefit. "They're just bruises. They'll heal."

Breeze found her voice. "We need help," she said, as though she'd just realized what they were up against. "We can't take on Ms. Rowe and that Death Squad of hers. We can't do this alone."

Mattie tried to sit up and couldn't. Her body felt stiff, like it would crack in two if she didn't hold perfectly still. The stiffness got worse by the minute. Soon she would be a living corpse. Rigor mortis was setting in while she was still alive.

"Whoever we told would go straight to Ms. Rowe," Mattie said, warning Breeze and Jane. "If she found out we'd ratted on her, she'd come after me again. Or Ivy. Or one of you! We can't tell anyone at this school. Ms. Rowe *is* this school."

"Then you have to run away," Breeze said. "You can't stay here."

Mattie bowed her head, trying not to be sick. The pain was that bad. Jane and Breeze went quiet, which she hoped meant she'd convinced them not to go for help.

"Promise you won't tell anyone how bad I am," Mattie

said, barely aware that she was pleading with them. "I don't want those asshole seniors to think they've won."

Breeze fought tears. "They haven't won, and it's not the seniors anyway. It's Rowe. She's the one who put them up to it."

Mattie eased her head back to the pillow and closed her eyes, groaning with relief. The room had a musty smell, and mingled with the overripe aroma of bananas, it was oddly comforting. She concentrated on that for a bit, clinging to anything that could take her somewhere less painful. Every once in a while her mother would bring home bananas from the store, and Mattie would eat them sliced in a big bowl of cornflakes. She fixed them herself, and it was one of the nicer memories she carried from childhood.

She opened her eyes to all three of them, watching her.

"What are we going to do?" Jane asked.

They weren't just worried about her, Mattie realized. They were depending on her, all of them in different ways. Their futures were inextricably locked with hers, and whatever she did affected them. Right now she was the weak one, and if she stayed, they had to figure out how to protect her. If she left, they only had to protect themselves. She could not put off her decision.

"I'm getting out of here," she said. "Tonight."

A flash of terror lit Ivy's haunted gaze. Mattie watched it happen and realized that Ivy would always think of herself as a victim. She didn't see Mattie as weak and vulnerable, even now. Mattie felt like she was abandoning her friend, but what else could she do? She couldn't stay, and she couldn't take Ivy with her. Mattie didn't know if she was strong enough to make it out of Rowe on her own. And anyway, they would all be better off with her gone. She had a problem with authority figures. She was belligerent. She couldn't help herself, and she was making it worse for all of them.

* * *

"Wait here!" Mattie gripped Ivy's arm, issuing the order as if Ivy were a pet prone to running away. She was still pissed at Ivy for slipping out of the dorm and following her into town tonight. Mattie had gone the long way around, taking the paved road that ran the perimeter of the peninsula. It would have been shorter to cut through the woods, but she didn't want to lose her way, and she wasn't sure how much punishment her body could take. One bad fall, and she could have crippled herself. She was bent over like an invalid now, but the pain had actually let up some. Maybe it was the adrenaline pumping through her system.

She hadn't noticed Ivy behind her until she reached the deep curve that rounded the point and led into town. They were too far from Rowe to send her back, so Mattie was stuck with the little sneak.

"Why can't I go in there with you?" Ivy asked.

They were hidden in the bushes near the police station, and it was late, after midnight. Mattie had already told Ivy about her plans to spill her guts to the authorities. That made more sense than running away when she had nowhere to go. She was going to tell them everything, and she was terrified, but she didn't want Ivy to see that. Mattie believed with all her heart that Ms. Rowe should be put in jail for what she did, but Mattie's only experiences with the police had been bad scenes when they'd come to the trailer because some guy was roughing up her mom.

"They might not believe me," Mattie whispered, "and there's no sense getting both of us into trouble. You stay here, and when I'm sure they're going to help us, I'll tell them where you are."

Ivy shook off Mattie's hold. "They *won't* believe you," she said. "Not if you go in there yourself. I can back you up. There'll be two of us. They'll have to listen."

There was an odd grip to Ivy's voice that told Mattie it would be useless trying to reason with her. There only seemed to be two options: knock her cold and leave her here in the bushes, or take her along.

"Come on then," Mattie said. "I just hope you're right."

"Did Ms. Rowe personally inflict any of your injuries?"

The female police officer sitting across the table from Mattie and Ivy reminded Mattie of a man. She had wide shoulders, strong features and a cleft in her chin, but there was something kind about her eyes, and she'd actually let slip a string of curse words when she saw Mattie's bruises. At that exact moment, Mattie had dared to hope that she might help them.

The three of them were alone in an interview room, where the officer had been asking Mattie questions for the past hour. So far she'd asked Ivy nothing, but that would come, Mattie was sure. At least she hadn't split them up. Mattie wasn't sure anyone could have unclamped Ivy's clinging fingers from the arms of the chair where she sat.

"Not these injuries," Mattie said, pointing to her midriff. "That was done by the Death Squad, a bunch of students Ms. Rowe uses to bully the rest of us. But Ms. Rowe was the one who called the Death Squad into her office and told them to teach me a lasting lesson. She made it happen."

"Did she ever hurt you herself?"

Mattie opened her mouth and exposed the scars on her tongue.

The officer seemed startled. "She did that? How?"

"I'm not sure. I was unconscious." Mattie told her how Ms. Rowe had knocked her out with the tea and put her in the crawl space. "My tongue was swollen and bleeding. It might have been acid or lye."

"Can you prove any of this? Did anyone see anything? Would they be willing to testify?"

The questions caught Mattie off guard. She couldn't imagine any of the Death Squad testifying on her behalf. "I guess it's Ms. Rowe's word against mine. But there was a man who pulled me out of the crawl space—the gardener."

"And he saw Ms. Rowe put you in there?"

Mattie was hesitant. "No."

"Was the gardener one of the men who abused you?"

Mattie shook her head. "I didn't see the men. It was always dark in the room."

"You *were* sexually abused, though? By these men?"

"No."

The officer looked at Ivy. "How about you? Were you abused?"

Ivy wouldn't answer and Mattie knew it was all over. She couldn't drag the other two girls into this. She'd run away to protect them.

"Did anyone see them?" the officer asked Mattie. "Anyone who could testify on your behalf?"

"I don't think so."

Ivy buried her face her hands, and Mattie sank into the chair.

"Don't send us back there," Mattie pleaded.

The officer tried to reassure her. "No one's sending you back anywhere. You're going to need some medical attention, young lady, and then we'll see that you both get a hot meal and a good night's sleep. Tomorrow, you'll be feeling a whole lot better, and by then we'll have had a chance to pay Ms. Rowe a visit."

Ivy scrubbed at her eyes and whispered, "She'll lie. She won't admit to anything."

Someone rapped on the door and opened it slightly. A young woman in civilian clothes, who might have been a secretary, beckoned for the officer to come out.

"Be right back," she told Mattie and Ivy as she rose from

the table. She pulled a couple of miniature Snickers bars out of her pocket and tossed them to the girls. "Munch on these while I'm gone."

As Mattie opened her candy bar, she noticed the door was ajar. She held a finger to her lips, warning Ivy to be quiet as she slipped out of her chair and went to investigate. Through the crack, she saw the woman who'd interviewed them talking with a man. He was wearing a dark suit, and something about him made Mattie think he might be running the place. He seemed important, although she couldn't have explained why. Just a feeling she had. Otherwise, the hallway was empty. The secretary was nowhere around.

Mattie couldn't see the man's face. He stood with his back to her, facing the officer. But when he raised his hand, she caught the glint of gold from the star-shaped object on his cuff.

She shut the door and turned, pressing her body against it. A mallet in her chest was pounding spikes. "Ivy, we have to get out of here. She's talking to one of Ms. Rowe's men, the one I spit on. He's here!"

Ivy stuffed the untouched candy bar in her pocket and got up. "How are we going to get out of here? There's only that one door."

Mattie didn't see any way of escaping, except perhaps to make a run for it. If she could create a diversion that would allow Ivy to get away, then Mattie could pretend to be gravely injured and fake a fainting spell.

She waved Ivy over and told her the plan. Poor Ivy looked as if *she* were going to faint. Mattie gripped her hands, trying to shore her up. She spoke to her in low, firm tones. Finally, Ivy nodded. She would do it. She was ready. But when Mattie tried the door again, the handle wouldn't give. It was locked.

Locked. From the outside.

Free fall. Mattie felt as if she were hurtling through space.

She turned to Ivy in despair, but neither of them said a word. They knew. It was all over. They walked back to their chairs and sat, facing each other, so weighed down with dread they could hardly breathe. After a moment, Mattie reached over and took Ivy's hands again, this time for solace. What option did they have but to provide each other what little comfort they could?

Some time later, the door opened, and Mattie looked up.

Ms. Rowe walked into the room and shut the door behind her. She was alone, and Mattie couldn't help but believe that was a very bad thing.

The headmistress came to the table, her raincoat billowing as she stood across from them. "I have bad news for you two," she said, her voice oddly soft. "There's been a robbery at Rowe Academy. Tonight, after everyone went to bed, the display cases were broken into and priceless Rowe family heirlooms taken."

"We didn't steal anything!" Mattie grimaced as Ivy's fingernails bit into her flesh.

"I think you did. When the police woke me with the news that you two were here, I knew my robbers had been caught. Did you bring your backpack, Mattie? Where is it?"

Mattie glanced over at the table where the officer had set their packs. Ms. Rowe followed her gaze and nodded. "Excellent," she said.

Mattie didn't speak. Her pack was marked with her name, per school regulations, and she wanted Ms. Rowe to look. They hadn't taken anything, and this would prove it.

Confused, she watched as Ms. Rowe unzipped the bag's main compartment and took something from inside her raincoat. Quickly wiping her prints with a tissue, Ms. Rowe slipped the objects inside and zipped up the compartment.

"What did you do?" Mattie struggled to make herself heard. "What did you put in my backpack?"

Ms. Rowe turned and clutched her coat together. Her lips trembled, unable to hold a smile. "You filthy girl," she said. "You have the gall to steal from me, *lie* about me, and now you're making accusations? My heirlooms are right there in your bag. You *stole* them."

Neither girl spoke, but Mattie's thoughts shrieked out an answer. *You didn't find anything in my bag. You planted it.*

"They know all about you, Mattie." Ms. Rowe's voice could barely be heard as she came back to the larger table, but there was hatred burning in her eyes. She probably wanted to kill them right here in this room, but she couldn't for fear of being overheard. There weren't any opaque windows or see-through mirrors, but there could be a microphone somewhere.

"I've told them how you bully the other girls and goad them into fights," she said, "how you leap out of towers and self-inflict horrible wounds to get attention. And Ivy, with her eating disorder and alienation. They know how sick and self-destructive the two of you are. I told them what constant torment you've been to me, despite all my efforts to help you."

Ivy whimpered, and Mattie tightened her hold on the other girl's hand. She glanced up at Ms. Rowe, trying to hide the hatred in her own eyes. She wanted to fly at the woman and rip her to shreds. She should have known the headmistress would stop at nothing, even this, *framing them.* Fury burned through Mattie's utter despair. She wanted to shriek at the headmistress and throw the lies back in her face, but she'd learned not to fight when there was no chance of winning. Ms. Rowe had taught her that.

"You will recant everything you've said to the officer who questioned you." Ms. Rowe bent toward them and hissed out her demands. "You will admit the truth, that you inflicted those wounds yourself, and you stole my precious heirlooms. If you don't I'll press charges against you and leave you here, at the mercy of the police and the courts. You will surely spend from now until your eighteenth birthday behind bars, if you get out then."

She fingered the lace hanky she'd tucked into the sleeve of her blouse, still speaking under her breath. "I've heard the older girls in juvenile hall take ownership of the younger girls and turn them into servants, and worse. I'm sure you'll be very popular, Ivy. Mattie will probably try her spitting trick and end up with her throat cut."

She waited until both girls looked up and acknowledged her.

"Are you going to recant or not?"

Mattie avoided the headmistress's gaze as she rose from her chair. Ivy barely made it to her feet. Silent, they followed Ms. Rowe out the door. Mattie had to concentrate on making her legs move. She was going numb. She couldn't feel the floor beneath her feet. She had no idea what Ms. Rowe would do to them when she got them back to school, maybe nothing immediately. She was smart enough to wait until the heat was off and the police weren't watching, but she would exact her revenge.

She had said they would die if they talked. Mattie wondered how. How would she kill them and get away with it? Because Mattie had no doubt that she could do it. If the man she'd seen had the authority, if he was running things, then Ms. Rowe could probably get away with just about anything, even dead girls in the walls.

24

"Ooh, Mr. President, shame on you!"

Jane smothered a giggle as her husband crept up behind her and gave her breasts a gentle squeeze. She let her head loll against his shoulder, abandoning herself to his caresses. She loved how his bare chest cushioned her with lovely, furry heat. Apparently he intended to wear only pajama bottoms to bed tonight. Always a good sign.

"The red satin?" he said, referring to her low-cut nightgown with its deep slit up the leg. "It's like a double dose of Viagra."

His smile beamed at her from the gilded mirror of the vanity, where she'd stopped to check herself out before joining him in their bedroom. His gaze caught hers, and she floated for a moment in the light blue pools of his eyes. His silvery hair and aquiline features aroused her in ways she still didn't understand.

She brought his questing fingers to her lips and kissed them. "I was hoping for a personal audience with the commander in chief," she said.

"You've got it," he assured her. "And you don't even have to salute."

"Oh, but *you* do."

She turned and laced her arms around his neck, very seductively nestling her pelvis into his. "My, my! Are we saluting already?"

He actually blushed. It was one of his most endearing

traits, in Jane's opinion. A shy president. The country hadn't had one of those in a while, nor a man as dedicated and determined to turning things around as Larry Mantle.

His restless hands roamed her back, searching for a home, and ended up with two handfuls of fanny. "A commander has to inspect his troops," he explained.

She retaliated by plunging her hands down the back of his pajamas and giving his manly tush a good squeeze.

His eyebrows shot up. "Oh, baby, cold hands!"

"Warm heart."

Jane whooped as he picked her up and headed out of the dressing room. She kicked her bare feet, abandoning herself to the silliness of the moment. "We could be a Doris Day movie."

"Only until I get you to bed," he warned. "Then we're a porno flick." He settled her on their elegant antique canopy bed and stood back to look at her. His voice dropped to a whisper. "You are everything to me, Jane."

Tears burned her eyes. "As you are to me," she said.

"I want you. I will *always* want you."

The very words she needed to hear. How did he know when she'd never told him? She drew in a breath, aware of the ache in her throat. She was safe now, for the moment, safe from her demons. And it was because of him, the man who'd given her the gift of seeing herself through his eyes. His love had stabilized and reassured her enough that she had no longer needed to prove anything. She'd felt complete with Larry in her life, and she couldn't lose that now.

"Countless presidents have bedded their wives in this room," he observed, gazing down at her, "but it has never seen a First Lady like you."

Thrilled at the husky caress in his voice, she sighed and melted into the pillows of their antique canopy bed. The bedroom of their private quarters on the top floor of the White House was decorated in cream satins, blue velvet damask and turn-of-the-century American antiques. It had been done by a former First Lady, but Jane loved the look too much to change it, which was just as well. In an era of triple-digit deficits, the country didn't take kindly to lavish redecorating in the White House. This was not Camelot, although Jane rather wished it was. Not so much for the decor as the romance.

As Larry joined her in the bed, she thought about how little private time they had these days. They'd met when she was a political science major at San Jose State. He was running for state congress, and his visionary ideas had so impressed her that she'd volunteered to work on his campaign. The rest was history. He liked to joke privately that she was responsible for getting him elected and foisting him upon the American people, so she'd better not desert him, or them.

That was fifteen years ago, and despite the stresses of public life and interminable global conflict, they'd managed to endure, to stay close, and in love. That wasn't easy under any circumstances. Jane often fancied that their relationship had begun in another life and they'd been reborn for the sole purpose of building on the blueprint that they themselves had designed. Their paths were meant to cross and their lives to intertwine. He was meant to save her from herself. And she was meant to make him great.

A question intruded on her reflections. It didn't seem to be related, although perhaps it was the reference to greatness.

"What's happening with the Grace project?" she asked him, curious about the status of an appropriations bill that would fund groundbreaking work in biotechnology. A major lab held the patent to a cutting-edge concept called Smart Sand, and its CEO, David Grace, was one of Larry's biggest backers.

He hesitated, perhaps because of the mysterious smile that had curved her lips, despite the serious question she'd asked. She wanted to touch his naked chest, but then all would be lost, and there was much she needed to talk about before they gave in to their animal passions. But he was damn near irresistible in pajamas bottoms, and he knew she loved them.

They tried hard to please each other. That was the secret, in Jane's opinion. As simple as that. They paid attention, and they tried hard.

"To answer your question," he said, "it doesn't look good. Smart Sand and its *intelligent* microscopic sensors are a bit too exotic for this bunch. We polled the House, and the votes aren't there."

Jane wasn't terribly surprised. She feared the idea of brainy sensors that could form their own self-organized networks would come off as science fiction, despite its potential for things as varied as detecting forest fires and discouraging shoplifting. Another great idea ahead of its time.

"Is there anything you can do?"

He sighed. "If it were close, I could call in some favors."

To hide her concern, she plucked up a satin pillow and toyed with the tassels. "How will you deal with the fallout? This could cost you Grace's support, couldn't it?"

"The same way I always deal with fallout. I try to avoid getting clobbered by it, and I keep going. No matter what I do, someone is going to be unhappy. That's the reality I live with."

"What about all the rest?" she reminded him. "The ones who are happy. That's a lot of people."

He smiled. "I thought we were going to have sex?"

"I hope so." She tossed the pillow aside, revealing breasts that were quite wantonly exposed by the deep neckline. "Otherwise, why did I endure that carnal inspection of yours?"

Jane rarely thought back on her finishing school experience with gratitude in her heart, but she had learned a few tricks at the hands of the headmistress, and she wasn't averse to using them. Long ago, she'd swallowed her pride and coaxed her husband to reveal his secret fantasy woman, which had just happened to be a vampy torch singer with long blond hair, à la Michelle Pfeiffer in *The Fabulous Baker Boys*.

Jane already had the hair. She'd thanked her lucky stars for that and had sprung into action. She'd gone in search of slinky lingerie, compiled a collection of torch songs and painted her lips and her nails the hottest shade of red she could find. She'd listened to nothing but R&B for a week to get herself into the mood—and finally, when she was ready to vamp the fabulous Mr. Mantle, she'd invited him to her modest little apartment and met him at the door in transparent black lace.

She smiled, remembering how impressed he'd been with her visionary ideas. Tonight, she intended to remind him that the old girl still had some vamp in her. He was just where she wanted him, on his back. She rose up on all fours and swayed over him, a purring sound in her throat. He caught hold of her undulating hips as she dipped her head and let her hair swing free. It caressed his face.

"This is no lady," he murmured as she lowered her mouth to his and drank. Or rather sipped.

She wouldn't let him kiss her, and it seemed to drive him a little wild. She could see the fires dancing in his eyes, but she paid no attention, satisfying only herself with her whispering words and her teasing lips. She was moist and inviting. She nipped him like a playful cat would a plump catnip mouse.

He groaned in anguish when she slipped her tongue in his mouth.

Her fingers stole under the waistband of his pajama bottoms and found the swollen heat between his legs. One tender squeeze, and the beast came pulsing to life. His intentions were shockingly obscene, and he gave her no chance to object. She couldn't even find the breath to squeal before she was on her back.

Jane was grateful the rooms were soundproofed as her commander in chief unleashed every weapon in his arsenal. He used his hands and his tongue and his trusty staff to ravish her within an inch of her life. In military terms, he kicked ass. *What would the country think of their shy president now?* she wondered as she laced her arms and legs around him and spiraled into ecstasy. What would the world?

His climax was so violent it frightened her. Jane clung to him protectively, and only as his tremors gradually subsided did she allow herself to relax. He hadn't had any chest tightness in weeks, but she couldn't shake the fear that it might be something serious. She was being morbid, of course. Her herbal remedies were obviously helping, which was more evidence that it was stress-related.

Even now, she was reluctant to get up and break the lovely sense of quiet and peace that enveloped them. He was drifting off to sleep anyway, and as they lay in each other's arms, she thought about her life now, and how it was consumed with protecting him. Today in an interview she had jokingly taken the blame for his silver hair, saying she ought to be more soft-spoken and First Lady–like. He would worry less. Tomorrow she would find another way to shield him from any hint of criticism. But how was she going to protect him from her past? That had to be done at all cost.

Mattie had left her several messages that day, but Jane hadn't found a private moment to call her back, although she'd probably been avoiding it. Mattie wanted them to meet again, all of them and in person. She had something important to tell them, and it couldn't be done over the phone.

Jane didn't want to take that chance. The media stalked her like a celebrity, and she couldn't afford to trigger their suspicions. Her husband was at the peak of his powers. His popularity ratings were at an all-time high, and he was almost certain to be reelected, unless something unforeseen happened…such as his wife being accused of murder.

Mattie was somewhere in Washington, D.C., and that was all she knew. When Jane had returned her calls at 6:00 a.m. that morning, she'd already made arrangements for Mattie and Breeze to come to the country's capital. They'd been flown into Dulles International and limo'd into the depths of a government building, then met by John Bratton himself and escorted up several floors in a private elevator to this conference room.

Mattie hadn't been happy to see Bratton. Breeze had. She'd shamelessly applied her attractiveness theory, and Bratton had fallen all over himself to make them comfortable until Jane arrived. With a couple of phone calls, he'd had a wine and cheese basket delivered, in case either of them was hungry. And now he was watching Breeze nibble a chunk of Gruyère with the drooling concentration of a dog watching a filet being consumed.

Mattie sipped her Merlot. Cheese or not, she didn't like Bratton. She didn't like him at all.

A buzzer sounded, the panel door clicked and slid open, and Lady Jane entered. Without so much as a nod to Mattie or Breeze, she went straight to Bratton, who was standing guard in the corner, and conferred with him briefly. Mattie didn't like that, either.

"I'm sorry," Jane said, all smiles once Bratton had gone, "but I couldn't manage these meetings without him. John understands how important it is that my husband conserve his energy and stay focused these days, and this peccadillo of ours would only worry him, so John has agreed to help. I hope no one objects."

Mattie put her hands on the conference table. "He *knows* about our peccadillo?"

"No! I suggested it was a bit of awkwardness about a boyfriend from the distant past, and that I intended to take care of it without involving anyone else. Now, can we get started?"

She spun around one of the cushioned conference chairs, sat down and yanked at the cuffs of her suit. It was a clear signal to move on and Mattie had already decided to let it go. She had an admission of her own to make, but not quite yet. First, the bombshells, two—no, three of them.

She took another sip of wine, wondering if it was too early in the day to be drinking. She'd lost track of time in the mad rush to get here, and then there were the time zones. Breeze, who was already on her second glass of Chardonnay, was doodling erotic flowers on the cocktail napkin.

"I've become aware of evidence that was never presented at William Broud's trial," Mattie said, "and if I'm right, it could save our butts. The trouble is it's missing."

Jane twitched as if a wire had shorted out somewhere in her nervous system. Breeze stopped doodling.

"What are you talking about?" Jane said. "What is this evidence?"

"A videotape from Ms. Rowe's collection. It's been missing since the first trial."

"How do you know this?"

The old Jane was back, peppering Mattie with questions and drilling her with suspicious looks. Mattie's energy began to flow back. The dynamic between the three of them had always worked on the same principle as an engine, powered by gears and levers. It still did. If any one cog jammed, the entire mechanism failed.

"I spoke with Broud's attorney, and she was more than forthcoming."

Mattie gave them a quick recount of her conversation with Tansy Black, and then got right to the point. "When I asked her why she pursued habeas relief for Broud, she talked about the evidentiary problems in his trial, including this missing tape. I don't think she realized she was telling me what to look for. She didn't seem to know that she was talking to one of the lonely girls, or anything about us, in fact."

"Which probably means we're not named in any of the reports," Breeze said. "Interesting, since we were each grilled for hours."

"Maybe someone on the prosecution's team didn't want us to be named," Mattie offered. "Maybe he was a part of the ring."

Breeze clicked her tongue. "Or several *hes*."

Mattie glanced at Jane, who was rigidly silent and fingering the pearls at her throat. "And speaking of the sex ring," Mattie added, "there's no mention of it, either, which is also interesting, given that the tape is called Ms. Rowe's Private Social Registry."

Breeze was as animated as Jane was still. "You think she taped the men, her own clients? Maybe she intended to blackmail them. I wonder if her mystery lover is on that video, the one who gave her the gifts and the flowers."

Which brought Mattie to her second revelation. Her shoulder bag sat on the chair next to her. She unzipped it and drew out a manila envelope, from which she drew a tattered letter, held together by yellowed Scotch tape.

"We may not have the tape," she said, "but we have this—the letter she wrote to her lover."

Jane blinked in disbelief. "You still have that after all these years?"

Mattie allowed herself a pleased shrug. "I stash things under my mattress, remember? We can be grateful that your

Secret Service contingent neglected to rip my bed apart. Maybe I showed up before Bratton could get that far."

It had taken a bit of searching, but Mattie had found the letter in an envelope with some other memorabilia from her Rowe days, notes from the girls, birthday cards, all of which had been stashed under her mattresses over the years, from the creaky dorm bed she slept in at Rowe to the Serta Perfect Sleeper in her Sausalito beach house.

Mattie had originally found the torn-up letter in a wastebasket in Ms. Rowe's apartment while she was cleaning as punishment for one of her many transgressions. Later, she'd learned it wasn't Ms. Rowe who'd put it there, but that didn't matter now.

Breeze rose and came over for a look. "Does she refer to him by name?"

"No, but that's not the point." Mattie read the letter, which was only a few lines long. "'My cruel and unusual lover, you may as well have shot me and left me for dead. Why didn't you? It would have been kinder. How could you not mourn our tragic loss with me? How could you leave me at a time like that? More alone than I have ever been in my life. I gave you the most precious gift a woman can give a man, and you turned your back on me. I lie in bed at night, thinking of ways to hurt you, as if it might ease my agony.'"

It ended there, but the writer obviously wasn't done. She may have been interrupted—or too devastated to go on.

"Precious gift," Breeze said, musing aloud. "What would that have been? Sex? Her body?"

"Her heart," Mattie suggested, "except that she didn't have one. What about her tragic loss? That sounds like a child."

"Ms. Rowe didn't have one of those, either," Jane cut in sharply. "What is the point, Mattie? What does the letter prove without his name?"

"It proves she was enraged at the man and looking for

ways to hurt him. He may have killed her to shut her up. This is exhibit A, ladies. It gives the mystery lover a motive."

"Which doesn't do us much good unless we know who he is," Jane pointed out.

Breeze was walking, thinking. "I saw a note on some flowers once. They were long-stem red roses—I remember that—a huge bouquet of them, and the note was signed with initials. I think they were D-something, like D.C. or D.G."

Mattie didn't recognize either set of initials, but she made a mental note of them as she returned the letter to the envelope. "I'm going back to the school and find Ms. Rowe's Private Social Registry. I've cleared my calendar. It's already done."

"Sounds like a plan to me."

Breeze's agreement seemed to be the final straw for Jane. "Excuse me, ladies," she said, "but that's a ridiculous idea. How do you plan to find this videotape? Go to the nearest haystack?"

Mattie smiled. Mysteriously, she hoped. "Maybe I have an idea where it is."

"After twenty years? You can't do this, Mattie. It will look suspicious and draw attention to all of us. You think Cross won't notice you're snooping around? He still lives there."

"Let the detective find it," Breeze suggested. "That's why you hired him, isn't it?"

Jane let out a soft gasp, and Mattie whirled on Breeze. "How did you know I hired a detective?"

Breeze lifted a shoulder. "Well, you did, didn't you?"

Jane was out of her chair now. "What detective? We agreed not to do that because it was too risky."

Mattie was getting a little tired of Jane's high-wire act. "I would trust the man with my life," she said, putting steely emphasis on the last word. "He got me some information about Cross, and that's as far as it went. You involved Bratton without telling us."

"Why can't we just let this thing die?" Jane pleaded. "If this Tansy Black person didn't find anything, then Cross certainly won't. He'll get bored and go away, unless you make him think we have something to hide."

"There's more," Mattie said. She didn't want to frighten either of them, but Jane stubbornly persisted in thinking that this could go away.

"William Broud was Jameson Cross's brother," she explained, "and Cross is out for revenge. He has a journal his brother wrote in prison that names all three of us as the lonely girls and accuses us of killing her. I don't know what else it says, but he seems determined to prove that we killed both of them—Ms. Rowe and his brother—and that we were the architects of some massive conspiracy to frame his brother."

"Good God," Jane breathed, sinking into her chair, "this is a nightmare."

Mattie sipped some wine to clear her throat. "If there's a tape out there, I want to get to it before someone else does, namely him. If anyone asks me what I'm doing, I'll say I'm giving a speech for the school's Distinguished Alumni Series."

"Or investigating the possibility of funding a scholarship for some deserving student," Breeze said, clearly thrilled by the idea. "You might even run into some of our classmates, those darlings, the Death Squad."

Mattie wasn't aware that she was smiling until Jane spoke up.

"Mattie, this isn't a revenge thing, is it? If you want to confront your tormentors, do it on your own time, all right? Some of us have a lot to lose."

Mattie didn't like that at all. "You don't think I have anything to lose? You'd rather stick your head in the sand until it's too late to do anything. That's far more dangerous than what I'm suggesting."

"Wait a minute." Apparently Breeze had another idea. She was out of her chair, everything bouncing, blond hair, breasts and the flouncy skirt of her wraparound dress as she walked and thought aloud.

"Cross is our problem, right?" she said. "If he goes away, the problem goes away. Why not bargain with Cross himself? Everyone has a price. I'd be happy to meet with him and find out what it is."

"Oh, brilliant," Jane said, "then he can put it in his book that we tried to bribe him with sex. You do have a point about his price, however. We have resources between us."

Mattie couldn't believe her two cohorts. They really did sound desperate—and dangerous. "Now we're buying him off?" she said. "A cover-up? Recent history should tell you what happens when famous people try to cover their tracks. Does Bill Clinton ring any chimes? Martha Stewart?"

Jane was up, too, her hands clasped at her chest. "Mattie, please leave it alone. If they should find out what we did— if anyone finds out—it's all over."

Mattie only wished she *could* leave it alone, but it was far too late for that. And even though the other two didn't realize it, she wasn't asking their permission. She was going back to Rowe Academy whether they wanted her to or not.

Tansy Black was easier to find than Jameson had expected. She had a small no-frills office in one of the adjunct buildings to the law school on the Stanford campus, and no staff that he could see. Not even a receptionist to run interference.

No one answered the closed door when he knocked, but he could hear voices coming from inside. Possibly she was on the phone. He tried the knob and found it open. Nothing ventured, nothing gained. He just hoped he wouldn't be shot. He'd heard that one would be wise to wear body armor around Ms. Black.

"Am I interrupting?" he said, speaking to the dark dish mop of hair that was buried in a computer laptop screen.

She whipped her glasses off and looked up, bristling. "Who let you in?"

"I'm Jameson—"

"I know who you are, Mr. Cross. I read."

"Ah…good." He hesitated, smiled. "Are you busy?"

"Do I *look* busy?"

Take a breath, Jameson. He'd expected the surly personality, but not the angelic face. Her eyes were magnificent, as black and melting as a doe's, her skin was fair and her jawline delicate. Based on her background, he'd prepared himself for Holly Hunter on steroids, but she was more Winona Ryder, before the shoplifting debacle.

"Mr. Cross, why are you here?"

Interesting husky voice. Another incongruity, but interesting. "I'd like a word with you, Ms. Black."

She slammed the laptop lid shut. "Don't make me say it again. Your brother asked me not to—"

"My brother's *dead*," Jameson practically shouted.

Her lovely frowning features registered some surprise.

Jameson continued in a calmer tone. "The day *before* Billy died he called me and said he wanted to talk. We had an appointment, but when I got to his hotel, I found his body. He was going to tell me the whole story, Ms. Black. And he would have if someone hadn't killed him."

That got him a spark of interest. She laced her fingers, studying him. "What whole story is that?"

"Who was threatening him? Who were the men in the sex ring? And who were the students who killed the headmistress, the lonely girls?"

"That's a lot of questions."

"Got any answers?"

"I'm afraid not. Your brother was innocent, and I'm glad I didn't give up until I proved it. That's *all* I know."

"Who killed him?"

Her face flushed a deep red. With anger? He couldn't tell.

"Why are you asking *me*, Mr. Jameson?" she said. "I'm the one who got him out of jail. Where the hell were the people who loved him? Where the hell were you?"

Jameson had no answer for her. Nor did he find it easy to hold her gaze. Her melting black eyes weren't doelike anymore. They were seeringly hot, embers ready to burst. The rumors were true. He should have worn his body armor.

25

"**I**'m pleased to announce that my family's heirlooms have been recovered and returned to the display case in the reception room, where they belong."

Millicent Rowe spoke from the assembly hall lectern in a clear, crisp voice, enunciating as if this were an elocution lesson. Jane had learned that everything Ms. Rowe did was a lesson, although she couldn't figure out why the entire student body had been summoned for an announcement about heirlooms that Jane hadn't known were missing, and had already been recovered.

Jane had more pressing things on her mind. She'd thought Ms. Rowe's announcement was going to be about Mattie, who'd sworn she was going to run away last night, and who hadn't come to the door this morning when Jane knocked. Jane hoped Mattie had changed her mind because of her injuries, and had decided to sleep in. She hadn't seen any sign of Ivy or Breeze, either. Maybe they were sleeping in, too.

And now, with all this unnecessary talk of heirlooms, Jane wished *she'd* stayed in bed. At least then she wouldn't have to think about her next interview, which she dreaded, even though after the last one, Ms. Rowe had taken her aside for a pep talk and promised to make her fatally fascinating, a femme fatale.

Jane didn't believe she had the fascinating gene, and she didn't think of herself as a particularly good actress, certainly not like Breeze, but she had resolved that she would learn how to fake it. Somehow, she would learn. Otherwise, her life promised to be nothing but one deeply humiliating experience after another with the opposite sex.

"I sincerely wish I didn't have to make the next announcement."

Ms. Rowe's bell-like projection interrupted Jane's thoughts. The headmistress seemed uptight this morning. Shrill, even.

"Rowe Academy," the headmistress said, "has never found it necessary to subject its students to invasive security measures, but we are now forced to change our policies. We won't be resorting to metal detectors, but students *will* be required to submit to random searches—and all because two of our own have disgraced themselves by showing complete disregard for personal property and for the law."

The thieves were students? Jane sat forward, really listening for the first time. She'd taken a seat by herself in a back row, but now she didn't want to miss a word.

The hall had begun to buzz, and the headmistress raised a hand, asking for silence. "We have common thieves in this school, I'm sad to say. Perhaps I should have let the police deal with them, but I don't believe in passing the buck. These students violated their school's ethical code, and their school should mete out the punishment. It's only fitting, in my opinion."

Jane glanced around the hall, trying to find her friends. She had a bad feeling about what was coming. Could it be a coincidence that Mattie was supposed to have sneaked out last night, and this morning they were hearing about stolen heirlooms? But Jane couldn't leave without being seen by Ms. Rowe and the staff.

"Matilda Smith and Ivy White have repeatedly mocked our rules," Ms. Rowe said. "You don't see them here among you today because as part of their punishment, they are being shunned. They've been confined to their rooms and will not take part in any campus activities, except for their classes. Until further notice, you are forbidden to look at them or speak to them. They have stolen from me—and from you. They are pariahs, and I want everyone in this school to treat them as such."

Jane didn't know what to do. She wanted to dash out the door before the crowd, but she couldn't move from her seat. An icy state of disbelief had overtaken her. Unable to look at the other students, she sat there as they filed out. When she did glance up, she saw that they weren't looking at her, either.

She expected sneers and hateful looks, but they walked by her as if she didn't exist. She could feel the poison emanating from them. They loathed her and her friends, but their gazes were locked on the door that would take them outside. They were shunning her, too, she realized. None of them would look at her, not even the staff.

She waited for Ms. Rowe to go by, hoping that the headmistress would glance her way and reassure her that this wasn't about her. But when Ms. Rowe made her exit, she walked briskly past Jane, never slowing down or acknowledging her in any way. Jane almost called out her name, but she had the feeling Ms. Rowe's disdain would turn her into a pillar of salt.

Jane had never felt more hated or cast aside. Even her life at home didn't compare to this. She was torn, ripped apart by a terrible impulse. She wanted to run after Ms. Rowe and apologize, beg her forgiveness, do anything to be in her good graces again. But how could she do that to Mattie?

* * *

Breeze opened the door to her dorm room and peeked out. The hallway was pitch-black. Earlier that evening, while everyone was at dinner, she'd loosened all the bulbs in the wall sconces on her floor, hoping the floor mistress would think a fuse had blown and not bother to check the bulbs. The school handyman took care of such things, and he wouldn't be back until tomorrow morning, which gave Breeze plenty of time.

It seemed to have worked. The house rules required students to be in their rooms by ten. Lights out at eleven. It was now a quarter after eleven, and the hallway was empty. And dark.

Barefooted and in her pajamas, Breeze darted down the hall to Mattie's room. She'd been stunned when Jane told her what happened at assembly this morning, but she couldn't convince Jane to come with her tonight. Jane hadn't wanted to talk about it, although she'd warned Breeze that she would be shunned, too. None of the students would talk to her. Breeze sensed that Jane was devastated by what was happening, but for Breeze it would hardly change anything. They all hated her anyway. She was too pretty, too boy-crazy, too something.

Mattie's door was locked, but Breeze managed to open it with an old-fashioned hairpin, a trick most of the students had mastered to avoid locking themselves out of their rooms.

She entered the alcove, feeling her way along the wall. It was pitch-black inside Mattie's room, too. She couldn't even see the window by the bed, which meant the curtains must have been pulled, probably to block the moonlight. Mattie never shut the curtains. Had someone else done that?

Breeze was afraid to call her friend's name. Not sure what she was dealing with, she carefully made her way across the room. Mattie always had a pile of clothing somewhere around, and she didn't want to trip. *Shit!* She rapped her shin against something and winced at the pain. It was the bed frame. She bent close to investigate, but couldn't see anything that looked like a human form. The covers were smooth. It didn't feel as if the bed had been slept in.

Had they taken Mattie away? Killed her already?

Breeze wished she could turn on a light, but it would show under the door and be spotted immediately. She stepped back and heard the floorboard creak. Terrified, she whirled and saw someone coming at her. She scrambled up on the bed, grabbed the window curtain and ripped it off the wall, taking the rod with it. She heaved the entire thing at her attacker, who dodged and batted it away.

Moonlight flooded through the window, revealing a ghost-white face.

"What are *you* doing here?" Breeze whispered, shaken to the core.

Mattie jerked awake at the noise. She was hidden behind the clothing hanging in her armoire. Despite the pain of her cracked ribs, she'd curled up in the small space, hugging the lug wrench to her stiff, aching body. It would have been suicidal to sleep in her own bed. She'd been expecting Ms. Rowe or the Death Squad, and now, here they were.

She opened the cabinet door a crack and looked out. She could make out two people in her room, and from the noises she'd heard, they'd been fighting. The one she could see was Breeze. The other one was going to get hit over the head with a lug wrench, if Mattie could get out of the damn armoire.

Every move was torturous, like crawling on broken glass. She fought back tears, dragging herself around until she was sitting up. But when her feet touched the floor, and she tried to stand, her legs wouldn't hold her. She collapsed in a heap, and a groan shook out of her.

She heard gasps, a scream, and when she opened her eyes, she saw Breeze crouching over her.

"Are you okay, Mattie?"

"Do I look okay?" Mattie growled.

"No, you look like hell."

"There's someone else in here." Mattie craned around to see who was hiding behind Breeze. "You were fighting with somebody. I saw her."

"It's me." Jane's pinched face came into view. "Breeze and I," she said, a funny catch in her voice, "we're here to— Hell, I don't know why we're here, to support you, I guess."

"I don't want your damn support," Mattie said as emphatically as she could. "Now, get out of here. *Vacate*. You guys aren't supposed to be here anyway. Nobody's supposed to talk to me or Ivy. They're not even supposed to look at us."

"We know." Jane heaved a huge sigh. "Ms. Rowe announced it at assembly. Come on, Breeze. Let's get her to the bed where she can lie down."

"You're not touching me!" Mattie curled into a position to kick at them, if they tried. It would kill her, but she was very serious about not moving. "I'm staying right here on the floor. I can lie down just fine."

Breeze dropped next to Mattie like a hound from hell, her face contorting in a ferocious scowl. "We're not going anywhere, you nasty, bad-tempered little witch, and you can't make us."

"Get out of here," Mattie croaked. "Go, please. I'm sick of people getting hurt because of me, and there's nothing you can do to help!"

"That's too fucking bad, isn't it?" Breeze jabbed back. "Now, shut up and tell us what happened last night. Did you and Ivy actually run away?"

Mattie collapsed with a groan of helpless agony. She was tired of hurting. Hell, she was tired of living. But these two lunatics weren't going anywhere. She could see that. They were going to torture her until they found out what happened last night, no matter how risky it was for them to be here. Rowe really would kill them all.

Mattie didn't understand how she could have fucked up everything this badly. She even had totally stupid friends.

"Mattie," Breeze snarled.

"All right," Mattie whispered, defeated. "We went to the police station in Tiburon." Somehow, she got through the rest of it, everything that had happened, including having seen the man with the gold cuff links.

Jane knelt next to Breeze, the two of them hovering like vultures.

"Did you and Ivy steal Ms. Rowe's heirlooms?" Jane asked. "What were you going to do? Hock them?"

"I didn't steal anything." Mattie desperately wanted to push them away from her, but she couldn't find the strength. "She planted them in our backpacks. Or maybe they were never stolen at all. Maybe they were in the display case the entire time, and she just told that story to scare us. Who'd ever know? And what the hell difference does it make now?"

She tried to sound savage. "Are you guys going to go or not?"

"Not," Jane said, her voice taking on conviction.

"You'd have to kill us first," Breeze muttered.

Mattie collapsed again. She couldn't fight the two of them. She didn't have the strength, and it wasn't right of them to take advantage of her this way. Damn, stupid idiots. She hated them.

She turned her face to the floor, fire in every blink of her eyelashes.

Jane seemed unaware of Mattie's breakdown. "I'll bet you anything that man with the cuff links and Ms. Rowe are in cahoots," she said. "He's probably the one who called her and told her that you and Ivy were there."

Mattie felt a surge of helpless rage. "That bastard let Ms. Rowe come and get us. He had to know what she was doing to us, and he still let her bring us back here."

"Of course, he knows," Jane said. "Do think he'd save your ass over his own? He's as guilty as Ms. Rowe, the pervert."

Mattie pushed up to her elbows, breathing hard. She had it in mind to try and stand, but she didn't get that far. The pain brought her to her knees. "Damn, shit, *fuck,*" she said, "I'm no good to anybody like this."

"Come here." Jane reached out to help Mattie up, and Mattie let her this time. With Jane supporting her weight, she got to her feet, and the two of them hobbled to the bed.

"Look what that bitch Rowe did to you," Jane said softly, sitting next to Mattie on the bed. "Somebody should kill her."

Suddenly Breeze rose to her full height in the gloomy dorm room, an avatar of justice. Her blond hair gleamed white. "*We* should kill her. We should all kill her and take the blame together."

"Like *Murder on the Orient Express?*" Jane said.

"Like murder, fire and sudden death at Rowe Academy."

Jane laughed. "Has a nice ring to it."

Mattie was beginning to feel a little better when the floor creaked again. She glanced at the door, but it hadn't opened. It sounded as if there was someone else in the room, but the shadows kept her from seeing into every nook and corner.

All three of them went silent.

"Who's there?" she asked.

Ivy crept out of an alcove near the door, her face flushed with heat. "Let me do it," she said. "Let me kill her."

No one responded, but there was something in Ivy's eyes that terrified Mattie. She had never seen her friend look like this before, so strong and determined. She'd never seen such resolve. Ivy had come back to life. Gentle, timid Ivy was bursting with life.

Mattie wondered if she should be relieved. Ivy had been withdrawn and listless for weeks. Anything that revived her was good, wasn't it? Even this? But Mattie was torn with conflicting emotions—fear and wonder, excitement and icy dread—and the strongest feeling rising from the quagmire of her feelings was a sense of impending doom.

It wasn't just resolve she saw in Ivy. It was deadly resolve.

One week later

Mattie awoke to a thundering noise in the hallway outside her dorm room. She fumbled for her battered Timex on the bedside table. Two-thirty in the morning? Much too early for the breakfast rush, but it did sound like a stampede.

She sat up gingerly. She was still tender in places, but she'd been up and around for a few days, and she'd returned to her classes. The ribs were mostly healed, as she'd predicted.

She could hear shouts outside.

"What happened?" someone called out. "Was there an accident?"

She felt the pain in her knee as she got out of bed and pulled on her robe. Lights spiraled across the ceiling of her room. They came from the window. She was on the fifth floor, and there were fire trucks down in the school's driveway. She hadn't heard the alarm ring or the trucks drive in.

Her door flew open and Jane burst in. "Mattie, come on, hurry! The paramedics are here. They're on our floor!"

"What happened?"

"I don't know. Come on!"

Mattie winced as Jane grabbed her hand and dragged her along. "I can't go that fast," Mattie protested, "my knee!" But

Jane didn't seem to hear. She was heaving like an exhausted runner.

Breeze was outside in the hallway, waiting for them.

Mattie took one look down the corridor and froze. Now she understood Jane's panic. Paramedics were streaming in and out of one of the dorm rooms. Mattie had never seen so many of them.

"It's Ivy," Jane whispered.

Not Ivy. Not *Ivy!* Those words echoed until they became a scream in Mattie's head.

Jane wanted to go down there and find out what had happened. Maybe Ivy was okay, she argued. But Mattie couldn't do it. She allowed very little to frighten her, but she had no control over this. Terror had gripped her like a knife to her throat. Something bad had happened to Ivy, and she couldn't let it in. She didn't want to know, ever. It would kill her.

Within moments the paramedics had roped the area off and asked the cluster of students and teachers to disperse. A group of girls came whispering back down the hallway toward Mattie, Jane and Breeze, but none of the girls would look at them. They weren't being shunned, Mattie realized. Something terrible had just happened.

Mattie's stomach lurched. She let out a low moan and Breeze gripped her hand, squeezing so hard it took Mattie's breath away. Pain. She welcomed it.

One of the approaching girls announced to her friends, "She's dead, poor thing. I saw them put the sheet over her head."

"Did she kill herself?" another asked.

"Yes," the first girl answered, "one of the paramedics said it was suicide."

A third girl chimed in. "I heard it, too. She overdosed."

Mattie shook her head. *Suicide? Ivy? No. I don't believe it.*

Jane grabbed Mattie's other hand, and three of them clutched each other in stunned silence.

Mattie didn't know who said what after that, but for the rest of her days, she would remember that the hushed words the three of them spoke had become prophetic.

"Goddamn her to hell! She killed herself?"

"I don't believe it. Ivy was depressed, but she wouldn't do that to herself. She wouldn't do it to *us*."

"I don't believe it, either. It was that evil bitch of a headmistress. Look, do you see her anywhere around? Where is she? Why isn't she here?"

"It was Rowe."

"Now we *have* to kill her."

Breeze had just ripped out every page of her Latin textbook, but it wasn't enough. She was surrounded by piles of shredded paper, and now she wanted to break everything in the room that could be broken.

She looked around the room, searching for something precious to destroy. If she didn't rip it all apart, everything that meant anything to her, then she would rip herself apart.

Ivy was gone. Ivy had nothing. Why did Breeze Wheeler deserve to have anything? Why did she deserve to live?

She swung around in a circle, desperate. She saw the gold bangle she'd been given by one of Ms. Rowe's men. She snapped it in two and threw it in the trash. Next, she swept the cheap glass lamp from her bedstand, flinching as it shattered on the hardwood floor. What else could she break?

When it was all over, she sat in the midst of the debris and stared at the blood on her hands, watching it run with the splash of a single tear. The anger was gone, but she wondered if the deep, lacerating ache ever would be.

26

Mattie was surprised at the beauty. She could remember only fear and ugliness, but a golden spire split the clouds overhead, haloing the campus in sunlight. She'd expected to feel revulsion, but it was burning sadness that rose inside her as she followed the tree-lined paths that rambled through groves of ferns and feathery greenbelts.

Summers here had been her favorite time. Ms. Rowe was usually away on sabbatical and with the day students gone it had felt like the campus belonged to the scholarship girls. Only Ivy had a home to go back to. She lived somewhere in the Napa Valley, but she never spoke of her family, not to anyone.

Mattie almost didn't mind having nowhere else to go. The long break was serene and hopeful, the way all her time at Rowe Academy should have been. It was the people, not the building or the grounds, she reminded herself. People made things ugly.

Raindrops brought her out of her reflections. One splashed on her cheek. Another hit her eyelash. The air smelled of dust from the paths, the way it did before a rainstorm. When the sky opened up, the grounds would get a good soaking, and everything would reek wonderfully of wet dirt and sweet green grass.

Mattie's senses mercilessly tugged her back, torturing her

with pleasure and pain. How would she deal with this? Memories would flood her, and she feared she wouldn't be able to handle them, even the good ones. Perhaps the good ones would hurt the most because they were so few and so precious, each a tiny diamond, bright and sparkling, chopped out of black carbon. A tiny diamond, sharp enough to cut.

Stop, Mattie, or this will overwhelm you. You're here to find the videotape, not reminisce.

She put her head down and dashed across a gravel parking lot toward the halls and buildings that surrounded the courtyard. The layout rather reminded her of a Norman fortress, but the flourishes were gothic, and today she was headed for the one with the corner bell tower, Steuben Hall.

She slowed to a walk as she entered the courtyard. It still felt too close for comfort here. Gray stone monoliths surrounded her on every side, looming guardians that blocked the light. Her legs grew heavy as she approached the crumbling brick tower where the headmistress had lived.

The slower she went the faster the rain came down.

From somewhere behind her drifted the coo of a mourning dove. Desolate, that sound. She'd never seen the bird, but she'd heard the haunting cry every day of her four years here. It couldn't be the same bird. Not twenty years later.

Her silk blouse and linen slacks were drenched by the time she reached the steps of Steuben Hall. She should have worn a jacket. She'd lived in the Bay area all her life, and nothing about the weather could be predicted, except its unpredictability. Her bare feet squished around in the spectator pumps that Breeze had insisted she wear.

A burst of white light confused her. She backed into the courtyard and saw lightning fork overhead. The jagged blue spikes dragged her thoughts all the way back to a suffocating crawl space in the attic of this tower, where a fourteen-year-old girl waited to be electrocuted at any second, and tried not to choke on her own bloody tongue.

Mattie wet her lips. Her vision went gray and spotty.

She turned and walked out of the courtyard, stiff with horror. When she reached the gravel lot, she broke into a run, heading for the only refuge she knew, the dark forest of pines that bordered the campus. As soon as she entered the forest, the branches formed a canopy above her, concealing her from view, and a bed of fallen needles muffled her footsteps. The abandoned toolshed was only a short distance, ramshackle black against the ashy gray trees. Relief nearly brought her to her knees when she saw it.

She jogged toward it, unsteady on her feet, and opened the door to one of the few places she'd felt safe at Rowe Academy. It was dark and dirty, a third-world hut, but three young girls had taken refuge here and forged a sisterhood strong enough to endure forces that could have crushed them otherwise.

She almost expected to see her friends waiting for her, huddled around a rusty barbeque grill, fanning a blaze made from dried pine cones. They'd papered the windows with newsprint to keep out the prying eyes, but allow a bit of daylight to filter through. Still, it was gloomy and dank—the perfect place to foment rebellion and revenge.

Her friends weren't here, of course, but she wasn't alone. There were ghosts in the room, ghosts everywhere she looked. She could see scratches etched in the cement floor that might have been writing and wondered if they were her own hieroglyphics. A wheelbarrow, tipped on its side, was nearly overgrown with ivy, and the voices whispering in her head were speaking of rites of purification and acts of desperation. They were whispering of things a young girl could never imagine herself doing.

Rowe Academy
Winter 1981

"We can't all be involved. It's too dangerous. The oldest should do it, and that's me."

Fourteen-year-old Lady Jane spoke with all the authority of her few months' advantage over the other two girls. A car coat draped over her shoulders, she sat cross-legged in a wheelbarrow that didn't look sturdy enough to hold her, but had become her throne.

"I'll write you in reform school," Breeze said. Wrapped in a blanket she'd smuggled from the dorm, she looked peaked and not at all happy to be there. Plotting murders wasn't Breeze's idea of fun, and Ivy's death had shaken her to the core. Breeze wasn't breezy anymore. She seemed sickened by the horrific turn of events, and it was affecting her ability to eat and sleep.

"I'll send toilet paper." Mattie barely noticed the chilly air as she crouched on the grimy floor, her plaid school skirt tucked under her butt. She madly scratched her thoughts into the cement, using the sharp end of a scale pulled from a pine cone.

"Very funny," Jane said. "I suppose one of *you* is going to kill her?"

Mattie kept writing. The ideas burning in her brain were brilliant. She didn't know where they were coming from, but they were so good it wouldn't have surprised her if they'd been sent by the devil. Her hand was cramping, but she couldn't stop.

"We agreed we'd all do it," Mattie told her. "If we're going to reform school, let's go together."

"Oh, you'll go," Jane informed her in a haughty tone. "You're here, planning the murder with me. That's conspiracy, and it carries the same penalty as the crime itself."

"How do you know so much?"

Breeze had asked the question, and Jane shot her a withering look. "Somebody around here has to know something."

"Stop bickering." Mattie rose and tucked the pinecone scale in her hair, as if it were a pencil. "We're going to do it together," she said. "It can be done, and we're going to do it, but it has to be all three of us or nothing."

The other two spoke as one. "How?"

"First, we take a vow of loyalty and solidarity, our very own oath of *omerta,* just like in *The Godfather.* We're doing this to avenge Ivy and to stop Ms. Rowe from killing anyone else, like one of us. Is that agreed?"

They both nodded, rapt at this point.

Mattie reached down and tugged up her knee-high stockings. She hated it when they bunched around her ankles, but rubber bands cut off her circulation. "Okay," she said, "so we have to do it right. We have to make it look like she could have done it herself."

"How do we do that?"

"We attack her on three fronts, the very things we hate most about her. Her phony airs, her disgusting immorality and her vanity."

"Disgusting immorality?" Breeze brightened.

Jane looked intrigued, too. "Tell us more."

"All in good time," Mattie said, enjoying the chance to be mysterious. "First, let's take the sacred oath. Come on. Get up, you two. I know it's silly, but we have to hold hands."

The others rose and they formed a ring. Mattie took the lead, solemnly promising to protect her sisters to the death and to take to the grave with her any words uttered in this shed. *"Trica juncta in uno,"* she said. *"Amicus usque ad aras."*

The other two repeated the oath, and when they were done, Mattie looked up. "Is that good enough?"

"No," Jane said, "we should take a final test of courage, and then we should ask for protection." She released Mattie's hand and dug a tiny vial from the pocket of her jeans.

Mattie saw the heartwine and felt an icy tingle of fear that took her back to when their tests of courage had started. It was during their second year at Rowe, a few months after Ms. Rowe returned from her summer sabbatical in Europe, an embittered woman. None of the girls had wanted to meet with the headmistress's "friends," the men she'd been grooming them for, especially when it became clear that these men would expect sexual favors, but Ms. Rowe had found the most terrifying ways to cajole and threaten them into it.

One evening Ivy had blurted that she didn't want some horrible man touching her, and the other girls had chimed in, but Ms. Rowe had hushed them, promising to show them a miracle that would change their minds. She'd filled an eyewash glass with a clear liquid from a perfume bottle, and then she'd set the glass on an open windowsill, along with some pumpkin seeds.

They all watched in silence as she carried the Victorian birdcage with her pet parakeet to the window, set it on the sill and opened the door. The bird made its awkward way out of the cage and went straight for the pumpkin seeds, devouring the feast. It then dipped its beak into the glass, drank its fill and dropped over dead.

Ms. Rowe had searched the girls' faces with her emerald-green eyes. "You see how quickly things can change? Mere moments ago my precious pet was in his cage without a thought of anything but his next meal. I think the lesson here is take nothing for granted, ladies. Nothing."

None of the girls had harbored any doubt about the lesson that evening. A bird had been sacrificed before their eyes, and they were no more safe than it had been, or so she wanted them to think. That was when they'd begun stealing vials of heartwine from Ms. Rowe's stash and taking it in small doses to build an immunity. They'd rubbed it into the skin of their hands and face as she'd taught them to do for cosmetic purposes, and then they'd sipped from the vial, tiny amounts at first, not even enough to kill a bird.

Today, Jane didn't bother with her hands and face. She sucked down some of the poison and grimaced, handing the vial to Breeze, who did the same. As Mattie drank hers, she wondered why they weren't dead yet—and why Ivy's immunity hadn't saved her.

"Wait, I have this," Breeze said, showing them a red ringlet of hair that she had tucked in her blouse pocket. "The night Ivy died, I asked one of the paramedics for a lock of hair to remember her by. He told me he couldn't, but the next day he brought me this. Maybe we can use it, too?"

Jane nodded. She gripped their hands and spoke in a husky voice. "In the ancient tradition of Greek mythology, this lock of our slain sister's hair will make us invulnerable to all attacks. As we strive to give meaning to her death, we humbly offer ourselves to Artemis, the huntress, protector of young women, who will watch over us and guide us in our battles."

"Artemis," they all murmured.

"One last thing." Mattie drew the pinecone scale from her hair and showed them the needle-sharp point. "We're going to need some blood."

Trying not to wince, Mattie plunged the point into her thumb pad on the theory that removing bandages hurts less when you do it fast. It hurt like hell. The other two watched, eyes widening as a bubble of nearly black blood formed.

"Now you," she said, handing the scale to Breeze, who swayed forward in a near faint before she caught herself. That was when Mattie began to worry about the perfection of her three-pronged plan.

* * *

Jane crept up the spiral stairway in her bare feet. She didn't dare make a sound, and shoes were treacherous. Ms. Rowe was supposed to be at a staff meeting in the admin building, and Jane had no reason to think there would be anyone else in her apartment in the middle of the morning, but she didn't like taking unnecessary risks. Shoes could give you away quicker than a sneeze.

She'd let herself in with the key hidden behind a loose piece of wall baseboard. Ms. Rowe had told her four lonely girls where to find it in case a VIP client requested an unscheduled date. That would have been arranged through Ms. Rowe, of course. The men weren't allowed to make their own dates. Nor would they ever have been that anxious to meet with Jane. Obviously.

The men could either observe the girls in the courtyard and take their pick or choose from snapshots Ms. Rowe had taken of each girl. Jane thought of them as their "Lolita" pictures, and she considered hers quite exotic, but it hadn't helped get her chosen. She'd been relieved at first, but it wasn't long before doubts crept in, and she'd begun to wonder what she was doing wrong.

She was too stiff, according to Ms. Rowe, not the type important men fantasized about. The news hadn't surprised Jane much, considering what her stepmother had forecasted. No, Jane had not been surprised about her lack of appeal—or that it was Breeze who was requested the most. Breeze seemed to glory in the bewildering power she had over the opposite sex, even if she didn't understand it. Ivy had been popular, too, but she had locked herself in her dorm room afterward, refusing to talk about it with anyone. And Mattie spit on any man who got near her. She may have been the only smart one of the group.

As Jane slipped up the stairs, she glanced down at Ms.

Rowe's apartment. The living room, which Ms. Rowe called a salon, took up one entire floor of the tower so that she could "entertain properly." She'd decorated the spherical area with pieces of real Chippendale and Sheraton, genuine Tiffany lamps and Oriental screens. Turkish rugs adorned the hardwood floor, and in the corner by the window, her potted Judas tree was in full bloom, its rich pink blossoms hanging on glossy, naked brown branches.

Jane knew the details because every year the headmistress gave the incoming class a tour as part of their education on appreciating the finer things in life. She told them the story of the Judas tree, probably as a cautionary tale, but Jane had sensed the myth's personal meaning when Ms. Rowe explained how the tree's pure white blooms had gone pink with shame after Judas had hanged himself from one of its branches.

Now the room looked undisturbed, much to Jane's relief. Breeze had already been here and carried out her part of Mattie's plan, despite a bad case of the shakes. She'd been exultant and near tears afterward when she'd found Jane on the campus. "I did it," she whispered. "I did it. She's not going to hurt anyone else."

Breeze's passion had actually helped Jane with her own uncertainties. And Breeze's timing had been perfect, too. She'd had a great excuse for skipping morning classes. Everyone knew she hadn't been feeling well, so she'd gone to the infirmary first thing, and the nurse had immediately excused her and sent her back to her room to rest. Once classes started she'd been able to slip across the courtyard—unseen, Jane hoped—and into the tower.

Jane had drawn yard duty this week, which meant picking up litter on the grounds and gave her a reason to be out wandering around now. Her next class was in Ogden Hall, the science building, and she would have to move fast to get back there. Mattie's excuse was almost karmic in its perfection. Cleaning the apartment during sixth-period study hall was one of her punishments for stealing and breaking school rules.

Ms. Rowe's bedroom was on the third floor, just above the living room. Once Jane climbed the last flight and entered the room that the headmistress called her black satin boudoir, she had no trouble finding the facial mister. She and the other girls had been there many times for coaching sessions with Ms. Rowe. Jane had actually enjoyed some of those sessions, especially when Ms. Rowe talked about grooming and makeup.

The girls had been fascinated when she prepared her exotic herbal beauty-and-health remedies. They'd all felt proud and special at having been singled out for her personal attention, until she'd sprung her grand plan on them, and everything had changed after that.

Jane fished disposable rubber gloves from her skirt pocket and pulled them on. Next, she took a small test tube of clear liquid from the same pocket, uncapped it and poured it in the mister's reservoir. She used the tube to give the mixture a swish, and then she closed the reservoir, hoping that Ms. Rowe didn't change the water every morning before she used it.

She was intimately familiar with Ms. Rowe's morning ablutions, as she called them. The headmistress had entertained them with stories about her mystery lover, a man who visited her one morning a week. Her preparations had included a cup of herbal tea made from honey and lilac water. She'd even perfumed the water in her facial mister and used a special vaginal lubricant that smelled and tasted of peaches, his favorite scent.

Breeze had already poisoned the lilac water that would be used for the tea. Now Jane had done the mister, leaving Mattie to take care of the vaginal lubricant. Jane smiled. Mattie had lost the coin toss.

As long as Ms. Rowe followed her normal routine tomorrow morning, she should get enough heartwine to bring down a whole flock of birds. *Consider it revenge for the parakeet, too,* she thought. And since Ms. Rowe used heartwine on a daily basis anyway, no one would know she hadn't accidentally overdone it. That's what the girls were counting on.

Ms. Rowe's tricks were about to do her in.

That was Mattie's brilliant idea.

Jane pulled off her gloves and put them back in her pocket, aware that nothing about this felt quite real to her. It seemed like a good prank more than anything else, and honestly, she didn't expect the headmistress to get as much as a sore throat from all the heartwine. You couldn't kill people like Ms. Rowe. They weren't human. They had evil powers and black magic. They didn't die like everyone else, like Ivy.

No one was really going to die. Not really.

They just desperately wanted her to.

The room got so bright it made Jane dizzy. The floor tilted beneath her feet, and she touched the vanity to steady herself. If she dwelled on all this, she might change her mind and undo everything that had been done. And she couldn't do that. They'd all sworn to go through with it. She'd taken a vow.

Get out of here, Jane. Take the spiral staircase all the way down to the front door and leave.

Perhaps it was because she took the stairs so slowly that she noticed a piece of paper lying on the living room floor near the writing desk. She'd already stayed too long, but curiosity compelled her to see what it was.

Ms. Rowe's private stationery, she realized as she knelt over the paper. She recognized the expensive linen by its watermark and by Ms. Rowe's initials at the top, elegantly embossed in eighteen-carat gold with flourishes on each side. Jane had often dreamed of having stationery like this someday, but she couldn't imagine how it would ever happen to her, a scholarship girl. That was sad in a way. If Ms. Rowe hadn't been such a horrible person, she could have been one of Jane's heroes. Jane didn't admire her greed or her cruelty, but she did admire her style.

The letter was written to an unnamed man, and the opening line told Jane that Ms. Rowe was angry, but that was as much as Jane was able to read. She heard the headmistress's voice through the open window. Ms. Rowe was down in the courtyard, chatting with a faculty member. Jane had checked her schedule for the day, and she was teaching a deportment class next, but Jane couldn't take a chance that she wouldn't come up to get something.

Jane intended to leave the letter where she found it, but realized she'd taken her gloves off too soon. Her fingerprints were on the stationery. It looked as if Ms. Rowe had intended to throw the letter away anyway, so Jane quickly ripped it up and stuffed it deep in the trash can. Mattie would dump the can when she cleaned and the evidence would be gone.

Now it was Mattie's turn.

27

Mattie stared up at the bell tower, clutching her bare arms. This was why she'd come back. She had to go up there. Maybe she shouldn't have revisited the old toolshed. It had brought back some bad moments, and she couldn't let herself be pulled apart that way. She had too much to accomplish.

Still, there was no way to avoid the past. It was everywhere.

Cast against stormy skies, the tower looked as forbidding today as it had twenty-three years ago when the police roped it off with yellow ribbon and declared it a crime scene. She could remember watching with her friends from across the courtyard as the forensics unit conducted their search. They'd probably done a reasonably thorough job, but they didn't know what they were looking for—or where to look. Mattie thought she did.

Moments later, she was inside the tower, her footsteps reverberating like the bell that no longer existed. She clicked up the spiral stairway in her spectator pumps, trying not to notice how hauntingly empty the apartment was without Ms. Rowe's lovely furnishings. Heavy cobwebs had replaced the blue damask draperies. Long strings of dust swung like moss from the walls and ceilings, and the windows were fogged with grime.

Mattie had done some research prior to the trip, and she'd learned through phone calls to the administration office that the tower had been closed down after Ms. Rowe's death. No one had lived here since, which seemed to explain the eeriness she felt. Maybe it was her state of mind, but it felt as if, like the shed, everything that had happened here was caught in a limbo of half-life, suspended and echoing still. It would have been better if the rooms had been filled with a new headmistress's furniture, a new life. As it was there was nothing to blunt the emanations from the past.

She tried not to look at any of the rooms as she climbed: the first-floor parlor that no one ever used, the magnificent living room on the second floor and the bedroom of many secrets above it. She climbed straight to the attic, breathing heavily by the time she got there.

The door creaked open with one twist of the knob. Not locked. Just as the front door had not been locked. Anyone could have had access to this room, she realized. She went straight to the crawl space and pulled free the vent, fanning away the dust that flew in her face. Ugh, how she hated tight places.

Stealing herself, she drew a flashlight from her shoulder bag and crawled inside, flat on her belly. The day he pulled her out of wall, William Broud had said that Ms. Rowe hid things up here. Why not a videotape?

She found lots more dust, a menagerie of bugs and the hanging wires that had tormented her. But nothing else. She felt around, grimacing at the thought of what she might touch. And finally, inching back, she pushed herself out with her hands and landed on the floor on her butt, much like the first time. Dust and cobwebs, ghosts everywhere. There was no beauty in this place. It was the rotting soul of Rowe Academy.

She brushed herself off and got up to scope out the room. The stacks of chairs she remembered were now gone, but there were half a dozen student desks and some rusting file cabinets that she hadn't noticed, which didn't mean they hadn't been there. It had been twenty years, and it was safe to say that she hadn't been paying attention to details.

She went through the desks, the file cabinets, everything, fighting dust and tears. It had to be here somewhere. She'd been so sure. Had someone beaten her to it, or was the needle in some other haystack? Some time later, frustrated and perspiring, she gave up. She'd even pulled up floor planks where she could and loosened the baseboard. If there'd ever been a tape hidden in this attic, it was gone.

Despair ripped through her as she realized that her Plan B sucked. Searching for the right haystack was crazy. It was sure to be fruitless. She needed a plan of action that made sense, something that got her the most information in the least amount of time…and there was only one way to do that, as far as she could see.

Jameson didn't see her coming until she was on top of him. She had her head down as she barreled around the corner of the Administration building, and he couldn't swerve fast enough. Even Sugar Ray couldn't have swerved fast enough. The woman was an eighteen-wheeler without brakes.

"Look out!"

Her cry was lost in the impact of their two bodies colliding. It all but knocked the wind out of Jameson. She was like a flying shoulder butt to his solar plexus. She plowed into him with her arms wrapped around herself, as if she was freezing and there was a blizzard on her heels.

"I've got you," he said, gripping her by the arms for leverage. Everything was wet from the storm that had passed over, and it was all he could do to keep them from tumbling to the ground. As it was, they were wedged against a dripping maple tree.

"Sorry!" Her shiny black hair was everywhere, but she seemed intent on untangling her shoulder bag from his arm. "I didn't see you."

She shoved the wealth of hair from her face, and Jameson's jaw dropped. "Mattie Smith?"

"Jameson Cross?"

She gave him a push, and they both nearly went over again. She was clearly shaken. He could see her lips working, but nothing came out, and just when he thought he might have to give her mouth-to-mouth, she visibly transformed. The color rushed back into her face, and she gathered herself together in a flash.

Jameson watched it happen with a certain measure of awe. This woman could have committed multiple murders. She was sharp-tongued, physically abusive, at least to him, and she either loathed men or sex or both. Why did he find that charming?

"Are you all right?" he asked.

"I'm fine."

Well, not quite fine. Her slacks looked soiled, the tail of her blouse was hanging out, and a couple of pearl buttons had popped, none of which she'd noticed yet.

"Our second collision," he pointed out.

"At least no one is bleeding this time."

She apparently had no comment other than that, but the stiletto point in her tone was clear. She had not wanted to run into him this way.

Why was he not surprised?

One of the many zippers on her purse was trying to eat the buttons off his jacket sleeve. Jameson gently pointed that out, and she seemed more than happy to set him free, even though it required some teamwork. Afterward, he got the hell out of her way while she straightened her clothing and her hair.

He tried to avoid weather metaphors in his writing, but she was a dead ringer for the dark clouds he'd seen the other day. She was a storm with a fringe of gold around the edges, where the sun fought to break through. You would never know what you were going to get with someone like that.

"What brings you here?" she asked him.

"I'm writing a book. What about you?" Her smile, which wasn't a smile at all, said touché. "Actually, they asked me to speak here," she explained. "The Distinguished Alumni Series. I'm very flattered."

"I'll bet you are. Will you be here awhile?"

"Perhaps. I have friends in the area."

"Friends?" He pretended to think about that. "Would one of them be Jane Dunbar? Oh, no, wait, Jane doesn't live here anymore. She's in Washington, D.C., now. On Pennsylvania Avenue, right?"

She patted her purse and dismissed him with a nod. "I need to get going, Mr. Cross. *Plans.*"

"Of course." He whipped a business card from his pocket and handed it to her. "When you get ready to talk."

The card could have been a red-hot poker. She wouldn't touch it. "I don't think we have anything to talk about."

"I think we do. The medical examiner's report is in."

"On your brother?"

There might have been the slightest glint of alarm in her eyes.

"Billy was smothered to death with a pillow," he said. "He also had an herbal toxin in his system, although probably not enough to kill him. Ring any bells? What if I said the herb was heartwine?"

"I would think an attempt was being made to frame someone, wouldn't you? Otherwise, why be so obvious?"

He couldn't help but smile. She was good. She was almost too good to be true. "How about dinner tonight?"

"Mr. Cross, you apparently believe I was involved in at least two heinous acts, both of which victimized your brother in unspeakable ways. How could you possibly want to have dinner with me?"

"I'm a good listener, Ms. Smith. Maybe you could think of me as your father-confessor."

"I'm not that kinky. And from what I can tell Jaydee is more your type." She actually pursed her lips at him.

He didn't get the opportunity to ask her to explain herself. She adjusted her shoulder bag with all its zippers, turned on her surprisingly fashionable pumps and made an exit, not bothering to say goodbye. Imagine that.

As Jameson stood in front of Rowe Academy's administration building and watched her walk to her car, he was struck by the clash of feelings that lived inside him. Maybe he would always struggle with guilt where his brother was concerned. Billy had been a troubled human being, who'd made life difficult for too many people, including his own family, but his punishment was wholly undeserved.

As for Ms. Smith, Jameson couldn't deny that there was an antagonistic attraction brewing, but he was at a loss to explain it under the circumstances. Maybe he should have been harboring hatred toward her. The night he found his brother he had hated her *and* her cohorts. Now he didn't know how he felt, or should feel.

She was damn clever, but he'd always admired cleverness. He also admired the way she didn't back down. She seemed a formidable adversary, and that intrigued him as nothing had in a long time. He didn't know whether she was capable of killing in cold blood and carrying out an elaborate cover-up. His gut seemed to be saying no, but his head wasn't so sure. He would have to rip himself down the middle to answer that one. She was a conundrum, and that stirred his juices.

She was also capable of making a mistake.

As she got in her car and drove away, he opened his fist to reveal a black, scarflike object. It had probably been in the zipper compartment of her purse. At any rate, he'd found the sash end stuck inside his jacket sleeve after their collision, and he'd concealed it in his hand when he'd realized it wasn't a scarf. The design had told him what it was. The front was thick and pleated like a cummerbund, narrowing to ties in the back. Maybe that's why she intrigued him. How many federal judges packed a blindfold for a short trip? It should be interesting finding out.

Mattie had never been so grateful for a traffic jam. Cars were stacked up as far as she could see on Highway 131. Morning rush hour was long over, so it might be road construction or an accident up ahead. She hoped it wasn't anything serious, but the longer the better.

She couldn't drive anyway. Nothing worked. Her rental car defied logic. She'd been forced to get a rental because her own car had stubbornly refused to start that morning, and she didn't want to add unreliable transportation to her list of concerns. So, now, she had this to contend with. The controls for the lights were where the windshield wipers should be. She couldn't find the air or the radio's power button. And despite the Post-it note with precise directions she'd stuck to her console, she'd gone the wrong way coming back from Rowe Academy and taken the long route, around the peninsula and through the middle of town.

She'd grown up in Marin County and lived there most of her life, although her mother's trailer was a far cry from the county's typical high-end real estate, as was her aunt's apartment in a rent-controlled building. Sausalito, where Mattie now lived, was just across Richardson Bay from Tiburon. Not far in terms of distance, but she hadn't been on the peninsula in years, and the place seemed as foreign as her car.

It surprised her how much even timeless Tiburon had changed. A cell phone store had replaced the ice-cream shop where she'd hung out with her three compatriots. And what was that futuristic-looking outlet mall on the hillside all about? Tiburon was as close to a quaint fishing village as you could find in the Bay area, and more significantly to Mattie, it was a school town.

Out of habit she inspected her fingernails. Anyone who'd taken the time to look at them twenty years ago would have known she wasn't tough. She'd gnawed them almost to the quick. Terror was her constant companion, and it had taken all her nerve to keep it at bay. It was almost that bad now. She was shaking, and her guts were in turmoil, but it wasn't the car or the area.

It was the inevitability. *He knew about Jane, which meant he knew how much was at stake in this. He could ruin them all, and he knew that, too.* His brother's killer had used the same M.O. as Ms. Rowe's. That seemed to have confirmed his suspicions about the lonely girls, but couldn't he see that someone must be trying to frame them?

Mattie rested her forehead on the steering wheel. The past. God, the past was an avalanche. It had broken loose from the mountain, and it was gathering speed and mass as it thundered down at them. There was no way to stop it, nothing she could do. She'd gone to Rowe Academy to find the missing video, but it wasn't there, and then she'd run into him.

A horn blared behind Mattie. The traffic was moving again.

She put the car into gear, gave it some gas and headed off in search of Highway 101, which would take her to Corte Madera. At least the gearshift was where it belonged. She'd already decided not to call Jane or Breeze. They shouldn't get the news over the phone, although she couldn't put off telling Jane for long.

She stopped and got directions at the first gas station she saw. According to the clerk, she wasn't far from her destination. The relief that washed over her felt like an omen. Maybe this wasn't going to be a complete disaster.

When she returned to the car, she dug in the zipper compartment of her bag, searching for her cell phone. She needed to give Jaydee a quick call to make sure he'd added her notes to the case files for the judge who would be replacing her. She'd gone over Jaydee's research, clarifying things and hoping to ease the load for whoever was assigned. She'd always appreciated that kind of help from the judges she'd replaced. She also wanted a report on the Langston case. She'd heard nothing since she left, not that she expected earth-shaking news this soon.

The traffic was rolling now, so she couldn't take her eyes off the road, but she found the cell right away. It was what she didn't find that concerned her. She continued to feel around in the compartment for the object that had taken on the significance of a talisman in her life. In some bizarre way it had come to symbolize both her terror and her struggle to master that emotion, and she never traveled without it. Sometimes just to touch it helped. But the blindfold wasn't there.

The weathered Cape Ann cottage had probably been very beautiful once. Its patchy gambrel roof was only partially hidden in the bows of a giant oak, and the dark green window shutters were in need of paint. Its lines would always be classic, but the house wanted care, and the woman who answered the door was in nearly the same condition.

According to Mattie's research, Nola Daniels was in her early fifties, but her shapeless shoulder-length blond hair had gone mostly to gray, and her gaunt features made her look a decade older.

"Is Chief Daniels here?" Mattie asked her.

"My husband?" Her fluttery smile revealed an eyetooth that had turned dark, marring an otherwise lovely mouth. "No, I mean yes, but he isn't well."

"Oh, I was hoping—" Mattie glanced over Nola Daniels's shoulder. She'd heard someone talking loudly inside the house. She could see into the living room and beyond, where an open doorway revealed a burly, balding man with a phone in his hand. If that was Chief Daniels, he was noticeably taller than his petite wife.

Mattie asked herself if she'd ever seen him before, either at Millicent Rowe's apartment or at the police station when she and Ivy ran away. He didn't look familiar, but it had been so many years. A flash of gold caught her eye as he paced, but it wasn't his watch as she'd first thought. It had come from the hallway wall, where his chief's badge was mounted and framed.

The bright gold star instantly struck a chord of memory, taking Mattie back to the police station—and to the dark classroom where a man who wore gold stars for cuff links reached out his hand to touch her mouth.

The flashback brought a visceral reaction. Mattie's stomach turned over with sickening speed, and if not for Nola's timid presence, she might have been sick right there. She did not have control of these memories. She'd held them off all these years with a combination of will and emotional voodoo, but that wasn't working anymore.

"Can we go outside?" Nola said, slipping out the door and pulling it shut behind her. "Do you mind? It's such a beautiful day."

It was a horrible day, gray and overcast, but Mattie was too rattled to object. She had to move smartly, or she would have had her toes stepped on. Nola Daniels was on her way out.

"Was that your husband in there?" Mattie asked. "Are

you sure I can't talk with him? I'll wait until he's off the phone."

"Shhh. Come with me." Nola beckoned Mattie with her as she moved toward the cover of the towering oak.

"Is something wrong?" Mattie asked, following along.

Nola drew Mattie close with a tweak of her wrist. She lowered her voice. "Danny thinks there's someone on the other end of the line. There isn't, of course. It's his condition. He thinks people are calling and making threats. I don't want to upset him."

"Your husband's condition?"

Nola stepped back to look at her. "I guess you're not the new therapist?"

"No, I'm here to ask him some questions about a case."

"You're a reporter then? We had one of those here just last week. Danny's not the chief of police anymore, you know. He retired several years ago."

Mattie made a mental note to ask about the reporter as she offered her hand and introduced herself by name. "It's a cold case that I'm interested in. I'm in the legal field and doing some research. I'm sorry to hear about your husband's condition. Do you mind telling me what it is?"

"It's bad," Nola said, glancing back at the house as if she expected her husband to walk out the door. "He's been diagnosed with early-onset Alzheimer's. I probably won't have him home with me much longer. Which case did you want to talk about? I remember most of them. We've been married for nearly forty years."

"Millicent Rowe's murder." Mattie had decided to risk the truth. Even if the retired chief was a member of the sex ring that didn't mean his wife knew anything about it. She might be more forthcoming than he would.

"The headmistress down at Rowe?" Nola's wrinkles deepened with the effort to remember. "That happened twenty years ago, didn't it? I'm sorry, Ms. Smith, but Danny can't remember what happened twenty minutes ago, and your questions would only upset him. He doesn't like to be reminded of his losses."

Mattie had been afraid of that. "Ms. Daniels, what about these threatening phone calls to your husband. Can you tell me anything about that?"

Nola's quizzical look warned Mattie that she was moving into personal territory. "I told you there aren't any threatening phone calls," she said. "He's imagining it, and your being here will only make it worse, just like that man who came by last week, the writer."

Mattie had meant to ask her about the reporter. Maybe he and the writer were the same person. "Was it Jameson Cross? Did he speak with your husband?"

"Oh, no." Nola glanced back at the house again. "I think his name was Cross, but I didn't let him in. Danny thinks everyone's against him now. He goes on and on, but it's his mind. His mind is making him say such hideous things."

Mattie wanted to know all about the hideous things, but she'd pushed as far as she could for now. It wasn't a total surprise that Cross had already been here. He was several steps ahead of her, but at least he hadn't been able to talk with the chief, either.

"I'm sorry," Mattie told Nola. "This must be very hard for you, and I didn't mean to take up so much of your time. I'll be on my way."

Mattie turned and started for her car, surprised to see that Nola was trotting along beside her. "I do wish there was some way I could help," Nola said. "Are you planning to talk with anyone else about the case?"

Mattie mentioned the medical examiner and the presiding judge. She was operating on the theory that at least some of the prosecution team may have been in the sex ring, given all the discrepancies in the trial.

"Both gone," Nola said.

"What?" Mattie stopped to look at her. "Gone as in dead?"

"The medical examiner just passed of a lingering illness. He'll be cremated later this week. The judge retired and moved to Florida earlier this year."

Mattie's disappointment must have shown.

"The D.A.'s still here." Nola offered the information in a hopeful tone. Her hesitant smile revealed the disturbing dark tooth.

"Do you mean Frank O'Neill?" Mattie asked.

Nola looked back at the house, and so did Mattie. Chief Daniels was standing at the living room window, looking out at them. He didn't have the vacant stare of a man who couldn't remember. He looked frightened and wary, like a man who didn't know who he could trust. Mattie understood that feeling.

Had she seen him before? Certainly she'd seen that expression, but it was only a gut feeling that he was the man she'd encountered all those years ago. His face had been concealed both times, but the badge on his wall would not leave her mind. It might be nothing more than a coincidence, but a pair of star cuff links seemed tailor-made for a man like that.

She finally managed to say goodbye to Nola Daniels, who'd been chattering as if she didn't want her to leave, and escaped to her car. Odd that a police chief's wife had come to have such a prominent disfigurement as an eyetooth, she mused, and even odder that she'd never had it fixed. So far Mattie's questions had only led to more questions, which brought a maxim from her prosecutor days to mind. Nothing gets clearer when you look beneath the surface. If you don't want to see the bugs, don't pick up the rock.

28

Mattie left the library, still scribbling notes on a legal pad. She'd spent the evening going through magazine and newspaper clippings of the Broud case, stored on microfiche. An elderly librarian had been delighted to tell Mattie that the material she wanted was readily available, thanks to Marin County's famous local crime writer, Jameson Cross. It seemed that he'd recently requested a search of everything that could be found on the case, and now Mattie was to be the beneficiary of all that largesse.

Sweet guy, she thought dryly, making a few last notes. She would have to make it a point to warmly thank him. Maybe she could accidentally put out his eye next time she saw him. But she grudgingly admitted that his slipstream wasn't such a bad place to be.

A shadow swept over Mattie as she walked around the building to the parking lot. She glanced up at the mountainous black-and-yellow storm clouds and saw that the sun had almost dropped out of sight. It was a little after nine. She'd stayed until they kicked her out of the library, never giving a thought to the weather or the dark of night.

The chill in the air sharpened as she walked, raising goose bumps on her bare arms. The back of her neck prickled, too, eliciting a shiver. Normally she would have taken that as a signal that something wasn't right, but tonight it was just the cold.

"Can you spell the word coat, Smith?" She had a jacket in the car, but she'd been too preoccupied to put it on.

She stepped up her pace, her thoughts preoccupied by the Broud case and its fascinating contradictions. Initially the case generated lots of buzz, partly because of the suspect's wild claims. The press leaped on the sex ring idea, speculating madly, but once the trial got under way, the judge shut things down by issuing gag orders and closing the proceedings.

Some of the early clippings mentioned Ms. Rowe's videotape equipment, implying that it may have been used for illicit purposes, but everything Mattie read confirmed what Tansy Black had told her. Neither the defense nor the prosecution had made use of the tapes in any way. Black had said Broud was considered unreliable, and the defense didn't want him on the stand. But Mattie was thinking conspiracy theory—and wondering how large the plot might have been and whether the defense was in on it, too.

She'd found no mention in any of the clippings of a missing tape, which could mean Ms. Rowe had removed it before she was murdered, or that someone at the crime scene had taken it. Mattie also wanted to talk to Frank O'Neill, the district attorney. She'd left him a message that afternoon, but she intentionally hadn't mentioned that she was a circuit court judge. She'd told his assistant she was a former prosecutor and left it at that.

It wasn't unusual for judges at Mattie's level to be accorded as much respect as the governor of the state, and she didn't want that kind of attention now. She needed to stay under the radar, and pulling rank on the district attorney would invite scrutiny.

Mattie glanced up at the dim overhead lamps as she walked. Someone should speak to the city about the lighting on this path. She could hardly see where she was going. As she reached the parking lot, she picked up the sounds of someone running. The rushed breathing and soft footfalls seemed to come at her from behind. Her heart broke into a painful sprint, urging her to run, too, but it was too late. She had Mace in her bag somewhere, but there wasn't time for that, either.

She spun around, prepared for anything.

Shocked, she realized the path was deserted. The parking lot was, too. It must have been the wind rustling in the trees. There was no one there. Still, her pulse was rushing, and she didn't feel safe. She was about to make a dash for the car when she saw someone coming toward her. A woman.

Mattie hesitated, confused by the woman's behavior. Her thin face was frozen in a smile of recognition, and she seemed to be heading straight for Mattie. She was model thin and fashionably dressed, and yet there was something distinctly menacing about her. Maybe it was the short, spiky blond hair. Or the deliberation.

"Mattie Smith, isn't it? How are you?"

She reached for Mattie's hand, gripping it with almost painful force.

Mattie produced a smile. "I'm fine, thank you."

"What brings you back to Tiburon?" the woman asked. "You moved away some time ago, didn't you? To San Francisco?"

Clearly the woman knew her, but Mattie couldn't seem to place her. There was something disturbingly familiar about her, but Mattie hadn't been back in so many years, and it was difficult to see in the low light.

"That's where I work," Mattie said.

"Wouldn't that be nice." She sighed, as if working in San Francisco were her fondest dream. "Are you paying us a visit? I didn't know you had relatives in Tiburon."

"I don't. It's business, partly."

"Oh, good. Have you dropped by our moldering alma mater yet?"

"No, I'm just—" At that point, Mattie was thumped on the head with the reality of the situation. She was having a polite conversation with the woman who had kicked the shit out of her in finishing school. This was Lane Davison, the leader of the Death Squad.

"Lane?" Mattie said.

"Of course. Lane. Who did you think it was?"

Mattie extracted her hand—and wondered if she should use what was left of it to give the evil witch an extreme makeover. "This is bizarre."

"Yes, isn't it. What were you doing in the library?"

Mattie shook her head, unable to pretend. "Lane, we're not *friends*."

"Don't be silly. That was twenty years ago! Bygones, and all that. Why don't we have lunch and bury the hatchet over a couple of martinis? I'd love to know what you've been up to."

Her smile was instant, dazzling. Mattie didn't respond.

"Oh, I see," Lane said.

With no rancor, Mattie replied, "I doubt it."

"Apparently, some people never grow up."

"Some people still bear scars."

"Whatever." Lane shrugged, seemingly bored with the conversation. "Good luck," she said as she brushed past Mattie and headed for the parking lot. When she reached her shiny black sports car, she called back, "You'll need it around here."

Mattie watched her nemesis drive off, aware that her last reference could have been taken as a threat. She wondered if Lane now ran the town on some level, as she used to run the school. More than that, she wondered who Lane knew and might alert to Mattie's presence. Did she know Jameson?

Might she have known about the sex ring? That seemed unlikely, but Mattie couldn't rule anything out at this stage.

By the time she got to her car, Mattie had already decided that nothing good could come of having run into Lane Davison. There was little Mattie could do except be on guard, and she was probably too paranoid for her own good. But who *wouldn't* be paranoid if they were being framed for multiple murders?

That question had begun to dominate her thoughts. It had already occurred to her that the lonely girls were convenient, a scapegoat for the real killer. But it was also possible that someone wanted them out of the way, now that Broud had been exonerated. Ms. Rowe had had plenty of enemies. Any one of the men in the sex ring may have wanted them silenced. Broud may have known too much about those same men. Then again, he may have had enemies Mattie knew nothing about. Or one she did, such as his own brother.

Jameson Cross. She startled herself with the idea, but it did make some kind of weird sense. The so-called vigilante crime writer was working on a book about his own brother's case. What a story to have a brother released from death row only to be killed during Jameson's quest for the real killers, and then Jameson himself tracks down the women who did it, one of them the First Lady of the country. Oliver Stone, watch out.

Mattie's nape prickled again, filling her with a thundering sense of danger this time. She scanned the area, but Lane was gone, and there was no one else in sight. Still, her breath got thick and sticky. Something was wrong, and the feeling grew until she finally understood what it was. It felt as if she were being watched.

Her car was no more than fifty feet away. Every firing nerve told her to make a run for it and lock herself in, but she refused to give in to the panic. She was in no immediate danger, and she could not let this feeling rule her life. Locked in place, she waited until the impulse had flashed through her, as bright as the lightning she'd seen earlier that morning.

God, what a nightmare. She was damp with sweat.

But moments later, as she drove out of the parking lot, she noticed a nondescript car parked down the block behind her. It pulled out as she did and followed her at a distance. So, she *was* being followed. She couldn't see the driver's face, but it was a man, and he wasn't trying very hard to hide his presence, and that gave her a damn good idea who it was. Cross, perhaps? He'd been doing his best to frighten and intimidate her since he barged into her courtroom.

Mattie drove slowly, one eye on the rearview mirror as she formulated a plan. She turned a corner and so did he. Good, let him tail her, she thought. Let him drive right into her trap. Maybe the voyeur would find the camera turned on him?

Mattie's anger was tinged with sadness as she thought about how people changed and possibilities died. It felt as if Cross had come out of nowhere, a sworn enemy. He was the man born to haunt and harass her. But it hadn't always been that way. What had ever happened to sweet, sexy Jimmy Broud, the boy born to awaken her? She'd dreamed her way through school, high on fantasies of the shy delivery truck driver. Ridiculous, but she had.

He was supposed to have been her first kiss, her first stolen caress and the one she surrendered her heart to on some dark night of secret sighs in the pine forest. Now she had to wonder if that boy ever existed. She mourned all those possibilities, but maybe they had never existed, either.

As Mattie neared the Rowe Academy entrance, she slowed and pulled the car through the gates. The car behind her pulled in, too. She could see the twinkle of its lights. The fish takes the bait, she thought.

* * *

Mattie knew the campus better than he did. She was counting on that advantage as she took him on a wild-goose chase through the maze of roads, lanes and access tunnels that was Rowe Academy. She went slow enough to make sure that he was following her, and once she had him at the heart of the labyrinth, she whipped through a tunnel and crossed the campus on a diagonal route, heading for where they'd started.

The goal was to lose him, and she did. She didn't have to worry about his finding her again. Unless he made a U-turn there was only one way out, and that's where she would be waiting.

Mattie sat there in her rental compact, blocking the exit road as his lights appeared. She keyed the engine and revved the motor. If he tried to broadside her, she could easily jump the curb in this little compact. She doubted he would try that, though. He didn't want to risk killing her. He wanted her in good enough condition to confess.

Besides, she wasn't afraid of him. It was time he knew that.

The other car pulled to a stop not thirty feet from her, its headlights trained on her car. Mattie stared directly at his windshield, wondering if he could see her. Apparently he wasn't getting out, the coward. But then what did she expect of a man who behaved like a stalker?

The minutes ticked by. Fortunately it was late in the evening, as well as summer break, and the campus was virtually deserted. She glared at him and gave him the finger, hoping to trigger a reaction. When she hit the horn, he did nothing. Apparently he planned to sit there all night.

She couldn't let that happen. She had a few things to say to him.

She took her canister of Mace from her purse. She'd carried it for years and never used it, but maybe she would get lucky, and he'd give her a reason to shoot him between the eyes. Where was her flak vest when she needed it?

"Come out of your car," she called to him. "We need to get some things straight."

Again, no response. Nothing. He didn't even roll down the window.

She could see the silhouette of his head, and it looked as if he was staring at her, but she couldn't see his features or his expression. Suddenly she was more uneasy than indignant. His lack of response was strange. Maybe that's what bothered her, but she'd come this far. Now it was a matter of pride.

As she walked up to his car, the driver door flew open and caught her square in the chest. The blow sent her stumbling backward, and the shock left her mind reeling. That was no accident. She ended up on the pavement, gasping for breath. It felt like she'd been hit with a sledgehammer. The pain was nearly disabling, but she had to get up. He had a knife.

She'd seen the glint of a silver blade as the door flew open. *Knives are more dangerous than guns.* She'd taken self-defense classes while working for the prosecutor's office, and her early training had stayed with her. A man with his knife already drawn could actually throw it and kill an officer before the officer could draw his weapon and shoot.

Where was the Mace? She couldn't find it in the dark.

She got to her knees, feeling for the canister. This time she saw him coming. He was out of the car and walking toward her. His face was covered with some kind of mask. But it *was* a knife in his hand.

She stayed low and rolled away as the blade caught the back of her leg, ripping her slacks. She felt no pain, but a blow to her side sent her sprawling again. Something had hit her with enough force to knock the wind out of her.

She moaned in agony, unable to scream for help. That might be her only weapon against him now. The school used to have security guards. She prayed they still did.

He came at her again, and she kicked him back, viciously jamming the heel of her shoe into his kneecap. The slashing blade caught her blouse and nearly ripped it off her, but at the same time, she heard a horrible snapping sound and realized she'd hurt him.

He doubled in pain, and she let out a blood-curdling scream. At the top of her lungs, she shrieked for help. Frantically she searched for the Mace. Desperate to find a way to defend herself, she grabbed one of the large rocks that lined the driveway. But he didn't attack her again. Instead, he hobbled back to his car.

Mattie watched him get in the car and turn on the engine. Was he going to run her over? She scrambled for cover, hiding behind the compact. A mistake, she realized as his motor revved and roared. If he hit her car hard enough, he would take her out, too. She would be crushed or beheaded by flying metal.

She cringed, waiting for the impact, but to her astonishment, he gunned his car over the curb, careened around her car and peeled off down the road. Had she actually scared him off?

That was the good news, she realized, watching him escape. In all the time she'd been waiting for him to get out of his car, she had not thought to take down his license plate number. And it was too dark to see it now.

It took a wad of gauze from the hotel's first aid kit to stop the bleeding. Once the oozing slowed, Mattie cleaned her wounds with soap and water and sterilized them with a tiny bottle of airline vodka. It stung like hell, but she wasn't taking any chances on infection.

She stood in front of the bathroom sink, staring into the mirror at the ugly purplish bruise on her shoulder, the laceration on her collarbone. She had scrapes on her arms, as well, from the fall, and her bad knee was throbbing. But the pain didn't even begin to match the damage to her sense of self-preservation and to her pride. How could she have been so reckless? She'd thought it was Cross following her, and that had been her first terrible mistake. Her second had been leading him into a dangerous labyrinth, thinking to outmaneuver him.

She touched her rib cage and winced. If Jameson Cross was capable of this, she had completely misread him. She'd taken him for a son of a bitch, not a fiend. Whoever she'd tangled with played rough. All she had was cuts and bruises. No broken ribs, thank God, but that didn't help the utter despair she felt at this moment.

She'd already dismissed Lane Davison as a possibility, unless Lane happened to keep a vicious thug on retainer. If it wasn't Cross, Mattie had no idea who'd attacked her or how to protect herself. That was the terrifying part. If she was right about the conspiracy, the suspects were all invisible, and short of finding the videotape, she didn't know how to expose them. Worse, if she told anyone about this, they would warn her that it wasn't safe to stay here. She couldn't call the police and draw attention to herself, and if she was trying to spare Jane and Breeze from worry, she should certainly spare them from this.

Not knowing what else to do, Mattie diligently bandaged the cuts. When she was done, she went straight to the room's minibar, where she crouched before the open door and removed all the bottled water. She needed to feel clean, but a shower would be painful with fresh wounds. Maybe drinking the water would be like an act of purification. She had a feeling it would take every bottle in the minibar.

By the time she'd finished the first bottle, she had decided not to call anyone. She wasn't going back. The very fact that she was attacked meant she must be getting close to the truth, or at least to something that someone didn't want discovered. That was good enough for her. Besides, if her assailant wanted to kill her, he could have, easily. His goal was to scare her, and he'd done a good job.

Hell, she was terrified, but she was going ahead with her plans for tomorrow. It was another hunch, and a long shot at that, but she couldn't go back when all the signs said she should be here.

No pain, no gain, she thought as she returned to the bathroom and turned on the tap to fill the bathtub. She knew exactly how Breeze would handle a situation like this, and her friend was the expert when it came to rest and relaxation. Mattie was going to take a bubble bath and to hell with everything else.

29

"Jane, what's that awful noise?"

"It's a secure line, Breeze. You're hearing the equivalent of white noise in the background. John Bratton arranged it for me here in my office."

Breeze lay naked on her stomach on the portable massage table, the cell phone pasted to her ear while a bronzed god of a masseur worked on her hamstrings. No need for further medical research, she'd decided. This guy's hands were the answer to all life's problems. She wondered what he would do if he knew who his client was talking to.

She smiled. Interesting life she led. Odd that she still felt restless, hungry almost, like a kid foraging through the refrigerator who couldn't decide what she wanted.

"Have you heard from Mattie?" Jane asked. "I can't reach her, and the medical examiner's report on William Broud is out. It's not good."

While Jane explained that Broud had died in exactly the same way as the headmistress, Breeze signaled the masseur to hand her the television remote. She clicked on CNN, looking for some breaking news on the case. Luckily, she was in the bedroom of her Four Seasons suite with everything she needed at hand.

As Jane talked in one ear, Breeze tuned in to the television with the other. Broud had been smothered, the commentator was saying, and some exotic herbal poison had been found in his system. It didn't sound as if the police had made any connection between the murders. Yet.

Breeze grimaced in pain. Either the masseur had hit a sore spot, or she had tightened up.

"Breeze, are you there?" Jane asked.

"Right here," Breeze said. She couldn't very well tell Jane what she thought with a third party in the room, but Jane wasn't listening anyway. To her it was obvious that someone meant to link the two murders. Random acts and coincidences had to be ruled out, she said, and most of all, they needed a plan for damage control.

Another sore spot. Breeze groaned and reached for a glass of champagne, thinking it would ease the pain. The masseur had arranged for an ice bucket to be set right next to the massage table.

"What's going on, Breeze? What are you doing?"

"Getting a massage."

"A massage? You're getting a massage while Mattie is risking her life, and I'm trying to salvage my husband's presidency? What are you thinking?"

Bubbles tickled Breeze's nose as she sipped, and she nearly sneezed. "I'm thinking you should have a massage, too. Now, what's this plan you mentioned?"

"The plan is to do nothing until we hear from Mattie."

"That's a *plan?* Why don't I go find her? She's been gone almost twenty-four hours, hasn't she? That's long enough to consider her officially missing."

"Breeze," Jane said sternly; "stay put. Get your massage. Get two. It's bad enough that Mattie went."

"Fine." Breeze set her champagne on the table, a little miffed at being so soundly rejected. She had a few things going on in her life, as well. The spa's VIP clients were asking for her, and the manager was afraid they might lose some of them, in particular the prince.

Normally that kind of news would have lifted Breeze's spirits. She enjoyed being sought after, and of the three women, she'd always thought she must live the most interesting, rewarding life. She had consorted with some of the most important men in the world, and a few women, as well. Some of them still paid a fortune for a little bit of time with her, just to talk. She knew how to make them feel good about themselves—and she never lied.

Things had changed now, of course. Her work had taken on different meanings and nuances, some of them less rewarding than others. "Jane, I have to go," she said abruptly. "This connection's bad."

"Breeze? What? Wait. Stay out of trouble!"

Jane's last words, Breeze thought, tapping the talk button. Immediately, she pressed a series of programmed keys, and a man answered, asking for her ID. "Worrywart," she said, enunciating for the voice analyzer. She'd chosen the word at random, although not really, considering Jane's mental state. Next, she hit several keys, initiating the number sequence generator on her cell. When the sequence came up, she keyed it in.

"Welcome," he said. "How goes it stateside?"

"They grow good-luck bamboo here."

"You need luck?"

"Always—and some information. I have three names to add to your list." She typed in Jameson Cross's name. "Find out what you can," she said as she typed in the next two. Jane Mantle and Matilda Smith.

There were no goodbyes, not with him. He'd been with her for three years now, and there wasn't anyone better in the intelligence business. She hit the off button and exchanged the cell phone for her glass of champagne. Stay out of trouble? Fat chance.

The masseur smoothed the backs of her calves with his palms, applying the most delicious pressure. Breeze let out a sigh, wondering if she ought to have a masseur sent up to Jane's office. These women. All they did was worry.

White smoke rose in a plume from the aluminum smokestack of the crematorium. Mattie didn't want to think about what that meant, so she concentrated on the chapel, where she was heading. Her entire body ached from the ordeal she'd been through last night, but she was trying to put that out of her mind, too. The chapel looked very much like an English country church, made entirely of rock-faced stone with rounded arches and dormer windows. A massive bell tower adjoined it, and both buildings sat in stoic grandeur on cliffs that overlooked San Francisco Bay.

Beautiful certainly, if you could handle the concept.

Mattie had already noted the signage that directed hearses to the crematory, a large, stark concrete facility behind the chapel. That was her objective, but first she needed some questions answered, and the chapel looked like the best bet. She'd called ahead and gotten a recording that said there were no services this afternoon.

She stepped inside the double doors, admiring the sanctuary's domed roof. Green marble columns ran along each wall with stained glass windows in between. It was as hushed and tranquil as a church, but there were no obvious religious symbols. An American flag hung where a cross or statue would normally have been.

"Can I help you?"

A smiling young man with glasses like Buddy Holly walked down the aisle toward Mattie. The broom and dustpan he carried told her he must have been cleaning up.

"Is there an office somewhere?" she asked. "I'd like to inquire about your services."

"It's right next door in the bell tower, but they left early today. Nothing to do." He twirled the broom and grinned. "You want to know about our no-frills package? Six hundred bucks total, and that includes one deceased in a corrugated cardboard container, ashes in a plastic urn, but no funeral services."

Suddenly the beauty of the place was lost on Mattie. She hoped they didn't normally let this guy loose on the bereaved. "I really wanted to know a little more about the cremation process."

"Ah," he said, clearly pleased. "Well, the bodies go into a brick chamber called a retort that can withstand temperatures up to twenty-one hundred degrees Fahrenheit. Even at that, it takes a couple hours, and not everything is ashes as they would like you to believe. There are bone fragments that have to be crushed. *Lots* of bone fragments. That's my—"

Mattie shook her head. More than she wanted to know. Unfortunately, she still had one question. "Are people ever cremated with their possessions?"

"Sure, all the time. As long as we can get the stuff in the box, and it'll burn clean, it's not a problem." He clicked his tongue. "Some of them believe they *can* take it with them. They want to be flambéed with their cash money. Can you believe that?"

Interesting way to get rid of a videotape, Maggie thought.

He blinked at her through the heavy glasses. "Are you a reporter?"

"I'm doing some research." She feigned a casual shrug.

"So...did I help? There's a lot more I could—"

"No, no! Not necessary. You did help."

She thanked him and left the chapel. Nola Daniels had told her that the man who'd been the medical examiner during William Broud's trial was being cremated this week. That meant he must be back in the crematory now, in storage. A corrugated cardboard box? That shouldn't be too hard to breach. If she didn't find a videotape, she might find something else, like star cuff links. She woke up this morning with the realization that other members of the ring might have worn them, too, as identification and to symbolize their membership in a secret society.

She slipped around the back of the building and spotted the facility's heavy aluminum doors. They didn't appear to be locked and as luck would have it, they weren't. She let herself in and cautiously checked out the warehouselike interior. There wasn't anyone within eyeshot, but you couldn't miss the row of ovens.

Their brushed-chrome exteriors had digital readouts and numeric keyboards to control the burners, fans and ventilation. The roller apparatus in front of each oven door seemed designed to smoothly roll the boxes in and out. The eerie similarity to oversized pizza ovens made Mattie queasy. She had to strike the image from her mind and get on with it.

Where would the bodies be stored? She spotted a huge vault door alongside the ovens, and as she walked toward it she saw a conveyance that reminded her of a luggage carousel. It looked as if the deceased were transported from the vault to the ovens on a conveyer belt.

Mattie reached for the door's lever, but her hand never made contact. A solid object exploded against the base of her skull. Her vision went blindingly white and a searing pain ripped through her head. She never heard it coming. Nor did she hear her own soft expiration of breath as she hit the concrete floor.

The deep, throbbing ache felt as if it had penetrated to some vital part of Mattie's brain. She couldn't move, couldn't see, even when she opened her eyes. Horror rose inside her, bringing a sob to her throat. She vaguely remembered the blow that had knocked her to the ground. Had she been paralyzed by it?

She tried to move her hands and felt the bite of thick, hard ropes, woven like cables. She would never be able to break them. Her feet were bound, too, and something had been forced into her mouth, a gag. Darkness pressed in on her, as heavy as a blanket, but she wasn't blindfolded. She was encased in some kind of box or casket. Sealed inside, where even light couldn't penetrate. The air she breathed was drenched with an odd antiseptic smell.

Terror swept her, wave after wave of it.

She was helpless, trapped. She couldn't breathe. She would suffocate inside this tomb before she ever broke these bonds.

Panic swirled through her and left her gasping. She felt it sucking, churning, swirling up again, but she couldn't let it take her over. She would pass out.

Think, Mattie, think. You're alive. You're not paralyzed. Use your head. Think this through.

Her heart was a constant wild flutter, like wings in a cage. A terrified child was shrieking. She was lodged in a crawl space, unable to breathe without feeling the burning air bounce back in her face.

That was twenty years ago, Mattie. You survived it then, and you're not a child anymore. Figure out where you are now.

Now, *Mattie. Where are you?*

Drenched in sweat, she forced herself to move her hands, even knowing that the dimensions of the tight space might send her into turmoil again. As far as she could tell, she was in one of the corrugated boxes the kid in the chapel had described, but there was no give at all. It felt as if the box was encased in something unbreakable, like a coffin.

A question seared its way into her consciousness. Who

had done this to her? She could still see the kid's grinning face in her mind, but it was hard to imagine him sneaking up behind her and hitting her hard enough to knock her unconscious. It had felt as if that blow could crack her skull, and if he hadn't done it, then it must have been the monster who attacked her last night.

Who would do this to her? Who?

She could feel the flesh rising on her body. Her skin burned, as if it had been rubbed raw with sand. But she wasn't hot, she was cold. Chilled to the marrow, which meant the storage room was refrigerated, and she'd been lying in this box a long time. She would die of hypothermia, if she didn't suffocate first. The panic rose again, and this time she was too exhausted to fight it. The antiseptic stench made her nauseous. She closed her eyes, surrendering to the chaos. Let it swallow her up, take her down and drown her.

Sometime later, barely conscious, she felt herself being lifted from the coffin and carried out of the storage area. She didn't have the strength to open her eyes, but she could hear the hiss of the ovens, and the inferno roaring in her ears told her that she'd been wrong. She was not going to freeze to death.

She would die by fire.

30

Mattie ached with cold. It cut to the deepest part of her being. The roar of the ovens was still in her ears, but she couldn't feel the heat. There was no searing agony. If she was going to die on a funeral pyre, then why was she quaking like this?

All she could hear now was chattering teeth and bones knocking together violently. She was a skeleton, dancing and rattling in the graveyard. The cold hurt. It did. Like blows to her spindly frame.

The faint noise of a zipper sent confusion spiraling through her. Cool air bathed her as she felt herself being lifted again, this time from a bag. A body bag? Was she already dead?

Cool air. Hot water.

She was being lowered into a steaming cauldron. Her skin prickled and stung. Here was the fire! She moaned and thrashed, but someone's arms held her tight. Someone's voice whispered to her.

Don't fight me. Let me help you.

She let go and a startled sound quavered in her throat. She knew that voice. She was fourteen, and he was the boy from town, the one who'd followed her into the pine forest.

Why are you running away? Come back! I just want to know who you are.

Jimmy? No, she must be crazy. Why was he saying those things? Touching her this way? But the image of a boy's dark eyes played in her mind as she sank lower in the tub, into welcome oblivion. The water swirling around her was as deep and warm as his voice.

So this was how it would be with Jimmy Broud. She had never been able to stop herself from wondering. She'd fought her childish notions, but there had been something about his cool, observing gaze and quiet strength that made her wonder if he would be the anchor she'd never had, the port in her storm, the strong shoulder. She had daydreamed her way through school on such childish notions. Mostly she'd wondered what would have happened if she'd let him catch up with her that day in the forest.

I just want to know who you are.

Mattie let out a strangled sound, fighting the arms that held her. Why had he said that? No one had ever been interested in knowing who she was. It killed her that he might have been making fun of her. Ugly, unkempt Mattie Smith. It was Ivy he wanted to know. Not her. Never her!

Did I frighten you away? Come back!

She'd wasted hours thinking about a boy who made a hobby of tormenting pathetic young girls. For two weeks she'd stayed up all night, every night, sitting by her dorm window so she could watch him make his first delivery at 5:00 a.m. Eventually her grades had begun to suffer, and the housemistress had caught her in the act.

Mattie had given up her watch in shame and gone back to bed. She was supposed to be tough. She wasn't supposed to have adolescent crushes, but for that two-week period she'd felt like Juliet on the balcony. She'd wanted him to see her up there and scale the wall to her room. She'd dreamed fervently of his touch, of his lips, and she had wanted him to kiss her as much as she had ever wanted anything in her life.

A shudder racked her. She stirred and moaned. She was still cold, but her thoughts were hot, delirious, *ridiculous*. She was delusional now, dreaming about Jimmy Broud again, just as if she'd never stopped.

When she woke up next, her legs were churning, but it wasn't water that weighed her down, it was a blanket.

Easy now. Go back to sleep if you can. I'll be here.

She was in bed with him, with Jimmy Broud. Was that possible?

He drew her into his arms and she didn't have the strength to fight him off. She was forced to let herself be held and comforted, and it filled her with a strange kind of agony. So alien, this feeling of helplessness. A moan rose inside her. She would have begged him to let her go, if she could. But she couldn't even manage that, and finally she gave up. She sank into him and disappeared. There was nowhere else to go.

That's it. No more fighting. Relax.

The bed was as soft and warm as the bathwater, and there were times when she couldn't tell which was which.

Why did you run away?

I don't want to run. I don't want to run anymore.

Don't fight me, Mattie. Let me help you.

Help me. Help me stay.

When did he kiss her? When had that happened? They hadn't kissed when she was in school. She was certain of that, but she could feel the imprint of his mouth on hers and it was like putting her lips to rose petals. His kiss was warm with life. Pulsing. Soft. She liked it. She liked it more than she'd imagined possible. She wanted more.

His arms weren't soft. They lifted her as if she weighed nothing.

His body wasn't soft. Anywhere.

Jimmy? Was this a dream or was he making love to her. Was he inside her? Was she crying his name? *Jimmy!*

* * *

Mattie opened her eyes to what could safely be called a nasty shock. She was in bed, but not with the boy she'd dreamed about. This was not her port in a storm. This could very well be the storm.

Jameson Cross was lying on the bed on his stomach, studying her, his arms wrapped around the pillows bunched up under his head. She turned to look at him and winced. The back of her head hurt, right at the place where it made contact with the pillow. But the pain had no chance of holding her attention with him around, especially when he looked as if he might be naked. There was a sheet covering him from the waist down so she couldn't be sure.

She *was* naked. A sheet covered her, too, all of her, but she didn't have to look underneath it. Some things you just knew. Nakedness was one. Another was when your head hurt. Hers did.

"What are you doing here?" she asked him, her voice low, strained.

"I live here."

She gave the disheveled bedroom a glance and closed her eyes, trying to make sense of the past twenty-four hours. "Then what am I doing here?"

He rolled up to sit, and she saw that he had jeans on. Thank God for that. While he poured a glass of water from a pitcher on the nightstand, she gingerly pushed up against the pillows and tried to get her bearings. If this was a bedroom, she'd never seen anything quite like it. There weren't any walls per se, just a room-size translucent hanging screen to her left and an enclosure of watery blue glass blocks to her right that seemed to house a bathroom. Opposite the bed was a teak console that ran the considerable length of the room. The mirror above it appeared to be hanging, too.

His house had no walls, she realized, spotting what

seemed to be a kitchen behind a wraparound granite counter across the way. An old-fashioned windup alarm clock on the nightstand said ten o'clock. It had to be morning because there was sunshine slicing through the strangest skylight she'd ever seen. The unzipped mummy-type sleeping bag draped over a chair stirred vague memories of a body bag. Was he trying to keep her warm in that?

Jameson handed her a glass of water with a straw in it, which she took, gratefully.

"Someone tried to kill you," he said. "I brought you here rather than a hospital. I didn't think you'd want to deal with the paperwork or the possibility of police reports."

Someone had tried to kill her. She'd been hit over the head and stuffed in a box to be cremated. *Twenty-one hundred degrees Fahrenheit...not everything is ashes as they would like you to believe. There are bone fragments that have to be crushed.*

Mattie left the glass on the nightstand, aware that she'd slopped water all over the place. She felt her face going hot and her chest tightening. Within seconds it was a struggle to breathe.

"Are you all right?"

She shook her head and closed her eyes again, as if she could control the reaction that way. "How long have I been here?"

"Since last night."

Last night? Then this was the second attack in two days.

"Mattie, you're shivering."

She found her voice. "Who did it?"

"I don't know. By the time I got to the crematorium, you'd vanished, but your car was still in the lot. I knew something had to be wrong, so I collared the kid in the chapel and made him open up every one of the cadaver boxes until we found you. I had to pay him off not to call the cops."

Her eyes snapped open. She stared at him hard. "How did you know I was at the crematorium? What were *you* doing there?"

"I've been following you."

"You've been following me?"

"Yes—and apparently I wasn't the only one."

"You were *following* me?"

"Let's say I was keeping an eye on you—and why wouldn't I, Your Honor? You're the prime suspect in two murders. This could very well be your return to the scene of the crime."

His shrug said he just didn't give a shit. He was going to bring her to her knees one way or the other. Mattie felt a sense of despair. Who was this man? And where was the Jimmy Broud she remembered? The one who visited sleeping girls in the infirmary?

"If I'm the killer, who's trying to kill me? Did that question ever occur to you?"

"It has now."

Her head ached all the way to the top of her skull. Every muscle fiber protested as she struggled to sit up, tugging the sheet along with her. It startled her when she saw the bruise on her shoulder and the cuts from the first attack. Still, she had to get up. Lying down shouted that she was wounded and vulnerable.

He left the bed and started tidying the room, picking up clothing and closing cabinets and drawers. There didn't appear to be any of her clothing in the array he draped over his arm. Her bag wasn't anywhere to be seen, either. She wondered what he'd done with it, but she wasn't quite ready to ask yet. He dumped everything in a wicker hamper, then went to an armoire and pulled out a fresh shirt, one with fluid lines and long sleeves, which he slipped on without bothering to button.

Black silk? Nice against his golden skin tones. She'd read that about him, that he was...what? Elegant? Immaculate? She didn't think so, not by the condition of his hair. It was a mop and a messy one. There were also a couple of sizable rips in his jeans where the material was worn.

Still, the dishevelment worked on him, she had to admit. On some people, messiness was elegant, even darkly elegant. He would be one of those.

"Let me see if I understand this," she said. "You followed me to the funeral parlor, waited awhile, and when I didn't come out, you got suspicious. That's when you went looking for me?"

He nodded, sort of.

"But you didn't see me come out of the chapel and slip around to the crematory? You're not a very good snoop."

"I didn't park in the lot. That would have been a dead giveaway, don't you think? I stayed down the road—and I waited for *hours.*"

"What about the night before last?" She kept her voice soft, not wanting to give anything away. "If you've been following me, then you know what happened on the Rowe Academy campus. You were there, of course."

He reached down and whisked up a newspaper, probably the *Chronicle,* and dropped it on the console. "I wasn't anywhere near the campus. I was at a dinner for collectors of rare and unusual magazines night before last."

"You collect magazines?" The console where he'd set the paper had a framed blowup of an old magazine cover. Mattie hadn't noticed it before. A woman, bound and gagged, lay wide-eyed with horror in an open coffin.

Her heart gave a hard, painful thud. "Is that a fantasy of yours?" she asked, "sealing up women in coffins?"

She snatched up the glass of water, slopping more as she tried to get the straw to her mouth. Good grief, what kind of game was he playing with her? It felt like some kind of terrible cat and mouse scenario, all this stalking and baiting and switching. It felt like she was dealing with a very sick man.

The glass missed the nightstand and landed on the carpet. Mattie didn't even look. She tugged the top sheet free, gathering it around her. Nothing hurt anymore. Not even her head.

"Where are my clothes?" she said, struggling to get out of the bed.

Her feet hit the damp carpet, but she tilted with the very first step. The floor lifted and swayed as if she were on a boat. She saw him coming around the bed and she thrust out a hand to stop him. She might as well have tried to stop a tidal wave.

She clung to the huge sheet as he whipped her into his arms and held her, supporting her tumbling weight with his frame. She was light-headed enough to float away. It felt as if her body had lost contact with the ground. She should never have tried to get up so fast, and if he hadn't grabbed her, she and the sheet would be spinning toward the ceiling.

Finally the room slowed its rocking.

"Was it you yesterday?" she rasped at him. "Did you attack me?"

"Christ, no. I found you. I brought you back here and revived you. You were half-dead of hypothermia."

She searched his lean, perversely handsome face, wondering if she could believe anything he said.

"It wasn't me," he said, giving her a little shake. "The question you should be asking yourself is who did do it. Who's trying to kill you, Mattie?"

Fear, again. It came in a burning flash that lit up every nerve ending, like lightning. She bowed her head. "I don't know."

He drew her close, and the warmth of his body heat felt so good it frightened her, too. After a moment, she pulled away, hobbling to catch her balance.

"What happened last night?" she asked him, determined to distance herself in whatever small way she could. "Did you undress me and give me a bath? Did we have sex?"

He looked at her long and hard, as if he could see right through her ploy. "Did you kill my brother?" he asked.

"You didn't answer my question."

"I will when you answer mine."

"No, I didn't kill your brother. And neither did Jane or Breeze."

"Then you wouldn't object to a lie detector test?"

"I certainly would. They're not reliable, but I'll submit to a DNA test."

"For what purpose?"

"To prove that the blood on Ms. Rowe's pillow isn't mine. Deal?" It was a tight, bitter question. "If I didn't kill her why would I need to kill him?"

He didn't respond and she had the feeling he was trying to think of a way to reject her offer. His arms were folded. He was frowning.

"All right," he said at last.

"I have just one condition. I want some answers, too. You've been evading me at every turn, maybe even lying to me about what happened last night, and I want to know now, starting with the sex."

His expression didn't change. He was still frowning, arms folded. But she sensed a change stirring inside him. The gray in his eyes was less steely, more lavender and sinister. He was thinking, calculating, measuring her, but for what? A coffin?

Perverse, she thought, and attractive. He might be wondering what he was dealing with, as well. A female psycho? A murderer? Maybe some gender confusion to boot?

Let him wonder. He would answer her questions first.

31

Jameson's tone was measured. "Maybe I should be making allowances for your mental state?"

Mattie bridled. "I'm not crazy."

"Crazy, no, but traumatized."

She was too wobbly to stand much longer, so she sat herself on the edge of the bed. He came and sat next to her, apparently determined to get close enough so that she could not misunderstand him.

"We did *not* have sex," he said.

"Someone took off my clothes and put me in a tub of hot water. Are you going to tell me that didn't happen?"

"The bath happened. I had to raise your body temperature, and that was the fastest way. The sex *didn't* happen."

His brows knit, confirming his perplexity. "Where did that come from? What made you think we did?"

"Never mind." Mattie wished she'd never asked. His denial was embarrassingly matter-of-fact. He sounded as if he couldn't even imagine having sex with her. Hell, furthest thing from his mind.

She made a point of looking the other way, even though it hurt.

"Can I get you anything?" he asked. "Something to eat, drink, a pain pill?"

"My clothes?"

"I'll get them on one condition. You stay here until you're in fighting shape, however long that takes. It's not safe out there, and you're in no condition to defend yourself."

"I'll be ready next time," she was quick to assure him. "No one's catching me off guard."

He reached over in a totally bold move and brought her head around so that he could look at her. His eyes were steel again, with a riveting hint of frustration and concern.

"Ready for what, Mattie?" he asked. "You have no idea who wants to hurt you. No idea how to protect yourself or who to protect yourself from."

"Other than you?"

"Touché." His raised brow acknowledged that she had a point. "However," he said, "you won't have any need to protect yourself from me unless you're not telling the truth. I don't want you—well, not in the sense of revenge. I want justice for my brother, his killer."

She had no idea how to respond, but something held her for a moment. It could have been the way he glanced at her mouth, or the stillness building inside her. No butterflies in this stomach. She was as deep and hushed as the nave of a cathedral. The only thing she could feel was the pulse ticking in her temple. This was nothing like her dreams as a kid. This was real.

He caressed her face and released her.

Mattie breathed easier as he moved away, and told herself it was a sigh of relief. That was too close for comfort. She was a wreck now, buzzing with inner noise. Her lovely sense of quiet had been obliterated.

His gray eyes warmed with a slight smile. "I'm getting you some food and some hot lemonade with whiskey. It's an old family recipe. Once you've had a mug of that, we'll talk about whether or not you're ready to leave."

Mattie found herself trying not to smile. It probably

looked ridiculous, as if she were chewing off the inside of her lip, which she was. Fighting impulses took so much more energy than going with them. The lemonade sounded different, but good, and she might even be hungry.

He crossed what could loosely be called a hallway to the kitchen. From her vantage point, the house looked like a mostly open gallery, with master bed and bath on one side and a workout area, kitchen and dining area on the other, all large and elaborate. She couldn't see what was beyond the smoky screen that walled off the bedroom, but she imagined it was some kind of great room.

Odd how safe she felt being here, even somewhat removed from the reality that someone had tried to kill her. Both attacks on her had taken place after her meeting with Lane Davison. Coincidence? More likely it had something to do with her visit to Nola Daniels's house. Especially since Nola Daniels had volunteered the information about the medical examiner's cremation. And the chief's furtive expression as Mattie had left struck her as ominous.

She had another thought about the attacks as she curled up in the blanket. Whoever came after her the first time had been injured. She'd landed a hard kick to his knee that had left him hobbling. It didn't seem likely she would get a chance to inspect Jameson Cross's knee, but he wasn't limping. She let out a deep breath that was at least part relief. Maybe she hadn't been taken hostage by the enemy.

She thought about checking her cell phone messages. Yesterday she'd left a message for Frank O'Neill, and she was curious to see if he'd responded. She also needed to find out what was happening at her office and touch base with Jane and Breeze to let them know she was still on the job. She hadn't had time to think about what her next move would be, but she was going to relax first, and block out all the noise, if she could.

Watching her host cook proved to be an interesting distraction. It wasn't a total surprise that he knew his way around a kitchen, and the smells already coming her way were delicious. She caught the subtle essences of saffron and bubbling chicken broth and something richer. Was that a chicken gumbo? The simmering lemonade gave off a piquant sweetness that made her mouth water.

A part of her wanted to think that Cross's concerns about her welfare were genuine, despite everything. But it still seemed like a risk to bring him into her confidence. Why was she even thinking about it?

He may have saved her life, but that didn't mean they were buddies. And yet a bond of some kind had been forged, and she had to acknowledge that, at least to herself. It was part of being able to tell friends from enemies, and right now he didn't seem to fall into either category, which made him very dangerous.

He seemed to be offering help, and she needed all the help she could get. But could she possibly enlist his aid in her cause? He wanted to bring his brother's killer to justice, too. And he *had* come to her rescue, but perhaps only to play God regarding her guilt or innocence. He was deeply suspicious of her, as she was of him. His brother had been the black sheep of the family. He and Jameson hadn't been close, and yet Jameson seemed bent on avenging his brother, despite what he'd said about justice. It was even possible that he'd set up the two attempts on Mattie, and then saved her life to win her trust so she would open up to him.

Extreme, but possible.

She huddled in the blanket, watching Cross.

In truth, she wasn't sure she could ever let herself trust him, and it wasn't just about him or the situation they were in. She had harbored a distrust of the male gender since earliest childhood. Her mother was a lush rose who had bloomed too early, and she'd used her sex appeal in the worst possible way. The men in her life were brutish and controlling, including Mattie's father, a truck driver who was gone before Mattie could crawl.

Lela Smith had given up her own child when Mattie was four in favor of her current live-in boyfriend, who'd shown an unhealthy interest in Mattie. That's when Mattie was dumped on her unmarried aunt, whose staunchly feminist views had eventually rubbed off. Before her transfer to Rowe Academy, Mattie had studied avidly, become an all-around honor student, avoided boys at all costs and played down the much-too-lovely features inherited from her mother.

She'd come to see beauty as a dangerous thing, and her ordeal at the boarding school and Ivy's death had seemed to confirm that. She didn't believe most men could be trusted to protect the vulnerability they seemed to crave in a woman, so she had decided to protect herself in the only way that made sense. She would depend on no one but herself.

Not much had changed, Mattie realized, except that at thirty-eight, it was getting harder to convince the world—and herself—that she could get along just fine without the opposite sex. And Jimmy Broud, whose eyes reminded her of the sky at dusk, was not shy anymore.

"I hope you like salmagundi," Jameson said.

Not gumbo, but close. Salmagundi was a spicy, savory chicken broth with summer vegetables and sausage. "Love it."

He carried a tray of food, but waited until Mattie had pushed herself to a sitting position before he positioned it on her lap. There was a crock of soup, a mug of lemonade and a small loaf of moist dark pumpernickel bread, steaming warm with raisins. The icy bottle of beer must have been intended for him.

Ravenous. Mattie did nothing but eat until she'd staved

off the hunger that gripped her from the first bite. Jameson seemed to take some kind of amusement from watching her as he sipped his beer.

The soup was ambrosia, and Mattie could cheerfully have died from an overdose of warm raisin pumpernickel bread. She didn't want to think about what it would taste like slathered with cream cheese.

A short time later, when she'd eaten all she could manage, she pushed the tray away, pleasantly flushed. She had given up fighting the urge to smile at him.

"Delicious, thank you. Now can I have my clothes?"

He collected the tray and set it on the console, next to the terrified woman in the coffin. "Rest, first," he suggested. "You're sleepy. I can see it. Your eyelids are getting heavy."

His hypnotic voice almost worked. Mattie was tired. She could have curled up and hibernated. But she had phone calls to make and some strategizing to do, and she couldn't do it in Jameson Cross's bedroom, no matter how tempting an idea that might be. She had to continue to think of him as the enemy. If she'd had only herself to consider, it might have been different, but her friends were counting on her, and she couldn't take any chances.

"I have to go," she said, assuming a firm tone. "I'll lock and deadbolt myself in my hotel room and alert the security guards. If that doesn't work, I'll hire a bodyguard, okay?"

"If that doesn't work, you could be dead."

"Lay off those detective magazines, Mr. Cross."

Mattie gingerly scooted to the side of the bed and was pleased at how strong she felt. She'd pulled the blanket around her for cover, but this time when her feet hit the ground, she heard a clicking noise.

"Shit," she breathed at the knifelike pain. Her knee had gone out. Even a little weight hurt. She gave the bathroom a measuring look, wondering if she could hobble that far. She would crawl if she had to.

The blanket made it tricky going, but she bunched it up and tucked it in here and there. Ignoring her host's skeptical expression, she limped toward the igloo of blue glass, some twenty feet away. She ignored the fact that Cross seemed to be channeling all the negative energy in the universe as he watched her with his steel-gray eyes. She was going to make it one way or the other.

She was breathless by the time she got there, but it was mostly from fighting with the bedding. He'd draped her clothing neatly over the hamper and set her bag next to it. Now all she had to do was get the slacks and sweater set on.

She sat on the toilet, draped the blanket over her shoulders like a tent and started with her underwear. Her bra was the worst, but her slacks were difficult, too, because she had to stand up and sit back down. She hadn't realized how swollen her knee was or how exhausting getting dressed could be.

"Are you all right?"

Jameson's voice startled her. She was pulling on the cardigan to her sweater set when he appeared in the doorway. She didn't want him to see how bad it was. "Of course," she said as she gripped the sink and pulled herself to her feet. "I just need to— Oh!"

Her knee wouldn't hold her, and she sat back down. "Give me a minute."

"I have a better idea," he said. "Let's get some ice on that knee. I may even have a pain pill."

It probably shouldn't have surprised her that he had great, sexy hands. His palm was wide and strong, his fingers long and tapered. He could have played the violin. Or basketball. She'd never seen a more gorgeous Mound of Jupiter, which was developed almost to the point of arrogance. She'd had a glimpse or two of that, firsthand. Of course, he might have said the same about her. Interesting that the smoothness of his fingers held the possibility of psychic abilities. It also indicated a sensual nature.

Mattie was stretched out on Jameson's living room couch, an ice pack on her bad knee as she cradled his hand in her own and studied it.

"Am I going to live to be a hundred?" he asked her. He was sitting on a table trunk in front of the couch, bent toward her and watching her analyze the relief map of his past, present and future.

"Well, let's see," she murmured.

She'd never really believed in the practice of palmistry. Her mother had used it to make money off people's hopes and fears, and Lela Smith had been particularly good with men, able to reduce them to drooling idiots when she traced their love lines with her shiny red fingernails and exclaimed at what wonderful lovers they must be.

Maybe that's why Mattie had agreed when Jameson asked her to read his palm. In a weak moment, she'd probably thought it would give her some kind of advantage. Of course, he hadn't asked about his love line. She almost wished he had.

"You're on borrowed time," she told him.

"Where does it say that?"

She pointed out the abrupt break in his life line and casually explained that it didn't mean he was going to die, just that there were some major changes coming. "Of course, it could also mean you're going to die."

Those lavender-gray eyes of his peered at her. "You liked telling me that, didn't you?"

"Of course not."

"Tell the truth. If a car ran over me tomorrow, you wouldn't be sorry."

She would miss the boy who'd delivered the supplies—

and called out that he just wanted to know who she was. Of course, she didn't say that.

"Taking the Fifth?" he said. "In that case, do I get another palmistry question?"

She shrugged. She probably owed him that.

"If I looked at your palm, would it tell me what you were doing at the crematory yesterday?"

Mattie adjusted the ice bag on her knee, in no hurry to answer his question. They'd moved to his living room because she'd insisted on a change of venue. She'd been in his bed long enough. He'd buttoned up his shirt. She'd insisted on that, too.

"Taking the Fifth again?" he probed.

"Fortunately, I don't have to," she said in her best finishing school voice. "This isn't a court of law, and I'm under no obligation to answer. But, since you asked, let's just say I was looking for something and leave it at that."

He hesitated, observing her. "A videotape, perhaps? The one that's missing from Ms. Rowe's instructional set?"

She drew in a breath. "What makes you think a tape is missing?" Thank God, the finishing school voice was still there when she spoke. It only made sense to play along, see what he said. He must want to get his hands on that tape, too, which posed an interesting dilemma for Mattie. If the men in the sex ring had been videotaped, there was a good possibility the lonely girls were on the tape, too. That didn't mean the girls had killed anyone, but it could ruin Jane, regardless.

"It was in my brother's journal," Cross explained. "He claimed the headmistress was running a sex ring, and the missing tape would prove it. It was supposed to have been her private social registry. I'd like to have a look at it."

He let that thought linger. "I imagine you would, too."

It almost sounded as if he was suggesting they join

forces. Interesting idea. Mattie had no intention of buddying up with Jameson Cross, but she didn't have to let him know that. This might be her chance to find out what else he'd gleaned from his brother's journal, even if it meant exposing herself a bit. Sometimes you had to give the fish a little line to land it.

"Who wouldn't want to see the missing tape," she said, "if there actually is one. I'd also like to know why the tapes were entered as evidence, but never used, and why no one seemed to notice that one was missing."

Jameson nodded. "Good point. I didn't know they'd been entered as evidence."

Mattie shrugged. Were they bonding? She hoped *he* thought so. Of course, he could be playing her as cleverly as she was playing him. She should never forget that.

He'd turned on a sound system earlier, and the music that played throughout the cavernous house was Latin in rhythm, a soft, dreamy samba that made you want to close your eyes and sway to the beat.

Very sensual, she thought, glancing down at his fingers. Why was she still holding his hand? The question made her stomach drop. Or maybe it was the heat of his skin. Suddenly he was too close for comfort.

She really should leave palmistry alone. It always backfired.

"Speaking of which," she said, dropping his hand, "I need to check my cell messages. I have a call in to the Marin County prosecutor's office. Maybe he's returned it by now."

"Who? Frank O'Neill?"

She reached down for her shoulder bag, which sat beside the couch and opened the zipper compartment. She had decided to let a little more play into the line, let the fish show her what he had.

"Yes, he's one of the people I came here to talk to," she

said. "I think the missing tape may have had exculpatory evidence that was overlooked at trial."

"Exculpatory for my brother or for you?"

She had just admitted that she was looking for the tape. Interesting that he'd brushed right over that. "Both of us," she said, "I hope."

She had her cell phone open, but he stayed her hand.

"How do you feel about a party tonight?"

"Are you serious? I can hardly walk."

He shrugged. "That's too bad. I'm sure Frank would love to have met you."

Cross seemed to be dangling some bait, as well. "Frank, the D.A.? You know him?"

"We've been friends for years. I'm invited to a party there tonight, his wife's birthday. I wasn't planning to go, no date."

She sighed. "I suppose I could be your date since you don't have long to live. This could be my only chance."

"To date me?"

"To meet Frank."

His dark eyes glimmered. "So that's a yes? From the woman who can hardly walk?"

"I'm *fine*."

"Your head is fine? You knee is fine? That's not what I heard."

"My head's much better. It hardly hurts at all." A stab of pain forced her to shut her eyes for a second. "My knee is…manageable. I'll use this ice bag on the trip to my hotel, and I'll take that pain pill you offered."

"Fine, but I'm driving you there."

Of course, she wanted to argue with him, but it didn't make sense. She couldn't drive herself, and her rental car was probably still over at the funeral home anyway. Plus, she didn't want to be alone yet no matter how much she'd protested earlier. She didn't feel safe in the placid little community of Tiburon.

He rose suddenly, leaving her to wonder what he was doing. She followed him with her gaze as he went deeper into the living room, stopping in an area that looked as if it might have been his office, and perhaps his library, too. The outside wall was a floor-to-ceiling bookcase with a thirty-foot wheeled ladder that looked as if it had come from the Library of Congress. Made of rich, dark polished wood, it had three standing platforms with guardrails, and Mattie had never seen anything so beautiful.

"It's magnificent," she said, certain he had no idea what she meant.

A collection of framed posters caught her eye, as well. She couldn't see them well, but they looked like they might have been vintage men's magazine covers.

"What are you doing?" she asked as he bent over a set of cardboard boxes that sat on the floor near his desk. He held up what looked like a videocassette.

"Now, I have a confession," he said, returning with the cassette in his hand. "This is one of Ms. Rowe's tapes. I have what I believe is a copy of the entire set, minus number fifty, the last one. Someone sent them to me anonymously."

"Who would do that?"

"No clue."

Her heart was pounding. She'd been probing for information, but she hadn't expected this. "Have you watched them?"

"I did, and they left me with lots of questions."

Obviously, she was supposed to ask what those questions were. She couldn't have done so with a steady voice. She felt almost violated that he'd intruded on the horrors of her past. He'd witnessed at least some of her humiliations, and no one was supposed to know about that except Jane and Breeze. Sometimes she even resented that they knew. These were the most private of degradations, buried in a part of her that she could barely reach. They were walled off, a part of the crippling chaos she had to protect herself from.

"What do you know about the sex ring, Mattie? Was she really selling young girls like you? Were you a part of that?"

She forced a brittle laugh. "Now, I am taking the Fifth."

"Yeah, I'll bet." A piece of black cloth trailed from the pocket of his jeans. He pulled the wadded black object free and showed it to her. "You're probably wondering what happened to this," he said.

Mattie's heart sank when she saw what it was. Her blindfold. He wanted to know if it had anything to do with the sex ring. He really would stop at nothing, she realized.

"I figured someone must need a blindfold more than I did," she said coldly.

"I guess that depends on how much *you* need it."

She shrugged to let him know she didn't care one way or the other, but the swiftness with which she snatched it out of his hand might have given her away. At least she had it back, and he couldn't use it as a weapon against her. Thank God he didn't know it *was* a weapon. She wondered if he knew how profoundly he had disappointed her.

32

There was an assassin on the guest list of Frank O'Neill's lavish birthday party for his wife. A wolf moved with easy lupine grace among the unsuspecting sheep. Complacent animals, those sheep. They had no idea how much easier they made this guest's task with their casual smugness. Why would they give a thought to their safety at the estate of Marin County's top lawman? Rarefied air, they all assumed. What evil could touch them here?

This guest scanned the crowd, a drink in hand, looking very much a part of the upscale scene, however, the quick, bright smile and friendly manner were a guise. This was work. Everyone was being observed and assessed. Some were being measured for their character flaws. Others for coffins.

The sprawling Mediterranean mansion bustled with activity, but most of the guests milled around the blue mosaic swimming pool. The birthday girl had not yet arrived to be surprised—and no one suspected a predator in their midst. They counted everyone here as a friend and, more importantly, as one of their kind, safe and properly enlightened... and that certainly included this guest. *Yes, it includes me.*

The assassin in sheep's clothing.

None of these complacent snobs would ever *suspect me. I look nothing like a predator—which is part of my unique skill set—but how could you reasonably call me anything else? I kill as necessary. Never randomly. Rarely with animosity. Assassins always say it isn't personal. They're doing a job. In my case, it is personal. I have to kill to protect the sanctity of my world, and because my world is a complex place, there are several more who must die. That's why I'm here. My next victim is one of the unsuspecting sheep, a guest at this lovely party, and the last person any of them would ever expect to meet such a gruesome end.*

The pain pill seemed to be working. Mattie's knee had settled down to the point that she could walk in sling-back heels without wincing, and her hair hid the bruising at the base of her skull. She'd been selective about her outfit, too, a silk capri set with three-quarter sleeves on loan from Breeze. The dizzy spells were disconcerting, but it was a small price to pay for some one-on-one contact with Frank O'Neill.

"Where is he?" she asked Jameson as they crossed the foyer of the palatial estate, took a long hallway, studded with recesses that housed an impressive collection of Chihuly glass, and entered the great room. Through an entire wall of French doors, thrown open wide, she could see the guests, grouped in colorful clusters on the terrace that surrounded the pool.

"I'll point him out when I see him," Jameson said. His glance lingered on Mattie's form-fitting outfit in sea shades of aqua and green. "That's nice. You're going to fit right in."

She felt a twist of pleasure that probably showed in the way she refused to look at him. Breeze had picked out several things she thought would look good on Mattie when she did Mattie's makeover, and she'd left them in the closet when she moved to the Four Seasons. This one had fit to perfection.

"Can I get you a drink?" Jameson asked as they walked out onto the terrace. At her nod, he reminded her that she'd just taken a pain pill. "Sip it slowly and stay low to the ground."

Jameson left to get the drinks while Mattie checked out the buffet tables. She pretended to be as excited over the food as some of the other exclaiming guests, but she was actually gauging the crowd. There were no faces she readily recognized, but it had been a lot of years. The names might ring some bells. As would hers. She'd already told Jameson she didn't want him to use her real name or her judicial credentials. For tonight she was Lela Smith. Her mother's name was her middle name, although she'd never told anyone.

Jameson was stuck in a long line at the bar so Mattie kept herself busy by putting together a plate for the two of them. Cracked crab, prawns and oysters on the half shell. He looked like a man who could appreciate a good raw oyster, she decided wryly. Maybe she wanted to pay him back for his grim insistence on chauffeuring her to her hotel room and waiting while she got ready for tonight. That had been hell. One dizzy spell as they left the hotel had convinced him she wasn't strong enough, and it had taken all her persuasive powers to get him here.

She'd also had to get free of him long enough to check her cell messages. She'd done that while locked in the bathroom. Jane had called several times from a very noisy phone, Breeze once and there were half a dozen calls from Mattie's office, but only the last one counted. It was from Jaydee telling her he had everything under control. She hoped that included the kidnapping case. Mattie had left messages for both Jane and Breeze. No details, but she'd assured them she was fine and making progress.

A waiter with a tray of champagne came by. Mattie set down the food she'd prepared in favor of the flute he offered.

It would be less obvious if she sipped while she spied. Beyond the terrace and the pool, there was a view of San Francisco Bay that included the famous bridge, and as the minutes ticked by, and the falling sun cast its amber spell over the waterfront, she could feel some of her tension easing.

The party crowd looked as though they were having a good time. They greeted one another warmly, with handshakes and hugs, but the chatter and laughter sounded a little forced. Mattie noticed a few singles here and there, mostly young men, although one of them, an attractive woman with dark hair, caught Mattie's eye and smiled.

Mattie felt a twinge of unease. Did she know the woman? She didn't want to stare, so she averted her gaze to the other end of the pool, where a distinguished, graying man, probably in his late forties, was chatting with a group in a spacious gazebo. The people around him were clearly admirers, and the way he held court made Mattie think he might be the party's host.

She set her champagne down and began to stroll that way. As she got closer to the gazebo, she heard someone call him Frank and compliment him on his beautiful home.

It was O'Neill. Mattie wasn't quite sure what to do. She glanced over at the drink line and saw that Jameson was no longer there. He seemed to have left the pool area, and she couldn't wait for him. She would have to deal with this herself, and she felt oddly naked without her credentials. What a power suit those judicial robes were.

Breeze's attractiveness theory came to mind. Mattie had worn her hair down, but she hadn't had time to do much besides brush it out and hope for the best. She gave her head a shake, hoping to create a bit of sexy wildness, and quickly licked her lips to wet them. What was she *doing?* She'd inhaled too much of Breeze's fairy dust. It had gone to her brain.

O'Neill seemed to have made the rounds in the gazebo and was on his way out. To Mattie's surprise, he descended the steps and came straight toward her. She'd been ready to intercept him no matter which way he went. Now, all she had to do was hold out her hand.

"Mr. O'Neill? Lovely party. I'm Lela Smith."

He looked confused, but only for a moment. "Ah, yes, Jameson called me about you earlier. He said you were a lawyer, and you had some questions about the discrepancies in his brother's case. Can I ask what your interest is in the case?"

"I love a good puzzle." She clasped his hand with both of hers and lightly stroked his wrist with her finger. "Is this convenient? Could you possibly take some time now?"

He glanced at her hair, her face. His breathing seemed to slow a little. "Certainly, Jameson is a good friend. How can I be of help?"

Breeze would love this, Mattie thought. She'd expected to be dodged and ditched. Of course, she hadn't asked the questions yet. "Can you tell me why the records in the Broud case are sealed?" she asked. "He was exonerated on DNA evidence. Why is access still being denied?"

O'Neill shrugged. "You need to ask that question of the judge who ordered them sealed. It could be because of the renewed interest in the case, or there may be information that's still sensitive after all this time. You know of course that it's sometimes necessary to protect the identities of the parties involved, like informants and witnesses, particularly underage witnesses."

Mattie did know. She'd had to order records sealed a few times in her judicial career, but it would have been a shame to interrupt him. Frank O'Neill wasn't one to hide his lawyerly light under a bushel, and she was happy to have some of it shed on her.

"Everyone seems to think I prosecuted that case," he said.

"I was a new hire at the time, green at the gills. They had me jumping through legal research hoops, but I didn't get near the courtroom. I was never in the loop, but I can tell you this. They believed they had their man. It was William Broud, open and shut."

Mattie had already eliminated him as a member of the sex ring. He'd been too young at the time, but it was interesting how he'd put that. *Never in the loop.*

"And you believed it was Broud, too?" she asked.

He folded his arms. "Based on the evidence at that time, sure."

"Do you know why the files were originally sealed?"

"Again, the judge of record is the man you'd have to ask, and I'm afraid he's retired and moved away."

Nola Daniels had already made sure Mattie knew that. O'Neill might know how Mattie could reach the judge, but she thought better of asking. She didn't want to seem more than curious at this point. And if she decided to track the judge down it shouldn't be too difficult with her connections in the field.

"Were you aware that Ms. Rowe had a videotape collection? It was introduced into evidence by the prosecution, but never used."

Mattie wasn't pulling any punches. She didn't have time, but if he was surprised at her grasp of the case's details, he didn't let on. "I'm aware of the video collection, yes," he said.

"Did you know that one of them was missing, possibly at the scene? Apparently it was the video equivalent of a little black book. It was called Ms. Rowe's Private Social Registry."

"A little black book? I hadn't heard it put quite that way." His smile was faint, but intrigued. "It does sound like a video log of possible suspects, doesn't it? A thing like that could break the case wide open."

Mattie stared at him. Could she and Frank O'Neill possibly be on the same page? She'd expected him to launch into a heated defense of his office. She hadn't accused the prosecution of screwing up, but it was implied.

Guardedly, she said, "That tape needs to be found, Mr. O'Neill. It may have disappeared because it reveals the killer."

His nod said he was in total agreement, and Mattie pressed on. "Could we meet and talk about this further? Tomorrow, perhaps?"

"Certainly," he said, spiriting a business card from the change pocket of his slacks. "Give my office a call in the morning. I'll tell my assistant to clear some time for you."

Mattie debated kissing him. She also debated telling him about Millicent Rowe's letter to the man who betrayed her. That would make an even stronger case for one of her lovers having killed her, but she'd probably said as much as she should tonight—and besides, something else had caught O'Neill's eye. The pool lights had come up as the sun went down, and he seemed to be looking over Mattie's shoulder.

"My God," he whispered, "it's my wife. We were supposed to surprise her. Excuse me, I have to go."

Mattie turned as he hurried away, hoping she hadn't spoiled the birthday party. Still, she couldn't bring herself to regret having approached Frank O'Neill. He'd been more forthcoming than she'd dared to hope. She might even have an ally in the district attorney, and that was her first ray of light in this frightening black hole of an investigation.

Her only concern now was the little paranoid voice in her head, wondering if she and her friends were on the video in some incriminating way. What a terrible irony if instead of freeing them, it could seal their fate. But she'd already decided to take that risk. She was dealing with a haystack at least the size of Marin County, and the needle could be anywhere. She would never find it on her own, but given what she already knew about the sex ring and her suspicions about the men involved, she might be able to get to it before anyone else did.

She watched O'Neill stride around the pool, and as her gaze transferred to the slender blond woman he hurried toward, Mattie breathed out a four-letter word.

O'Neill raised his hand and called out to the crowd. "Excuse me, everyone. My wife, Lane, has arrived and surprised all of us when we were supposed to surprise her."

Laughter and applause broke out. There were congratulations and calls of happy birthday, but Mattie was too astounded to join in. Lane Davison was married to Frank O'Neill?

Mattie wasn't sure her legs would hold her. She tried to step back, but her bad knee felt as if it had frozen at the joint. Where was Jameson? She had to get out of here. She searched the pool area, but couldn't find him. He may have gone inside, but she couldn't possibly risk going in to look for him. She would have to walk by Lane.

Mattie found her footing and began to creep backward, melting into the crowd. There must be some side or back way out of this place. If Lane saw her and called her by name, all the goodwill Mattie had created with Frank O'Neill would be lost. He couldn't know she'd been a student at Rowe Academy.

Without too much difficulty, she found a gated wall behind the gazebo and let herself out. The rocky terrain of the bluffs led to rugged cliffs that dropped to the water, and the last flickers of waning sunlight made it difficult to see. It would be dark in moments, and a low-lying mist had crept up from the water. Mattie could see it swirling around her ankles.

She slipped off her heels and tread carefully, making her way among the embedded rocks and the bushes. The estate's guest parking area was on the other side of the house, if she remembered correctly.

Darkness fell swiftly, and thick, silvery clouds blocked the moon. Only the lights from the house illuminated her way, and the mist was thickening, swirling up her legs. She couldn't see her own feet, and she was terrified of losing her balance again.

A rustling sound rose from the bushes behind her. The wind, she told herself. Or a small animal. She couldn't see well enough to safely walk any faster, but she sped up her pace anyway. At least her knee didn't hurt. Adrenaline, probably.

The rustling continued. It sounded as if something was following her, but she wasn't going to let her mind go there. This was a party at someone's home. She'd come with Jameson, and no one would have expected her to be out here by herself, alone and vulnerable. All she had to do was get around to the front of the house where the lights were.

The moon seemed to brighten and then go dark, enveloped by clouds. She strained to see the ground as the mists thickened, closing around her. It was hard to imagine that people as obviously wealthy as the O'Neills didn't have more security lights on their property. Interesting that O'Neill was wealthy in the first place, she thought. On the district attorney's salary? Maybe it was Lane's family money.

"Mattie?"

"What?" She hesitated, thinking someone had whispered her name. She wasn't sure where it had come from, but the rustling had stopped, and in the sudden quiet, Mattie heard her own galloping heart. Someone had spoken to her, she was sure of it. As she glanced around, she saw a shadowy form on the path behind her, not twenty feet away.

"Who's there?" she said.

The form moved closer, and for one crazy second in time,

Mattie thought she saw a face she recognized, features she recognized.

"Ms. Rowe?" she whispered.

Mattie dropped the shoes she was carrying and ran, flying over the ground, heedless of her knee. She was a child, running for the pine forest, running to safety. Running for her life. That couldn't be Ms. Rowe back there. Ms. Rowe was dead. But Mattie had seen her pale, ghoulish face. She had seen it.

Somehow she made it around to the front of the house and found Jameson's Escalade in the first row of the valet parking. The door was unlocked, and she slipped inside to check the console between the front seats. She was looking for a car key, which she hoped would fit the ignition. When Jameson had opened the console to get the valet key for the attendant, Mattie had noticed an extra key, but now, the dim light made it difficult to see.

Her heart surged against her ribs, seeming to expand with every beat. She feared it was going to explode. Had she seen someone behind her? She prayed it was only shadows, but she had to get away from here. Once she was safe, she could call Jameson on her cell and leave him a message.

She found the extra key, and it was for the ignition. The car started immediately, but as she wheeled back, she saw someone in the rearview mirror. It was Jameson, but she couldn't hit the brakes fast enough. The car shrieked and shuddered, plowing into an object before she could come to a stop. Mattie collapsed against the wheel, sobbing. Please don't let it be him she hit.

33

She got out of the car and saw Jameson coming straight at her. There wasn't time to say anything. His grip on her arms nearly lifted her off her feet. "What the hell's going on, Mattie? Are you all right? You just ran my car into that Mercedes."

"I didn't see it. I didn't see you, either." She couldn't force her voice above a whisper. "I'll pay for the damage—or my insurance company will. Both cars."

God, he held her tight. His hands were anchors. She couldn't tell if he was angry or determined not to let her fall apart. Either way it felt good. She *was* falling apart.

"*Are* you all right?" His fiery breath bathed her face. "Where were you going?"

She shook her head, unable to explain. She kept expecting the parking attendants to show up. The car crash had sounded thunderous to her, but maybe the noise of the party had drowned it out.

"Let's go inside," he said. "I'll get you a drink, and we can talk."

"No, I need to leave. Can we go? Please? I'll tell you about it in the car."

His response was immediate. Once he had Mattie settled in the passenger seat, and he'd tucked his business card under the Mercedes's windshield wiper, they were on their way.

The accident didn't seem to be much more than a fender bender, but it had jarred the hell out of Mattie, especially when she'd seen Jameson back there.

By the time they drove through the gates of the estate, she'd collected herself enough to confront him. "You disappeared," she said. "I couldn't find you anywhere at the party."

"I had an accident, too."

Mattie lifted her head. A mysterious essence filled the car. "What is that smell? It's you," she said, peering at him. "You smell like…"

"Margaritas? The lady in front of me was juggling four of them, and I made the mistake of trying to help. Now I'm wearing two of them."

With a pained expression, he plucked at the shoulder of his shirt. It was still damp enough to cling to him.

Mattie laughed softly. It sounded like something he might make up, except for the smell. "Is that why you left? Why didn't you tell me?"

"You and Frank seemed to be hitting it off. I didn't want to interrupt the flow."

He turned south on Highway 131, which made her wonder where they were headed. The darkness outside was so thick the road couldn't be distinguished from the hills or the sky. A black cloak could have been thrown over the car. The only light glowed from the dash, and it illuminated Jameson's face in a way that startled her.

His profile was cut out of shadows. It reminded her of the house he lived in, half light, half dark. Not that she hadn't noticed his looks before. They were striking, but it wasn't something she allowed herself to dwell on, and she didn't want to go there now. He could be the devil for all she knew. He probably *was* her devil.

He seemed to sense her eyes on him, and his quizzical glance elicited an icy sensation in her gut. She didn't understand why he'd swooped into her life in the first place, and now she had a hunch he was taking her back to his house. She didn't have the energy to deal with that at this moment. One thing at a time.

"I have an appointment with Frank tomorrow," she told him. "He's not only willing to discuss the video, he seems anxious."

"So it wasn't Frank who scared you off?"

Mattie saw no reason not to tell him. "It was his wife, Lane. We were at Rowe together, but she wasn't a friend." Lane Davison had struck the most vicious blows in the head-mistress's office that day. She'd bared her teeth like an animal and kicked Mattie in the ribs, cracking several.

"She frightened you that much?" Jameson asked. "What did she do?"

"It wasn't Lane who frightened me." Mattie bent over and brushed dirt from her bare feet. She wasn't eager to clear up the confusion. "I thought she might recognize me and blow my cover, so I slipped out the back gate. It was dark, and— This is embarrassing. I guess I panicked. I heard someone whisper my name, and I thought I was being followed."

Mattie's underarms were drenched. "It was probably nothing," she said. "I am sorry about the car."

"I'm not worried about the car."

They both went silent, and Mattie listened to the low roar of the air rushing past the car windows. It was almost as loud as the air rushing through her nostrils and into her lungs, her brain. What was that roaring inside her, fear? Dread? It felt as if she was hyperventilating, bringing on another one of those damn anxiety attacks.

The part of her brain that was still logical told her that someone was trying to frighten her. Not kill her, frighten her. She *had* heard her name out there, and she *had* seen a face.

But the headmistress was long dead, and Mattie didn't believe in ghosts beyond the kind that her memory could conjure. It had to be someone who wanted to terrify her. They were still trying to scare her off.

"We're going to my place," Jameson said.

She didn't even try to protest. There was no point. His voice said he wouldn't budge—and she didn't know whether to be glad or afraid. Maybe he hadn't been laying traps for her with the tapes or the blindfold. Maybe he was just trying to solve a mystery, as she was. She'd never partnered up with anyone in her life, except Jane and Breeze, and even then she hadn't depended on either of them to fight her battles. Most of the time she'd fought hers *and* theirs. She couldn't take the chance of anyone getting in her way, slowing her down. That was dangerous.

Now, she seemed to be weakening, letting him help her when she desperately needed to keep her wits about her and be stronger than she'd ever been. She felt like that bleeding kid in the dorm again, the one who wouldn't let Jane look at her wounds. When things got tough, she had always split off and handled it alone. It was just safer alone.

Jameson rested a shoulder against the door frame, watching Mattie sleep, and wondering why he was doing this—rescuing birds with broken wings, treed kittens, whatever needed rescuing most. He had a bad habit of picking up strays and dropping money into every open palm. It had to do with making up for Billy. A lifetime of saving lost souls as penance for not saving his brother's. That was Jameson's sentence.

But this one was something else. No ordinary stray, she. This could be his brother's killer. Mattie Smith, the crusader judge, might very well be hiding her own crimes. And the ironies didn't stop there. She put people in jail, and he tried to get them out with his books. Now he wanted to put *her* in.

What the hell was he doing?

If he'd had any thoughts of keeping his enemy close they'd gone out the window the night he'd bathed her and slept next to her. *She'd called out his name in her sleep, and he'd had no idea what to do…so, he'd done nothing except whisper that he was there.*

"I just want to know who you are."

She'd said that in her sleep, too.

Apparently he wasn't satisfied with saving her life. Tonight, he'd taken her as his guest to the party, consoled her when she'd racked up his car, brought her home and given her his bed. He'd stayed up to get his thoughts down on paper, and then he'd sacked out on one of the living room couches. Hours ago, actually, but sleep hadn't come. Now the entire loft was dark, and he felt like a ghost, wandering his own home. He'd gone from room to room until he ended up here, in his own bedroom doorway, aware that this was where he wanted to be all along, watching her.

What the hell was he doing?

She looked more like a newborn filly than a kitten, curled up on her side, favoring her injured knee. An ice pack lay on the floor, probably soaking his carpet by now. Naturally he hadn't failed to notice that the sheet had slipped away and the shirt he'd loaned her revealed the curve of her butt and the tuck of her legs.

Nice, he admitted. Too nice. His body was suddenly generating warmth as if for a long winter, starting with the hopeful little blaze in the pit of his stomach. His jaw had heated up, too. And muscles were tightening where they shouldn't be.

Clearly his mind wanted to take him somewhere he shouldn't be going. It was straining at the bit, urging him to imagine what it would be like to make love to a spitfire like her. Fiery expiation? Or fiery death? There would be no saving him then. No saving either one of them.

He'd made the grave mistake of getting too close to one of his causes once, and she had almost taken him down with her. A prominent banker in the Bay area had been viciously slain, and the police had charged his two teenage sons. Jameson became aware of the widow when he saw her on TV, denying that her sons were involved and begging for their lives.

Grief had seemed to cover the woman in a shroud of grace and beauty that she might not otherwise have had. Jameson was taken with her at first sight. He'd contacted her and offered help, which she'd eagerly accepted. But in a bizarre twist, it was Jameson who discovered the evidence that would eventually convict her sons, and he'd had to break the news to her. She'd pretended to accept it, but that very night she'd overdosed on sleeping medication, apparently unable to bear the grisly truth. He'd been half in love with her, and he hadn't seen it coming. For years afterward, he'd felt responsible and had questioned his career choice. Maybe he still did.

He seemed to be attracted to tragedy in the flesh, and here it was again, in his bed. Of course, he was drawn to Mattie Smith. He was drawn to everything doomed, and if anyone had ever been that, she was.

What the hell was he thinking about?

Frank O'Neill's office was in the county courthouse in San Rafael, about a half hour north of Mattie's hotel in Tiburon. Mattie had already been there before so she had no trouble finding it, but she was uneasy about the meeting as she pulled into the courthouse lot. Fortunately, she was early. There was time to collect herself and get her bearings.

She'd called the car rental agency this morning and had them pick up the Dodge Stratus at the funeral home. Afterward, Jameson had driven her over to the agency so she could get a new car. It was an expensive trade-off. They charged her a transport fee and tacked on additional costs, but worth every penny. She'd picked out the most nondescript four-door sedan she could find, but it had made her feel as if she were starting out fresh.

Now she drew on her linen jacket—the day had started out typically chilly and overcast for this time of year—and let herself out of the car. Her knee was still sore when she put weight on it, but she'd taken two extra-strength over-the-counter pain pills at Jameson's.

He'd been different this morning, a reserve about him when he'd offered to fix her breakfast. She hadn't wanted anything but toast, and she'd fixed it herself, sensing the tension between them. The timing of his mood had made her feel as if she should back off, too. The night before she'd actually thought about the possibility of opening up to him, confiding, trusting, even just a little. Strange, how the mere notion had been enough to frighten her off, and yet there was a part of her that was exhausted from carrying every burden alone. But already that glimpse of vulnerability was gone. Maybe he'd sensed the change in her, too.

She glanced around the lot, checking out her surroundings. It was broad daylight, but if she'd learned anything the past couple of days, it was that she couldn't be too careful. She'd dressed for the weather in gray linen slacks and a silk blend turtleneck. No Breeze getups today, although she had taken time with her hair and makeup, including a smudge of shadow to enhance her blue eyes. That attractiveness thing seemed to have merit, whether Mattie liked the idea or not. She doubted something so superficial had much impact beyond first impressions, but she was still at that stage with Frank O'Neill.

On her way into the building, Mattie checked the directory to verify that O'Neill was there. She'd done a great deal of thinking about her talk with him at the party. His candor and openness had impressed her, but she'd also realized that this could be his star turn. The William Broud murder had received some media attention, but finding the real killer of Millicent Rowe after twenty years would be quite a coup, especially if it required him to probe into the workings of his own office.

He had everything to gain if the videotape was found. But Mattie might have everything to lose. That was the tightrope she'd walked this entire investigation. She and her friends were not blameless. The evidence she sought could either exonerate or incriminate them. She wouldn't know until she saw it, and by then it might be too late.

She had to find the video first. That was the only safe way.

As Mattie walked through the lobby of the building to the elevator bank, she saw a wall-size plaque commemorating contributors to a building fund for a new courthouse. What caught her eye was the name showcased in the center. He was one of the wealthiest men in the country, Silicon Valley venture capitalist David Grace.

Mattie knew very little about Grace, except that he had very shrewdly seeded start-ups that thrived, despite the nineties tech crash, and that he was a scientist himself. But for some reason the name wouldn't leave her mind, and by the time she'd reached her floor, she thought she knew why.

David Grace. D.G.? It was far-fetched, but she couldn't completely discount the possibility that he might be the man who'd given Ms. Rowe the flowers. It also occurred to her that he could be the same Grace who'd endowed the scholarship fund that got her and the other girls into Rowe Academy. They'd been called the Grace scholarship girls.

Mattie checked her watch as she entered the waiting area. She still had a little time, and she needed to make some phone calls. The receptionist, an older lady with dyed black hair and a rosy complexion, greeted Mattie with the news that

Mr. O'Neill was running a few minutes late, so Mattie excused herself and slipped back out into the hallway.

She checked her voice mail first, skipped messages from Jane and Jaydee—she would get to them later—and listened to one from Tansy Black. Tansy was convinced someone had wanted to silence William Broud. She remembered reading in the trial transcript that the headmistress used heartwine for cosmetic purposes. Tansy didn't think it coincidental that Broud had the poisonous herb in his system. Mattie deleted the message.

She called Jane and Breeze next. Neither answered, so Mattie left messages with just enough information to let them know that she may have identified Ms. Rowe's mystery lover. The way her heart raced told her she was onto something, but it was too soon to get excited about anything.

Just as she turned back to the reception area, her phone rang. The sudden shrilling alarmed her. Jane's voice alarmed her more.

"Mattie? I need you and Breeze here as soon as possible. There's a plane waiting at San Francisco airport. Can you come?"

"Jane, I'm about to meet with Frank O'Neill, the D.A."

"Reschedule, Mattie. This is serious. I'm not asking you now, I'm telling you. Be on that plane."

"What is it, Jane?"

"I can't say now. We'll talk when you get here."

"Did you get ahold of Breeze?"

"She's already at the airport. The pilot is waiting for you."

"Jane, what the hell is going on? Did you get my message?"

"I did. We'll talk about it when you get here. Dammit, Mattie, get your butt on that airplane. I'll see you in a few hours."

Jane clicked off, and Mattie stood there, stunned. There

was no question what she had to do—and no time to fall apart. She took a couple deep breaths to compose herself, and then she walked into the waiting area and cancelled her appointment with Frank O'Neill. She'd been called out of town on an emergency, she told the receptionist. She would reschedule when she got back.

34

Mattie was taken by limo into a back entrance of the White House, swiftly ushered up to the private quarters on the second floor and taken to a small, but lavishly appointed drawing room. Breeze was already there, and Mattie had never been so happy to see anyone as she was her friend.

"Holy shit, look at you," Breeze said, flinging out her arms. "You have on makeup?"

Mattie's throat ached as they embraced, and the emotion surprised her. She fought back the sting of tears. So much for the smoky eye look.

Breeze broke the hug and held Mattie at arm's length to examine her. The woman had her priorities.

"Is that eye shadow? And lip gloss? What color? It's good, but I'm thinking a little more emphasis on the red tones. You are a brunette, Mattie."

"Breeze, listen to me. I need your help. It's important."

"And lip gloss isn't?"

Mattie gave her a little shake to shut her up. "Did you get my message about David Grace? I have an assignment for you. I need a deep background check on Grace, but you have to be discreet. No using Google. Use my detective friend, if you like. Vince Denny."

"Mattie, I know how it's done. I have clients who are royalty, world leaders. The spa's security is hermetic. We do deep background on everyone from the pool guy to the president of Gambia."

Her heavily lashed gaze narrowed, and she touched Mattie's face. "You really should rethink the blush. Is that coral? It's giving your skin a yellow cast, and the hepatitis look is so last year."

"Breeze, someone may be trying to kill me."

"I know."

"You *know?*"

She smudged away a bit of Mattie's blush with her thumb. "There were two attempts, neither of which succeeded," she said, intent on reconfiguring Mattie's cheekbones, "possibly because my operative scared the assailant away, but more likely because your death was never the goal."

Mattie pushed Breeze's hand away. "Your *operative?* What kind of crap is that? Did you have me followed?"

Breeze sniffed, pretending to be offended. "Do you think you're the only one with access to an investigator? And by the way, whoever attacked you was too good to miss twice. He wasn't trying to kill you. He was—"

"Trying to scare me off," Mattie broke in. "I figured that much out. But if you had someone there why the hell did he let me get conked over the head and stuffed in a cadaver box?"

"You have your friend Jameson to thank for that. He confused the issue. My person thought Jameson was the assailant and kept him under surveillance. That's probably why the real assailant was able to execute his mission."

"Please, let's not use the word execute. Did this *operative* of yours actually see who hit me?"

"As I said, the assailant was good. My person wasn't able to ID him."

"But you know it was a man?"

"Not necessarily."

"Breeze, who *is* this person of yours? I want to talk to him."

Breeze's brown eyes were suddenly chilly. "No, Mattie, you don't. Believe me. He's well-trained, ex-military intelligence, and that's all I'm going to say. I won't let my people be compromised."

"But you'd let *me* be compromised, not to mention almost killed?"

The chilliness became disbelief. "That's not fair. He scared the assailant off the first time, and Jameson was an unwitting decoy the second. My person would certainly have intervened if he'd known what was going on."

"Why didn't you tell me about this before?"

"The same reason you kept quiet about Denny."

Mattie would have said no, obviously. Not that Breeze knew the meaning of the word. At the moment, Mattie's indignation was getting her nowhere. It seemed her friend had a security team on retainer. Apparently the spa business was high-risk these days.

"You're not angry, are you?" Breeze smoothed Mattie's eyebrows. "Let's get you a wax when we're done here. Jane must know someone. And we can get rid of that moustache while we're at it."

Mattie ducked out of Breeze's range. "I do *not* have a moustache."

"You *are* angry."

Mattie sighed. "Just call off your dogs, okay? If I want a tail, I'll arrange it on my own."

"Fine, fine." Breeze stepped back, tapping her lips with a perfectly manicured nail. "Are we sure you haven't already arranged for some? Tail, I mean. That Jameson Cross thing is pretty interesting, eh?"

She knew about Jameson. Why was Mattie not surprised?

"Whatever Jameson wanted, it wasn't that," Mattie said,

knowing Breeze wouldn't believe a word of it. Mattie wasn't sure what she believed, but she was now questioning the wisdom of having given Breeze a task as important as David Grace. Security team or not, Breeze had an amazing way of reducing everything to the urgency of a broken nail, even brushes with death. Mattie just hoped her blithe disregard didn't get them all killed.

Jane swept in, looking flustered but chic in her pale pink jacket and skirt. The jacket's gold braid trim and buttons shouted Chanel. She definitely did the First Lady thing to perfection, although she put her own spin on it. How many presidents' wives showed that much leg? The skirt was dangerously close to a mini.

"I'm sorry," Jane said, hurrying over to give Mattie and Breeze a quick hug each. She gestured toward an elegant brocade settee and a tray of refreshments sitting on the occasional table next to it.

"Have some iced tea and a sandwich," she said. "I thought you might want something after your whirlwind cross-country flight. Are you both all right? Did I scare you to death? I'm sorry, but there are some things you can't tell people over the phone."

Breeze helped herself to a cluster of grapes from a heaping fruit bowl. "Someone attacked Mattie," she said. "Twice."

"What?" Jane's face flushed as if she were angry. "That's not very funny, Breeze."

"Unfortunately, it's true." Mattie spotted a turkey sandwich and took a wedge. She was starving actually. They'd only had snacks on the chartered plane. Plenty of booze, but not much food.

"It's under control," she added, wishing she'd impressed upon Breeze the need for discretion where Jane was concerned. The last thing she needed was Jane going parental on her. "He was trying to scare me off, and it didn't work. I'm here. I'm fine. Now let's hear your story. Why are *we* here?"

Mattie's tone said, *Ask me another question about it, and I'll be forced to attack* you. Breeze saluted. Jane resigned herself with a shrug.

"Very well." Jane picked up a glass of iced tea and took a drink, as if preparing for an ordeal. "I have something to tell the two of you, and this is particularly hard for me. I should have told you long ago."

Breeze looked intrigued. "Jane has a secret?"

An odd crackling noise stopped the conversation. It sounded like a bad connection on a telephone line. Jane rose to have a look around. But Mattie had already spotted an old-fashioned rotary dial phone on a writing desk by the window. She picked up the receiver and listened to the line. It was quiet, but just to be safe, she unplugged the phone from the jack.

Meanwhile, Jane was on her cell, speaking to someone in a hushed voice. Mattie watched her with rising concern. Were her fingers trembling? She appeared fragile, almost breakable, and Mattie didn't know what to think. She'd had a glimpse of Jane's vulnerability once, and it had frightened her. Jane was their Gibraltar, if she could crack, they all could.

"It's safe to talk," Jane told them, seeming much more relaxed as she hung up the phone. "I checked the room myself, and I just verified that Larry won't be back until much later. He's at a fund-raiser tonight. I was supposed to go with him, but I begged off." She touched her forehead. "One of my headaches."

Breeze had a grape halfway to her mouth, but her arm appeared frozen. "Jane, cut the drama. You're driving me crazy."

Jane shot Breeze a glare. "First of all, I'm not surprised that someone went after Mattie, but I don't think they meant to kill her, either. We're being toyed with, all of us. Whoever killed Broud is sending signals that we're about to be exposed. He, or she, wants us to panic and do something stupid to incriminate ourselves. We're being flushed out."

Mattie could have argued that being stabbed wasn't her idea of a prank. But it wasn't easy to dismiss Jane's point that it was all a game. Someone wanted to shake her down and make her talk—and Jane knew who it was, or thought she did.

The crackling noise again.

Mattie's spine rippled as if something cold had touched her. She put her uneaten sandwich back on the plate. There was only one person Jane could be talking about. Mattie had already played out that paranoid fantasy, and decided it was too far-fetched. She didn't want to think Jameson would go that far, but he had plenty of reason. He seemed determined to avenge his brother, and there was probably a big book deal involved, especially now that he knew who Jane Dunbar was.

Maybe there was no way to tell friends from enemies. Anyone could be a friend or an enemy, depending on the situation. She didn't like that thought. It made her feel more alone than ever.

She met Jane's gaze and wondered if they were thinking the same thing. "Is that the secret?" she asked.

Jane touched the pearl necklace at her throat. "No, the secret has to do with the man who brought Ms. Rowe flowers, the D.G. on the card. Your wild guess was not so wild, Mattie."

"What do you mean?"

"Ms. Rowe's mystery lover was David Grace."

"How do you know that?" Breeze asked.

"I heard some things, saw some things."

Breeze popped the grape she'd been holding and crunched down. "You spied on her?"

Mattie sat forward. "You spied on Ms. Rowe?"

Jane nodded. "Remember the day you were too sick to clean her apartment, and I did it for you? She showed up as I was about to leave, and I ducked in the hall closet. She called a man on the phone and confirmed their date for the following day. I figured it had to be her mystery lover, the one she went through all the elaborate rituals for, so the next morning, I skipped class and let myself into her room while she was taking her shower."

"You never said anything?" Mattie asked.

"I thought you might try and talk me out of it, and I was scared to death as it was. Besides, I didn't know who David Grace was at the time—and I didn't find out until it was too late."

"Too late for what?" Mattie asked.

"To say anything."

Mattie sprang from the settee. "Jane, he could be the killer. She died the morning she was supposed to see her mystery lover. We timed it that way when we came up with our plan to poison her. It wasn't Broud. It was David Grace, and you've known all this time?"

Jane hushed Mattie with frantic hand signals. "It wasn't Grace. I have proof of that. He didn't keep his appointment with Rowe that morning. He was in the hospital."

Breeze had gone quiet, but Mattie was angry. She'd put herself in harm's way for these two women. "How do you know all this?"

Jane touched her throat protectively, entwining the pearls in her fingers, worrying them. "After they took Ms. Rowe's body away, I panicked. I was certain they would discover the heartwine and connect it to us. I didn't want to frighten the two of you, so I came up with a plan I thought would protect all three of us."

Mattie could understand that much. She was withholding information from the other two women right now because she didn't want to scare them.

"You went after Grace?" Mattie already had a hunch working as to what had happened.

Jane's nod was tentative. "I tracked him down, found out he was in the hospital and went to his room. He suffered from bronchial asthma, and he'd had an attack so severe he required a breathing tube."

Mattie persisted. "And you blackmailed him?"

Breeze squeaked, "Oh, please tell me you did!"

"Blackmail is such a unpleasant word. I warned him he should be careful because if *I* knew about him and Ms. Rowe, there might be others who did, too. That was really all I needed to say."

"Gutsy," Breeze enthused. "Weren't you afraid he might turn you over to the cops?"

"I figured he'd have me killed or kidnapped and sold into slavery. I could see myself vanishing without a trace, and neither of you would know what had happened to me. But given that his paramour had been murdered, I clung to the belief that he would want his secret trysts kept a secret, and I was right."

"What did he say?" Mattie asked.

"You'll never believe it." Jane's expression was almost a smile, almost wistful. "He asked me what my dreams were. When I recovered from the shock, I told him I wanted to make a difference. Politics, possibly state government. He said I didn't dream big enough, that I could run the country, if I wanted. He could see unrealized potential in me. Those were his exact words, unrealized potential."

"Did he offer you money?"

"No, Breeze, he's a *little* too classy for that. But listen to this—apparently he had a daughter who was a terrible disappointment to him. He said she had no vision, no guiding star, and he couldn't reach her. But he told me not to worry about anything, that he was going to help me with *my* dreams. And, if you can believe this, he apologized for the Grace scholarship program. He said it hadn't worked out the way he'd intended. I didn't know until that moment that he *was* the Grace scholarship program."

"Did he know about the sex ring?" Mattie asked. "Was he part of it?"

"I didn't speak of it, and neither did he. In fact, we haven't spoken of it to this day."

Mattie felt a wave of dizziness. She didn't know if it was what Jane had said or a recurrence of her head injury symptoms. "You're still in touch with him?"

"Who do you think introduced me to Larry?" She held out her ring finger.

"Oh, my God," Breeze whispered.

"Who do you think paid for my Bryn Mawr education and set me up with a very chic state department job?"

Mattie whistled under her breath. Jane was clearly enjoying herself now. She'd made what sounded like a deal with the devil all those years ago, and it had gotten her everything she wanted. Mattie couldn't say she was totally surprised. Unlike Grace's daughter, Jane had grand dreams and the drive to carry them out. But Mattie had trouble imagining that all Grace wanted in return was Jane's silence.

"What was he like?" Breeze unfurled, raptly attentive. "I've heard he's a recluse. He rarely gives interviews, never allows photos. Is he ugly and ogrelike?"

"No, actually, he's a very attractive man, then and now."

Mattie glanced at her nails and saw the impact of the past two days. She had splits and hangnails, which distressed her, but not for the reason it should have. Why was she compelled to indulge in such a childish habit? Did she want her hands to look ugly because her mother had once said they were small and sensual, exactly the kind of hands a man would like?

"Does he know our secret, Jane?"

Mattie asked the question, and Jane's fingers began to flutter again. She tugged at the necklace repeatedly, drawing it tight against her neck. The pressure was too much. The string snapped and pearls flew.

Breeze was on her feet. This, apparently, was a big deal. "You didn't tell him? Jane?"

Jane's silence was answer enough. She knelt, searching for her pearls, anything to avoid Mattie's question.

Now Mattie understood her vulnerability. It was about risk and loss. Jane wasn't unbreakable, but the bond between the three of them had been, and Jane had just put it at terrible risk. At one point in their lives, all they had was each other. It was that way now, and it was crucial that they could trust one another completely. Mattie would not have questioned that allegiance until today. Even a seemingly small lie was huge, especially one kept all those years. It meant that Jane's bond with Grace was stronger than her bond with them.

Don't let this be happening, Mattie thought. God, what a blow. She needed these two women. She needed their bond to be unbreakable. She had taken tremendous strength from that. It might be the source of her strength.

Jane picked up pearls. "David Grace changed my life. He gave me a chance. All he's ever done is help me, but I couldn't tell you without breaking a promise to him."

"We promised not to lie to each other," Breeze said.

"But we also promised to protect and support each other, to the death, if we had to. Remember that pledge? It was the lie that allowed me to do that, and if I had to make the choice again, I'd do the same thing."

She clasped the loose pearls in her hand and looked up at the other two women. "It's not just me he's helped. It's all three of us."

Silence. Neither Mattie nor Breeze managed to speak a word as Jane rose and brushed off her skirt. She put the pearls in a lead crystal bowl, placing them so carefully they didn't make a sound. The sudden quiet was terrible. It carried the weight of a guillotine blade about to fall.

"Please, can we all sit down?" she said. "There's more."

Once they were seated on the settee, Jane told them the rest of it. Head erect, hands clasped, she blurted it out. She and David Grace had not been idle over the years. He had anonymously been helping both Mattie and Breeze, simply because Jane asked him to. How else could Breeze have negotiated a hefty business loan without any collateral? And did Mattie think she got appointed to a prestigious judgeship with no connections beyond Larry?

The shocked silence persisted, even after Jane finished with her confession. Mattie wasn't even aware of the other two women anymore. She was lost in her own empty echo chamber. She'd been naive enough to think she got her position because of her merits. Now she didn't even have herself to believe in.

She drew in a breath, fighting against the spinning sensation that made her feel as if she'd just stepped off a merry-go-round. There was a terrible ache at the base of her skull, but worse was a sense of helplessness, as if she'd had no control over her own fate all these years. She didn't know which decisions were hers and which were someone else's. She didn't know what she'd achieved and what she hadn't. Could a man like David Grace rig a jury?

She could still hear that odd crackling, although no one

else seemed to notice it. It sounded almost exactly like the noise she lived with, the static that built inside her, and for a second she wondered if she was imagining it, having some kind of flashback.

Eventually, she became aware of Jane, trying to stay her hand.

"Mattie, look at what you've done," she said.

Mattie stared at the fingernail she'd nearly bitten off and felt a wave of revulsion. She was her own person, no matter what David Grace had done. He may have pulled some strings on her behalf—and who didn't have a benefactor, or several, when it came to these things—but he had not ruled on the cases, and he had not swayed her thinking or altered her quest for the truth. Whatever effect he'd had on the outside had not changed the inside.

"Mattie, talk to me, won't you? Tell me what you're thinking. I'm afraid. *Please* talk to me."

Mattie's head snapped up. Her famous glare turned Jane chalky. "Are you done? Can I go now?"

Jane struck back with equal force. "No, you can't," she said, rising from the chair. Her tone summoned all of the vast authority she had wielded as their leader. "You're not walking out of here. I won't let you. What I did, I did for us. I've never done anything to hurt either of you, not intentionally. I only tried to help. Breeze, tell her, please."

Breeze's voice was light with disbelief. "I couldn't be happier," she said. "If David Grace was here, I'd plant one on him. The man gave me my start, and I love him for it."

"A spa is a little different than the Ninth Circuit Court of Appeals," Mattie countered.

Breeze didn't seem to think so. "What about all the good you've been allowed to do since you took that position. Aren't you grateful for the opportunity?"

"I'd rather have earned it on my own."

"What, and lose all that time? He gave you a head start, for heaven's sake. Give the guy a break."

Mattie wouldn't look at either of them. They had done this to her too often, ganged up on her. "I don't like being lied to, dammit."

"And I don't like lying. I won't ask for your forgiveness, but I am asking for your understanding—and one more thing."

Mattie sighed. She couldn't summon her glare as she looked into Jane's big beseeching brown eyes.

"Mattie, David wants to help us," she said. "And if anyone can do that now, it's him. He's out of the country on business, but he'd like to meet with you as soon as possible. Will you do it?"

The room crackled with static. A loud pop startled all of them. Darkness engulfed the far corner of the room, and Mattie realized a floor lamp had gone out. She wasn't hearing things. It was nothing more than a lightbulb blowing out. A short in the wiring, maybe. Thank God.

She got up from the settee, needing to move around and clear her head. Jane had asked her a question, and she didn't have an answer.

Twenty years ago, Jane had made a desperate choice. No matter what her reasons, she'd crossed the line and ventured over to the dark side to barter with Minos, king of the underworld, and in many ways the bargain she'd made had brought them to this. Now she was asking Mattie to go there, too. But this wasn't twenty years ago, and Mattie wasn't a fearless fourteen-year-old anymore.

35

I am not crazy. I do not terrorize and torture people. I don't violate their corpses for sexual gratification. I remove obstacles, and occasionally those obstacles are people. All of the great figures in history have had to deal with the impediments blocking their path. Moses had to part the seas. Jesus removed doubts with his miracles. Mother Teresa fought poverty and ignorance with love, healing one person at a time.

Not Hitler, of course. Wars and mass killings are excessive, the product of disjointed, paranoid minds. People learn well by example. Only a few have to be removed to reeducate the masses. People can learn, even the sheep.

I pride myself on being efficient and organized. Some of us in this life were born to get things done. I'm one of those, a doer. My mind simply operates that way. If others fail to see that, if they don't have the sense to get out of my way, they give me no choice but to take them out.

It's all for love. Why else would I go to such extremes? I know what's important. I wonder if she does. I'd rather not kill her, but I don't think she's going to give me a choice, and she is too strong an adversary to leave standing. She will be an example to the others, the tipping point that turns things in my favor. But first, there is someone else to deal with—and he has already sealed his fate. I won't mind so much taking him out. In fact, I may rather enjoy it.

Now it's time to sleep, to escape this machine that is my mind for a while, if it will let me. Most of the time it won't. I don't torture others, but there are times when my mind tortures me. I don't know what rest is, and at weak moments when my emotions control me, I find myself hating those who do, the complacent sheep who take everything for granted. They believe life owes them health, wealth and happiness, safety, even peace of mind.

Life owes them nothing. It has given me nothing. I strive. I struggle to understand. I never rest. Why should they? Nature is the only pure system, but humans in their quest for control have thwarted the natural balance, distorted it. Happiness is not a birthright. It must be earned, pursued. Even our constitution affirms that.

I'm not Moses or Jesus, certainly not Hitler. I'm a teacher of men, and my sense of accomplishment comes in knowing that a few of them will learn the truth about this life. Before I'm done, a few of them will learn.

Mattie glanced at her watch again. Just 7:00 p.m., but the darkly tinted windows made it look as if the sun had already gone down. Jane had arranged for the limo to the airport, and Mattie was using the time to catch up on her phone calls. There'd been several from her office, most of them from Michelle with questions about the upcoming cases being juggled, one from Mattie's gynecologist, confirming an annual exam she'd forgotten all about, and half a dozen from Jaydee, all of them regarding the Langston case.

He'd had bad news. Two of the three judges on the panel scheduled to hear Langston's appeal had issues with Mattie because of dissenting opinions she'd written early in her judgeship. She'd not been as careful to spare egos in those days, and that could be coming back to bite her now. Mattie hated the thought that her errors were continuing to complicate the case.

Damage control, she told herself. She would find a way to fix it when she got back.

There was a voice mail from Jameson, too, but she hadn't listened to it yet. She'd left him a quick message during the meeting with Breeze and Jane to let him know she'd been called away on an emergency. Apparently he'd returned her call, and for some reason, she was holding his message for last.

Because it was the least important, she told herself.

She wished that were true, but she was burning with curiosity. There'd been a strain between them when she left his place that morning, and she'd told herself it was better that way. She needed her distance, especially from him. She was a loner. That was how she'd always operated. And maybe she would have convinced herself if there hadn't been this odd feeling of something lost.

She'd actually felt pressure in her chest, a need to take a breath.

She had to be crazy. What had she lost? She'd never had *anything* with him but conflict and adversity.

A sign for Dulles Airport flashed by the window, and her stomach tightened. She would soon be there, and she was still uncertain about the decision she'd made. Jane and Breeze had *not* let up on her. They had begged, pleaded and cajoled her to meet with David Grace.

She took a swig from the bottled water she'd found in the limo's bar. Unfortunately, there were no snacks, and she could have eaten just about anything at this point. She'd already returned all her other calls, leaving voice mails for everyone. There was only Jameson's call left.

The thought made her face hot. Why was she so curious about a phone message from a man who could so easily wreak havoc in her life, a man who'd accused her of murder? Life had been much simpler when everyone thought she was a lesbian, and she'd been happy to let them. This man could as easily be her arch enemy as her lover. An emotional involvement with him would only complicate things. And yet—

She pressed the voice mail button and typed in her password.

"Mattie, it's Jameson."

He said her name in a voice as rich and textured as a shot of aged liquor. Her throat burned as if she'd been drinking whiskey instead of water, but a burst of static cut him off for several seconds—and when it cleared, something had happened to his glorious voice. It had gone hard, cold.

"I don't know what you're up to, Mattie, but you have forty-eight hours to prove to me that you and your friends are not cold-blooded murderers. A national newspaper has asked me to write a series about my brother's case. They're waiting for the first installment, and I intend to name names. It's up to you now."

The limo slowed and Mattie looked up in confusion. It was hard to breathe in the enclosed space. She had no idea why Jameson would turn on her this way. She hadn't been able to leave him a detailed message. She couldn't have explained where she was and still have protected Jane's privacy. This was only supposed to have been a one-day trip, Dulles and back.

"We're here, ma'am," the driver called back. "What airline?"

Mattie was torn. She didn't doubt that Jameson would carry out his threat, but she didn't understand why he'd made it. Maybe the smartest move was to go straight back and confront him.

She tapped out his number on her cell and was startled when he answered. "Jameson, is that you? I don't have much time, but I didn't understand your message. Why did you give me a forty-eight-hour deadline? Hello? Are you there?"

"Where are you, Mattie?"

"I'm at the airport. Jameson?"

Mattie heard the limo driver calling, "Ma'am? The airline?" His voice sounded tinny and faint. A buzzing noise told her the phone had gone dead. She'd lost Jameson, and there was no time to call back. What did she do now? This was insanity. Sophie's choice. She had to tell the driver something, but it felt like she was taking a risk no matter what she did. The wrong decision could be disastrous.

The noise in her ears reached a painful pitch. It blocked out everything, even the driver's voice. Mattie gathered her things, refusing to be immobilized. Her body jerked like stick-figure animation, but sheer force of will broke through the cacophony. By the time she had her cell phone in her bag and her jacket in hand, the noise had been walled off. She could still hear the chaos, but it was outside her now, somewhere far away where it couldn't hurt her. Nothing could hurt her.

"The international terminal," she told the driver. "Alitalia."

With those words, she changed the course of her life. She was not going west, back to San Francisco International, to Jameson and Tiburon. She had a ticket to Heathrow with connections to Rome. She was on her way to the Amalfi coast to meet with David Grace.

Mattie was afraid to look down. The silver Bentley's growling ascent up the cliffs was nearly vertical. A glance out the window made her think she was still on Alitalia. A hundred feet below, the Tyrrherian Sea thundered against the rocks, and there didn't seem to be any road beneath the car.

It was as terrifying as it was breathtaking. Unfortunately, her Italian driver spoke little English, so she was reduced to hand signals, which he seemed to find amusing. At least she'd picked up a guidebook at the airport that had a section on common Italian phrases.

"Siamo quasi là?" She had to raise her voice over the noise of the engine. With luck, she'd asked him if they were almost there.

"Three kilometers," he called back in heavily accented English.

Three kilometers. That was less than two miles. They *were* there. Mattie had begun to think it would never happen. She'd had connections through London to Rome, where Grace's limo had picked her up. The drive to the coast had taken two and a half hours on some very challenging roads.

As the hill crested, the driver turned away from the cliffs and onto a white gravel driveway that was lined on both sides with trees and classical statuary. Mattie wasn't prepared for the magnificence of the estate they approached. Apparently Grace had many homes. Jane had described this one as a villa, but it was much grander than that.

The entrance reminded Mattie of a Roman senate building. Marble steps led to a circular portico, supported by alabaster columns. Granite creatures, possibly griffons, sat on either side of the double doors, and bright green topiary trees magically assumed the shapes of circus animals.

The Bentley rounded the driveway, where a tall silver-haired man awaited them. Not David Grace, Mattie realized. This was a footman or butler in livery.

Very grand, she thought. Grace must be quite the lord of the manor.

Mattie checked her watch, which was still set to Pacific time, and added ten hours to account for difference in time. It was now midafternoon in Italy, and she hadn't showered or changed clothes in over twenty-four hours. Jane had loaned her all the essentials for the trip, and fortunately they were close to the same size. Mattie had freshened up in the airplane bathroom as best she could, but she didn't feel terribly presentable under the circumstances. She would have killed for a bath and a nap before meeting her host.

Douglas, the English butler, directed the driver where to take her bags, and then he led Mattie into the villa's foyer. The domed ceiling was painted with Italian frescoes reminiscent of the Renaissance era, and the walls had lush green landscape murals between alabaster columns. Beyond the foyer, Mattie could see a sheet of black marble that gleamed like a dance floor. It led to a glass wall that overlooked the cliffs and the sea in the near distance.

A cobalt-blue sky dominated the glass room, as Mattie instantly named it. Her first impression was of silk chaises in gold-trimmed Versace prints, a grand piano and willowy stands of bamboo in lacquered boxes. It was a dizzyingly vibrant tableau, and at the center of it all stood David Grace.

"Your Honor, welcome," he said, coming over to greet her.

Mattie had expected him to be tall, immaculately groomed and patrician in manner. She hadn't expected him to be warm and friendly. If he noticed that she was massively jet-lagged and crumpled, he hid it well. But he wasn't able to hide the sadness that misted his cloud-gray eyes.

Mattie was immediately caught, intrigued.

"Jane said you were beautiful." His smile erased some of the shadows. "She didn't do you justice. Your eyes rival the horizon for brightness."

Mattie didn't know quite what to do when he kissed her hand. He started in again about how beautiful she was, and she almost believed him.

"You must be tired," he said. "Would you like a quick tour of the house before Douglas shows you to your room, or would you like to go there immediately? When you're rested, I'll have something served on the terrace and we'll talk. I have some news for you."

"News? Really?"

"Good news," he assured her, "but it can hold until we're alone."

Mattie wasn't sure she had time to be rested. Besides, she wasn't going to miss a chance to be shown around and get the layout of the place. It looked big enough to get lost in several times over.

"The tour first," she said. "I'd love to see the rest of your home. It's so beautiful."

He led her through rooms that were furnished with priceless antiques and museum-quality art. She tried to absorb the rich variety of colors and fabrics, but the predominant hues were blue and gold, very much like the waterscape beyond the windows. The last place he showed her was an interior courtyard that reminded her of the courtyard at Rowe Academy, except that this one was completely enclosed in glass.

The centerpiece, a lily pond, had a waterfall created by a mermaid sitting atop miniature steps and emptying the pearlescent seashell in her arms. Delicate ferns reached toward a glass ceiling that let in the light, but not the weather.

"Whose are these?" Mattie asked, noticing the artwork that rested on easels around the room. He'd turned the area into a gallery of charcoal sketches, she realized, and every one of the pictures involved the same figure, a bereft young woman whose features were concealed by shadows, except for her eyes.

Mattie felt an eerie sense of recognition as she studied them. It didn't seem possible that she could be looking at Millicent Rowe, but yet Mattie now knew she'd had a relationship with David Grace.

"They're mine," was all he said.

Mattie walked over to one of the pictures, drawn to the woman's distant, downcast gaze. "This is beautiful," she said. "It's haunting. Who is the artist?"

She turned to look at Grace and wondered if she was supposed to ask that question. "The work isn't signed," she explained.

"As I said, it's mine."

"You drew them? They're all the same woman, aren't they?"

Footsteps came clickety-clicking down the hall toward them. Douglas appeared around the corner with an air of expectation. "Sorry to interrupt. It's a phone call for you, sir. Important."

Mattie continued to study Grace, and he acknowledged her with an apologetic smile. He seemed to understand that she was waiting for an answer.

"I have always believed that art gives way to the inexpressible," he said. "Now, if you'll excuse me, I'll take that phone call."

Mattie watched him walk off, aware that she didn't know what to make of David Grace. He looked to be in his fifties. He was obviously cultured, handsome, intelligent, soft-spoken. But like the subject in his paintings, he had eyes that could rend the soul with their sorrow. Was that the emotion he couldn't express?

The whole experience had left her shaken. She hadn't even realized that Douglas was still hovering.

"Ms. Smith, would you like to go to your room now?"

"Thank you, Douglas," she said. "I really am tired."

Mattie's mouth began to water the moment she saw the fruit arrangement. Her stomach rumbled loudly. Berries, green grapes, mangos and white peaches spilled from a cornucopia that rested on the gold velvet bench at the foot of her bed. Next to the cornucopia, on a wicker tray, sat a vase of fresh-cut flowers, a wedge of Irish black wax cheddar and a carafe of rich red wine.

She would feast this fine afternoon.

Her room was beautiful, too, a bedchamber fit for a princess. The feather bed looked as if it could bounce her to the ceiling, and the window's wooden shutters let in just enough light to give the room a rosy glow. But Mattie barely had time to admire the delicate lace spread and pillow shams. She helped herself to a ripe peach and headed for the bathroom, intending to eat as she bathed.

She didn't expect a modern, three-headed shower with gold fixtures. She left the peach to wait patiently for her on the marble vanity while she deluged herself from all sides in a shower stall made from pink marble slabs.

Afterward, snuggled in a thick terry robe, she arranged herself on a velvet chaise and devoured the juicy fruit, eating it all the way to the pit. The only good thing about being famished was how exquisite food tasted. The explosion of flavors made her sigh with pleasure. Next she tried the wine and a thick slice of cheese. Delicious. The wine had a spicy hint of cinnamon, and the cheddar was creamy and surprisingly pungent.

"I should do this more often," she murmured, her lids barely open as she cupped the goblet in both hands and sipped. Perhaps this was a mistake, imbibing wine when she was already so tired, but it rivaled ambrosia, she was sure. She'd never actually had ambrosia...

She didn't remember setting the glass down. She didn't even remember laying her head down. She must have done both, however, because within seconds of swallowing her last sip of wine, she had rested her hands in her lap and she was gone.

Mattie wondered what she was doing in a funeral procession. She heard the music, a dirge so heavy with sorrow it weighed down her every step, but she couldn't see anyone's face. They were wearing dark hooded robes, all of them, everyone but her. The pallbearers had set the coffin by the altar and opened the lid. As the mourners filed by to pay their respects, Mattie wondered who was inside, and why the church was so dark.

Ms. Rowe came to her mind, perhaps because she'd looked so sad in the paintings. The dirge had grown louder, taking on a strangely dissonant tone. Suddenly there were candles everywhere, Mattie realized, tiny white votives floating in the air.

She heard someone whisper, asking who the deceased was. Another voice whispered back, "It's that Broud boy."

William Broud. Now Mattie understood. She had not gone to his funeral, and this was her chance to explain that she had never meant him any harm. To apologize and beg his forgiveness.

Expecting to see the handyman's terrifying face, she approached the coffin and looked in. But the face she saw was beautiful, dark, still.

Not William. Jameson. There was a cut on his forehead where she'd hit him with the bracelet, and somehow she knew that she was responsible for this, as she was responsible for everything terrible that had happened in her life—her father's leaving, her mother's self-degradation, Ivy's death, Ms. Rowe's, Broud's.

"No!" She whispered the word that keened inside her mind. Desperate, she tried to wake him. But when she touched his face, he turned into Jimmy Broud, the shy delivery boy who had just wanted to know who she was. Now he never would.

Tears rolled down her cheeks.

Behind her the mourners began to moan and howl. It sounded like cries of anguish, and Mattie turned to see them rising from the pews and removing their hoods. The nave of the church was filled with students from Rowe Academy, and the emotion blazing in their eyes wasn't anguish. It was hatred.

36

A gasp caught hard in Mattie's throat. The sharp sting of it brought her awake. She opened her eyes in confusion, blinking away what might have been tears. For several seconds, she could see nothing but hazy brightness, as if someone had turned a snow globe upside down. Everything was afloat, glittering. But gradually the room came into focus, and she realized where she was.

David Grace's villa. A continent away from her everyday life, where people were either trying to kill her or threatening to ruin her.

She sat up in an effort to clear her head. If she wasn't crazy, she ought to be. She had tears in her eyes and her chest felt as if it were bruised. It was only a dream, but knowing that gave her little sense of relief. The emotions were painfully real, and she had no idea what they meant. Was she mourning the loss of a childhood dream? Jimmy Broud was dead to her? Never coming back? Or was the dream trying to warn her that Jameson was in danger?

Maybe she *wanted* him dead. Both of them. The delivery boy and the predatory adult he'd grown into. That would make some sense. They'd each made her life hell when you came right down to it.

Deep golden rays sliced through the shutters, telling her it was either late afternoon or early evening—and she'd slept for several hours. She rose stiffly from the chaise in search of her carry-on bag.

She found her cell phone in the zipper compartment of her bag. It was probably the middle of the night in the States, but she had to make one last attempt to reason with Jameson. He was asking the impossible of her, and he could so easily destroy everything she was trying to do.

Her cell was programmed to change with the time zones. It was six-thirty in the evening in Italy, from which she could have calculated Pacific time, but she didn't take the time. It took all her concentration getting the codes right. The connections were slow, but she finally got through to Jameson's voice mail. She'd wanted to talk to him, not a female android who droned on about how important Mattie's message was, but at least she knew she'd dialed the right number.

"Jameson, it's Mattie again," she said. "I had to make an emergency trip to Europe, but I'll be back in a couple days. Jameson, I need more time. I'm asking you to wait until I get back, and we can talk this out."

A beeping nose signaled she had voice mail. She ended the call to Jameson and brought the message up, surprised to hear Breeze's voice. She and her military intelligence guy were running a background check on David Grace, and they'd already come up with something.

"David Grace's wife, Cynthia, died in childbirth over twenty years ago," Breeze said. "He's never remarried, but listen to this. Rowe was murdered six months after his wife died. Cynthia Grace was admitted to a clinic in Ravello, not far from the villa where you're staying. That's where she *and* the baby died. Maybe you can do a little nosing around while you're there."

Breeze left Cynthia Grace's maiden name, which was how the clinic had her registered, and the date of her death, then signed off, promising to call back if she got anything else.

The headmistress and David Grace's wife died within six months of each other? Mattie calculated back from Ms. Rowe's death in February of 1982 to Cynthia Grace's death, which would have been in the summer of the previous year. Was it also a coincidence that in the months before Ms. Rowe's death she'd begun a distraught letter to Grace that talked about a precious gift and a tragic loss? Mattie had to wonder if both women had lost babies.

She didn't have time now to sort that out, but she had every intention of doing some sleuthing. If possible, she would check out the clinic in person. Meanwhile, she had a date on the terrace with her host.

Twenty minutes later, dressed in a black summer sheath, her hair clean and swinging, Mattie walked out to the balcony that fronted the living room. It was actually the middle of three conjoined balconies that ran the entire length of the villa. If she remembered the way the house was laid out, the other two were off the master bedroom and the dining room.

The view was breathtaking. The balcony overhung a perfectly manicured lawn with topiary gardens and reflecting pools, bordered on both sides by marble colonnades that were reminiscent of Roman ruins. Beyond that were the rugged mist-covered cliffs of the Amalfi coast and the Gulf of Salerno. The mist's vibrant shades of pink were courtesy of the setting sun.

Her sandals clicked on the marble tiles, but if Grace heard her coming, he didn't acknowledge it. He sat at a large verdigris iron table, gazing out to sea. His tropical-print silk shirt, sand-colored slacks and woven sandals were the casual chic of a wealthy European. But the melancholy she'd noticed earlier was deeply etched in his face, even in repose.

Mattie felt certain it had something to do with a woman. Ms. Rowe perhaps, or his wife. Was she the beautiful shadowed creature he'd painted repeatedly? Or was that Millicent

Rowe, which would explain Mattie's sense of recognition. It didn't seem possible that those forlorn eyes were Ms. Rowe's, but something had driven the headmistress to do the things she did, some unbearable pain.

"Lovely," he said, glancing up as she joined him. He gave her dress an appreciative once-over with his discerning gaze, and Mattie felt both flattered and relieved, as if she'd passed inspection.

"Join me, please," he said, rising to pull out a chair for her. "Douglas should be here soon with our first course. He counts cooking among his many talents, and he spent the afternoon in the kitchen in honor of your visit. Would you like some champagne?"

Mattie nodded, and he poured them each a flute, murmuring *"Salute,"* as their silver glasses clinked. Moments later, Douglas appeared, carrying a platter of caviar canapés, a colorful antipasto salad and a sampler of other delicacies from the region. Mattie helped herself to the canapés and baptized them with lemon juice from a wedge wrapped in cheesecloth.

She nibbled ecstatically, savoring each piquant morsel until David coaxed her to sample the calamari. Squid had never been her favorite dish, but this was tender, drenched in olive oil, sautéed tomatoes and lots of garlic.

Before they were nearly through, Douglas returned with a second platter. This one had a chafing dish heaped with scallops, shrimp and crab legs in a buttery, bubbling hot sauce. There was also a skillet of pan-roasted sea bass with braised truffles and fresh baby asparagus.

David suggested that Mattie start with the sea bass so its delicate flavors wouldn't be overwhelmed. She took his advice, saving just enough room for some tender scallops and another glass of champagne. She wanted to groan it was all so good.

She noticed him watching her during the meal, and his expression told her that something as simple as watching a woman enjoy good food brought him pleasure. She had the sense that he might spend a great deal of time alone.

Over a light dessert of Italian ices, she floated a question she'd been waiting to ask. "Jane told me that you were instrumental in both of my appointments to the federal courts. May I ask you how that worked?"

He rested his elbows on the table. "In your case, very smoothly. Your record speaks for itself, of course, and Congress couldn't find much to object to since you don't dabble in partisan politics. Actually, Mattie, you represent what I like to think of as the ideal in judicial appointments. We have too few jurists willing to set aside their personal biases and rule on the merits of the case. You do that routinely, and it's...refreshing."

He tipped his head to her, admiration in his eyes, and Mattie was quite sincerely flattered.

"Thank you so much for everything," she said moments later as they sipped decaf espresso from demitasse cups. "I leave tomorrow." She was hoping to prompt him to share his news.

"It's a shame you can't stay longer," he said. "You've seen nothing of the area. But, duty calls. I understand. I have business myself tomorrow morning, so I've arranged for my driver to be at your disposal. He'll take you to the airport whenever you're ready, and if there's anywhere else you'd like to go, don't be afraid to ask him. He's a native and could as easily have been a tour guide as a driver."

"That's very kind." She set the cup in its tiny saucer. "You said you had good news."

"Well, not in the typical sense." He rose and crossed to the ledge, just a few feet away. "Jane shared with me that the three of you are being harassed by a writer named Jameson Cross. If there's one thing I've learned in life it's that most of us have secrets we don't want discovered, and we will go to extremes to protect them."

"Jameson has that kind of a secret?"

"His work has made him a public persona—and vulnerable to blackmail. It's the price of fame."

Mattie was caught completely off guard—and not entirely certain she wanted to hear Grace's news. Was he going to tell her that some of her fears about Jameson were true? Maybe he really was a night stalker, and he'd done some of the terrible things the art on his walls depicted. Or worse, he was the one who'd attacked her. Of course, she had to know, and if it came down to using the information, she would.

"Why are you doing this?" she asked him.

"Because Jane is my friend, and she asked for help."

It was never that simple, but Mattie couldn't very well challenge him.

"Have I overstepped my boundaries?" he asked. "If you'd rather not have the information, just say so."

"No, please, tell me what you know."

He returned to the table and refilled their champagne flutes. As he sat down and began to reveal what he knew the sky turned from pink to purple to indigo and the quarter moon bounced its grinning reflection off the wine-colored sea. In Mattie's periphery, the horizon grew more beautiful with every passing second, and the man across from her proceeded to tell a tale so disturbing she fervently wished she hadn't asked.

Mattie woke up to breakfast in bed. A tray of rolls, coffee, fresh fruit and juice had been left on the velvet bench at the end of her bed, and she hadn't even heard Douglas enter the room. That struck her as a little creepy, but perhaps the rich were used to having people wander around, attending to things while they slept.

Last night's feast had left her uncomfortably full, and she

couldn't touch the breakfast, other than to sample some tart green apple slices while she got ready. She'd never really unpacked so there was nothing to do but shower, dress and be on her way. She would ask the driver to stop in Ravello long enough for her to do some sightseeing. Of course, her plan was to visit the clinic and glean whatever information she could about David's wife.

The drive to town went quickly, despite a hair-raising descent down the rutted road that ran along the cliffs. The driver let Mattie off in a quaint town square with plans to pick her up in an hour. He was barely out of sight before she'd hired a taxi to take her to the clinic, which turned out to be a lovely, rambling old country estate, set among flower-filled gardens and breathtaking views of the sea.

Her first impression was correct. La Serena Clinica catered to the wealthy and security was tight. Fortunately, the staff's English was good, but Mattie's story about being put up for adoption as a baby and needing to see her biological mother's medical records because of a mysterious genetic illness fell on deaf ears. The stony-faced administrator couldn't even be coaxed into revealing whether they'd kept records from twenty years ago or how long she herself had been on staff at the clinic. Mattie wasn't certain the woman would have given her name if there hadn't been an engraved plate sitting on her desk.

On her way out, Mattie approached an elderly desk clerk with the same story. The woman was sympathetic, but also unable to help. "I wouldn't know where to find a file over twenty years old," she explained as she walked Mattie to the door. "The only one who's been around here that long is Alessandro, our gardener."

Mattie thanked her and went outside to have a look around the grounds. Obviously, someone took very good care of the place. She wondered if one gardener could do it by himself.

The sloping greenbelts were perfectly mown and edged, and the dogwood trees were in full flower. She took a white gravel path through beds of bright summer blooms and ended at a grotto recess with a bubbling fountain and cool stone benches.

Mattie sat for a moment, hoping the serenity would ease her sense of frustration. She probably shouldn't have expected anything to come of this visit, but she couldn't believe the clinic didn't have client files going back twenty years. Private clinics like this one were hotbeds of jealously guarded secrets. It was their stock in trade. If they couldn't promise privacy they couldn't attract the kind of clientele that could pay their bills. Too bad it was broad daylight, and she couldn't break into the place and search it.

She rose to leave, aware that her knee wasn't bothering her. There was something to be grateful for, she thought ironically.

On the walk back, she noticed a weathered specimen in a ratty straw hat, soiled jeans and rubber boots. He was down on his knees in a patch of huge pink oleanders. Alessandro? At least she should stop and compliment him on his flowers. She doubted he would remember a patient from so long ago, but she'd learned not to dismiss even remote possibilities, especially with tough cases.

"Bella fiores," she said to get his attention.

He pulled off his hat and peered up at her with suspicious brown eyes. The pruning sheers in his hand took on a menacing cast as he sprang to his feet.

"What you want?" he asked in heavily accented English.

Mattie glanced at her watch. She still had some time. "I'm looking for information about my mother," she said, deciding to try her story on him.

"She is here? You try office?"

Mattie took a slightly different tack with Alessandro, who looked as wise and world-weary as any patron saint.

"I did," she said, speaking slowly so that he could follow her, "but they can't help me. No one remembers her. It was twenty-four years ago that she stayed here. I never knew her. She put me up for adoption when I was a baby."

She hesitated to make sure he understood, and he nodded for her to continue. "She stayed at the clinic for several days, and that was the last time anyone saw her alive. I was told that she died in childbirth, but the bodies were never returned to America, not hers or the baby's."

"She die here? Your mama?"

"Yes," she said, pleased that he seemed to be following her. "On the seventh of August," she said, remembering Breeze's detailed message.

"*Il sette d'Agosto?*" His eyebrows furled in a question. "She's an American woman, like you?"

"Yes, an American. Do you remember her?"

He dropped the clippers in his bucket of tools and waved for Mattie to come with him. She found it difficult to keep up as he bolted off in the direction of the cliffs.

"*Il sette d'Agosto,*" he said, pointing to a graceful cypress tree that stood near the edge of the cliffs. "The date I remember exactly because I'm the one who found her."

Mattie didn't understand. "You found her by the tree?"

"No, where she fall from the cliff. I find her on the rocks below."

"Was it an accident?" Mattie asked, eager for all the details.

"Some say yes, but me, I never believe it."

"Did someone push her or did she jump?"

Mattie was being much too matter-of-fact for a grieving daughter, but Alessandro didn't seem to notice. He seemed eager to unburden himself, as if he'd been waiting all this time for someone to ask.

"Your mama, she walk the cliffs every day. I see her myself. She open her arms like she could fly. When I find her that morning, her arms were open and there was peace on her face."

"She jumped then?"

He explained it patiently. "If she fall, she no look peaceful. But your mama, she made a choice, she look happy."

Mattie's forty-eight hours were already up by the time she landed in San Francisco that evening. One of her flights had been cancelled and another delayed, but she wouldn't have made Jameson's deadline anyway. Of course, no driver waited for her at the airport in a sleek black luxury car, and she'd turned in her rental when she'd flown out to Washington, so she hailed a cab, gave the driver Jameson's address and told him she had to get there yesterday.

"Try not to land us both in the bay," she cautioned as he tore across the Golden Gate Bridge a short time later.

The jangle of a cell phone startled her. Her first thought was of Jameson and the deadline, but she'd already checked her messages, and there'd been nothing from him. She fished out her cell and hit the talk button, hesitating a moment before she said hello.

A woman's soft voice could barely be heard over the roar of the car's engine. "Ms. Smith, is that you? This is Nola Daniels. You gave me your phone number."

"Chief Daniels's wife?" Mattie said. "How are you? Is everything all right? I can barely hear you."

Nola spoke up a little, but the words were muffled, as if she'd moved the mouthpiece closer to her lips. "It's my husband," she said. "He thinks he's remembered something. He wants to talk to you. Could you come over here? Could you come over here now, please?"

Mattie glanced at the time on the display panel. She *had* to confront Jameson. "I can't, Mrs. Daniels. I have an appointment. It's urgent, and I'm already late. Can I call you as soon as I'm done?"

"I don't know, Ms. Smith."

"I'm sorry, I really am, but that's the best I can do. An hour. Give me an hour, can you?" she pleaded.

"I'll talk to him," she said.

Mattie said a quick goodbye as the taxi pulled up in front of Jameson's loft. She drew in a deep breath, let herself out of the cab and paid the driver, who was already pulling her bags out of the trunk. As an afterthought, she tipped him generously for not killing them both.

37

I know what you did—and it was monstrous.

Knowledge was power, Mattie told herself as she dropped her bags on the stoop and knocked on Jameson's door. She steeled herself for the confrontation, but nothing happened. The door stayed solidly shut. No lights came on. No noise could be heard. The house was as quiet as a tomb.

She spotted the doorbell and tried that. Still nothing.

Writers kept odd hours, but it seemed too early for him to have gone to bed. He could be out for the evening. That would explain why he wasn't answering, but she couldn't shake the feeling that something was wrong. Could that dream of hers have been a premonition? She didn't know how to feel about that now. She didn't know how to feel about anything, except that there was going to be a car wreck, one of those accidents you could see coming, but couldn't avoid.

The house had a full-length skylight and windows in the front, but none along the sides, where his bedroom was.

Maybe there was a way to get to the skylight by climbing a trellis or fire escape ladder. As she stepped back to look, a burst of light blinded her. She heard a loud pop and ducked, covering her face. More hits and popping. It sounded like flashbulbs going off, only a thousand times louder.

"What are you doing out here?"

Jameson's voice boomed in her head and the blinding

light went dark. When she looked up, he was looming above her. She could just make him out through a sea of white dots. Apparently he'd turned on a security spotlight and now he was blocking its beam.

"You're late," he said.

It seemed Jameson Cross was alive, well and every bit the bully who'd left the forty-eight-hour deadline on her voice mail. Tyrant. *Coward.* Mattie felt like a fool for having worried about him. She had actually considered trusting and confiding in this man. They should have wanted the same thing, to bring justice to the guilty, but he seemed determined to bring *her* down, as if this were some kind of personal vendetta and to hell with any evidence to the contrary. He was doing to her exactly what had been done to his brother.

She rose and faced him, the fight flowing into her.

"I want to talk to you," she said. "We can do it here, but I'd suggest we move inside. This may not be something you want to share with your neighbors."

His gaze narrowed, and so did hers. His eyes bore into hers and hers bore back. She had been intimidated by the best, and he would find that out. She did not give.

At last, he stepped back from the door, making way for her to enter, which she did, walking past him as stiffly as if it were enemy territory. Only one light shone inside the cavernous room, and it was at the far end where he had his office and an extensive library.

As he brought her bags inside, she headed for the light, unwilling to engage him in the dark, which was probably the preferred territory of a night stalker. She had barely completed the thought before she saw the detective magazine covers, framed and arranged on the translucent screen that was his bedroom wall.

Jameson's prized collection. This was what David Grace

had warned her about. Her stomach turned over as she looked
at the vintage covers, blown up to poster size, with some of
the campiest, most lurid artwork she'd ever seen. Women re-
strained seemed to be the recurring theme, all of them in
skimpy clothes. There weren't many exceptions, but a desperate blonde caught Mattie's eye. She was clutching a red
sheet to her bosom as she concealed a gigantic gun near her
inner thigh. The seen-it-all guy in the doorway had to be the
detective. Who else?

Another poster caught her eye, possibly because the arc
of the woman's spine reminded Mattie of an archery bow.
Her hands and feet were tied together behind her back and
somehow linked to another rope that seemed to be wrapped
around her throat. There was a certain bizarre grace to the
pose. Mattie could only imagine the agility involved, but it
was the menace that struck her. This one was much darker
and more troubling than the others.

She turned away from all of it. She'd seen enough.

"How does the son of a minister come to have so much
smut?" she asked Jameson in her best prosecutorial style.

"One man's smut, another man's art."

His shrug drew attention to what he was wearing, as well
as what he wasn't. Blue boxer shorts and a black kimono.
Nothing else. The kimono wasn't tied, and from what she
could see, he was lean, muscular. Probably a fitness nut.
That went with the control freak profile.

"And yourself?" he said, his tone sardonic. "Back from
Europe so soon? Did you get the emergency taken care of?"

"Even if that were any of your business, it's not why I'm
here. I want to know why you're making crazy threats. I'm
supposed to prove my innocence in forty-eight hours? Would
you like to tell me how?"

"You meant to put that in the past tense, didn't you? The
forty-eight hours is up."

He cut around her and walked across to the kitchen, where he opened the refrigerator and took out a bottle of water.

She followed right behind him, refusing the bottle he offered her. "What are you saying? You submitted the article? You threw us to the wolves? All three of us, or just me?"

He took a swig of water and crossed his arms. "I'm not the one who has to explain myself, Mattie. I'm not a murder suspect."

"That's true, you're not a suspect." She retreated to the countertop opposite him. "But you are a murderer."

His only visible reaction was a slight narrowing of his eyes. "I'd be very careful about making accusations like that, Your Honor. They can backfire."

"It's not an accusation. It's a fact."

"And you're going to explain this fact to me. *Now.*"

She permitted a smile. "Looks like it's your turn to twist, Jameson—and I didn't know it until this minute, but the thought has a certain appeal."

She'd assessed the risk in confronting him before she decided to take it. She didn't regret that decision now. It was something she needed to do for many reasons. However, if he perceived her as a threat to his career or his professional reputation or anything else, she could be in real danger. She knew things about him now that she wished to God she didn't.

"I don't like being fucked with, Mattie."

"How does it feel?" Her eyes must have looked evil because she had never wanted to hurt anyone more, not even Ms. Rowe. "Apparently, I'm not the only one with deep, dark secrets."

His head lifted, but he said nothing.

Mattie's heart surged so hard she felt faint. She was afraid she might not be able to get the rest of it out, but she had to. If for no other reason than that he deserved it for playing such depraved games.

"You're bluffing," he said. "What are these secrets? Who am I supposed to have killed?"

She could either look at him or the door. It was an easy choice. His front door was her only escape route. She turned just enough to keep it in view.

She repeated what David Grace had told her, almost word for word. "You're responsible for an innocent young woman's death. You tied her up and left her in a cave on the beach to teach her a lesson. When the tide came in, she drowned. Her body was discovered two days later, still bound."

He said nothing, and the silence built until all she could think about was him, behind her. She didn't know where he was, how close. But she didn't dare look. She did not want to give in to fear. He might think he had her exactly where he wanted her, but the worst he could do was ruin her life. She could damn his soul to hell. She knew what he was.

She did not turn around.

His voice was hoarse. "That was an accident."

"Really? That's not what I heard. She was your girlfriend, and you were crazy about her, but she was having sex with your brother."

"I didn't kill her. It wasn't like that."

Mattie detested men who hurt women. She'd grown up with that, and she considered them the worst kind of cowards. "You were in a jealous rage and you wanted to teach her a lesson. You were hell-bent on it."

"Who told you that?"

"It's true, isn't it?"

His silences wore on Mattie terribly. She'd expected anger and defensiveness, maybe even fear. The endless quiet was agony, and when she could stand the wait no longer, she came around, preparing herself for the worst.

He met her gaze, but only for an instant. He seemed more

stunned than angry. His gray eyes were dull, and he had tied his robe, as if he didn't know what else to do.

"Billy gave her drugs and had sex with her," he said. "He got her hooked, and she was willing to do anything for more drugs." His voice dropped off until it was hard to hear him. "I was a stupid fourteen-year-old kid, and I thought I was going to save her."

Mattie steeled herself. She did not want to hear that he'd done something noble and foolish. She didn't want to feel anything remotely close to forgiveness.

"I was only fourteen when *my* life fell apart," she said, "but you have no compassion for me."

"That isn't true."

Maybe she wanted him to fight with her. She wanted anger, outrage, self-defense. He was making her feel cruel, and that wasn't fair. He wasn't fair. He didn't fight like a man.

"You don't have to believe me," he said, "but I was trying to keep her away from Billy long enough to have it out with him. Unfortunately, I lost the fight. Billy knocked me cold, and I was out for most of the day."

Mattie stared at him. "That was when the tide came in?"

He nodded. "No one knew where she was, and I couldn't tell them."

The enormity of it stunned her, but within moments, the anger had crept back. "That *doesn't* absolve you."

"Christ, don't you think I know that? I would have done hard time if my father hadn't had friends in high places. As it was, I got community service and probation."

She sensed that she was ripping at open wounds, but she couldn't seem to stop herself. Maybe it was all the years of watching men hurt her mother.

"Now I understand how deep the rift went between you and your brother," she said. "He stole your girlfriend, and you couldn't forgive him. You even abandoned him when he needed you most, at his trial. Your father blamed everything on William, including this girl's death, didn't he? He banished William from the family and forbade you to have anything to do with him, and you went along with it."

"Stop," Jameson said. "Don't say anything else."

Her laughter had an icy bite. "You can't take it? You can't handle having the tables turned on you?"

"Mattie, I want you to leave. Now, before—"

"Before what? Before you hurt *me?*" She faced him down. "Do you think that frightens me coming from a man who turned his back on his own brother? A man who—"

Finally, rage. It fanned through him like a torch fire. His face contorted and he turned away, but Mattie had already seen the damage she'd done. His shoulders locked, they shuddered. He was torn with guilt over his brother's life, and death. And maybe even more over the girl.

She had gone too far.

"I'm sorry," she got out. "I shouldn't have done that. There was no need. I know it won't stop the article. I only did it to hurt you, and I'm—"

She couldn't say anything else. She had come back hurt and angry, but all she'd accomplished by lashing out was to injure someone else. Now there were two of them bleeding. They were both betrayed, and a part of them withered. This kind of careless retaliation ate away at the soul. It killed by degrees one's faith in human nature.

"I'll get out of here," she said. "Do whatever you have to. I'm done with this investigation anyway. All I've done is make a mess of it."

She didn't intend to say anything else to him, even goodbye was too much to manage. She just wanted to get out of there. Her bags were heavy, but she slung the carry-on over her shoulder and picked up the weekender. She could handle them herself. She'd been doing it for days.

She got as far as the door before a loud click sounded. Her knee! The bags went flying, and she went down, gasping in pain.

She didn't even try to get up. Her knee was throbbing, and she didn't want him trying to help. Instead, she grabbed her shoulder bag by the strap and dragged it to where she sat. Her cell was in the small zipper compartment.

Jameson was there, hovering as she began to dial the cell. "What are you doing?" he asked.

"Calling Jane. I can't let her be blindsided."

"Don't."

She looked up at him in disbelief. "Her world is about to explode because of you, and you won't let me warn her?"

"There's no need to warn her. I didn't submit the story."

"What?"

"There is no story."

Relief washed over her, making it even more difficult to get to her feet. But she had to. "I can do it," she said, slapping his hand away as he tried to help. It took some effort, and she had to use the wall as a prop, but finally she was able to stand and face him. "Why?"

"It seemed like the right thing to do."

"Really?" She shook her head, confused by his inexplicable change of heart. Several awkward moments passed before she had the presence of mind to say, "Thank you."

"Don't be so quick to thank me, Mattie. I didn't do it for you."

"Why then?"

He shrugged. "Why write an article when I can write the book? It didn't make sense."

She thought about that. "You're lying."

An eyebrow lifted. "Now I'm a liar? You're brutal with the accusations."

His robe gapped open. She felt a strange twist of excitement, and that pissed her off, too. What had he done to deserve her prurient interest? Nothing, except maybe a few sit-ups. In fact, everything about him pissed her off, if she was being honest. He was too damn pretty, and he'd been calling the shots plenty long enough.

"An article would be the perfect publicity for your book," she said. "You could have done a series of them as a lead-in to the book's debut."

"You're talking me into it."

"Tell me why you didn't submit the article." She pushed off from the wall and took a stumbling step toward him. "Why did you give me that deadline and force me to come back?"

"I told you, it seemed like the right thing to do."

Another step. God help her, she was going to fall over, but something was driving her to face him down, to make him admit it, whatever *it* was.

"I don't believe you."

He stared at her, silvery-eyed in the low light. "That much is clear."

"Is it me?" she said. "Is this about me? Why are you stalking me, watching my every move, haunting my footsteps? Why are you doing that, Jameson? Do you think about me? Do you? All the time?"

"What?"

"You heard me. You watched me sleep the night I stayed here, didn't you? Did you want me?"

"Want you?"

"Don't play dumb. Did you want me? Sex? Did you want to make love to me? Is that why you've become my fucking shadow?"

"No, I think you committed a crime, maybe several."

"That's not what this is about." She took two steps and wobbled. Took two more and couldn't go any farther. She was never going to get there at this rate. Her knee clicked again. "Oh!"

He lunged and grabbed her as she was about to tumble.

"Are you afraid of me?" she said.

"Yes," he hissed, "because you're a *criminal*."

"No way." She was close enough to kiss him—and he seemed to have noticed that possibility, as well. His gaze dropped to her mouth, and his expression had the same wanton boldness as when he'd touched her face and made her look at him.

Her stomach dipped, a terrifying feeling.

"Yes, I think about you," he said. "I think about you all the fucking time. About putting you in jail. About kissing your unbelievably foul mouth."

"Oh, and yours isn't foul?"

"I'm not a defender of the public morals."

"Do it."

"Defend the morals? Or kiss you?"

He captured her face in his hands, and bent his lips to hers.

Mattie moaned against his mouth. She clutched him and fought for breath. She couldn't distinguish one heartbeat from another after that. All restraints seemed to be ripped away.

She wasn't aware of anything but her senses. Taste and feel and smell. The sound of his breathing, the sexy rumble in his throat when his lips brushed her ear. God, luscious. Hot and luscious.

"Do you think about it?" he asked.

"Never."

"Liar."

He pulled her into his arms and brought her with him, stumbling backward. She had to hold tight not to get tangled in his legs, and when her knee wouldn't work, he lifted her up and carried her. Amazing that she felt no pain.

And suddenly her shoulders hit the wall.

They came to a breathless stop, their bodies pressed together.

He groaned anguished words in her ear.

"I think about you like this," he said.

"Because criminals turn you on?"

"Yes." He set her down, and his hands slid down to her butt, hot and frantic. Crazy with need, she began untying the sash around his waist. As her fingers fumbled with the knot, she felt the erection beneath his robe, hard and massive, even though confined in his boxers.

It had been too long. Too long since she'd surrendered herself in any way. She wanted her body entered, hard and fast. Never mind afterward, she needed now.

At last the knot gave way and she pulled the sash from around his waist. It was soft and silky as she handed it to him. "Are you going to tie me up?" she asked him. "That's what you like, isn't it? Tying women up and putting them in coffins?"

Jameson's eyes narrowed, and Mattie realized what she'd said. How could she have been so careless and stupid? "I didn't mean—"

"No, that isn't what I like," he said. "But this much is true, Mattie. If I were to tie your hands to my bedpost tonight, you wouldn't be sorry."

The sash fell to the floor. His kimono followed. His breath was hot and quick.

They never even got her out of her clothes. She kicked off her shoes, and he unbuttoned her blouse, but let it fall from her shoulders. Her jeans pooled on the floor, but only one leg was free as he slipped between her thighs and lifted her up.

He pressed her to the wall, and Mattie raised her leg to accommodate him. She bit into the muscle of his shoulder, muffling her cry as he entered her. It wasn't a gentle thrust.

It was quick, hard and possessive. Exactly what he needed. What she needed.

When her feet touched the ground afterward, they wouldn't hold her, and she ended up on the floor again. Jameson landed there with her, breathless.

"I did it for you," he said.

"The story or the sex?"

"The story."

"I know," she whispered.

A sound caught in her throat as he kissed her mouth. Laughter? Yes, and something else. Sadness, perhaps. He freed her from the rest of her clothing and carried her to his bed, where they lay under the cover of a crisp white sheet. Somewhere in that span of time, Mattie remembered a thought she'd had.

Where was sweet, sexy Jimmy Broud? The boy she used to know?

If she really let herself go crazy, she could almost imagine that he was lying right here next to her. Was he as surprised as she was by the strange turn of events?

With some hesitance, she touched his arm, struck by the simple fact that she was in bed with the boy she'd pined for as a young girl.

"I know you're exhausted," Jameson said, feathering the dark silk of her brow with his thumb. "But out there…" His gaze shot toward the front door. "That was too fast. I need more of you, Mattie."

She *was* exhausted. The trip back had seemed endless, but that wasn't the problem. She couldn't do it again. That would be crazy and risky. It had been risky enough the first time. She was still buzzing. And look at her, stroking his arm. Purring like a satisfied cat. The sex had opened her up. It had pried apart the shell she lived in, and now it was time to go back inside. Close herself off.

"I am tired," she said, glancing at him. Could he read the conflict in her eyes? Could he see what she was really thinking? It had felt strange clinging to him, strange and good. She'd never really had anyone to grab and hold on to. But more than anything else, she'd been driven by the need to feel something other than fear.

Anything other than fear. Sleep was the easy part. It was only a matter of closing her eyes and drifting off in his arms. Tomorrow would take care of itself. She had to believe that and push all the worries away, just for now.

She drew a deep breath and settled into the warmth of his embrace, content except for the one errant thought that wormed its way into her consciousness as she nodded off. She had never returned Nola Daniels's phone call.

38

A terrible clamor woke them both. Mattie nearly flew out of the bed and took the sheet with her before Jameson could get ahold of her. The crashing and banging was bad. He wasn't surprised it had startled her.

"It's just the morning paper," he said. "Remind me to plug that mail slot with something, like cement."

She turned to face him. "You wake up to that every morning? I'd be in a padded cell."

The conviction in her voice made him realize the extent to which he'd become oblivious to his daily life. He put up with these things because there didn't seem to be a reason to change them, even if they *were* disrupting his sleep, and his existence. The kamikaze newspaper carrier was the least of it. Writing was a solitary profession, and as his career had grown, he'd become more isolated, but it was starting to border on extreme. In the past few years, there hadn't been much in the way of meaningful human contact, except through his work—and that wasn't about him, it was about whoever he was trying to help.

It was easier saving other people from extinction than himself, he realized. Over the years, his investigations had freed the innocent and helped bring the guilty to justice. By focusing on the dark side of someone else's life, he didn't have to focus on his own.

And now here he was with her. What did that mean?

"Mail slots can be fixed." His breath lifted a dark tendril of her hair. "I'll fix it." He seemed to be promising her something, although with only the vaguest sense of what that might be. He was operating on instinct, he realized, testing more than promising. He'd just exposed a damp finger to the air to see which way the wind was blowing.

She burrowed into his chest. "What have we done?"

He laughed at that. "You're not sure? We could do it again, if that would help."

She glanced up at him as if she might be receptive—and he would have taken her up on it, but there were too many clouds in her blue eyes. Naked like this and wrapped in a sheet, she reminded him of the battle-scarred girl in the infirmary, sleeping peacefully, despite her ordeals.

He'd had no idea back then how she'd sustained those scars.

"Mattie," he said, "the tapes I watched gave me some idea what you went through at Rowe, you and Ivy. If you ever want to talk about it—"

Her wariness also reminded him of the battle-scarred girl. She had secrets. Everyone did, but he'd just realized that hers were a barrier to whatever might be possible between them. Interesting that he was thinking something might be possible. Good sex could do that to a man.

"I guess you're not gay."

She laughed out loud. "I hope that won't put me out of the running for Superhottie."

"God, woman," he said with utter sincerity, "you're a sure thing." He touched her hair, letting the raven-black skeins run through his fingers. The gesture seemed to make her curious. She searched his face.

"Was there anything going on with you and Ivy?" she asked him. "I always thought you were smitten with her."

Jameson quickly put an end to that idea. "Despite my

past transgressions, or maybe because of them, I'm a sucker for damsels in distress. Ivy was the one in distress in those days. You—well, you were just quick and mean."

"Gee, thanks." She touched a knuckle to her lips, seeming to be mired in thoughts. Never a good sign, as far as he was concerned.

"So, am I the one who's in distress now?" she asked.

He hadn't noticed her fingernails before. Several of them were bitten down to the quick. "It sure looks that way," he said, indicating her hands.

Her face went scarlet. "Oh, that's nothing," she said, trying to hide the evidence.

"You bite your fingernails. I collect depraved art. Everyone does something weird. It only makes you more human, and to me, more beautiful."

Her eyes brightened with disbelief. No way was she buying that one. He wasn't even sure he meant it. But he was reasonably certain that that no one in her life had ever looked at her scars and told her she was beautiful. He doubted anyone saw much beyond the black judicial robes.

"Do you ever wonder how she died?" he asked.

Her face went ashen as she mouthed the words, "Ms. Rowe?"

"No, Ivy."

"Oh…yes, of course. I've been wondering about that since it happened. It was the heartwine. I think she may have accidentally overdosed."

Jameson found it difficult to conceal his curiosity. "Heartwine is a poison. How could that have been accidental?"

"Well, as bizarre as it sounds, all four of us were taking it, trying to build an immunity so Ms. Rowe couldn't poison us. She'd done a little demonstration in her apartment once and killed her own pet bird right in front of us."

Jameson swore under his breath. But at least some things

were starting to make sense, like the time he'd seen the four of them on campus, hiding out in an alcove and sipping from a vial. Now he wondered what other things they'd done in the name of self-preservation. He had the feeling she was on the verge of revealing more of her secrets, perhaps all of them. That scared him a little.

He was asking her to incriminate herself with every question.

"About your brother," she said, catching him totally off guard.

"What about Billy?"

She hesitated, as if preparing herself. "I'm sorry about what happened to him. He didn't deserve it, not any of it."

She rushed on, as if she'd been waiting her whole life to get this out. "I think he wanted to be a good man, but people were frightened of him. He helped me once when I was at Rowe, and I never got to thank him for it. I was frightened of him, too. I just wanted you to know that he did something good."

Jameson was touched, but not quite sure how to respond. He needn't have worried. She had no intention of letting him.

"I'm going to go get that paper," she said.

"Wait!" He grabbed for her, but this time she was too fast for him. She disappeared into the hallway, where he could hear her bare feet on the slate tiles. It sounded like she was running.

He settled back on the pillows with a sense of contentment that he hadn't felt in years. Strange, because nothing was resolved. He didn't even have a plan at the moment. The only thing on his mind was maybe making some coffee and having a cup while they read the paper in bed. Then they could clear up some of her questions about what they'd done. He'd be happy to give her a refresher course.

He'd just dragged himself out of bed and was pulling on his shorts when he heard her scream.

* * *

"Oh, good, you're still here!" Jane Mantle rushed into the dining room where she and her husband breakfasted when they were both in town.

"That Cokie Roberts can talk," she said, flattening the stubborn white lapel of her navy suit jacket with her fingers. The damn corner curled up every time she took her hand away. "And she calls at such inopportune times."

The President looked up from his discussions with his reelection campaign manager, a sturdy woman with a cap of curly graying hair and a warm smile. "Jane, say hello to Muriel. We're working on a short list of campaign contributors. She's lined up some deep pockets, haven't you, Muriel."

"Kangaroo pouches," Muriel Dickerson said with a sly smile.

Jane blew the woman a kiss. "If I wasn't married, Muriel, I'd be dating you. You're my hero and never forget it."

Larry chortled. "Perhaps you should skip the coffee this morning, my love. You're already levitating."

Jane sank into her chair, making a noise like a punctured tire. She was always running, always. Sometimes she didn't realize how exhausted she was until she stopped, particularly since she'd quit taking her pills. She hadn't had one, or even a sliver, since the day she saw her psychiatrist, and her nervous system felt as if it were on automatic pilot. She was flying just above an abyss, endless and black. If she stopped, she dropped.

She glanced over at Muriel. "You have David Grace on that list, right?"

Muriel checked the paper in front of her. "How could we have missed him?"

"We may have lost him," Larry advised. "I spoke with him this morning, and he's not happy about the possibility of having the plug pulled on his pet project."

Jane had feared this was going to happen. But maybe it

wasn't too late. She would make a phone call to David and try to smooth things over, although she wasn't nearly so certain about her ability to do that now. She wasn't at her best, and this project of his was his life.

"Coffee, ma'am?" Felicia, a relative newcomer to the second floor staff, appeared with a thermal carafe of coffee and Jane's newspapers. Jane and Larry had tried to preserve as many relationship rituals as possible when they moved to Pennsylvania Avenue, including the simplicity of starting out their day with coffee, rolls and the morning news, although lately Larry had quit the rolls for his health and Jane for her figure. He'd wisely substituted grapefruit. She'd gone for one square of decadently dark chocolate. Not wise, but it got her engine going like grapefruit never would.

No coffee or chocolate today.

Felicia set down the stack of newspapers, and as Jane plucked one from the top, she absently covered her coffee cup with her hand, signaling she didn't want it filled. She glanced at the headline and caught back a gasp. Reflexively, she jerked her hand back and hot coffee splattered everywhere. It drenched her navy blue pantsuit.

Felicia hadn't caught Jane's signal not to pour, but Jane's sharp cry had less to do with pain than with shock. The newspaper on the top of the stack was the *San Francisco Chronicle,* and Jane was stunned by the headline that blared from its banner.

She flipped the paper over, not wanting anyone else to see it. She couldn't believe what she'd read.

"Mrs. Mantle, I'm so sorry!" Felicia was near tears as she attempted to blot Jane's jacket dry. "Did it burn you? Should I get some ice?"

"Jane, are you all right?" Larry asked. Muriel Dickerson echoed his concern, but neither of them seemed to have any idea what to do.

"Of course," Jane said, soaking her napkin in ice water. "I'm fine." Felicia was now trying to blot the linen tablecloth, but Jane gently shooed her away. She just wanted people to stop fussing and gaping at her like she was an embarrassment to the civilized world.

They were looking at the napkin in her hand. It was dripping, shaking. Jane's mouth was so dry she could barely speak.

"The stain will wash out," she told Felicia. "You go ahead and change. You have coffee all over you, too. It was my fault, totally mine."

Felicia slunk away, but her husband and Muriel were still watching Jane with some concern. "Go back to your list," she told them. "I'm sorry to have messed up everyone's breakfast. I can't imagine what made me so clumsy."

But no matter what Jane said, they couldn't seem to tear themselves away from her plight. They could hardly ignore her without appearing to be insensitive clods, she supposed. Manners were such a pain in the ass! She had brought all this attention on herself at the worst possible time. The newspaper headline was still screaming in her head.

The ugly dark stain came into full view as she rose from the table. "I'll go change," she said, "and send someone with fresh table linen."

Larry smiled. Muriel smiled. Everyone smiled and acted as if things were perfectly fine. Just some spilled coffee, a minor glitch in the great scheme of things. But Jane feared differently. Somehow she had to smuggle the newspaper out of here and find a private place to read the article. If it said what she thought it did, her husband could stop planning his campaign right now. It was all over.

Mattie's grip on the newspaper had crumpled it beyond recognition.

Jameson tore into the living room, panting. "What's wrong?"

She turned it around and showed him the front-page headline: Retired Police Chief In Sex Ring With Minors.

"I never called Nola Daniels back," she told him. "She said he wanted to talk to me."

"Who wanted to talk to you? What are you talking about?"

"Chief Daniels, but I couldn't. I was on my way here." There wasn't time to tell Jameson the history. All Mattie could do was relate the thoughts running through her head. "I asked her to give me an hour, and she said that might be too late. It doesn't matter now."

Jameson took the paper from her hands, snapped the wrinkles out and began to read aloud.

"'Daniels refused to name the other participants in the ring or the underage girls, but he admitted they were students from Rowe Academy, a local finishing school, and that he'd been involved with at least one of them himself.'"

"Does it say anything about Ms. Rowe?" Mattie asked.

He skimmed the piece. "Here's something. 'The confession seems to corroborate the claims of William Broud, the school's groundskeeper, who was convicted of murdering the school's headmistress, Millicent Rowe, in 1982. Broud's claims of a sex ring were dismissed at the time, but he was recently exonerated of the murder and released from prison. The week he was released, Broud was murdered in the same manner as the headmistress.'"

"Daniels's wife told me he had Alzheimer's," Mattie said, "and he suddenly remembers all that?"

"There's no mention of Alzheimer's here. It says his health is failing, and that's why he may have felt compelled to confess. Oh, wait—Jesus," Jameson whispered. "Daniels claims he's being blackmailed by Frank O'Neill."

"The D.A.? That O'Neill?"

Jameson didn't respond. He was fixed on the newsprint,

devouring the rest of the article. Rubbery-legged, Mattie turned and headed for her bags. She dropped to the floor, heedless of her bad knee, and rifled through her shoulder bag.

Her cell was in the zipper compartment where she left it, thank God. The message light was flashing, but she didn't have time to check voice mail. She hit the smart button repeatedly, which took her through a log of incoming calls. When she found Daniels's phone number, she hit Redial.

Nola Daniels answered on the first ring.

Mattie fought to calm her voice. "Mrs. Daniels, this is Mattie Smith. I wasn't able to call back last night. I had an emergency, but I can talk with your husband this morning. Now, in fact, if it's conven—"

"He can't talk to anyone." There was no rancor in Nola's refusal, just despair and a weariness that sounded like resignation. "His attorney has advised him not to comment on the case."

"The paper said he was being blackmailed by the district attorney. Do you know how O'Neill found out about the sex ring?"

"I know nothing, and even if I did, I couldn't tell you."

"Are you sure? Your husband seemed to think it important that he speak to me last night. Maybe I can still help in some way."

"You can't help him, Ms. Smith. No one can. It's too late."

The phone went dead, and Mattie felt a flash of desperation. Nola Daniels had hung up without giving her a chance to make her case. Mattie hadn't pleaded, and she would have done that, she realized. She would have begged. She'd made a mistake, and there was nothing she wouldn't do to fix it, including break every vow she'd ever made to herself.

She stared at the phone, aware that a shadow had fallen over her. Someone had come up behind her.

"Who are you calling?" Jameson asked.

"No one. It's too late," she said. "The media's involved

now, and it's only a matter of time before everyone knows who the minor girls were. There's nothing I can do."

He came around and stood in front of her. His bare feet were brown and strong and firmly planted. They said he was a solid presence in a world of flux. Odd that she could take any comfort from that awareness, but somehow, she did.

"Listen to me," he said. "I've known Frank O'Neill for years. I'll see what I can do to stop this story, or at least the details involving the three of you. I'll talk to Frank."

Mattie glanced up at him, confused by his generosity. He had wanted to write this story for his brother. Now he was offering to try and stop it altogether? It should have been *his* story to write.

She didn't know how to thank him. She couldn't even bring herself to try. She rarely allowed herself to be in the position of needing help, and now she didn't know how to accept it. But that seemed to be changing, even if she didn't want it to. Moments ago she'd wished for the opportunity to beg Nola Daniels, and now she was letting this man make what amounted to a great personal sacrifice.

Fighting dragons was easy, she realized. This was hard. Letting people in. It terrified her to the core. She would rather have gone on alone. She *had* to go on alone. It was the only way she knew. Maybe there was a part of her that longed to let someone in, but she couldn't. She would always be wondering what he wanted. Why he'd done it. It couldn't be the kindness of his heart. The men in her life had not been kind. And there was just too much at risk.

She rose to her feet. "We didn't kill your brother," she said. "And we didn't kill the headmistress, either. We all believed that he'd done it. I wish there was some way I could prove that to you."

"Me, too," he said, engaging her with a gaze that could cut like a blade.

She fended him off with more information. "I think it's possible that Frank O'Neill has the video," she told him. "Chief Daniels claimed that O'Neill was blackmailing him—and O'Neill's wife, Lane, used to work the videotape equipment for Ms. Rowe. Just the classroom stuff, as far as I know, but she maintained the tape library, and she was the only one who had access to it besides Ms. Rowe."

He seemed surprised. "You think Lane and Frank were blackmailing people? Is Lane capable of that? I'm not sure I believe Frank is."

"Lane is capable of anything, in my opinion. She used to threaten to steal the tapes and blackmail the kids she didn't like. There was plenty of humiliating material, especially to teenage girls."

"I can't promise I'll get it back," he said, seeming to have overcome his hesitance, "but I'll try. Is that what you want?"

Emotion stung her throat. She bit it back. "Thank you."

"Will you wait here?" he asked.

"No, I have to go home, then probably back to Washington. My friends and I have to make some decisions."

"I don't suppose I could stop you, could I?"

"Not short of sealing me up in a coffin."

She smiled but he didn't. His expression turned grave. "Mattie, do not get yourself killed. I wouldn't like that."

Mattie let herself into her house and took a quick look around. She'd insisted on taking a taxi back from Jameson's. She didn't even have a rental car right now, but she hadn't wanted him to drive her. She had to be alone, to think. Her mind felt as if it was running in place, sprinting frantically. Her own car was still sitting in her garage since she hadn't been able to start it. She would have to do something about transportation, get another rental.

Nothing seemed to have been disturbed in her place since

she was here last, but that had been quite a while. She was having her mail held at the post office and hadn't picked it up yet. She'd closed the blinds and turned the heat off, too, but the chill she felt was odd, clammy, as if she'd left a window open.

The wall sconces came on when she hit the light switch by the door. The soft light allowed her to see the way to her bedroom. It wasn't far, but she had her bags in hand, and they were growing heavier by the minute. Her poor knee had been through too much and didn't like the extra weight at all. She was limping by the time she got to her room.

She dropped the bags on the bed and went to turn on the nightstand lamp, a Tiffany replica she'd picked up at an estate auction. Maybe that would warm the place up. She'd been gone so long she felt as if she didn't belong here, as if the house had disowned her for neglect.

The light flickered when she pulled the chain, but didn't quite catch. She yanked again, bending down to get a look inside the shade. Moments later, she was on the floor with the lamp, doing some quick repairs, when she heard a scratching sound. It sounded like a cat's claws on a wooden floor, and it was coming from the doorway to the bedroom.

Mattie didn't turn. It was too late for that. Someone was in the house. They were in the room with her. Coming up behind her. She'd been attacked twice. She wasn't going for thirds.

Gripping the lamp by the base, she ripped it out of the wall socket as she sprang to her feet. Someone was going to fucking die this time, and it wouldn't be her.

"Who's there?" she shouted, wielding the lamp like a club. The intruder stepped out of the shadows, and as Mattie saw who it was, she dropped the lamp. An ear-splitting scream rent the air.

39

It might surprise people that I am not a fastidious eater. I inhale French fries, bunches at a time, licking the salt and grease from my fingers. I prefer tacos made of hamburger meat that ooze orange juices when I eat them, and I always ask for the grated cheese, sour cream and onions.

When I'm hungry, food is heroin. Eat or suffer the agonies. Eat or die. I'm a salivating wolf, a predator, but I only gorge when I'm starving. That's when the smells and tastes and textures are exquisite. That's when my mouth waters and my jaw goes slack with desire. Other than that, I rarely bother. I can do without food for days.

No one would be surprised that I'm fastidious in other ways. I clean up my messes. Always. That should be the golden rule, but the world is full of pigs. Pigs and sheep. They leave their garbage around for others to pick up. They litter the streets and ruin what's natural and beautiful. There's a plan to all things, a perfection they completely fail to see.

The thing is I have faith in human nature. I haven't given up in despair or become numbed to the possibilities. I believe people can be shown another way. Given a chance, they'll see the perfection, too, and they'll do the right thing. The sheep can generally be counted on in this way. They're docile, for the most part. Malleable.

The pigs? Let them live in the swill. I walk around them

if they let me. If they don't, if they make me walk through their
garbage, then it becomes my garbage, and I have to clean it
up. Some people create so much waste they have to be shown
the error of their ways. Unfortunately, that's not pleasant for
anyone. But I don't go looking for it.

That's what's happening now in this culture of pigs and
sheep.

So many messes to clean up, none of them mine.

Breeze nearly fell backward, trying to keep from being hit
with the Tiffany lamp. Her blood-curdling scream sent Mattie spinning backward, too, onto the bed. Mattie's grip on the
lamp was so tight, she couldn't let go of it. Otherwise, her
prized possession would have been in shards all over the
floor.

Mattie couldn't catch her breath. "What are you doing
here?" she asked between gasps. Nearly hitting her friend
had frightened her more than dealing with an intruder. She'd
been ready for that.

Breeze couldn't seem to breathe, either. She was quite a
vision, cowering in her white slacks, tangerine tube top and
stiletto sling-backs. She looked like a *Baywatch* babe, having a heart attack.

Maybe that's what made Breeze giggle. She clapped a
hand over her mouth and made rude hissing noises.

Mattie didn't see the humor. She didn't see it at all, but
somewhere inside her a tight rubber band snapped and gave
way completely. She dropped the lamp on the bed and laughter foamed into her throat. It could have burned holes it was
so hot. Hysteria, obviously.

"I'm sorry," Breeze said, finally. "I came over to get one
of the outfits I loaned you, that sweet little Tahari wrap dress
with the ruffle on the hem. I didn't know you'd be back
today."

"How did you get in? I had this place locked up tight."

"The doors are locked, but you forgot the guest bedroom window. I checked them all and found it already open, so I climbed in. Not easy, either. I ripped a nail right off." She held up her hand as proof. "Wait, Mattie? Where are you going?"

"To check the window." Mattie brushed past her friend on her way to the window. If someone really had broken in, neither one of them was safe.

Mattie saw immediately that the window on the far side of the bed had been jimmied. The shutters were hanging open and the lock was unlatched. A wicker wastebasket that normally sat beneath the window was lying on its side, the contents spilled out.

Mattie pointed to the basket as Breeze followed her into the room. "Did you do that?"

"Please, I'm a much neater criminal than that. I did mess up your backyard a little, though. I couldn't reach the window without some help, so I dragged the trash can over to the ledge and crawled up on that." She wrinkled her nose. "It's in need of a good hosing, that can."

Mattie was already deeply engrossed in what could have happened here. She hadn't left the window open. Someone had broken in. Last time it had been the Secret Service, but that seemed unlikely. She hadn't entertained Jane here, and had no plan to.

Jameson probably knew where she lived, but she'd been with him. As far as she knew, Chief Daniels was in custody and David Grace was in Italy. She couldn't think of anyone else, other than the invisible members of the sex ring. That left her nemesis, the one who'd attacked her. *He knew where she lived.*

"Where are you going *now?*" Breeze demanded.

"Back to my room," Mattie said. "Lock the window, would you, and close the shutters."

Mattie sprinted down the hall to her bedroom and went straight to the armoire to check the combination-lock safe. She found the safe open and her gun missing. The last time she'd unlocked it had been for John Bratton, the Secret Service officer. He'd insisted she show him the contents, but he must not have closed the door. Intentionally, she wondered?

She locked the safe, shut the armoire and set about searching the rest of the bedroom with Breeze trailing after her, asking what she was looking for.

Mattie didn't try to spare her this time. She didn't have the energy or the concentration to lie. "Someone is stalking me, and it looks like he's been here," she said. "He took my gun."

Breeze pitched in without a word. They went through the entire house, room after room. Neither of them found anything missing, except the gun, but that was plenty.

"We can't stay here," Mattie said.

Naturally, Breeze was several steps ahead of her. "Darling, no offense, but I wasn't intending to stay here. I have a suite at the Four Seasons, remember? Want to join me? Massages? Champagne? Beautiful men? There's an extra bedroom."

"Do you have a car?"

"Of course, a rental Mercedes. How do you think I got here?"

Suddenly life didn't look quite so bleak to Mattie. She'd always wanted to stay at the Four Seasons. She hadn't imagined it would be under these circumstances, but leave it to Breeze to turn a nightmare stalking experience into a dream vacation.

Mattie felt rather like visiting royalty as she settled herself in the black cashmere chair and put her feet up on the matching hassock. Breeze's suite had turned out to be the presidential suite, and she was now freshening up in her own room while Mattie checked her voice mail messages.

Mattie did have her own bedroom, but she hadn't wanted to leave the elegant living area. Everything was so gilded and regal that she couldn't imagine anything going wrong here. She hadn't felt this safe since she was in the White House itself.

She hit the smart button on her phone, checked her messages and found several from Jane. She was probably freaked about Chief Daniels's confession, but Mattie'd had no chance to return calls until now. She had hoped to hear something reassuring from Jameson that she could pass on to Jane, but there was no word from him yet.

Jane had given Mattie a number to call that she said was a secure line for their conversations, as well as safe for leaving messages. Mattie got her voice mail on the first try. She apologized for not getting back sooner and asked Jane to call as soon as possible.

While Mattie waited for Breeze to appear and for Jane to call back, she used her handheld computer to send an e-mail to the Italian *municipio* in Ravello, requesting a search of birth records. She made it a point to use her judicial credentials, hoping that might speed things up. The story the gardener at the clinic had told her about the woman he found on the rocks had given her an idea. She'd decided to narrow the search to the year that David Grace's wife died, and to a baby born of an American mother. It was probably a wild-goose chase, but she had to try.

Another piece of Breeze's research had stayed with her, too. She'd said that Cynthia Grace died in August, which was when Ms. Rowe was in Europe for an extended sabbatical. In Italy, if Mattie remembered correctly. A connection seemed far-fetched, except that Ms. Rowe *was* having an affair with Cynthia Grace's husband, and when the headmistress returned to school in the fall, she was different. She'd always been cold and controlling, a frightening figure to a fourteen-year-old, but after that summer, she seemed angry and dangerously obsessed. The idea of turning her lonely girls into teenage hookers became a mission she was willing to do almost anything to achieve, even if it meant sacrificing them. As Mattie thought back on it now, she'd seemed almost self-destructive in her quest. And there was that letter to her lover that had talked about tragic losses and precious gifts. To David Grace, according to Jane.

Far-fetched, maybe, Mattie reasoned, but two people were dead, and she herself was under attack. It felt crazy not to follow through.

Jameson drove by Frank O'Neill's gated Mediterranean estate and saw the media parked out front in their mobile units and unmarked cars. Some of them had already set up shop on the grassy areas and the sidewalk, waiting like enemy troops with their shoulder-mounted cameras and boom mikes.

Instead of stopping, Jameson called the house on his cell and got Frank's wife. He knew Lane casually, only because she and Frank had been married for some time. Jameson had never formed an opinion of Lane one way or the other, but now that Mattie had given him some background information on her, he was curious. He didn't know how she and Frank met, but their marriage had never seemed like a love match, and they'd always pursued separate interests. Frank typically came to business functions alone. Jameson had first met him at their athletic club, and he'd interviewed Frank many times over the years for articles and books.

Lane told him Frank wasn't home, but didn't volunteer where Jameson could reach him. It surprised Jameson that he picked up no hint of distress in her voice. Maybe she was putting on a good front, but she sounded calm and collected. He took a chance and expressed his sympathies anyway.

"I read about Frank's troubles in the paper," he told her, "and I was hoping to offer support as a friend. This isn't a professional call, so if there's anything either of you need, please let me know."

Now she sounded relieved. "I'm sure he could use some support right now, but I really don't know where he is. He said he had to get away, be by himself. I'm worried," she admitted.

"Could he have gone to the lake cabin?" Jameson had been out to the cabin on Phoenix Lake, where Frank often spent spring and summer weekends fishing.

"Possibly, although I don't know why he wouldn't have said so. I tried to call him there and no one answered."

"I'll check it out and get back to you. I'm sure he's all right."

She thanked him and once they'd said their goodbyes, Jameson wheeled his car around and headed southeast toward the cabin, which was about an hour away. It made sense that Frank might have gone there. It was a great place to hide out from the world. A bunch of them used to get loaded and go native spear fishing in the lake at night. It was a wonder they hadn't all speared each other and drowned. Then Frank began drinking too much, and it stopped being fun.

Jameson had taken that as one more sign that Frank's marriage wasn't working. But Frank never talked about problems. He got his drinking under control, and he'd been flourishing ever since. Of course, blackmail money could explain that. He'd always lived like a millionaire, well beyond the means of a D.A. on the county payroll. Were he and his wife sidelining in blackmail?

Jameson checked his cell for messages. Still nothing from

Mattie, and his concern was growing. He'd tried to talk himself out of his fixation with her safety, but no amount of reasoning had a chance. He was hooked into another fatal attraction to the tragic, hooked like a fish, it seemed. But he couldn't blame this one on his pattern of avoiding his problems by immersing himself in someone else's. He was right in the middle of the problem. He *was* the problem. Since getting involved with her, he'd been forced to face himself, his feelings for her and his feelings for his brother.

There'd been no avoiding anything. Hell, maybe that was why he had to follow this through. It was territory he'd dodged his whole life, and until he dealt with it, the Fates would keep bringing him right back to the same place.

Gravel popped and crackled, chunks of it spitting into the air like bullets, as Jameson drove down the winding access road to Frank's cabin. The Escalade was still in the shop, getting bodywork, so he'd had to use his second car, an older four-door Jaguar that he enjoyed working on himself. It might need a new paint job before he got to the end of this road. The area was sparsely populated, except for cabins, trailer parks and summer rentals. Frank's wood shake cabin was one of the nicer properties, but still small and rustic compared to his mansion.

Jameson was relieved to see Frank's Range Rover parked in the driveway. He let himself out of the Jaguar and headed for the front door at a jog. No one answered when he knocked, and he debated whether to use the key. He knew where it was hidden.

He knocked again, but he'd already made the decision. Frank's car was there, so Frank must be. Jameson couldn't leave without talking to him.

Moments later, he let himself inside the shadowy cabin. The sun was fast falling, yet no lights had been turned on. Visibility was so low Jameson had difficulty finding his way around. He thought about calling out Frank's name, but didn't. Something about the cabin's strange hush filled him with trepidation.

Even the smell of the place was wrong, musty and cloying.

He bypassed the kitchen, dining room and bedrooms and went straight to the back of the house to the den, where Frank spent most of his time.

Jameson stopped in the doorway, struck by the sight of the man resting in his chair, staring out the window at the lake. The room was suffused with lavender twilight. It was a peaceful scene that should not have filled Jameson with quiet horror. It should not have pulled beads of sweat from his forehead or made his stomach turn over with revulsion.

His friend's eyes were open, but he wasn't looking at the lake. He couldn't see anything but eternal darkness. Frank O'Neill was dead.

40

Suicide, Jameson realized. As he entered the room, he saw the open fifth of liquor and the highball glass lying on its side. Beside them on the desk was an empty bottle of sleeping pills. A heavy sadness pressed on him. That could mean Daniels's blackmail charges were true, which was even harder for Jameson to accept. No one would have accused Frank of being a saint, but he'd always seemed like a decent guy.

Jameson came around the desk, aware that he had discovered his brother's body just days ago. Billy and Frank could not have been more different, in their lives or their deaths. Despite his fetal position on the bathroom floor, Billy had seemed at peace, as if the end were in some way welcome. Frank's face was a fright mask. Jameson found it hard to look at him.

In the dim light, Frank had appeared to be gazing at the lake, but now, straight on, he looked like a man being menaced by hell hounds. He was one of Van Gogh's grotesque self-portraits. The stark, staring eyes and the grimacing mouth, now gone slack. The spittle and mottled skin.

He had not been dead long, Jameson realized. His blood had stopped circulating and because of his upright position, it was beginning to drain from his head cavity. That explained the splotchy color. Jameson estimated that it might have been less than an hour.

He wanted to close Frank's eyelids and end his horror. Let the man rest, for God's sake, but he couldn't. If the police were called in, they would not want anything to have been touched. Jameson wasn't licensed, but he'd done plenty of investigating. He knew the ropes.

Jameson glanced at his watch. He should call Lane and find some way to break the news to her, but something stopped him. Frank was dead, but there was nothing resolved in this room, nothing finished. Even Frank's posture had the immediacy of a freeze-frame, where the action is stopped for an instant before resuming.

Jameson could see Frank's arm and hands, his neck, but the muscles weren't slack. They still appeared to be engaged in some action. There didn't seem to be any letting go anywhere in his body. Jameson touched his skin and felt the warmth. He'd guessed right—Frank hadn't been dead long. Still, it was odd that he hadn't slumped over, hadn't unlocked from whatever had driven him to this act of self-destruction.

Jameson tried to imagine what it could have been. The fear of exposure, perhaps. Shame. Guilt. Jameson hated the idea that people could be pushed to this extreme, and for all the wrong reasons. Usually they couldn't live with their own gnawing sense of failure, but their only real failure was in not seeing that it was someone else's standard they were trying to meet. In Billy's case, it was their father's. Harlan Broud was so invested in preserving his own illusion of goodness and piety that he would sacrifice a son to maintain it—and Jameson had participated in that.

Harlan couldn't have a rebel around, embarrassing him and proving that he wasn't God's emissary here on earth. He'd had the sense to marry a soft-spoken woman who worshipped him right up until the day she died, her body eaten away by multiple cancers. He'd also had a second son who, once he'd seen the error of his ways, was more than prepared to make up for the prodigal firstborn.

Jameson had accepted his role, unaware that it was all in the service of preserving his father's self-image. Egotistical asshole. Why hadn't Harlan died? He'd driven his innocent son to the brink of suicide and emotionally abused his gentle wife every day of their marriage. Why didn't the assholes ever die young, and tragically?

Life *was* fair, Jameson reasoned. People weren't. They were pigs, selfish, egotistical and ruthless in the preservation of their own egos.

Shadows lengthened and flared, throwing the room into swimming darkness. He was running out of time. As much as he disliked the thought of violating Frank's space and his dignity, even in death, Jameson had to search the room. This would be his only chance to find the video, if it was here.

He took a Kleenex from a box on the desk and used it like a glove to avoid contaminating the scene. He started with the desk drawers, but didn't even get the first one open. There was a cassette box on the floor. It looked as if it had fallen from Frank's hand and landed on the floor next to his chair.

"Jesus," Jameson whispered.

He knelt for a closer look. He'd planned to call Lane as soon as he was done here, but maybe he should call the police instead. A wild thought occurred to him as he read the label on the box. What if Mattie was right and Lane was in on the blackmail scheme with Frank? Lane was the one who'd sent him here, but maybe she'd wanted him to find Frank's body. If Frank had decided to confess and give up the videotape, Lane may have killed him to stop him from implicating her.

On the other hand, there were lots of people who might want this tape, including anyone in the sex ring, assuming it existed. He knew Mattie wanted it. She'd told him. Either one of her friends would want it, too. And so would anyone who wanted to protect a member of the sex ring.

He hadn't noticed a suicide note anywhere. His blood ran cold. Had he interrupted a murderer in the process of killing Frank?

Jameson reached for the tape, but he wasn't fast enough to pick it up. A blow from behind struck him hard enough to crack his skull. His last thought was of dead bodies, his brother's, Frank's, his own. The last thing he saw was a brilliant red fire inside his head and the floor of the cabin hurtling toward him. The pain was indescribable. And then it was gone.

"You're going to wear out your finger, girl. Who are you calling?"

Mattie snapped her cell phone shut. "Jameson. He isn't answering."

Breeze eyed her suspiciously. "Is there something you haven't told me? You seem to have a one-track mind tonight, the Jameson track. Here, have some of this and relax."

Breeze poured fragrant tea into a bone china cup and handed it to her. She'd just joined Mattie in the living room for some girl talk before retiring, and she'd ordered a bedtime snack from room service—a plate of gingersnaps and a pot of Artist's Blend tea, probably to make good her claim that the Four Seasons could do anything. Mattie had been hoping for the Cristal and the chocolate strawberries.

"Actually, there is something I haven't told you." Mattie gave a thought to her posture and graciously accepted the tea, balancing the cup on her knees. Ms. Rowe would have been proud.

"And that is?" Breeze poured herself a cup, expertly wielding the pot and keeping one eye pinned on Mattie as she did so.

In an understated voice, Mattie said, "He's helping us."

"Jameson Cross is helping us? Last I knew he was accusing us of serial murders."

"He seems to have had a change of heart." Mattie sipped the tea just as she'd been taught, with lightly pursed lips and a smooth, serene brow. She held the saucer in her left hand, the cup in her right, nothing touching the delicate handle but thumb and index finger. Too bad her fingers were sticky with perspiration.

Well-brought-up young ladies glow with excitement. They do not perspire, they certainly do not sweat. They flush, they blush, they glow.

It was one of Mattie's favorite Ms. Roweisms. *Are you flushing with excitement?* the scholarship girls would whisper to each other from their lavatory stalls.

"Mattie, did you hear me?"

Apparently Breeze had had enough of the tea ceremony. Her cup and saucer hit the sterling silver tray with a none-too-delicate clunk. "Tell me more about his change of heart. Did it start somewhere a little lower? You didn't get naked with him, did you?"

Oh, and how. Mattie set down her cup, too, before it slid right through her clammy fingers. She conjured up a half-hearted glare, certain it wouldn't give Breeze so much as one qualm.

Steeling her voice, she said, "For once, don't go there, all right? Not everything is about sex. Jameson volunteered to speak to Frank O'Neill about playing down the sex ring angle of the police chief's story, or at least keeping our names out of it."

"Listen to yourself talking about sex rings and telling me everything isn't about sex. More to the point, why would either one of them do anything to help us?"

"O'Neill and Jameson have been friends for years. And

Jameson would like to find his brother's killer as much as we would. He's actually cooperating with me on my investigation, and we should all be damn thankful."

Breeze did not look thankful, and Mattie couldn't say she was surprised. Jameson wasn't your typical Good Samaritan, and she didn't fully understand his generosity, either. She hadn't told either of the other women about her alliance with him for obvious reasons. They would think she'd gone nuts. She had.

"Anything else on David Grace?" Mattie asked, hoping to change the subject. She'd already told Breeze about her thoughts on Cynthia Grace's death and Ms. Rowe's sabbatical, and Breeze had promised to work on it herself.

"Grace is a magician," Breeze said. "My people have never had more difficulty getting background information. There are circles within circles, trails that lead nowhere. No false identities, but false paths everywhere. My security expert thinks he's created paper trails in the way that people do dummy corporations. It's impossible to tell what's real and what isn't. It's a challenge." She winked. "Of course, I'm up to it."

Mattie's cell shrilled, startling them both. She flipped it open and checked the number. It was Jane. Thank God.

She hit the talk button and barely got out, "Hello."

"Mattie, we have a crisis on our hands."

"Jane, it may not be as bad as you think."

Out of the corner of her eye, Mattie saw Breeze pick up the remote and turn on the TV. Oh, for that kind of nonchalance in the face of disaster. Maybe she should have Breeze take Jane's calls. That would be interesting.

"It's worse," Jane was saying, "you have no idea how bad, but I can't go into detail. You and Breeze need to get back here right away, tonight, if possible. Meanwhile, be thinking about a worst-case scenario strategy. I don't have to tell you that Daniels's confession is the tip of the iceberg."

Given Breeze's reaction, Mattie wasn't sure she should mention Jameson's offer of help. She spoke soothingly. "Worst-case scenario strategy. Good idea. I'll go to work on that."

"Mattie?" Jane's voice went soft, desperate. "Please hurry. Can you find Breeze? How soon can the two of you get here?"

"I'm here with Breeze now at the Four Seasons. We'll catch the first flight out to D.C. There may still be a red-eye."

"Thank God," Jane said. "My life is over, Mattie. It's all over."

A dial tone buzzed in Mattie's ear. Jane had hung up, but her frantic words reverberated with such force that Mattie sat up and sucked in a gasp of alarm. "What was that all about?" she whispered aloud.

Breeze was engrossed in something on television and didn't seem to have heard her. Mattie collapsed forward, catching herself with palms pressed against her forehead and elbows on her knees. She didn't have the energy to try and explain Jane's call, even to herself. The fatigue she felt made her ache in every fiber, and she was filled with despair at the thought of another cross-country trip.

Where was Jameson? Why hadn't he called? And what the hell was going on with Jane?

"Mattie, look, look!" Breeze waved the remote, trying to get her attention. She pointed at the television where there was breaking news of a high-profile suicide. "Do you mean *that* Frank O'Neill?"

On the screen a team of paramedics carried a stretcher out of a rustic cabin made of wood shingles. What appeared to be a man's body was draped from head to toe, and the commentator, a local news reporter, expressed her shock and grief at the loss to everyone who knew and worked with Marin County's district attorney.

"The paramedics are saying that it appears to be suicide," she explained, shouting over the noise of the fire engines. "We don't know why a dedicated public servant like Frank O'Neill would have chosen to end his life this way, but it's a sad day for all of us."

Mattie listened in stunned silence. She waited for the woman to say that they'd found a videotape that revealed the identity of every man and every underage student in the sex ring. She waited to hear them say her name.

Mattie glanced in the rearview mirror, checking for patrol cars as she exited the Golden Gate Bridge in the rental Mercedes at a speed that would have set radar equipment screaming. She had to get to Jameson's place and make it back to the airport in time to meet Breeze and catch the red-eye flight.

Jameson still wasn't answering his phone or returning his calls, and she didn't know whether or not he'd attempted to talk to Frank O'Neill. He might not even know what had happened. The news had called Frank's death an apparent suicide, which made unfortunate sense given Daniels's accusations of blackmail, but Mattie had a bad feeling that foul play was involved. She had a bad feeling about almost everything. People were acting oddly, including her two closest friends. Breeze had broken into her home and frightened her half to death, and she'd seemed strangely detached about things, even for Breeze. She'd told herself it was a coincidence that Breeze was in her house the night it was broken into, but something still didn't feel right. Nothing was a crisis to her, and yet everything was a crisis to Jane, which was out of character, too. But Mattie feared Jane was in real trouble—and may have been holding something back for years.

Mattie let up on the gas pedal. Too much was happening too fast. She felt as if she were careening toward a body on a dark road and wouldn't be able to stop in time. And worst of all, somewhere out there a missing video was waiting like a land mine for someone to step on it and explode.

Who was going to turn up dead next? Please, not Jameson.

His house was dark when she pulled into his driveway. She left the car running and dashed to the front door, but he didn't answer the bell. She rang several times, wondering how on earth she was going to find him. He couldn't have gone to bed this early, and his car wasn't parked in the driveway, where he normally left it.

She glanced at her watch, aware that she'd run out of time. If she missed the red-eye, there wouldn't be another flight out until morning.

She backed the Mercedes onto the street. As she headed for the airport, she tried to sort through all the recent events for any connection she could find, any sign of a pattern. It was only then that she realized something beyond her understanding was at work here. William Broud's ramblings about a conspiracy seemed very real to her now, possibly a conspiracy beyond anything she could have imagined.

When this all started, Jameson was the only one she couldn't trust. Now, as impossible as it seemed, it felt as if he was the only one she could.

41

"Stop, Mattie. Stop right there and turn left, maybe twenty-five degrees. The boards aren't nailed together straight. Oh, shit!"

Mattie's arms flapped wildly, like a bird desperate to keep itself aloft. Jane's cry brought her to a teetering halt on the plank, but Mattie couldn't see where she was going. A blindfold covered her eyes, and the plank was narrow. She could only put one foot in front of the other. Worst of all, she knew what lay below. A thirty-foot drop to the cement. She would explode like a watermelon.

She reached to the left with her foot and felt nothing but air.

"Too far!" Breeze squealed.

Mattie lurched back, arms flailing. Jane shouted at her to stop, and Breeze shouted at her to keep going. Mattie could do nothing but rock like a tightrope walker.

"Shut up," she told them, fighting to concentrate.

Within moments she had her footing, but sweat poured down her face, soaking the blindfold. Her legs shook. This was the stupidest idea she'd ever had. It was supposed to have been a test of her courage and trust in her friends. Negotiating the scaffolding that braced the old Residency Hall was something Artemis would have asked of her followers. But the renovations had been abandoned years ago, and the scaffolding was falling apart, along with the building. Worse, it was Mattie's idea, so she'd had to go first.

Her friends were on either side of the ten-foot bridge, giving her instructions on how to get across it. It wasn't walking the plank that took the courage, she realized. It was trusting that they wouldn't accidentally send her to her death.

"Try it again," Breeze shouted, coaxing Mattie over to her side. "Point your body left first, then step."

"Mattie, come back," Jane implored her from behind. "It's too dangerous."

Jane was closer, but Mattie didn't dare try to turn around. She blocked out their voices, both of them, and focused on the move. This was what she was good at, visualizing, hitting the target. She adjusted her body slightly, caught her balance, and sent up a prayer to the protector of young women.

"You're good," one of them shouted at her. "Go!"

With arms outstretched for balance, Mattie mentally negotiated the turn. She saw it in her mind, but when she put her foot down, the plank wasn't there. Her weight came down on thin air, and she fell forward, plunging into a dive.

The wind whistled in her ears and whipped at her clothing. She couldn't see the cement she was hurtling toward, but she could already feel it breaking her bones. The shrieking she heard came from above her, from Jane and Breeze, their frantic cries drowning out the sigh that eddied in her throat.

* * *

The White House
Present Day

Mattie bent over the bathroom sink, her hands planted on the porcelain rim. The tap water was running full blast so that no one would suspect that she was fighting to hold it together. She was in the bathroom adjoining Jane's bedroom in the private quarters of the White House. She'd ducked in here the moment she and Breeze had arrived, even before Jane could drop her bombshell.

They were waiting for Mattie to rejoin them, but she wasn't sure she could. She'd been traveling nonstop for the past several days, and she was beaten down by exhaustion. On the plane trip here, fatigue had hit her from behind, a blow she hadn't been braced for, and now it took all her strength just to support herself. She had nothing left. The few hours she'd had in Breeze's suite had not been enough to gird her for what lay ahead, or even for what awaited her outside.

Mattie had known within seconds of arriving that Jane was falling apart, too. She'd looked as if a touch could shatter her. Even Breeze had been silenced at the sight of her. And Mattie was beyond the ability to soothe either one of them. She couldn't even soothe herself.

Her nails were bitten to the quick, her ability to focus, lost. She couldn't find the way inside herself to that still center. It was gone, spinning off like everything else. She was immobilized, defeated, with no way out of the hole she'd slipped into. As ridiculous as it seemed, the only thing that had ever brought her back from despair was the black piece of cloth she used to tie around her eyes.

Her blindfold. She'd searched her bag and it wasn't there. It was lost, like her courage, like Jameson. Everything. Lost.

Mattie stared at the water rising in the basin. She cupped some in her hands and splashed her face, the cold stinging her eyes.

If she'd had the blindfold, she could have hidden inside its darkness until all the screaming was gone, hers, Breeze's and Jane's. Once her mind and her heart were quieted, she would be whole again, reassembled like a broken toy. After the fall from the scaffolding, the blindfold had come to represent all her fears. Just the sight of it had sent her into a paralyzing panic. She'd thrown it away, but had suffered such terrifying dreams of falling, she'd finally had to go fish it out of the Dumpster and face her fears.

The fall she'd taken that day should have killed her, but the only injuries she'd sustained were rope burns. At Jane's insistence, they'd rigged a safety rope and tied it to her ankle. That had stopped her plunge. But the real terror hadn't come from the fall. It had come from not being able to trust her friends.

And there was no rope tied to her ankle now.

She blotted her face dry, aware of her reddened eyes and sallow skin. She looked like hell. She wasn't going to be able to fool anyone about her state of mind, so she wouldn't even try. Breeze's attractiveness theory didn't apply when your world was crumbling.

She let herself out of the bathroom to the deathly quiet of the presidential bedroom suite. Jane hadn't yet changed out of the seersucker suit she'd worn all day, and even though nothing was obviously out of place, her outfit looked crumpled and ill-fitting, as if she'd lost weight since putting it on that morning.

Breeze was seated at Jane's vanity, busily examining the vast array of perfumes and cosmetics. Mattie picked an antique secretary and stationed herself there. The land mine she'd imagined seemed to be right here in this room with its heavy velvet draperies and presidential crests. At least Larry

Mantle was out of the country on a diplomatic tour, so they had the place to themselves.

Mattie pushed up the sleeves of her linen blazer and waited for someone to speak. It was possible Jane's news had something to do with Frank O'Neill's death, but Mattie didn't want to press her. Jane was too fragile.

Breeze opened a perfume flacon, dabbed some of the scent on the inside of her wrist and sniffed it. "Look on the bright side, ladies," she said. "We're in the White House. We've come a long way from that ramshackle shed where we used to plot Ms. Rowe's demise."

Jane was at the foot of the canopy bed, her fingers tightly wrapped around the bedpost. "Shut up, Breeze," she said. "Just shut the fuck up."

Breeze set down the perfume. "Excuse me?"

"I'd rather be in that ramshackle shed," Jane snapped. "At least we had some hope that we could fight our way out of that mess. At least we had each other."

"And we don't have each other now?" Breeze said.

Jane's voice sparkled with pain. "I'm trying to find a way to tell you about this ghastly thing I've done, and you're making quips. My life is about to shatter in a million pieces, if anyone cares."

She released the bedpost and stepped away, but her balance was off.

Mattie sprang from her chair as Jane staggered. "For heaven's sake, sit down," Mattie implored.

Jane waved her away but sat down on the far side of the bed, her back to the two other women. Her fingers were at her throat, twisting an imaginary string of pearls.

Mattie stayed where she was. She had a sick feeling about what Jane was going to say. Earlier that evening, in her panic at not finding Jameson, Mattie had attempted to sort through the chaos of the last days—and years—and eventually she'd been able to see some patterns emerging. Things that had appeared coincidental at first glance may have been anything but. It was still speculation on her part, but some of her mental detective work seemed to be paying off—only not in a good way.

Jane spoke up at last. "William Broud didn't kill Ms. Rowe. I've known he was innocent for twenty-three years."

"How could you have?" Breeze asked.

Mattie's heart nearly ripped free of her chest. "Shut the fuck up," she said, echoing Jane's own words. "Shut up, Jane!"

Breeze sprang to her feet. "What the hell's going on here?"

"He didn't do it," Jane whispered, her voice breaking.

"Shut up! Goddammit, Jane." Mattie was frantic, but she couldn't outshout her friend. Jane's whispering drowned out everything else.

Breeze walked over to Jane. "What are you talking about?"

"He didn't do it. *William Broud didn't do it.*"

Breeze stood there, staring at Jane, unable to comprehend. She dropped to her knees and gazed up at her friend for several agonizing seconds.

Breeze's hand flew to her mouth. "Jesus," she whispered. "You did it? *You* killed Ms. Rowe?"

Jane bowed her head. She nodded.

Mattie had known something terrible was coming. Jane had all but begged them to let her confess. Still, Mattie's reaction ricocheted from shock to disbelief. It couldn't be true. Jane was breaking down under the stress. She wasn't even rational. *They were all breaking down.*

"That isn't possible," Breeze said. "Ms. Rowe was smothered. We gave her poison, but it didn't kill her."

"I think I'd know whether I killed someone or not," Jane got out. "That was my blood on her pillow. *I* smothered her."

Mattie approached the bed, but Jane didn't turn around. Breeze stayed where she was, apparently unable to do otherwise. Jane's posture forbade either of them from getting any closer. There might as well have been barbed wire surrounding her.

Now Mattie was starting to believe it.

"How could you have done it?" Breeze asked. "You were in French class, weren't you?"

"I cut class—" Jane drew in a breath and began to unburden herself. Clearly, she had been waiting a long time for this moment, and was probably dreading it as much as she wanted it over with. "I went back to her apartment," she said. "I had to see whether the poison worked. There's a dormer window in the back that's hidden by a chimney, so I watched her through that. She was clearly ill, but still alive. I was leaving to find you guys when somebody knocked on her door."

"William Broud?" Mattie asked.

She nodded. "His hand was bleeding. He'd wrapped it in a handkerchief, and he asked her for a bandage, but she was too weak to get one for him. He helped her into the bedroom, and then he went to the bathroom. By the time he found a bandage, she was lying down, and her eyes were closed. He probably thought she was asleep, so he left, but his fingerprints and blood were on the bathroom sink and cabinet."

Breeze still didn't seem convinced. "You said it was your blood on the pillow."

"It was. I thought she was dead, and I went down to make sure. When I realized she was still breathing, I must have gone into shock. It frightened me so badly I got a nosebleed. I was certain she'd killed Ivy and would kill us if I didn't do something, but I couldn't even hold the pillow. So I shut my eyes and put the pillow on her face, and then I laid on it and counted to a hundred."

Mattie began to ask questions, one after the other. It was the safest thing to do right now. "The blood was from your nosebleed?"

"Turns out my blood type and Broud's are the same, B-negative."

"Why didn't you tell us?"

"I wanted to, but they picked up Broud the same day, and everyone was convinced it was him, even you guys. I didn't know what to do. I couldn't ask you to keep a secret that horrific. I didn't want you to have to live with that."

Mattie wondered if she was protecting them or herself. But then she reminded herself that this was Jane, and Jane protected everyone she loved. Fear had driven her to finish what all three of them had started, and she hadn't told anyone. She'd been shielding them from the truth all these years and carrying the guilt herself, probably because she believed it was the lesser of evils. If she confessed, she exposed her friends to criminal charges, and she ruined her husband's promising career. She might even have rationalized that she was protecting the country. She believed deeply in her husband's vision for a better America.

What an agonizing choice she'd had to make, Mattie thought.

"Why are you telling us now?" Breeze asked. "You didn't have to."

Jane drew herself up. When she turned to them, she seemed to have regained her balance, but she was pale. Frighteningly pale.

"I can't live with it any longer," she said. "At first I stayed silent out of fear, and then later because of what it would do to Larry's political chances. But none of that matters anymore."

"What do you mean? Have you told Larry?"

"No, not yet, but I will when the time is right." Her chin

trembled. "He's not going to run again anyway. His health won't permit it."

Her shoulders dropped as if something were weighing on them. Sadness swept her, and her beautiful features seemed to disintegrate right before Mattie's eyes. Mattie was struggling to take in what she'd heard, but she was also afraid that Jane might collapse.

"Jane, do you realize what you're saying?" she asked. "There is no statute of limitations on murder, and it won't matter that you were a minor. You could do prison time—or worse. And William Broud is dead."

It's too late, Jane. You've lived with it this long.

Mattie, the seeker of truth, wanted to tell her friend to keep living a lie. But Jane had the look of a penitent who had made up her mind to confess everything.

"That's just the point, Mattie. If I'd done this twenty-three years ago, William Broud would be alive now, and he wouldn't have spent what life he had in prison. I know I can't help him, but I can put a stop to this witch hunt for Millicent Rowe's killer—and to whoever is trying to expose us."

"Jane, it's okay," Breeze said. "It isn't that big a deal."

Mattie whirled on Breeze, ready to grab her by her skinny neck and wring it. "Easy for you to say. You're not the one going to jail. What the hell is wrong with you that your only priorities are clothes and makeup? This *is* a big deal. Jane needs us to step up to the bat. Grow up, Breeze. It's time you stopped thinking with your tits."

Breeze's eyes narrowed to slits. She circled Mattie and faced her, hands on her hips. "You're telling me to grow up? You still bite your fucking nails!"

She grabbed Mattie's hand and held it up for Jane to see. "Look at that mess. Someone should spray these hands with that foul-tasting stuff they use on little kids and dogs!"

Mattie yanked her hand free and fought to catch her

breath. Outrage made her pant like a runner. How she wanted to smack that smug expression right off Breeze's face. The woman needed a good lesson in life, and Mattie was just the one to teach her. This was a wake-up call two decades overdue.

Mattie reached for Breeze's shoulders, but Jane was suddenly there, right in her face.

"How is this helping anything?" Jane glared at her. "You two fighting like alley cats?"

"Tell *her* that," Mattie snapped. "I didn't start it."

"You certainly did." Breeze yanked on the lapel of her blouse, setting it straight. "You insulted my intelligence *and* my breasts."

Jane got in between them and pushed them apart like a referee, although Mattie had no intention of roughing Breeze up. All she'd had in mind was a little talk, albeit a forceful one.

"Are we all right now?"

Jane turned from Mattie to Breeze, drilling each of them with a look that said they had better be all right. Mattie might have found it amusing, except that she was still pissed. It was just like the old days when the younger, headstrong ones got carried away, and Jane threw a bucket of cold water on them. Jane was no slouch in the glaring department, either.

"Just dandy," Mattie muttered, setting her slacks and blouse straight. At least her energy was flowing back. She could thank Breeze for that much. She pushed her blazer sleeves back up where they belonged, thinking that it might still be possible to reason with Jane, but that turned out to be a waste of time. Jane had not yet emptied her bag of tricks.

"I think I know who killed Broud," she said, "and possibly Frank O'Neill."

Mattie and Breeze spoke in unison. "Who?"

Jane had begun to look like herself again. There was a hint

of color in the ashen cheeks. "This is so important," she said, emotion catching at her voice. "Before I go to the police with my story, there's something I want us to do, all three of us. I guess you could call it another mission."

Jane brushed at her own clothing, absently smoothing it as she spoke. Mattie was pleased to see signs of the Jane she knew. But she still wondered about her friend's stability.

"Our last hurrah," Jane said. "Are you with me?"

Now Mattie was nervous. "Do I have to kill anybody?"

"I hope not."

Breeze held up her hand. "If you need someone killed, I'm your girl."

Jane turned her laser focus onto Mattie, who refused to be coerced. "I'm in, I *think*. Now tell us who did it."

"David Grace."

"Are you sure?" Mattie wished she hadn't left the secretary. She needed to sit down.

"He has the motive, two of them, in fact, and a man with his kind of money always has the opportunity. Broud had become a threat because of what he might know, and Frank O'Neill was blackmailing Grace, along with the other men in the ring, like Chief Daniels. That's my theory."

"We don't know that Grace was in the ring," Mattie pointed out. "You said yourself that you never asked him."

"He may not have been in the ring, but he likes to have sex with young women who dress up like schoolgirls."

It was Breeze who'd spoken. She flashed them a smile, the first smile Mattie had seen all night.

"What's that supposed to mean?" Mattie asked her.

"He's been to the spa," Breeze explained. "He's on our records as David Cerga, which is a rearrangement of the letters of his last name. He's been there several times, as recently as this spring, and he always asks for the same thing, a woman dressed up as a schoolgirl."

She shrugged, as if it was all in a day's work. "I vote for Jane's theory."

Mattie didn't have a theory, but as she searched her mind for other possible suspects, one name did come to mind. Frank was dead, and Jameson seemed to have disappeared. If he'd found the video, he could sure as hell use it to write a blockbuster.

Mattie hated her suspicions, but she couldn't seem to make them go away. They got worse every time they surfaced. William Broud's murder would make that book even more of a bombshell. Who better to write the story of the man the legal system sacrificed than his crusading, bestselling brother? Jameson had motives for both murders.

God, the thought made her sick. Jane's idea was starting to sound good to her.

Jane reclaimed her attention. "Even if I confess what I've done, I can't prove that David killed either man. Nor can I prove he was in the sex ring, so he gets away with it, all of it. I can't have that on my conscience, too. Can you?"

She looked long and searchingly at Mattie and Breeze. "Can you?"

Mattie glanced at Breeze, whose eyes were much too bright. Both of these women were making Mattie nervous.

"Grace called me tonight," Jane said. "He offered to help us *resolve* our problem. He wouldn't go into detail, however, I'm sure he was telling me that he'll back off, the harassment will end. But he wanted something in return."

"Like what?" Breeze said.

"He wants Larry to step down—and to endorse the replacement candidate that he, David, has in mind."

Mattie cut right to the heart of it. "What was your answer?"

"His replacement is no one Larry would be willing to

back, but rather than turn David down and risk his wrath, I stalled him. I told him I needed some time to think."

She walked to the dresser, where a crystal decanter sat on an elegant glass tray. With a steady hand, she filled three liqueur glasses to the brim with what looked to be amaretto. She'd made a remarkable recovery for someone about to break. Mattie could have questioned that, but she was already paranoid enough, and besides, she'd made up her mind that if she had to trust someone in this crazy game, it was going to be her friends.

"Grace is angry because Larry failed to secure congressional support for his brainchild," Jane said, "a concept called Smart Sand."

Breeze put in her two cents. "We turned up plenty on Smart Sand. It'll be worth a fortune, if he ever perfects it. Theoretically, you could weave sensors into the thread of cashmere sweaters that would make them as difficult to steal as cars with security devices."

Jane brought the drinks on a tray. "It isn't money he's after," she explained as she handed Mattie and Breeze their glasses. "He has more than he'll ever need. It's recognition as the creator of Smart Sand. Larry's only failure was in feeding Grace's insatiable ego."

She raised her glass. "Twenty-three years ago, we took an oath of *omerta,* and we vowed to stop a tyrant. Now I'm asking you to help me stop another one. Friends to the last extremity?"

Breeze raised her glass, but Jane was speaking directly to Mattie, and Mattie caught Breeze glancing her way, too. They had both made up their minds. But Mattie had done no such thing, and she wasn't going to be pressured into some wild scheme to get retribution. Jane ought to know better. What was this? Another conspiracy? A personal vendetta of Jane's?

"Bring down a *tyrant*," Mattie said, hoping they could hear her emphasis. "Bring down *David Grace?* Sure, no problem. Would it be silly of me to ask how you plan to do that?"

Mattie caught the tiny glint of what looked like pure unadulterated evil in Jane's eye. And Breeze was fighting a smile. What the hell? Did these two know something she didn't? It appeared they already had some kind of a strategy cooking, but Mattie didn't see how that was possible. There'd been no chance to discuss it. Mattie must have missed something somewhere along the line, something very obvious.

Desperation crept into Mattie's voice. "Why are you two looking at me like that? You do realize we're not kids anymore? This isn't Rowe Academy."

Nothing about this appealed to her. They *weren't* kids anymore, and it wasn't a tyrannical finishing school headmistress they were planning to overthrow. Careers were at stake. Lives were at stake. And somehow she had to make them see that. It was time to go to the police. Time to own up.

It was pain that brought Jameson awake. His skull felt as if someone had cracked it with a hammer, but his body was wailing like an injured child. Every muscle fiber shrieked with fatigue. Wrenched behind him, his shoulders throbbed and burned. He lifted his head and felt something cinch tight around his neck. Jesus, what was that?

Rope. Looped around his neck. A noose?

He fought to concentrate, but his thoughts swam with confusion. Where the hell was he? He couldn't move his hands or breathe through his mouth. And he couldn't see. A blindfold? He could feel the canvas fabric rub against his cheek. Some primitive level of his brain registered all this vital data. And one more thing. He'd been this way a long time. His limbs were stiff to the point of cracking.

He remembered being in Frank's cabin, bending to pick up the videotape. He'd been hit hard across the back of his head, possibly by a metal pipe or a gun barrel.

His body felt as if it were semiparalyzed. Nothing seemed to want to move or work when his brain willed it. He was on his side, crammed into an incredibly small space. The trunk of a car? His legs were folded back, and his hands and feet were bound tightly behind him. The rope around his neck cut into his windpipe.

Dread filled him as he realized he knew this lethal hogtie. It was one of his detective magazine covers. Jameson moved his feet, and the noose around his throat tightened. He was *in* that hogtie, and if he continued to move he would strangle himself.

Even the small of his back stung. It felt like there were splinters embedded in his skin where his shirt had pulled loose. Had someone dragged him across the cabin's wooden floor to get him outside and then into the trunk of a car?

The pungence of rubber told him there was a spare tire close by. He could also smell gasoline and motor oil in the stale air. It reminded him of every garage he'd ever been in. The coolness on his face meant the trunk lid was probably open. Did that mean his captor didn't want him to suffocate?

Lethargy swept him, muddying his thoughts and weighing his body down. The pain deepened, and the urge to let himself drift off to sleep was nearly overwhelming. It would be so easy to sink into a place where nothing hurt.

Think. Make yourself think. Who wanted that videotape bad enough to kill Frank? And who would have had to drag you to get you out of the cabin?

Someone who wasn't strong enough to throw him over a shoulder and carry him out. A woman? That didn't explain how she got him into the trunk, unless she backed a car up against the wooden porch and rolled him into it.

His foggy brain didn't want to concentrate, but he forced himself to come up with a list of women who might have wanted the video. Lane Davison, Mattie or one of her girlfriends? Maybe even Nola Daniels in a belated attempt to help her husband? Those were the names he knew, but only one of them stuck in his mind. Mattie.

He'd done a background check that revealed she had a gun license, and she had as much motive for wanting him out of the way as the others, possibly more.

He rolled forward a little, groaning at the fiery pain in his shoulders. The noose pulled tighter, reminding him he was in a deadly hogtie. She was the only one who knew about that tie and how it worked. Mattie was the only one who had seen the cover photo in his house. It all led back to her.

Jesus, no. A part of him wanted to go with the evidence, to find her guilty and convict her of heinous crimes. But his mind wouldn't go there. Some things a man knew in his gut and if he didn't go with them, they could take him down. Just like these ropes could take him down. He'd turned his back on William all those years ago, and it had been the gravest mistake of his life. He couldn't make that mistake again, with Mattie.

Footsteps brought him out of his thoughts. They came closer. Steady and determined footsteps. He couldn't tell whether they were a man's or a woman's, but whoever it was made no attempt to sneak up on him. The footsteps stopped just inches away.

Without warning, a sharp, needlelike pain pierced the fabric of his jeans and entered his thigh. This wasn't a knife that had nicked him. He was being injected with something.

Heartwine?

He didn't hear the footsteps recede. Whoever had injected

him was waiting, probably to watch him die. When the drug took hold he would no longer be able to control his limbs. His legs would relax, pulling tight on the rope, and he would be strangled while he slept. That was how this tie worked.

Moments later, he felt himself being dragged down into a dark morass, and it hit him that he would never wake up from this descent. He was going to die and he would take with him a heart full of regrets. In all the years that he had been seeking his brother's forgiveness, he had never once told Billy that he loved him. That thought hit him now and plunged him deeper into the depths. He would never have that opportunity.

Nor would he ever again watch a woman sleep in his bed or make sweet, angry love with her against a wall. Thank God, he had known those things with her. Thank God for that, at least.

42

I have him. I bagged the big one. I would never have counted him among the sheep, but he was remarkably easy prey. What better distraction than a crime scene? It's almost not fair. He was immobilized for several seconds, horrified at the sight. He couldn't hear anything, see anything but his dead friend.

One rock-solid blow to the head with my gun is all it took because of the way he'd bent over. I suppose I could have shot him and saved myself some effort, but I have a much more interesting way to remove this particular obstacle. And besides, I get no thrill out of killing people point-blank. I much prefer finding ways for them to kill themselves. I mean, it's their demise. They should be in on the action.

Surprise, lover boy! My greeting must have been painful as hell, but you have to admit, you did get in my way. I forgave you because you forced me to think on my feet, and I'd almost forgotten how good I am at that. I like improvising, and I also like some of the ideas inspired by your appearance at my crime scene. Killer ideas.

Isn't it interesting how people so often stumble into traps of their own making? Human nature is endlessly fascinating, don't you think?

You see, it's like this. The key to survival is flexibility. Don't ever get rigid. Roll with the punches. Those punching bag dolls that won't stay down no matter how hard they're hit? That's the general idea.

You don't even know I'm here, do you? You're out like a light, but you don't look very comfortable in that position. I wish we could talk, discuss this pickle you've gotten yourself into. I'd love to hear how it feels to be the famous crime writer and crime fighter, all tied up like the sick and twisted picture on your wall.

Flexibility, Lover Boy. Remember that next time. Except that there won't be a next time, will there? No more hot sex with the judge. No more hot sex with anyone.

I haven't quite decided what to do with you. Maybe I'll use you as bait if you don't strangle first. But ultimately, one way or the other, you will *bring her down. I love it when someone else does my work for me. It's only fair. I mean look at everything I do, all my services to mankind.*

The way I see it, I'm owed.

Mattie winced at the fiery pricks of pain. "Ouch!"

"Sorry, drew blood with that one." Breeze hovered over Mattie with a wicked looking pair of tweezers. She closed one eye, as if to get better aim as she mercilessly plucked the stray hairs from Mattie's brow.

"Remind me again why we're doing this?" Mattie grumbled.

"Because we can't *not* do it. It's too good. It's poetry. Trust me on this."

Trust Breeze. Now there was a concept.

Mattie was going along with Jane and Breeze's lunacy only to prove to them that their idea couldn't work. There'd been no talking them out of the scheme they hatched up, and Mattie hadn't had the energy to fend them off, so she'd agreed to let Breeze try and transform her.

For just the second time in her life, Mattie was sitting at

a froufrou vanity table with makeup bulbs bright enough to burn her corneas as she endured the efforts of a crazed make-over fairy who was determined that she be beautiful and alluring to the opposite sex.

Mattie didn't want to be beautiful. She had never wanted that. But the gods seemed to demand it of her, and her destiny seemed to require it of her. There was your poetry. Bad poetry.

Breeze stepped back, sizing up Mattie's brows. She set down the tweezers and Mattie breathed a sigh of relief. "Am I done?"

"Don't be silly. We're fine-tuning now, which is time-intensive. There. Look at me. Purse your lips."

Breeze pursed hers, apparently as an example. Mattie felt like an idiot making fish faces, but if it would get her out of Breeze's clutches...

"The lipstick's wrong." Breeze turned to her well-stocked makeup case and began to sort through the tubes. "It's too dark. Should be gloss, pink-tinted. Nothing more. Purse, purse," Breeze said as she came at Mattie with makeup remover pads, smelling of rubbing alcohol and citrus.

For the next several minutes, Mattie suffered through the lipstick removal and reapplication process, which was followed by another dusting of blush to bring out the apple in her cheeks, and finally, Breeze's fingers fluttering about in the riotous curls of her new hairdo.

Breeze stepped back again. "Shake it out a little," she said, giving her own head a shake.

Mattie gave her a stone face.

But Breeze was engrossed. She smoothed Mattie's newly shaped brows and gave her auburn tresses a few more tweaks, then stood back to gaze at what she'd wrought. Her pleased smile went through a swift transformation. From surprise to something Mattie couldn't quite describe. Awe, perhaps.

"Unreal," was all she said.

Jane walked into the bedroom before Mattie could ask what that meant. Jane's energy and drive seemed to have been restored now that they were working together to right things. She'd been out all morning on First Lady business, but whenever she could steal the time, she'd also been taking care of the last-minute preparations for their plan. Breeze's job had been to prepare Mattie. Jane's had been to prepare David Grace.

"How did it go?" Mattie asked.

Jane was busy making notes on her PalmPilot. She frowned at the screen, tapped in an instruction with the stylus and glanced up. "So far, so good," she said, going back to her screen. "The plane's been arranged, and there's a car waiting to take Mattie to the airport. When she gets to Oakland, which is a little closer to Napa Valley than San Francisco, a limo will pick her up and drive her to Grace's home."

A split second later, the stylus stopped moving. Jane's head snapped up, and her gaze locked onto Mattie's face.

"Oh, my God," she whispered.

Her expression actually frightened Mattie. Breeze was gaping at her, too. "What's wrong with you two?"

The laughter that pealed out of Jane had a slightly hysterical edge. "Mattie, that's astounding. If not for that husky voice of yours, I'd never have known you. Breeze, what a job you've done. She looks amazing."

Mattie turned around to look at herself in the vanity mirror and her breath caught. Amazing didn't cover it. She couldn't take her eyes off the reflection in the glass. The resemblance was uncanny. She'd seen those makeover shows on TV, but she hadn't realized it was possible to make a person over so completely. Or in this case, to make one person into another.

The hairpiece Breeze had dyed and styled was a stroke of

genius. It seemed to have changed the contours of Mattie's face. The night before, when Breeze had revealed to them the dark side of David Grace's sexuality, Mattie had found herself thinking back to the time she'd spent in his house, and the female subject in his gallery of paintings. It hadn't taken her long to form a hunch about who that woman really was, and she'd shared it with the other two. That was what Breeze had recreated here, the face of the woman in the paintings.

Mattie touched her full, glistening lips. The aquiline nose was perfection, and the eyes, misty and sad. Breeze had done her job. The resemblance was uncanny, even to Mattie. But would David Grace buy it? And more to the point, could Mattie do it?

The problem wasn't with how she looked, it was with who she was. Jane and Breeze had done their best to convince her that she was the *only* one who could do it, but they didn't seem to understand what was involved for Mattie. She'd been fighting dragons the better part of her life, but she didn't know how to fight this way, using wiles and deception and a person's secret longings against them, no matter how twisted those longings might be.

Breeze came over and sat next to Mattie at the vanity, fussing with her clothing. She undid Mattie's blouse another button, then smoothed a drop of perfume on her throat.

"He'll melt," she promised in a low whisper. "If I liked women, I'd melt."

Mattie's only thought was to change the subject. "Is everything set with Grace?" she asked Jane.

Jane fingered her imaginary pearls, looking almost pleased. "I told him that Larry is stepping down for health reasons. I think he's a little disappointed it wasn't because of him, but I assured him that Larry would endorse his candidate. I also told him that the three of us were grateful for anything he could do to help us, and we wanted him to have a token of our appreciation. He's expecting the gift to be delivered this evening. That's where you come in, Mattie."

"He doesn't smell a rat?" Sometimes Mattie had trouble understanding why people weren't suspicious of everyone, all the time. She was.

"Not when the rat's wearing *J'adore.*" Breeze waggled the tiny bottle of the pricey perfume. "According to my sources, this is the scent Grace prefers on a woman."

Mattie glanced in the mirror again, and her stomach began to churn. "Do you guys really believe this can work?"

"Of course, how can it not? We know his fatal flaw."

Breeze exuded utter confidence, but it wasn't Breeze who would be facing the lion in his den. Perhaps it should have been. Breeze was a sorceress when it came to men, but her stature and manner were too different. As were Jane's.

Mattie rose and approached the room's antique Cheval glass. When she stood in front of it and took in the entire transformation, she felt almost dizzy. Anyone would be fooled, she thought, even him. But she also knew that while she might be the most physically suited, she wasn't psychologically suited. Breeze could have seduced Grace in her sleep, and Jane had a bit of vixen in her, too. Mattie had none that she knew of.

She couldn't have made much of an impression on Jameson. He'd upped and vanished the day after their wild sex. It didn't seem possible he was avoiding her because of that, but she'd left him several messages and heard nothing back. She'd gone from thinking he'd blown her off to worrying that something terrible had happened to him. Now she didn't know what to think.

"Are you going to do it?" Jane asked her.

Mattie touched the crest on the pocket of her blouse. Her friend's voice tugged at her. There was so much at stake, especially for Jane, that Mattie felt as if she *had* to do it.

Twenty-three years ago, when they went after their first ty-rant, Mattie had come up with a plan that had pitted the three of them against their nemesis. They'd all been in the belly of the whale. This time Mattie went alone. Jane and Breeze would be with her in spirit, but she would be the siren, se-ducing him onto the rocks...unless he should notice her fin-gernails.

Why did this feel like guaranteed failure?

"We don't even know if Grace is our man."

It was Mattie's last pitiful plea, and she barely got it out before Jane's face showed up in the mirror next to hers. "Ex-actly," Jane said. "That's why we're doing this."

Mattie's sigh must have sounded like an affirmation.

"Was that a yes?" Breeze asked.

"Excellent." Jane clasped her hands. "Let's get on with it then. I have a car arranged to take you to David's whenever you're ready, Mattie. Do you want to do some deep breath-ing? Do you feel comfortable with what you're going to say? We could role-play."

Jane, ever the life coach, ever the mother. "I'm fine," Mat-tie said. "Role-playing would only make me nervous." She knew exactly what her mission was: to get as much incrim-inating information as possible out of David Grace. Jane be-lieved that Grace had killed O'Neill for the videotape, which meant that Grace either had the tape or knew where it was. With any luck, Mattie would finally get her hands on Ms. Rowe's Private Social Registry.

"Wait," Breeze said. "I just thought of something. We should take the sacred oath first, the one we did in the shed. It will confer protection from the goddess."

Mattie's faith in rituals had gone the way of her blindfold. But she had no objection if the other two felt strongly. She doubted they would have been able to carry out their desper-ate mission back at Rowe if it hadn't been for their vows.

True, they were kids then, full of ideals and illusions. They believed in secret oaths and blood bonds, but now, as she thought back, she could still remember the sense of empowerment that came from their ceremony.

Breeze joined Jane and Mattie, clasping their hands and forming a ring. She took the lead, speaking softly. "I will protect my sisters to the death and take to my grave any words uttered in this room."

Mattie was surprised when Breeze remembered the Latin phrases perfectly. She said them first, letting Mattie and Jane translate them in union.

"Tria juncta in uno."

"Three joined in one."

"Amicus usque ad aras."

"Friends to the last extremity."

As they finished, Jane excused herself, promising to be right back. She returned from the bathroom with a vial, which Mattie recognized immediately as the heartwine she'd had at the academy.

Breeze called a time-out and went to get her purse. "Look what I have," she said, drawing out a tiny satin pouch. Inside was a perfect red corkscrew curl. Ivy's.

They had all saved something from the first ceremony, Mattie realized. She had the pinecone scale they'd used for the blood oath. She carried it with her on her key chain as a good luck charm.

They each sipped from the vial, and then Jane spoke in a solemn voice that reminded Mattie of twenty-three years ago.

"In the ancient tradition of Greek mythology," she said, "this lock of our slain sister's hair will make us invulnerable to all attacks. As we strive to give meaning to her death, we humbly offer ourselves to Artemis, the huntress, protector of young women, who will watch over us and guide us in our battles."

"Artemis," they all murmured.

Mattie supplied the scale and pricked her finger, drawing a tiny bright red bubble. Jane did the same, and Mattie took it as a good sign that Breeze didn't faint this time.

When they'd touched fingers and mingled their blood, and the ceremony was complete, they drew each other close and held on tightly. Mattie felt an unwanted surge of emotion, but there was little she could do to stop it. Unshed tears burned her eyes and she struggled to clear her throat. She had no family. This was it, these friends from decades ago, linked by their childhood scars, as much as by their will to survive.

It struck her as they broke the embrace that she should be glad to help Jane, who had helped her so many times, and quietly protected her and Breeze for most of their lives.

"I'm ready," she said, aware that her smile couldn't be anything but grim. She was ready, but as she picked up her bag, she heard three signal beeps from her phone. She had voice mail.

"I just need a sec," she said, walking away from the others for some privacy. She fished her cell from her bag and quickly checked the messages. There was one from Jaydee, letting her know there'd been no change in the status of the Langston case. That wasn't good news, but at least it wasn't more bad news. She would catch up with the other messages on the way to the airport. Right now, she was looking for Jameson's name, and wondering why her phone hadn't rung.

It wasn't there. He hadn't called. Why? He may have been out of range. She couldn't let herself start imagining all the reasons now, or it would immobilize her. Sudden anger burned through her dread. If she made it through this, if she ever saw him again, he was going to be in deep shit for frightening her like this.

As she was about to put the cell away, she saw the icon

telling her that she had e-mail. They'd never communicated that way, but she checked anyway. The address said it was from the *municipio* in Ravello. They were responding to her request for a records search. Her disappointment was so sharp that she didn't take the time to read it, but she promised herself she would once she got in the car. She was concerned they might have turned down her request, and she couldn't absorb another blow right now.

43

In the quiet of the limo, Mattie was finally able to focus in on her new identity. Her goal wasn't to convince Grace that she was the woman in the sketches. That wasn't possible for several reasons, but it didn't mean she couldn't give him the reenactment of his life.

Her greatest concern was that Grace would recognize her as Mattie Smith before she'd had a chance to seduce him with his own fantasies. She needed time to coax him into letting down her guard, and the way to do that was to be psychologically mesmerizing, the way a magician mesmerizes the audience into thinking they've seen what they haven't.

The muted ring of cell phone startled Mattie out of her meditative state. She found the phone in her evening bag and snapped the lid open, hoping it might be Jameson. "Hello?"

A whispering voice laughed softly in her ear. "Jameson is next."

"What?" Mattie asked. "Who is this?"

The caller didn't answer, and Mattie quickly checked the display. The number was already gone—and so was the caller. The dial tone buzzed in her ear as she hit a button to bring up the incoming numbers. As she was searching through them, she realized the number must have been blocked.

She also realized what the caller had been telling her.

Jameson was next. He was going to be killed.

Mattie froze in place, unable even to think for an instant. This was beyond the chaos. It was nothingness, a deep, glacial silence. She could feel a painful vibration in the delicate threads of her spine, but couldn't move. If the threat was real, then she understood why Jameson hadn't answered his cell. The caller already had him. But Mattie had no idea where to find him or how to save him.

And what if David Grace had left the message?

She steadied her hands enough to dial her cell. She tried Jameson's number, knowing he wouldn't answer. Next, she dialed Breeze and quickly filled her in. "Put your people on it," she told her. "When I last talked to Jameson, he was on his way to Frank O'Neill's house. It was the same day Frank turned up dead in his cabin. Find him, *please.*"

Breeze assured her that they would, and Mattie hung up. She didn't know what else to do. Asking someone else to find him had been wrenching. She wanted to go herself, but she had to believe that Breeze's intelligence person was better equipped than she was.

Still, Mattie was torn with indecision. And finally, it was the e-mail from the *municipio* in Ravello that convinced her to go on with the mission. She'd written to request a search of the birth and the death records, specifically for infants during the year Cynthia Grace had been at the clinic. The response had stunned her. Cynthia Grace had not lost a baby during that time period. But Millicent Rowe had given birth to one, a baby girl born just one month before David Grace's wife had died there.

Questions burned in Mattie's brain, and only David Grace could answer them. What if Cynthia Grace had never been pregnant at all?

And what had happened to Millicent Rowe's baby?

* * *

David Grace stood on the third-floor balcony of his Tuscan-style mansion, watching the purple rope of a road that wound through the deep green hills of his Napa Valley estate. A shimmering black sedan had just been admitted by his guards at the entry gates, a quarter mile away, and was now snaking its way toward the house.

David could have watched the entire process on the security monitor in his bedroom, but he preferred to observe this stranger bearing gifts in person, and without being seen. It never hurt to have the advantage, even in life's more pleasant pursuits. And he was curious how the women of Rowe Academy planned to show their appreciation.

The car curved around a stand of Russian olive trees and came into full view. The windows were impenetrable, of course. David had always been intrigued—and possibly challenged—by anything that shielded itself from him. His security cameras couldn't see inside the car, but he was already working on a way to remedy that with a unique optical lens. He also had his own shields to prevent industrial espionage, both at his lab and this estate, one of them being an invention that blocked transmission signals. It was one of the advantages of being a scientist and an inventor. When you had a need, you didn't have to wait for someone else to fill it.

The car pulled into the entrance court and stopped at the marble columns of the front portico. David's attention fixed on the passenger door as the driver came around and opened it. The passenger's legs swung out, lovely legs with sleek bare calves descending from the knee-length pleated skirt.

She took the hand the driver offered and rose to her feet, not entirely graceful under the circumstances. But David quickly forgot about that. He'd never seen such a vision as the exquisite young woman who emerged.

His throat tightened as he said her name. The lining of his

mouth burned. He recognized her immediately. She was the girl immortalized in his art, the fourteen-year-old who died despite everything he did to save her. Now he understood what the three women from the finishing school had done, even if he didn't understand why. His thank-you gift was an almost perfect replica of Ivy White.

Il Casa Tranquillo. That was the name on the iron gates that Mattie's car passed through. The house of tranquility.

Hardly a house, she thought as the car pulled up to the front portico of a property every bit as palatial as Grace's villa in Italy. The sprawling stucco mansion had several wings, cascading balconies and regal palms that shaded the dark red tile roof.

There was no one in sight when the driver let her out of the car. She hadn't expected a footman, but she'd thought there might be someone at the entrance. She grew even more alert when no one answered the bell. The double doors were massive, but she could see that one of them was slightly ajar. Was she meant to go on in?

She waited a few more minutes, wondering if she was walking into a trap. The house might be tranquil, but she was not. Her pulse was unsteady, her mouth dry. She should never have taken the heartwine, even a tiny amount on the tip of her tongue. The ritual called for it, and she had hoped to bring back the magic of the ceremony, but the herb was highly toxic, and her system wasn't used to it. She had no immunity to it anymore, if she ever had.

She rang the bell again and listened for any reaction.

You're not going to get another chance at this guy. Open the door and go in. Act surprised if someone's there.

The door opened with a determined push, and Mattie entered a great hall that looked as if it had been designed specifically to make mere mortals feel small and insignificant.

The vast two-storied chamber gleamed with white travertine tile and marble statuary that reminded Mattie of a temple built for the gods.

The back wall was ringed with interior balconies, their marble facades highly carved and inlaid with gold tracery. A black granite fountain in the center of the hall had two rearing unicorns. Water flew from their horns, creating a rainbow effect as the sprays crossed in the air like swords.

Mattie thought she heard footsteps and looked around. Had someone entered the room? The splashing water seemed to absorb all sound.

"My apologies for not coming down to greet you."

A man's voice pulled her attention back to the fountain. She made out a dark form through the spray, and Mattie realized there was a grand staircase to the second floor on the other side of the cavernous room.

As David Grace descended the stairs and came into view, Mattie braced herself. He looked perfectly congenial in his white silk shirt and linen slacks, the ideal host. But she had no idea what to expect, especially if he saw through the charade and recognized her. She almost wished for the glacial silence to return and anesthetize her from the fear. But as she registered the expression on his face, she realized that their massive efforts had worked.

Breeze's cosmetics and Mattie's inner magician had transformed her.

David Grace could have been staring at one of the hall's statues come to life, Venus probably. He was that entranced. Silently he took in Mattie's crisp white blouse and plaid skirt, a Rowe Academy uniform down to the Italian loafers she wore. But it wasn't so much male desire she saw in his eyes as it was reverence. He seemed to be in awe of her shy smile and her awkward attempt at visual seduction, as if he were in the presence of a fairy-tale princess.

"The lonely girls wanted to thank you," she said, hoping the sound of her voice didn't break the spell.

"I see." He got out the words, but they were rough. "But how could they have known?"

She shrugged, as if to say she had no idea. There was no safe answer, given that she didn't know the nature of his relationship with Ivy. She was reasonably certain that Ivy was the woman in his sketches, but that Grace was not the artist, as he'd implied. Ivy herself was the artist. That had come into Mattie's mind as she'd talked to Breeze and Jane about the sketches. Mournful faces had been Ivy's passion in school. She hadn't shown her work to anyone, but she'd probably had sketch pads full of them. Mattie was just surprised she hadn't made the connection sooner.

Mattie fingered her hair, wishing she could push the wild scatter of curls off her face. Breeze had found a full wig of exquisite red hair that perfectly matched Ivy's fairy-tale Guinevere look. She'd also found contacts in a shade that approximated the emerald green of Ivy's eyes.

Makeup had done the rest, and Breeze was a wizard at that. She'd outdone herself. Mattie was Ivy White, all grown-up and ready for an evening out.

"Come with me," Grace said, beckoning her to follow him.

They entered a room smaller in size than the great hall, but no less breathtaking. The ceiling was vaulted, the walls lined with antique mirrors of every type, but the focal point was a fireplace of gleaming black glass. Mattie was reminded of all the glass in his Amalfi villa, and wondered what the significance might be.

"I let the staff go for the night," Grace said, "but I think I'm capable of fixing us a drink. Would you like one?"

He raised an eyebrow, half-smiling as he waited for her answer. "Maybe I should have asked if you're old enough."

She toyed with the neckline of her blouse, running her finger along the opening. "Old enough for what?"

His faint smile didn't change as he went to the liquor cart and began preparing a drink. "What would you like?" he asked.

She took this as a signal to pour it on. David Grace may have had a schoolgirl fantasy, but he'd never requested a school*girl* at Breeze's spa. He'd always asked for a woman costumed as one, so Mattie hoped this would work. Still toying with her blouse, she began to stroll toward him, and when she was close enough to claim his attention, she began undoing buttons.

Grace glanced up at her, and his smile vanished. Her attempt to be seductive seemed to repel him.

"What kind of sick joke is this?" he asked her.

Mattie realized she'd miscalculated. Either she was as bad at seduction as she feared, or they had all miscalculated. His obsession with Ivy might not be sexual.

She apologized profusely. "It's such a warm night," she said. "I only wanted to cool off."

"What is that scent you're wearing? Ivy never wore perfume."

"You don't like *J'adore?* I'll wash it off."

"It's fine," he said, but his voice was still cold. "Let's get you that drink then. I'm having gin and tonic. What about you?"

"That's fine." Mattie found herself with a tall iced drink in her hand and no idea what to do. Seduction obviously wasn't going to get her the information she wanted. Possibly she could goad him into a reaction, but that seemed risky to the point of recklessness. It would only work if he was deeply conflicted enough about Ivy to drop his guard. Mattie wanted to know about Ms. Rowe's baby and his wife's death, but that wasn't part of the original plan.

She'd come for incriminating evidence, and perhaps even the videotape. A dangerous plan, but she was wired. She had Secret Service backup in the form of John Bratton and one of his men, although they were a half mile away, outside the gates of the eighty-acre estate.

She left her untouched drink on the fireplace mantel and walked to the nearest mirror, a Venetian masterpiece with a frame that looked to be carved from pure gold. "Do you collect antique mirrors?" she asked him.

"My wife did. She was an avid collector."

His wife. He may have given her another opening, but she didn't want to misstep. There was no time for another mistake.

"The mirrors are lovely. So is the fireplace." She turned back to Grace just in time to witness an entrance that silenced her.

A young woman emerged from the shadows behind Grace, and Mattie's brain performed a split-second assessment. She looked uncannily like Ivy. She didn't have Ivy's curly red hair or her haunted beauty. Her hair was short, a cloche of black swirls that softened her angular face, but the frame and the carriage were similar. And she was carrying something in her hand.

Mattie had hoped to make Grace think he was seeing a ghost. Now she was seeing one. She tried not to give the woman away, but Grace seemed to sense her presence. Perhaps he'd seen her in one of the mirrors.

"Tansy, put that gun away," he ordered. "Do it now."

Mattie's mind flashed to the law school student, Tansy Black. How many women were named Tansy? What the hell was going on? Was she here to kill Grace?

Mattie couldn't let her do that before getting the proof she needed.

But as Tansy came into the light, Mattie realized the gun was pointed at her, not at Grace.

Grace stepped in front of Mattie, shielding her, which

seemed to enrage Tansy. Her eyes filled with angry tears, her mouth contorted.

"What did she ever do for you?" she accused, sounding like a heartbroken child. "Nothing but kill herself! Ivy was *weak*. She was afraid, everything you hated."

Tansy Black's voice never rose above a whisper, but as she continued to agonize about Ivy White, Mattie realized that she wasn't a romantic conquest, she was David Grace's daughter. *And Ivy's younger sister.* Mattie also realized that Tansy was as obsessed with Ivy as Grace was. Mattie could only surmise that his guilt over his older daughter's suicide had stirred terrible envy in his younger. And psychosis.

Tansy had regained her composure, but her eyes were as cold and dark as the fireplace glass. "I killed for you," she said. "Did she do that? Could she do it?"

Grace could barely speak. "Tansy, what are you talking about? Killing for me? That's crazy."

Tansy's face flushed red with fury, but her voice was frigid. "Crazy, is that what you think? Do you have any idea of the risks I've taken for you?"

"Risks? What are you talking about?"

"You've reached the limits of your influence, Father. Money won't buy you your dream. But *I* can get it for you. I can get you the recognition you deserve because I'm not afraid. Of anything."

She pointed to her reflection in the mirror on the opposite wall. "Look at me. I'm everything you say you've ever wanted in a child, everything your father wanted *you* to be. Fearless, without limits, in control of my destiny. And of yours."

She turned to him, and her voice dropped back to a whisper, but nothing could hide the anguish that permeated every word. "Why aren't you grateful? Why don't you love me? Why do you still cling to Ivy as if you could bring her back to life?"

Grace didn't answer, and Mattie was stunned to silence, too. Tansy's whisper made her realize that Tansy may have been the one who called her in the limo and warned her that Jameson was about to die.

In a state of shock, Mattie listened to Tansy rant about the standards Grace set for himself and his daughters, how he despised fear and vulnerability, everything that Ivy was. How he tested them repeatedly, forcing them to prove their mental and physical strength because he wanted avatars, not daughters. How he named them Ivy and Tansy for graceful vines, but forced them to choose new surnames before entering school so they couldn't "get by" on the Grace name.

"I chose Black because Ivy, the *saint,* had chosen White." Tansy's voice broke on what could have been a sob, except that it was choked with rage. "But none of that hurt me like knowing that you held me responsible for my own mother's death."

"Your mother died giving birth to you," Grace said. "I didn't blame you for that."

"No, but you let me blame myself! And then Ivy took her life."

"I didn't blame you for that, either."

"Then why didn't you console me? Why didn't you sit down with me and talk to me? You were too despondent to know I existed. I was left with a father who had nothing to give me, even when I was an infant."

"Tansy, I'm sorry."

"Sorry that you never spoke of my mother? That you focused all your grief on Ivy and made me feel as if I could never live up to the ghost of my beautiful older sister?" Tansy's voice reached a hysterical pitch.

"That isn't true," he insisted.

"Oh, but it was. The only way to get your attention was to be everything that Ivy wasn't. I had to be her opposite in the extreme."

In the extreme, Mattie thought. Tansy was a homicidal killer, whereas Ivy couldn't have hurt a fly. Tansy also had it wrong. She believed her mother died in childbirth, when the certificate said otherwise—Cynthia Grace hadn't been pregnant when she died.

Tansy cocked and locked the gun, a sound that collided with every glass surface in the room. She took a step toward her father, a smile tightening her mouth.

"People think I'm a Good Samaritan because I got William Broud sprung from death row," she said, "but I did it for you. There was no other way to implicate Jane Mantle in the murder and force her husband out of the White House."

"Who killed Broud then?"

Grace asked the question that Mattie had been thinking.

Tansy's expression held nothing but disdain for William Broud. "As far as I'm concerned, he killed himself. He took for granted everything I did for him, and he broke his vow of silence. Once I did the math, it was a no-brainer. His death was another handy way to drag Jane and her friends into it, so I used the exact M.O. as in Millicent Rowe's murder case.

"Always thinking," she told her father. "Always one step ahead."

Grace was silent, frozen. Either he didn't know before this that his daughter had been killing on his behalf, or he'd been in denial. But Tansy had his attention now.

"O'Neill had to die once he'd been exposed as a blackmailer," she told him. "Surely you realize that? How could you buy him off after that? And someone had to get the videotape."

Grace could do nothing but gape at her.

"It's all right," she said. "No one will know you're involved in any of this. I made it look like suicide."

"Tansy, don't— You don't mean what you're saying. You can't."

·"Oh, but I do. It was easy, Father, so damn easy. I held the gun to his head, and I told him to wash down the bottle of sleeping pills with Scotch. He blubbered like a baby, but he did it. I didn't show him the antidote, Syrup of Ipecac, until he'd swallowed every last pill. I told him if he gave me the videotape, I'd give him the syrup. Of course, I never did."

"Jesus, Tansy."

"What did you expect? You admitted to me that people were threatening you, blackmailing you. Did you think I'd do nothing?"

Grace begged her not to go on, but she didn't seem to hear him.

"I picked up the phone," she said, "and overheard a man threatening you. It was the day after my sixteenth birthday, and it took me weeks to work up my courage, but when I confronted you about it, you told me the truth. You admitted you'd been with the headmistress at Rowe, and when Jane Dunbar came to you, you helped her cover up the murder. You said the D.A. was blackmailing you, and you had no choice but to pay him off."

Her countenance gradually transformed as she went on talking. Her eyes burned with the pride of a child, her voice softened.

"Do you remember telling me there was a lesson in the terrible things life did to people? A lesson I would have to learn, you said, and it might as well be now. You told me the price of being your daughter was that people would try to take advantage of me, and I shouldn't let them do that. I hung on to your every word, but all I could think about was someone taking advantage of my exalted father. I was still just a kid, but I knew exactly what I was going to do. Fix it for you, of course. What other chance did I have to do something you couldn't do for yourself?"

Tears welled in Grace's eyes. "Tansy, my God, why didn't you just talk to me? Why didn't we ever talk?"

Her smile was fleeting, sad. "Yes, why didn't we?"

She shrugged the emotion away. "It doesn't matter now because I fixed it. Me, *I* fixed it. You don't have the killer instinct, Father, but I do. Someone should have taken Frank O'Neill out a long time ago. He was *blackmailing* you."

An edge sharpened her voice. "Don't you see it yet? Money has failed you again and again, but I haven't. I'm the only thing you can count on. You'll *always* be able to count on me."

"I know," he said. "I know that. I had no idea you'd taken such risks for me. Now please, Tansy, let me count on you again."

His hand was shaking almost uncontrollably as he reached out to her. "Give me the gun."

Her eyes narrowed. "Come and get it," she said, suddenly contemptuous. "You don't believe me. You're placating *her.*"

She shot Mattie a murderous glare. "Don't you realize the woman you're shielding is a fake? Are you protecting her because she looks like Ivy? How ridiculous can you be? You don't understand what I've done at all. You're willing to give it all up."

Her voice rose to a shriek. "You are, aren't you?"

"For God's sake, Tansy," he implored, "let her go. She hasn't done anything wrong."

"Of course, she has. Mattie Smith is the enemy. She has to die now—here!—or I'll go to prison, and you'll *never* have what you want."

"Tansy, *no.*"

"I can do it. You don't believe me? I'll prove it to you, Father. Watch me kill her."

With a horrible scream, she turned the gun on Mattie and fired.

44

Jameson flinched. His eye stung as if someone had touched it with the lit end of a cigarette. The pain was excruciating. Even submerged in a well of darkness, he could feel that pain, and gradually he realized it was the only thing he could feel. The rest of his body had gone numb and lifeless. His arms and legs were gone. They could have been amputated.

It took tremendous energy to open his eyes. He was no longer blindfolded, but still in total darkness. There was no cigarette shoved into his eye. Sweat. Sweat had rolled down his forehead and into his eye, stinging him to wakefulness.

Duct tape covered his mouth. Waves of nausea rolled in his stomach from the drug his captor had used to keep him unconscious. He was still tightly bound, and the noose around his neck had cinched tighter. But something had kept it from strangling him when he was unconscious.

He felt pressure against the tops of his shoes, as if his feet had become lodged against an object in the trunk. That must have kept his legs in the folded position and saved him. Jameson shifted slightly, testing the object, and his feet slipped away from the support. The cord tightened instantly, choking a gasp out of him.

A slipknot held the painful pressure steady around his throat. A couple more of those and he'd pass out. A couple more after that and he'd be dead.

Somehow he had to hold perfectly still and reason this through. Not easy when he couldn't feel his legs or will his brain to hold them in place. The noose was tightening.

The trunk lid had been closed, he realized, and the car moved. That might be how his feet became wedged and saved him. Gasoline fumes had leaked up into the car's trunk, adding to his queasiness.

If he vomited, he would die.

If he didn't regain his footing to release the pressure on his windpipe, he would die.

If he didn't get relief from the toxic fumes surrounding him, he would die.

He was in a battle for his life against his own body.

Mattie.

Her name sounded in his mind. It felt as if some higher power was speaking to him, making itself known to his oxygen-starved brain, even through the mind-numbing gas fumes. Was she in some kind of danger? Even in his drugged state he knew that was crazy. *He* was the one in trouble, but he'd heard her name, and his deadened nervous system had released a spurt of adrenaline.

Had she done this to him? Condemned him to death?

His legs began to prickle and burn. He could feel them getting heavier by the minute, drawing on the ropes, and there was nothing he could do to stop them. His body wouldn't obey his screaming brain. He let his head fall back a little, hoping it would ease the pressure. God, a terrible mistake. The noose cut into his flesh this time, severely constricting his windpipe.

Jameson knew he had one chance to save himself. He had to find that object again and support himself against it. That was the only way he would ever get out of this tie without killing himself. He also knew one slip, one mistake and it was over.

Steeling himself for the worst, he shifted again, praying his feet came up against the object that had saved him before. There it was, the pressure he needed! He quickly groped for the knot securing the cord that ran from neck to feet. This was the key rope. This was the one he had to free up.

Blackness swirled up to greet him as he deliberately cut off his own oxygen supply by arching his back in order to reach the knot. He had it, then lost it. The swirling blackness coalesced around him, within him.

"Mattie?" He mouthed her name, hoping for another burst of adrenaline, anything to keep him conscious. He reached again, groping, choking. Dying. Where the hell was that knot? The pressure wouldn't lessen, even if he stopped now. It was too late for that. He had set his own death in motion.

On the very brink of passing out, he found the knot again. Then lost it.

Mattie saw Tansy turn and fire, but there was nothing she could do. She stumbled backward, aware that she couldn't possibly dodge a bullet. A loud click brought her crashing to the floor. She hit hard, but didn't feel the flesh-searing pain she expected. Didn't hear the whine of the bullet as it pierced skin and hit bone.

The ache radiating up her leg told her what had happened. Her knee had brought her down. Her crazy knee had saved her. If she could just hold on, the Secret Service should be here. They must have heard the shots.

Tansy seemed to have lost all interest in Mattie. All she cared about was her father's reaction. Apparently she thought she'd hit Mattie, and so did David Grace. Their eyes were locked on each other.

Mattie stayed down as David Grace dropped to his knees to beg his daughter's forgiveness. There was a remote bug hidden in her clothing, and she needed to get this on tape.

"Tansy, please," he said. "It's me you want to hurt, not her. And I deserve it. God knows I do, but I don't have any control over the past. I can't change what I've done. All I can do is apologize and ask your forgiveness."

Tansy stared at the man on his knees as if she didn't know who he was. Whatever she had wanted from him, it wasn't this.

Grace went on with his desperate explanation. "I just wanted to make you strong," he said, "so you wouldn't suffer the ridicule I did. I hated my father. He laughed at the things that terrified me and dismissed the things I loved, the science and the math. I was a failure to him, a weakling. He wanted me to be a businessman, but he never bothered to show me how to take what I was good at and make it pay off in the business world. I had to do that on my own."

He reached out a hand to her. "I cared, Tansy. I wanted both my daughters to conquer their fears and be invulnerable to pain so you would never have to go through that. It was for you. And you were right about Ivy. She was too much like me."

Tansy seemed to flinch at the mention of her sister's name. She steadied the gun with both hands, training it on her father.

Mattie waited for an opening, aware if she moved that Tansy would shoot her. Where the hell were those agents? Had Tansy somehow sabotaged their signal? People were going to die.

"I couldn't change her," Grace said. "I couldn't save her, either. And it was really me I wanted to change. When I buried Ivy, I mourned my own death, as well as hers."

He began to talk about how his parents killed him, killed the real David, and turned him into the scion they wanted, a soulless deal maker, a machine. But Tansy was different. She'd always been different. Tansy was everything he'd thought he wanted to be.

Mattie didn't know the details of Grace's background, but she could make an educated guess. He hadn't molested or physically abused the girls. He'd destroyed their identities, their egos, with his own inhuman drive to be perfect. He'd projected his self-loathing onto them and made them prove themselves as he couldn't. They had to make up for all his perceived failures. Ms. Rowe didn't kill Ivy. Ivy escaped her father's control by killing herself, and Tansy did it by going crazy. She might be everything Grace wanted in a child, but she was completely beyond his reach now.

Mattie took a calculated risk. She pushed to her feet as Tansy whirled on her. "Wait!" Mattie held up her hands, signaling she had no weapons. "You didn't kill your mother, Tansy. I know exactly when and how she died, and it wasn't giving birth to you. She wasn't even pregnant."

She told Tansy the place, date and time of her birth to the minute. She also told her the circumstances. Her father was having an affair with Millicent Rowe, and Tansy's mother found out. She threatened suicide and was sent to a private clinic on the Amalfi Coast for intervention, where she leaped to her death from the cliffs. Later that month, Millicent Rowe delivered her baby prematurely in the same clinic. Rowe was told her baby was stillborn, and that David's wife had died in childbirth, but the baby had survived. She never knew Tansy was her child, and neither did anyone else. David had been able to have the medical records altered for a price, but not the public records. He had counted on no one bothering to check.

Mattie was bluffing about some of the details, but she had documents to back up her theory—copies of the death certificate and Millicent Rowe's letter in her bag. She dug them out and showed them to Tansy.

Tansy took the certificate and read it. "You lied to me?" she said to her father. "You let me believe that I *killed* her?

You let me carry that cross my whole life? And she wasn't ever my real mother?"

"I didn't know you were holding yourself responsible," he said desperately. "I would never have let you think that if I'd known."

Mattie watched as he walked over to his distraught daughter, soothing her with explanations. He told her that her mother was weak and emotional. She couldn't deal with reality, and sadly, Ivy had taken after her. But when he reached for the gun, Tansy reared back.

"Get back!" she screamed.

He tried to wrestle the gun from her hand, and she squeezed the trigger. David Grace fell to the floor, mortally wounded. His last deal, and the businessman had failed to close it.

Tansy dropped the gun, seemingly in shock. Mattie lunged for the weapon before Tansy could react.

"Stay where you are!" she shouted at Tansy.

Tansy merely smiled at her. As casually as if she'd been to church, she pulled off the pair of surgical gloves she wore and tucked them in her jacket pocket.

"You're welcome to the gun," she told Mattie. "It's yours anyway." With that, she headed for the front door.

Mattie shouted at her to stop, and Tansy turned, an odd smile on her face. "There's a dead man on the floor," she pointed out, "and your fingerprints are all over the gun, Your Honor. I don't think you're going to kill me."

She opened the lapel of her jacket and flashed the small automatic weapon she kept there. "A girl can't have too many," she said.

Mattie had been framed. She reached for the remote bug and realized that it had fallen off, probably when she lunged for the gun. She could only hope that everything was recorded and her backup was on its way because Tansy had already disappeared out the door.

Mattie knelt next to David Grace and checked his pulse. She could find none, but there wasn't time to call the paramedics. She left him there and reached the front door just in time to see Tansy key open the trunk of a four-door sedan. She lifted the lid, staggering as it flew open and clipped her under the chin.

A man was in the trunk, Mattie realized. Jameson? He kicked open the lid and fought his way out of ropes that still clung to him. A blindfold hung around his neck. He ripped it off, but by the time he was free, Tansy had caught her balance.

"Watch out!" Mattie cried as Tansy took aim and fired.

Jameson rushed Tansy, charging right into the gunfire. He took her down with him, pinning her underneath him. They didn't seem to be struggling, and Mattie thought he'd been spared until Tansy pushed her way out from underneath him and made a break for the car. Jameson lay slumped on the pavement.

Mattie ran down the steps and into the road, trying to stop Tansy. She planted herself in front of the car and aimed the gun straight at the driver. Would she now be charged with two murders? Or did this make it three?

She shattered the windshield with bullets, and as she did so, she realized it was her own car she was shooting at. She recognized the license plate number, but there was no time to even question what that meant. She riddled the engine. The motor whined, turning over frantically but not catching.

Tansy couldn't start the car.

"Get out of there, you crazy bitch!" Mattie screamed at the top of her lungs. "Get out of that car before I kill you!"

Tansy let herself out, ducked behind the open door and crept around toward the back. She wasn't returning fire, Mattie realized. Was she out of bullets? Mattie shouted at her to stop, but Tansy broke into a run.

Mattie saw her go down and realized that Jameson must have tackled her. She rushed around the car to help, but couldn't get a clear shot. Tansy ripped and snarled at Jameson like a wild animal, and blood gushed from his wounds. He was gravely injured, but he fought like hell to take the gun away from her.

Mattie didn't know what to do. He might subdue her, but at what cost? He was bleeding to death. This was not how it was supposed to end. Mattie should have been the one fated to pay for her sins in this grotesque way. Jameson had committed no crime. He'd been trying to help her, and now he was going to die trying to protect her.

"Jameson, stop!" Mattie screamed, "I have a gun."

But Mattie was afraid to shoot. She could hit the wrong person.

Finally, enraged at all the pointless carnage, she waded into the fray herself. Tansy was struggling to get away from Jameson, and Mattie didn't care whether she got shot. She grabbed Tansy by the collar, savagely dragged her free of Jameson's hold and cracked the gun handle against her skull. Tansy hit the ground in a heap, unconscious.

Jameson dropped to his hands and knees, drenched in blood. As he slumped forward, Mattie caught him. Dear God, where was her backup? Had they heard any of this?

She noticed a black length of fabric on the asphalt next to her. The blindfold. It was hers, she realized as she picked it up. There were no identifying markers, but she knew it was hers. Tansy must have stolen that *and* her car, although Mattie didn't know she'd done it.

She rolled Jameson over on his back and saw that he'd been shot in the stomach, possibly more than once. His thigh was bleeding profusely, too, and immediately Mattie began creating a tourniquet from the blindfold. At least she could stem some of the blood loss.

Moments later, she was vaguely aware of a siren wailing as she cradled Jameson's head in her lap. He had no pulse.

45

They had come to Breeze's suite at the Four Seasons on the pretext that no one would be looking for them here. None of them had raised the question of whether they would ever be staying at the posh hotel again, but it hovered in the balance of their many silences. Breeze loaned Jane and Mattie slinky nightgowns, and they were drinking champagne by the magnum, but there was little laughter and nothing to celebrate. Still, Breeze couldn't seem to resist an attempt to lighten things.

"Let's play Top This," she said, rising from the Cleopatra chaise where she'd been reclining. Both straps of her camipajamas slid down her bare arms as she pulled their second magnum of champagne from the ice bucket and went about refilling their flutes.

Mattie gave thought to a smile, but the effort involved seemed to rival climbing Everest. Apparently Breeze wasn't aware that her silk camisole top was just barely defying Newton's laws of gravity. Mattie was reasonably sure she enjoyed the shock value of all that bobbling cleavage, especially when John Bratton was around—and right now he and his Secret Service contingent were stationed next door in the suite's living room.

Bratton had turned out to be both loyal and reliable where Jane was concerned. He'd kept her secrets and made sure his men were as discreet as he was. Mattie couldn't figure out whether he was the perfect bodyguard cum personal assistant, or if Jane had something on him. Mattie was just glad he was on their side.

"The subject is personal disasters," Breeze said. "Anyone want to start?"

She dropped the magnum back into the bucket. "Okay, I'll go. Top this, if you can, ladies. I'm almost certain to lose my international spa and the clientele it's taken me the best part of my adult life to build. No one will come near my place once my face is splashed on newspapers and television screens across the country."

"I didn't know you *had* an adult life," Jane said with no rancor whatsoever. Elegant in her flowered sarong, she slurped champagne like it was fruit punch.

"Now, now." Mattie had probably had too much champagne herself. With great care, she placed her own flute on an odd-looking sea sponge coaster.

"Breeze has a point," she said. "Her clients depend on her to protect their anonymity. How can she do that if she's under investigation for murder? They'll be terrified of exposure and run for the hills, so to speak."

Breeze planted her fists on her hips. "That's not how the game is played. You're supposed to top me with the details of *your* downfall, not mine."

Mattie was sitting Indian-style on the bed in the black lace teddy that Breeze had provided—no, insisted—she wear. "Well, my downfall *is* worse. I'm going to be disbarred, of course. And then impeached. I'll lose my lifetime appointment to the bench, and—" her throat tightened up, making it difficult to say the rest of it "—a good friend of mine is gravely ill."

Jameson had been in a coma since being admitted to the hospital over a week ago, and his condition was still critical.

Mattie had spent long hours at the hospital, and felt she should be there tonight, but now that she was in the company of her sisters, she knew it was the right choice. Just being with them had muted the pain and worry. The champagne had probably helped, too, and Breeze's craziness in the face of certain catastrophe.

Tonight they would decide whether or not to turn themselves in. Tansy had been taken into custody, but charged with only two capital crimes: first-degree murder and attempted murder. She'd done such a thorough job of trying to frame Mattie for Jameson's kidnapping that a grand jury had voted not to indict her. Jameson had never seen his abductor, and all the physical evidence had pointed to Mattie—the hogtie, the gun, the car and the blindfold. Fortunately Mattie'd had an alibi. She was on the other side of the country when the kidnapping took place.

There wasn't sufficient evidence to link Tansy to O'Neill's or Broud's deaths, either, but she'd wasted no time identifying the lonely girls and accusing them of murdering Ms. Rowe. The police hadn't acted on her claims yet. Nor had the media, but Mattie figured it was the quiet before the storm.

"Good gravy," Breeze whispered. "That *is* dreadful. I don't think it can be topped. Jane and I don't have a gravely ill man involved. Not fair, Mattie."

"I do, too," Jane said, apparently miffed at the omission. "Larry's health is in crisis because of all this stress. I've let down everyone in the entire country. Probably the world. And worst of all, an innocent man went to prison because of me. I should be hung."

Breeze whistled. "No contest. Jane takes home the gold."

Mattie unrolled from the position she was in. A loud click resonated as she straightened her legs. "How about this knee," she said. "Top that."

No one smiled at her effort to distract them. Jane stared into her champagne as if she were counting the bubbles. Even Breeze seemed to have run out of steam, but apparently she wasn't quite ready to give up.

"Want to discuss disasters of a more private nature?" she said. "Anybody game?"

Without a breath's hesitation, Jane said, "I can top you there, too. For this one we should have a confessional booth. I'm an addict. My habit was pills, and—God, this is harder than I thought—anonymous men. And I'm terrified I might relapse."

"Jane." Mattie gave out a soft groan of disbelief. "No more confessions, please. I don't think I can stand it."

Breeze was more reflective. "An all-woman's prison would take care of the anonymous men problem, unless they have male guards."

"It's the pills I miss," Jane said, "but thanks."

Breeze glanced at Mattie as if it was her turn, but Mattie had done all the sharing she was going to do for one night. "Jane, are you all right?" she asked.

Jane shrugged and set down her champagne glass. She looked philosophical, and if not calm, then resigned. "Confession is supposed to be good for the soul, isn't it?"

Mattie laughed. "Yours must be spotless by now."

It was quiet for several contemplative moments. Finally, Breeze walked to the bedroom window and gazed out at the city. "I'm not looking for sympathy," she said. "I've had a damn good life, for the most part, but in one way, it's been empty. I've made love to many men, so many I've lost track, to be honest, but I've never been *in* love."

In a soft voice, she added, "I think I'm incapable."

"Or afraid," Mattie said. "You can't love and I can't trust. It's a miracle that any of us could have a normal relationship with a man, given our past. You have that to be grateful for, Jane."

Jane sighed. "I am grateful for Larry. Hurting him is my greatest concern. To be honest, it's breaking my heart."

The quiet fell again, as did whatever gloom Breeze had managed to dispel with her games. Terrible things had happened, some of them to good people, and there was no way to lighten that load for more than moments at a time. Emotionally, they would all have to live with it for the rest of their lives, and in reality, they were about to face the consequences of actions that, however they may have seemed justified by the circumstances, had drastically changed the course of people's lives.

To Mattie it felt like the end of the line, and she knew her friends must share her frightening sense of finality. They were three women on top of the world—and in danger of losing everything they cherished and loved in life. Everything they'd worked so hard for. They'd all had a little help behind the scenes in the form of David Grace, but Mattie knew that she'd worked her heart out to achieve her goals. She knew the same was true of Jane, and Breeze, too, although that one would probably never admit it.

Mattie had decided not to share the good news she'd received that day from Jaydee. This wasn't the right time for it, but she was privately overjoyed. Ronald Langston's father had come forward and admitted to the abuses his son accused him of. He'd confessed everything. Apparently Ronald's conviction had brought about a crisis of conscience in the father. He'd lost both his sons, and his wife had walked out on him after the trial. Alone, and forced to face the monstrous things he'd done, he'd broken down. Ronald would go free, and he and his little brother would live with their mother. The father would receive counseling, but there was no guarantee he would get his family back.

There were no guarantees about anything, Mattie had realized. You did what you believed to be the right thing, and you summoned up your faith. That was the way of this world, and it was all you had in the last analysis, even if she wanted it to be different. Faith. The most ephemeral of virtues. And possibly, just possibly, the most powerful.

Of course, it was Breeze who broke the silence. She'd been lost in thought and sipping her champagne, but was probably the most sober of them all.

"For the first time in my life, I don't know what to do," she said.

Something in her voice frightened Mattie. It was weak, defeated.

Mattie didn't know what to do, either. There was no good plan this time. No tyrant to bring down or ritual to inspire them.

She sprang up. "Come on, ladies, what is it they say? When you're up to your chin in shit, you...what the hell do you do?"

"Take a shower?" Jane suggested.

Jane hadn't moved from the love seat the entire evening. Now she planted her feet on the floor, sat up and squared her shoulders. She could have been addressing an assembly.

"Neither of you has to do anything," she said. "Your spa will be fine, Breeze, and so will your judgeship, Mattie. This is *my* last hurrah, not yours. I did the crime and I deserve the time. I'm going to confess to the murder I committed, and neither of you will be involved in any way, do you hear me?"

"Jane, don't be silly."

She hushed Mattie, blinking away tears. "Don't argue with me, please. I don't have it in me to fight the two of you. Just let me do what I have to do. You both know it's right. I acted alone, and I never told anyone but David Grace. What a ghastly mistake that was, but I made it, and I'm the one who has to deal with it."

Mattie was torn. She glanced at Breeze, who looked conflicted, too. Jane seemed adamant, and on a practical level, it probably didn't make sense for all three of their lives to be destroyed. It was true that Jane had acted on her own without their knowledge and kept it a secret for over twenty years.

Mattie found herself wondering if Jane wanted to face this alone. She did have a Joan of Arc complex and maybe a bit of the martyr in her, but she couldn't have thought through what she'd just said. If she was tried as an adult, she faced life in prison.

"And you're not allowed to visit me in jail, either," Jane said.

Mattie sighed inwardly. That was so Jane, the mother lion, protector of the cubs.

Breeze wasn't all that impressed. Hands on her hips, she walked over and got right in Jane's face. "This is not me arguing with you," she said. "This is me telling you that you're not going down alone."

"Hear! hear!" Mattie grabbed the champagne from the bucket and joined Breeze in braving the fearless leader of their youth. With her free hand, she tugged Jane to her feet. It took more courage than strength.

"We started this together," Mattie said. "We'll finish it together."

Maybe Jane saw the futility of arguing, but she didn't give up with a whimper. She glared at them both, stretching her protest out to the breaking point. Finally, she took the bottle from Mattie, swigged some champagne from the dripping magnum and passed it to Breeze.

They drank without speaking, but within moments, the three women were laughing and had formed an unsteady football huddle. No one needed to say anything. They all knew they were in it together.

Tria juncta in uno. Amicus usque ad aras.

Three for one. Friends to the last extremity.

As the ancient phrases passed through Mattie's mind, she felt a stirring of resolve within her and a tiny wild spark of something else. Insanity, maybe. Was there a chance they'd get out of this? It was the first moment since Grace's death that she'd felt any sense of control at all.

Mattie was on her way down to the old courthouse when her cell phone rang. She fished through her bag in search of it, one hand on the wheel. She wasn't officially returning to work, given the sword of Damocles hanging over her head, but she wanted to go through her mail and clean up whatever paperwork had piled up on her desk. She hoped to be able to think more clearly in the quiet of her chambers than in the ICU, where she'd spent a long night with Jameson.

He still wasn't responding. This was the eighth day, and the doctors were becoming more guarded about his condition. Mattie couldn't get any straight answers, and she didn't understand how medical science, with all its miraculous advances, was completely stymied by a patient in a coma. How hard could it be to wake someone up? Why hadn't they figured that out yet?

"Where is that phone?" Mattie felt around blindly, unable to take her eyes off the road. One more ring and it would go to voice mail. There it was. In the wrong zipper compartment. She fished it out and flipped it open, one-handed. "Hello?"

"Ms. Smith?" a male voice said. "Could you come to St. Luke's as soon as possible? It's about Jameson Cross."

"I'm on my way," Mattie said, wheeling her car into the left lane to make a U-turn. "Is he all right?"

"The doctor would like to speak with you," the man said. "He'll explain."

Nothing about that sounded good to Mattie, but she didn't

argue. She was already calculating the time it would take her to get there. Had they lost him? Would she get to say goodbye to him at least?

Those thoughts consumed her as she pulled into the hospital's parking lot a half hour later. He was on the fifth floor. She took the stairs rather than wait for an elevator, and when she got to the ICU, she opened the door to find his bed empty.

"Oh, God, no," she whispered. She hurried from the room, desperate to find out where they'd taken him. The horrors of the crematorium flashed into her head, but she couldn't let herself get snagged on that thought. She would never get free. She would unravel like a cheap sweater.

"Mattie?"

Someone called her name as she raced down the hallway toward the stairs. She halted and looked around, but saw no one except a janitor who was mopping up a spill on the floor. It must have come from one of the patients' rooms. As she retraced her steps, peering in the doorways, she came to a room with a hospital bed partially blocked by a pulled curtain.

Mattie drew the curtain all the way back—and nearly fainted. "Jameson?"

He was lying in the bed, looking worn and pale, but very much alive. Her first impression was that he couldn't have called her name. Maybe she'd imagined it. He seemed confused, wary, even distant, as if he'd just awakened from a bad dream. Her second impression was of white pillowcases. They set off perfectly the dark, tousled elegance of his hair.

"They said someone brought me here." He seemed to be searching her features for answers. "A woman. Was it you?"

After the doctor had come and gone, predicting a complete recovery for Jameson, Mattie sat next to his bed, still trying to take it in. She had begun to lose hope, she realized, so much so that it was bewildering to have him back.

"Do your injuries hurt much?" she asked him.

"Only when I breathe, as they say."

Maybe it was the pain, she told herself. He was still distant and guarded, not himself. But then what did she expect? He'd been gravely injured and unconscious for days. He'd been in hell.

She couldn't seem to quell her fascination with the contrast of the white bedding against the dark hues of his complexion. His arms lay at his sides, and she wanted to touch the one nearest her, perhaps to reassure herself of something. Was his flesh warm? His body hair still silky? She did nothing, of course. It seemed odd that just days ago they'd been physically intimate. Wildly intimate. And utterly naked together. They'd seen and touched each other with complete freedom. Now, she couldn't lay her hand on his arm.

"You know your life line predicted this," she said, trying to lighten the mood. "Remember that break I told you about?"

"Ah, yes, the accident that could kill me."

"Except that it didn't."

A faint smile. "Does that mean I'm home free now?"

"Absolutely."

While he rested against the pillows, she told him what had happened in the Grace mansion, and that Tansy Black may have killed several people besides her own father, including his brother.

"She had something to prove," Mattie said, "and apparently it didn't matter who had to die. You're lucky to be here."

He studied her. "There was a moment when I thought it could be you," he said. "Tansy used a lethal hogtie on me, just like the magazine cover in my collection."

Maybe she shouldn't have been shocked that he'd suspected her, but she was. That was why she'd been picking up strange vibes from him. She didn't understand how he could have come to that conclusion, even with the evidence. Then again, she'd been haunted with suspicions of him, even after Jane had made her case for David Grace as the murderer of Broud and O'Neill.

Mattie returned his searching gaze, aware that for all their physical passion, they had never been emotionally intimate. She might have wanted that, but she hadn't allowed it. They didn't trust each other, perhaps even now.

Not knowing what else to do, she continued to fill him in.

"Tansy must have been spying on both of us," she said. "She probably wanted you to think it was me. She stole a gun out of my house and killed her father with it, but I don't believe she set out to kill him. That was a crime of passion. Obviously, her plan was to frame me for your murder."

His hand curled into a fist. "What twists a mind into something so hideous it has no regard for human life?" He seemed to be referring to Tansy's killing spree.

Mattie shuddered. "Thank God, they'll put her away for a long time. Hopefully forever."

She went quiet, dreading what had to be done next. She glanced at her fingernails, which were in terrible shape, but for a different reason. To keep from going crazy, she'd been working on her rock garden, weeding and reorganizing. And she'd also planted some actual flowers in her front yard, succulents and other lovely things. Flowers were friendlier than rocks, and they smelled better.

"Are you all right?" Jameson looked her over, taking in her wrinkled blouse and khaki slacks, her worried expression.

"I hope so," she said. "There's something I need to tell you."

He didn't respond. Even a simple "What?" from him would have made it easier. She plunged on anyway, telling him about the lonely girls' failed attempt to poison Ms. Rowe with heartwine. The hard part was admitting that Jane had come back to finish the job that his brother went to prison for.

He struggled to sit up, grimacing at the pain.

"Jameson, stay down," she implored. "You'll rip out your stitches."

"It was Jane, and you never told me?" He fell back against the pillows.

"I didn't know." Mattie explained that Jane hadn't told anyone, except David Grace, and she had gone to him only because she knew he'd had a relationship with Ms. Rowe.

Jameson made no attempt to hide his bitterness. "Jane could end up in San Quentin with Tansy Black. It's probably where she belongs."

Mattie couldn't defend Jane's actions, even though she might understand them, everything considered. One day perhaps she would try to explain the fear and desperation her friend had felt, the burning-in-her-soul sense of duty, but not now.

"Jane may have done it, but that doesn't absolve me, or Breeze," she told him. "We're guilty, as well, of attempted murder."

He went silent again. "Surely they'll take into account that she abused you and tried to sell you to the highest bidder. You were underage, a minor. You'll have to tell them everything."

A bell tone sounded in the background of Mattie's thoughts. The hospital intercom system, probably. She could hear the creak of a gurney's wheels and people talking in hushed tones as they passed by the door.

"It's not me I'm worried about," she said. "It's Jane. She's determined to turn herself in, and it looks bad for her."

"Why? She'll get a big gun attorney. She'll be fine, probably never serve a day."

Mattie wasn't so sure about that. Jane might well refuse high-profile representation, just on principle. "You must hate her," Mattie blurted, wondering if his feelings for Jane would spill over to her—or already had.

"It wasn't just Jane who put my brother in jail and kept him there. It was an entire conspiracy that included his family. Jane can take her share of the blame, and I'll take mine."

But only Jane would be charged with a crime, Mattie thought, still fearing for her friend.

Another cart rattled by outside, and a doctor was being paged. Mattie was glad she didn't have to worry about those sounds anymore. When she'd been waiting for Jameson to wake up, every burst of the hospital P.A. system had alarmed her.

He watched her, his gaze intent. "Why did you swear to me that you had nothing to do with Ms. Rowe's death? Why didn't you tell me the truth?"

"I didn't know Jane had done it," she explained. "And I couldn't have told you anyway because of Jane and Breeze. If I'd been the only one involved it would have been different."

That wasn't quite true, and they both knew it. Once again, it all came down to trust. She hadn't trusted him enough to tell him. She didn't trust easily, and she might never be able to. She suffered from the same syndromes that many abused children did, a form of post-traumatic stress disorder that made it difficult for her to embrace the most basic things in life, the things most people took for granted, like ever trusting anyone again.

She didn't even trust herself. She'd wanted to touch his arm. It should have been such an easy, innocent thing after the racy, sweaty sex they'd had. But she couldn't do it. *That* would have been intimate. It would have meant something after everything they'd been through.

She wondered if he knew that, too.

She *was* emotionally involved with Jameson Cross. As agonizing as it was to admit, she was probably falling in love with him, but she couldn't tell him that. She couldn't even look at him right now. And she had no idea what the future held, except that one of them was going to make a complete recovery.

"I'm glad you're all right," was all she said.

46

Eight months later

Mattie sipped a heavily doctored cup of coffee as she waited in the courthouse lobby. Of course, the caffeine would only make her more jittery. She should have had some breakfast, even a chunk of the stale raisin bread in her refrigerator would have been better than the roiling emptiness in her stomach.

Couldn't. Nerves. Terrible nerves. She'd raced over here from her place in Sausalito as soon as she'd received the call that the jury had come to a verdict. How long had she been waiting for this? It felt like her whole life was caught up in this trial and that nothing could go forward until it had been resolved. Most of the country was caught up in it, too, based on the media interest.

Mattie had found an inconspicuous spot in a shallow alcove, where she could watch the milling crowd. Part of the defense team was huddled nearby, probably trying to divine the verdict. She knew most of them, and the prosecutors, as well, but there'd been no contact beyond polite greetings.

It was widely known that she'd taken a leave from the bench until her legal and personal issues were resolved. The missing videotape had documented the physical, emotional and sexual abuse at Rowe Academy, and no charges were ever filed against Mattie, but she still needed time to sort things out. Lane Davison had come forward to corroborate her part in the physical abuse in exchange for reduced charges. She'd been arraigned as a co-conspirator in her deceased husband's blackmail scheme, but she'd admitted only to taking the videotape from its hiding place in the attic after Ms. Rowe was killed.

Mattie wasn't sure she believed Lane's story about secreting the tape because a family friend was on it, and then, some years later, having a crisis of conscience and turning it over to her husband to handle. Lane supposedly believed that Frank had quietly resolved everything among the parties involved without any need for prosecution. But, fortunately, that wasn't Mattie's problem to solve. She was here today as a spectator only.

Outside, the press had been herded into a roped-off area on the courthouse steps, where microphones were set up for a press conference. Mattie glanced at her watch. Maybe that's what had held up Breeze. Getting past the crowds and the media.

She'd half expected to see Jameson here. She couldn't imagine that the outcome of this trial didn't interest him. Mattie had been here for every session, but there'd been no sign of him so far, which had left her heavyhearted. She still regretted the way their relationship had ended, although one could argue that a couple weeks did not a relationship make, or that it had ever officially ended.

They'd been in touch since he was released from the hospital, but it was mostly casual and unsatisfying contact. Mattie had called him as often as she dared to check on his recovery, and he'd given her updates. He'd called her to see how she was holding up under the public scrutiny that hit after Jane turned herself in to the authorities. Mattie had pretended to be doing fine, even though it was hell dealing with the press, and especially painful watching her proud friend's fall from grace. But she had never told Jameson any of that, and he hadn't probed. Of course, neither of them had suggested seeing the other.

Mattie knew she'd been holding back. She was afraid of rejection. She'd always thought it was her confession that created the wedge between them. But she'd sensed him holding back, too. He'd claimed to be immersed in the writing of his brother's book, but he hadn't discussed it except to say that he needed to finish it so that he could put that part of his life behind him and move on.

That she understood. She needed to do some moving on herself.

"Did I miss anything?" Breeze rushed up to Mattie, breathless. Her eyes widened as she took in Mattie's sleek pinstripe pantsuit. "You look beautiful for an unemployed ex-juvenile delinquent. How about me?"

She did a twirl, showing off a green cashmere poncho and skirt ensemble that made her eyes shine like rich dark chocolate. "Do I look like a travel agent to you? It could be my new thing."

"I'd hire you on sight," Mattie said. Breeze was reconsidering her career path. As she'd predicted, the publicity had dealt her spa business a mortal blow, so she was pursuing other options. Fortunately, she was free to do so. No charges had been filed against her, either. Jane had not been so lucky, but it was partly her own doing. She'd done everything short of confessing, and she'd insisted on taking the stand during the trial.

Mattie spotted a trash can and went over to discard her coffee cup. Breeze followed along, and when Mattie turned to her, she saw the fear in Breeze's expression.

"Are you okay?" Mattie asked.

Breeze gripped her hand, and at first Mattie thought she

was going to inspect her fingernails. But her hold was tight. It hurt.

"What's wrong?" Mattie asked.

"What if Tansy doesn't get what she deserves? Mattie, what are we going to do?"

"Of course, she'll get what she deserves. Have some faith."

"In what? The legal system? Are you serious?"

Mattie didn't have a chance to answer her. The doors to the courtroom opened, a signal that they were ready to reconvene. She and Breeze slipped inside and took seats near the back in the spectator gallery. A hush fell over the room as the twelve jurors filed into the jury box, and the judge entered from the door behind the bench.

The proceedings were brought to order, the defendant, a woman in an orange jumpsuit, asked to rise, and the judge queried the jury, asking if they'd reached a unanimous verdict.

"We have, Your Honor."

"Thank you, ladies and gentlemen of the jury. Would the marshal please bring the verdict to me."

In silence, the judge read the piece of paper the marshal brought to him, then nodded and handed it to the marshal to be returned to the foreman, a heavyset woman in pale pink.

"Would the duly elected foreman of the jury please read the verdict?"

The woman took a moment to calm herself. "On the count of murder in the second degree," she said, "we, the people of the state of California, find the defendant guilty."

The gavel sounded, echoing like a gunshot.

Mattie gripped Breeze's hand. The verdict had stunned her, even though she'd expected to hear it. The defendant had expected it, too. Her spine was rigidly straight, her expression stoic, despite the sadness etched into the lines around her eyes. The woman in the orange jumpsuit, about to be consigned to a prison cell, was Jane Mantle.

One month later

"You say you saw Tansy Black shoot her father in cold blood, and yet the murder weapon has your fingerprints all over it, Judge Smith—and *only* your fingerprints. It is, in fact, your gun, is it not?"

The lead attorney on Black's defense team fixed his accusatory gaze on Mattie, who sat in the witness box. He was a short, wiry man with coarse hair, dyed shoe-polish-brown, and this wasn't Mattie's first experience with him. He'd staged a bombastic oral argument appealing a bank robbery conviction, but the circuit court had upheld the trial court's decision to find his client guilty. Mattie had written the opinion, and it appeared he held a grudge.

"The gun was stolen from my house, yes," she said.

The attorney snorted indignantly. "Your Honor, would you please instruct the witness to answer the question I asked?"

Mattie knew the judge only by reputation, but she respected his rulings and his sense of fair play. Of course, he had to grant the attorney's request, but Mattie didn't get a chance to answer the question about her stolen gun before the attorney had bellowed out another one.

"The gun is registered in your name, and you were there, at David Grace's home, for the purpose of trying to find a videotape that you believed would absolve you of a murder, isn't that true?"

"Yes."

"And you were dressed up like a schoolgirl, Judge Smith? Lying to David Grace, deceiving him and entrapping him into confessing to crimes that you had absolutely no proof he'd committed?"

"Objection, Your Honor." The assistant district attorney came to her feet. "That's several questions, and Judge Smith isn't on trial here."

The objection was sustained, and Mattie tried not to show her relief. As it had turned out, there was no proof connecting David Grace to anything. If he'd ever been on the videotape, Tansy had erased any evidence of it. And worse, the electronic bug Mattie had worn to Grace's mansion hadn't picked up anything that could be used as evidence. Grace had some sort of blocking device that had sabotaged most of the transmission.

"Your Honor," Black's attorney persisted, "I'm attempting to show that the witness has credibility issues."

Tansy Black was watching her, Mattie realized, had been watching her with the intensity of a military laser since she took the stand. The woman's eyes burned with icy outrage, apparently at the supreme indignity of having to stand trial and be questioned in this way. Her eyes were as dark and disturbed as her soul, and Mattie had avoided her throughout most of the trial. Now, she made it a point to return Tansy's fire, laser for laser—and was surprised at what she saw.

That night at Grace's mansion, Mattie had seen only Ivy's delicate features, but in the bright lights of the courtroom, Tansy Black was a younger Millicent Rowe. She looked far more like her mother than her half sister, so much so that she could easily have been the ghost who terrified Mattie at Frank O'Neill's party.

Mattie broke from Tansy's malevolent energy, only to come into contact with another disturbing gaze. Jameson Cross's. Earlier that day, he'd been a witness for the state, and now he sat on that side of the gallery, observing her, but not without sympathy. Concern glimmered in every facet of his expression, and it was almost more debilitating to Mattie than Tansy's hatred.

Her heart ached with the awareness of how much she needed his support, his friendship, if nothing else. Up to this point in her life, she had managed to get through every catastrophe on her own, sometimes dragging her friends with her, but always feeling as if she were responsible for their safety along the way. Mattie, the pit bull, Mattie, the woman warrior. She'd done it with Ivy, with Jane, even Breeze. Jameson, Ronald Langston and Jaydee, of course. She'd done it with everyone in her life.

But this catastrophe had been different in ways she didn't yet understand. Some inner tumult had cracked the plate armor of her famously stubborn will and transformed her. She had come to depend on people, to need them. She could feel that need in the very depths of her being, and Jameson was one of those people.

The blindfold was not going to work anymore. She'd grown up.

She had also sympathized with Jameson's ordeal in court. They'd both been witnesses at the grand jury, but their testimony had not convinced the jury that Tansy should be indicted for his kidnapping. Thank God, Tansy had been indicted for attempting to murder him when he escaped the trunk of Mattie's car, but she would never face charges for the horrors she'd put him through while she held him captive.

It saddened Mattie that the man who'd worked so hard at seeking justice for others couldn't get justice for himself.

The defense attorney's voice jolted Mattie back to the proceedings. "In fact, Judge Smith," he said, coming at her from another angle, "your knee went out on you, didn't it? You fell to the floor in terrible pain, and you didn't see anything, did you? Yes or no, Judge Smith."

Mattie was caught. Either answer would confirm his assertion that she'd seen nothing. She glanced at the prosecutor's table, waiting for an objection that never came. The assistant D.A. and her co-counsel were huddled in conversation.

"Yes or no, Judge Smith. Which is it?"

"I fell earlier," Mattie said. "I was down on the floor, and I saw—"

He cut Mattie off with a wave of his hand. "Thank you, Your Honor. That's all."

Mattie cut back instantly, but not at him. She turned to address the jury. "David Grace asked Tansy Black for the gun, and she shot him in cold blood, her own father. I saw *everything*. I saw him fall, I saw him bleed and I saw him die."

The attorney whirled on Mattie with a glare almost as frightening as Tansy's. Mattie wouldn't want to meet either of them in a dark alley.

"Your Honor, I move to have that stricken," he shouted.

While the defense attorney ranted about Mattie's outrageous courtroom tricks, Mattie glanced over at Jameson again. She couldn't seem to stop herself. This time he was smiling. He gave her a thumbs-up.

It meant more to her than he could possibly know.

Two months later

"Order in the court!" The gavel cracked several times as the judge attempted to quiet the packed courtroom. "The verdict will not be read until I can hear a pin drop and bounce three times in this room. Take your seats, please."

Already seated at the back of the gallery, Jameson checked his watch. The jury had been out just four hours. They'd come to a decision quickly, and he didn't know if that was good or bad. Two rows down, Mattie Smith glanced at her watch, too.

She looked frail to him, as if she'd lost weight, and possibly even something more essential, a sense of direction or purpose. Probably his imagination. He hadn't spoken with her in some time. She didn't call anymore, and the distance building between them had begun to seem insurmountable to him. He hadn't stopped thinking about her, worrying about her, but he didn't want to impose, and he'd been busy.

Finishing the book about Billy had consumed him. It was a rough emotional journey that he'd had to make on his own, and he'd exorcised some demons on the way. Not all of them, certainly, but his life was beginning to make more sense. He wondered about her life.

Her clerk, Jaydee, had called him recently to talk about one of Jameson's books, and Jameson had slipped in a casual question about Mattie. Jaydee had said she was still on leave. He didn't mention what she was doing, only that he missed her like hell. Jameson could relate.

He wondered if her pensiveness had to do with her two friends. The former First Lady was doing five to ten at Club Fed in Danbury, a minimum-security prison for women where Leona Helmsley had done her time, and where Martha Stewart would have landed, if she'd had her first choice of facilities. According to the papers, Jane's charge had been reduced to manslaughter. Other than that, she'd refused to let her conviction be appealed, but Jameson doubted she would serve more than four years, with time off for good behavior. He'd read an article that said she was making the most of her confinement, organizing women's groups and lobbying for better classes and occupational training for the inmates. He didn't know what had happened to Breeze Wheeler, but he couldn't imagine her not pursuing the constitution's guarantee of happiness.

He'd never seen the point of holding grudges, and he had already forgiven the lonely girls for what he believed was their attempt to defend themselves against Millicent Rowe. They were terrified kids, fighting for their lives. It hadn't been as easy to forgive himself.

"Thank you," the judge said, addressing the quieted courtroom. "Now, we'll proceed." He asked if the jury had reached a unanimous verdict on all counts. The foreman said they had and gave the written verdict to the marshal. Once the judge had seen the verdict, he asked the foreman to read it.

The foreman's voice rang out in the silent hall. "On the count of murder in the first degree, we find the defendant not guilty. On the count of attempted murder, we find the defendant...not guilty."

Jameson was too stunned to move. Tansy Black was going to walk on both counts. In a reasonable world, it did not seem possible that Jane Mantle was doing time for a crime committed over twenty years ago, and Tansy Black was going free. Apparently the jury had not been convinced beyond a reasonable doubt that Tansy killed her father, despite Mattie's testimony. They believed the defense's argument that it was accidental. The gun had gone off when Grace attempted to disarm Tansy, fatally wounding him.

Jameson couldn't seem to shake off the shock that buzzed in his brain. Obviously, the jury didn't believe Tansy had tried to kill him, either. The defense had made the case that it was self-defense because of the way Jameson had charged into the fire. And with the kidnapping charge thrown out, the state had been hard-pressed to come up with a motive for attempted murder. This was a death penalty case, and juries tended to cling to the doubt rule when capital punishment was involved, but still, Jameson couldn't believe what he'd heard.

And neither could anyone else. The entire courtroom was up in arms. But Mattie hadn't moved. He knew she must be as shocked and disbelieving as he was. He wanted to go and ask her if she was all right. She didn't look all right. He wanted to go. But he didn't.

Epilogue

Tansy Black was having an identity crisis. A copy of her father's will sat on the desk in front of her. She'd cracked the combination on his office vault to get the document because she didn't trust his lawyers. She wanted to see it for herself. But she hadn't been prepared for what she would find.

He'd left her everything. Everything.

Most things in life bounced off her as if she were solid rock. And in many ways, she was. She did what she had to do, and she was rarely hampered by doubt or uncertainty. But this had blown her away. What did it mean?

I entrust my sole remaining heir, Tansy Grace, with all of my worldly goods, possessions and property, including my life's work in the belief that she will ensure the company's tradition of rigorous scientific research and development.

She walked around his desk and sat in the chair, still shaken. She was vibrating, levitating. She couldn't feel her hands or feet. Nothing was connected. He'd even given her his business, and there was nothing more precious to him than that, except possibly Ivy.

Ivy. The thought of her sister didn't bring lacerating pain this time.

Tansy let out a gasp of laughter that verged on hysteria. She cracked her bare knuckles against the sharp edge of the walnut desk, and winced at the sting. She had to get control.

None of this meant he loved her. It didn't even mean he cared. But he must hold her in some esteem if he'd left her his empire. There might even be a chance that she'd earned his respect.

God, that was enough. He had entrusted her with his life's work, believing that she could carry on with it. Yes, enough.

She reached for the document, intending to read it again. She would read it until it was real, a part of her. Devour it. There were pages and pages of details. If she went through them slowly and meticulously, this would begin to make sense.

Intent on her mission, she ignored a faint snapping sound. It was the wall or the floor, wood expanding or contracting. Whatever wood did. But gradually, she realized someone was in the room with her. When she looked up, she saw a man in a full-length black trench coat. A Halloween mask hid his face with a skeleton's eerie grin. His hands were gloved, and in the right one he held a handgun with a silencer. It was not aimed at her, but she knew that it would be.

"I don't want to die," she whispered.

"Neither did they, Tansy—the people you executed. They didn't want to die, either."

She didn't recognize his voice, but that didn't surprise her. There were so many people who might want revenge. The lonely girls, of course, but there was also Jameson Cross, and the soon-to-be ex-president, Larry Mantle, or anyone associated with him. Nola Daniels, if she'd figured out it was Tansy who tortured her husband with phone calls, or Lane Davison because Tansy had orchestrated her husband's death and then harassed Lane with anonymous threats to keep her quiet about the blackmailing scheme.

Any of those people might want her dead.

She thought of one other, and her blood turned to ice. Even her own father, if he could reach from the grave.

Bitterness flared as she glanced at the will and realized there was no legacy here. Her father had entrusted his company to the daughter he thought he knew, the brilliant lawyer. She was the person he respected. Not the woman who would have sacrificed everything for him. He was a liar and a hypocrite. He talked about fearlessness, but he had no clue. He'd even begged for his life, something she would never do.

Fuck him. Fuck them all. Rage burned in her chest, and a tear rolled down her cheek, but it wasn't sadness at the thought of dying. How could she die when she had never lived? She wasn't sure she'd ever had a moment's happiness in her life, except at the possibility that her father would be proud.

"Shoot me," she whispered. "Get it over with."

The intruder stared at her through the mask's eyeholes, revealing the eternal coldness of an assassin's eyes. There was no hope there, no compassion, no life. She could have been looking at herself. He eliminated people who were in the way, just as she did. He did it efficiently and without remorse.

"Kill me," she sobbed. "Do it."

"No, I'm sorry," he said. "It's not going to be that easy. Turn around."

She turned, wondering if perhaps he was going to brutalize her in some way. Tie her in a knot that would slowly strangle her? Was this Jameson Cross?

"Put your hands behind your back."

He wanted to be sure she couldn't fight. He needn't have bothered. There was nothing to fight for.

When he had her wrists secured with what felt like cuffs, he told her to lie down on the floor, prone. She felt pressure on her legs—he'd pinned them somehow—and then the searing sting of a needle. Her right glute seized like a fist under the assault. He'd injected her right through her clothing. Heartwine? No, a powerful sedative. She could feel it fuzzing her thoughts already. She would be out in minutes.

So, a humane assassin. She wasn't to be tortured. But he'd said it wouldn't be easy. She didn't understand....

She woke up to blackness, to the shriek of a fire, and heat so intense it could have melted rock. The air reeked of antiseptic and musty cardboard. She was in a cadaver box. She was being cremated. If the assassin had been a woman, Tansy would have guessed Mattie Smith.

Tansy should have let her burn, the bitch.

She would like to have known her killer's identity, but she took pride in the certain knowledge that he couldn't have done this if she'd wanted to live. Some might say it was a fitting end. All her victims had been sent to their graves without knowing, except Frank. And it had been interesting watching him figure it out.

It was the drool that had terrified him the most. He couldn't wipe it off his chin, couldn't even lick it off with his tongue. He was paralyzed, and only his eyes would work at that point. They got buggy and huge. Tears soaked his sad, frozen face.

There would be no one to witness Tansy Black's death, but at least she wouldn't leave a mess, like her sister did.

She smiled. *If you're burning in hell, Father, move over and make room for your baby girl.*

"They strip-search me before and after every visitor's session," Jane said, lowering her voice.

"Is that good news or bad?" Mattie asked.

"Depends on who's doing the search."

Jane cracked a smile first. Mattie's was slower, wider.

They sat across from each other in a boxy room with a table and chairs. The male guard stood outside, observing through a sheet of mirrored glass. Jane had added Mattie to her defense team, which meant they didn't have to stick to the visitors' hours Jane had mentioned, although they were observing them today because they were expecting some-one else.

Mattie wasn't at all surprised that Jane looked good. She'd lost weight, but the hint of gauntness suited her. Plus, she had a mission. Prison reform. Jane was always at her best when the problems were seemingly insurmountable.

"Your team is ready, willing and able," Mattie reminded her. "Just say the word and an appeal will be filed."

"The word is no." Jane was firm.

"Seriously? You're up for three more years of this?" Jane had already served nearly a year of her term, including the four-month trial. Her defense team had argued for a four-year sentence on the grounds that she was fourteen when she committed the crime, and at eighteen would no longer have been the jurisdiction of the juvenile court, therefore the max-imum she could have been charged with was four years. The judge, who'd been inclined toward leniency, had agreed.

"Well, look at this place," Jane said. "There's so much to do, Mattie. I've already organized a women's group, and—"

The door swung open, and Breeze sailed into the room, flanked by a female guard. As soon as the guard left, Breeze slipped into a chair, her eyes sparkling with intrigue as she glanced from Mattie to Jane. "She's dead. The wicked witch is dead."

"What?" Mattie said. "Who?"

"Tansy Black."

"She died? How?"

"According to the noon news, the police were tipped by an anonymous caller that her remains could be found at the crematory in Tiburon."

Mattie's jaw dropped. That was where Tansy had attacked her. "Who did it?"

Breeze shrugged. "Could have been one of legions, given the murderous swath she cut."

Mattie thought on the possibilities. "True, but why would they have tipped the police?"

"To make a statement?" Breeze suggested.

"I don't know." Mattie's newly manicured fingernails tapped the table. "Sounds like there was some organization involved, maybe a mob hit or...the government?"

They both looked at Jane, whose eyes sparked with indignation. "You can't be thinking what I think you're thinking. Me? In prison? Paying my debt to society? I'm a poster child for time off with good behavior."

Mattie nodded, still musing the possibilities. "It could have been a vigilante intelligence group," she said, eyeing Breeze.

"How could you even think that?" Breeze tried to sound offended, but there was a lilt to her voice. There was a lilt to her entire person.

Mattie couldn't very well grill her friend inside prison walls, but she wouldn't have been at all surprised to learn that Breeze's little agency did contract work. They seemed to do everything else.

"Any truth to the rumor that you're seeing John Bratton?" Mattie asked her.

Breeze just smiled.

Mattie had her answer. Maybe to both questions. From what she'd seen of Bratton, he was more than capable of some cleanup work. And he was hot for Breeze. Mattie wouldn't have been surprised to see them go into business together. She would have been afraid for modern civilization, but she wouldn't have been surprised. But she wasn't going to ask any more questions. The world was a much better place without Tansy Black in it. Knowing that was enough.

She glanced around the room, thinking about the last time the three of them were together. "This isn't the Four Seasons, is it?"

"If it was," Jane said, "we'd be pouring champagne."

"Because of Tansy?" Breeze asked.

"No, Ivy. Tomorrow's the anniversary of her death."

Mattie glanced at her watch and saw that Jane was right. Twenty-three years ago today of causes that were still unknown. Mattie felt all the bittersweetness of that time flood her. She hoped her friend was at peace now that so many of the unanswerable questions had been answered. Her death would always be a mystery.

Mattie held up an imaginary glass and the other two followed suit.

"Alis volat propriis," she said. "To Ivy, she flies with her own wings."

"A *Girls Gone Wild* video collection?"

Jaydee whooped as he held up Mattie's going-away gift. "I expected something boring like a briefcase."

"You may find something boring in the other package," Mattie said, then added, deadpan, "you'll need the videos more. Stress relief."

Jaydee had passed the California Bar the first time out, and he was off to be a prosecutor for the organized crime unit in the Attorney General's Office in Washington, D.C. A job he was born for, Mattie knew, even though she wished he'd gone for something less *exciting*.

Jaydee set his video collection on Maggie's desk and accosted her with a bear hug. "I should have gotten you a present," he said as he released her.

She pretended to gasp for air. "Why? I'm not going anywhere."

"I know, poor baby. You're stuck here, in the Ninth Circuit."

Mattie had given some thought to leaving months ago, long before Jaydee made his announcement. She'd considered traveling or teaching, but eventually had realized she couldn't, not with a clear conscience. She was like Jane in that way. Sitting on the bench was a responsibility as much as a privilege, and there was still work to be done.

"You keep in touch," she said, giving him a stern look.

"Try getting rid of me. You're at the top of my speed-dial list."

Mattie's buzzer rang, but before she could get around her desk to answer it, the door to her chambers opened. She glanced up to see Jameson Cross coming across the threshold. Apparently he'd breached security. Again. And got past her receptionist. Michelle hadn't had a chance to announce him.

"Sorry," Jameson said. "Your receptionist was on the phone, so I let myself in."

Well, that was progress, Mattie thought. He hadn't bothered to explain his intrusions before. Her first impression was that he looked a bit worn, tired around the eyes. She hadn't seen him since Tansy's trial, which was months ago. She'd often wondered why she didn't just call him. But somehow, it would have seemed like an overture, and she didn't have the stamina, even if he'd been interested. It had been too turbulent.

"How are you?" he asked Mattie.

"I'm surprised...to see you."

He came over to the chair by her desk, and as the light from the window struck him, she saw that he wore well. There were a few more lines, but he was as darkly attractive as ever in the black trench coat. She could see why Michelle hadn't been able to stop him. It was the intimidation factor. He was still one of those people who gave off enough animal energy to signal their intentions. Mattie had discovered that about him the hard way, in her own courtroom.

Jaydee scooped up his videos and his unopened present.

"I was just going," he said. "Nice to see you, Mr. Cross. Mattie, my flight to D.C. is at seven tomorrow morning. Can I bum a ride?"

"You could, if *I* was going to the airport. Get out of here, Jaydee. Good luck with your life."

Jaydee shot her an exaggerated frown and slunk out the door. Mattie expected she'd be hearing from him very soon.

For some reason, which could only be nerves, Mattie went around her desk, retreating to the protection of its gleaming breadth. Her office felt like a fortress, unless Jameson Cross was in it. The desk was now her last stronghold.

"What brings you here?" she asked him.

"I thought you might be interested in this." He set what looked liked a bound manuscript on her desk. "It's the galleys of my book, the one about Billy."

She looked at it without touching it, trying to assess the damage it might do, if any. "Am I in it?"

"You're prominent."

She looked up at him, temper flaring. "I still have a panic button," she warned, wondering if he would remember what she'd said the first time he'd surprised her in her chambers, and she'd pushed the red button on the underside of her desktop.

Goodbye, Mr. Cross.

"No need to panic this time," he said. "It's not going to be published."

"Why not? They didn't like it?"

"They liked it a lot. Said it would be a blockbuster, considering the cast of characters. But that's what I had to do, consider the cast. It's not the right way to honor Billy's memory. My battles with Billy were private, and they should stay that way."

A moment passed. "My battles with you were private, too," he said. "I don't want them exposed to prying eyes."

She didn't quite know what to say, but her sense of relief brought a memory of the night he'd told her he wasn't going to file his story, and she'd bullied him into admitting that he'd done it for her. She had rather enjoyed that.

She hadn't realized that her finger was still hovering near the panic button, ready to eject him. One of many fail-safes in her life. Maybe she could forgo this one. Maybe she could let him in.

She placed both of her hands on the desk.

"Hello, Mr. Cross," she said, aware of the smile in his strange lavender-gray eyes.

AUTHORS AT SEA

www.authorsatsea.com

Join top authors for the ultimate cruise experience. Spend 7 days in the Mexican Riviera aboard the luxurious Carnival Pride™. Start in Los Angeles/Long Beach, CA and visit Puerto Vallarta, Mazatlan and Cabo San Lucas. Enjoy all this with a ship full of authors and book lovers on the **"Authors at Sea Cruise"** April 2 - 9, 2006.

Mail in this coupon with proof of purchase* to receive $250 per person off the regular **"Authors at Sea Cruise"** price. One coupon per person required to receive $250 discount. For complete details call **1-877-ADV-NTGE** or visit **www.AuthorsAtSea.com**

PRICES STARTING AT $749 PER PERSON WITH COUPON!

MIRA®   HQN™

*proof of purchase is required, sales receipt with the book purchased circled plus applicable taxes, fees, and gratuities.

Carnival The Most Popular Cruise Line in the World.

GET $250 OFF

Name   (Please Print)
_____

Address _____ Apt. No. _____

City _____ State _____ Zip _____

E-Mail Address _____

See Following Page For Terms & Conditions.

**For booking form and complete information
go to www.AuthorsAtSea.com or call 1-877-ADV-NTGE**

Prices quoted are in U.S. currency.

AAS05A

Carnival Pride℠
April 2 - 9, 2006.

7 Day Exotic Mexican Riviera Itinerary

DAY	PORT	ARRIVE	DEPART
Sun	Los Angeles/Long Beach, CA		4:00 P.M.
Mon	"Book Lover's" Day at Sea		
Tue	"Book Lover's" Day at Sea		
Wed	Puerto Vallarta, Mexico	8:00 A.M.	10:00 P.M.
Thu	Mazatlan, Mexico	9:00 A.M.	6:00 P.M.
Fri	Cabo San Lucas, Mexico	7:00 A.M.	4:00 P.M.
Sat	"Book Lover's" Day at Sea		
Sun	Los Angeles/Long Beach, CA	9:00 A.M.	

ports of call subject to weather conditions

TERMS AND CONDITIONS

PAYMENT SCHEDULE:
50% due upon booking
Full and final payment due by February 10, 2006

Acceptable forms of payment are Visa, MasterCard, American Express, Discover and checks. The cardholder must be one of the passengers traveling. A fee of $25 will apply for all returned checks. Check payments must be made payable to Advantage International, LLC and sent to: Advantage International, LLC, 195 North Harbor Drive, Suite 4206, Chicago, IL 60601

CHANGE/CANCELLATION:
Notice of change/cancellation must be made in writing to Advantage International, LLC.

Change:
Changes in cabin category may be requested and can result in increased rate and penalties. A name change is permitted 60 days or more prior to departure and will incur a penalty of $50 per name change. Deviation from the group schedule and package is a cancellation.

Cancellation:

181 days or more prior to departure	$250 per person
121 - 180 days or more prior to departure	50% of the package price
120 - 61 days prior to departure	75% of the package price
60 days or less prior to departure	100% of the package price (nonrefundable)

US and Canadian citizens are required to present a valid passport or the original birth certificate and state issued photo ID (drivers license). All other nationalities must contact the consulate of the various ports that are visited for verification of documentation.

We strongly recommend trip cancellation insurance!

For complete details call 1-877-ADV-NTGE or visit www.AuthorsAtSea.com

---

For booking form and complete information
go to www.AuthorsAtSea.com or call 1-877-ADV-NTGE

Complete coupon and booking form and mail both to:
Advantage International, LLC,
195 North Harbor Drive, Suite 4206, Chicago, IL 60601

Prices quoted are in U.S. currency.

AAS05B

A remarkable new novel by
USA TODAY bestselling author

JODI THOMAS

Every house has a secret.

Everyone assumes Rosa Lee Altman lived a life without
passion. But buried secrets are meant to be revealed. And
no one is prepared for what they discover beneath Rosa Lee's
overgrown roses—or how her legacy will change their
lives with love.

THE SECRETS OF ROSA LEE

"Jodi Thomas will render you breathless!"
—*Romantic Times*

Available the first week of August 2005 wherever paperbacks are sold!